DEADLY GRACE

TAYLOR SMITH

DEADLY GRACE

MIRA®

ISBN 1-55166-829-7

DEADLY GRACE

Visit us at www.mirabooks.com

Printed in Canada.

First Printing: December 2001
10 9 8 7 6 5 4 3 2 1

ACKNOWLEDGMENTS

A work of historical fiction like this owes much to many people,
especially to the Allied veterans of World War II,
to whom I offer profound thanks for their sacrifices.
Among those, in addition to my father and my father-in-law,
I owe a particular debt of gratitude to three people who were kind
enough to share their personal memoirs with me: Ben Ward,
U.S. Army glider pilot; and Jean Grant and Pam Orford, British nurses.

My dear friend, Holocaust survivor Louis Posner, was unfailingly generous
with his extensive research library, as well as his memories of the events
of that tragic period. Sadly, he died suddenly during the writing of this
novel and never got to see the finished product, but for a spellbinding
true-life story of his gripping experiences, I highly recommend Louis'
published memoir, *Through a Boy's Eyes: The Turbulent Years 1926–45*
(Seven Locks Press, 2000).

The character of Miss Vivian Atwater is loosely based on real-life
British spymaster Vera Atkins. After extraordinary wartime service with
Britain's Special Operations Executive, Miss Atkins (unlike her fictional
counterpart, happily) lived to the ripe old age of 92 in a cottage
overlooking the English Channel where, on a clear day, it is said,
she could see the coast of France.

Special thanks to Special Agent Gary L. Price,
U.S. Army Criminal Investigation Command, who graciously answered all
my questions on his discipline and his branch of the Service. Thanks also
to my writing buddy, Doug Lyle, M.D., for his medical advice, as well as
former FBI Special Agent Jack Trimarco, who gives all G-men a good
name. Deepest thanks also to my agent, Philip Spitzer, and to my editors
Dianne Moggy, Amy Moore-Benson and Valerie Gray, who've been
incredibly understanding through this past tough year. I'm very grateful.

It may be noted that the town of Havenwood bears a certain similarity
to another prairie town I frequent and love, and that some of
Havenwood's colorful characters seem to possess the same spunk
as my Lac du Bonnet aunties, who never fail to inspire me
and lift my spirits. Thanks to them all (and the uncles and cousins, too)
for so many years of love and laughter.

And last but never least, love and thanks to Anna, Kate and Richard,
who agonize with me through every page and rewrite, poor souls.
Lucky me, to have you guys in my corner.

This is dedicated
to my Auntie Olly Campbell,
who wrote the book on love & loyalty—
with thanks from the heart for all you do and all you are.

CHAPTER 1

Havenwood, Minnesota
Tuesday, January 9, 1979

She had no memory of her own death. No idea when it might have happened, or how, or how long she'd lain insensible in the netherworld between life and death. But when Jillian Meade awoke, she had no doubt she was in hell.

It was exactly as Reverend Owens had described in the fire-and-brimstone Sunday sermons that had terrified her as a child: acrid smoke that singed the nostrils and choked the lungs. A dry, searing wind that burned the skin like acid. Flying soot that stung the eyes so that she had to blink back tears to see. She was in a place of utter desolation, the darkness relieved only by the flickering of red and orange shadows writhing in the roiling smoke. A low vibration echoed around her, like the menacing growl of some great beast ready to spring for the kill.

And her bones ached, she realized. She was lying on a hard surface, and something was digging into her hip. Jillian shifted position painfully, and like a dreamer slowly awaking, she began to make out shapes in the murky shadows around her. She puzzled at what she saw. Furniture. She was on the floor, wedged into a corner, a tipped-over chair beneath her. She rolled to one side and pushed it away, the hellish light tracing the familiar spindles of its ladder back.

How many times had she sat on the hard, unforgiving seat of one of those chairs as a child, hands stubbornly behind her, fingers clenched around those spindles rather than around a spoon containing pale, woody lima beans or slimy Cream of Wheat? Stifling a cough, Jillian lifted her head. How was it that hell looked so much like her mother's kitchen? The simple explanation was, of course, that she wasn't dead, but back at her mother's house in Minnesota. But why was she lying on the floor? Why was the house in darkness, except for that odd, menacing red flicker coming from down the hall? And why—

Oh, God! Fire!

"Mother!" Coughing and choking, Jillian tried to rise, but when she placed her hands on the ceramic tile floor, her palms, wet and slick, skidded out from under her. She propped herself on her elbows, instead, and screamed again. "Mother! Where are you?"

Blinking through tears, she could just make out the shapes of the other three kitchen chairs, still upright around the oval oak table. A thick, gray brume was circling the room, wafting across the face of the cabinets, undulating under the ceiling like toxic silk.

Avoiding her slippery palms, Jillian used her wrists and elbows to brace herself as she struggled to her knees. Through the archway leading to the front hall and the rest of the house beyond, the subtle pattern of the flowered Victorian wallpaper had taken on a gaudy orange glow. The fire seemed to be coming from down the hall, toward the living room.

She scrambled to her feet. "Mother!"

Her voice was a strangled bleat. A claw of pain ripped at her lungs, and she doubled over, spitting up thick phlegm, coughing and choking, hands on her knees. When the spasm finally passed, she held her breath and unrolled the collar of her turtleneck sweater, covering her nose and trying to take small, filtered breaths.

"Mother, where are you?"

This time there was an answer, but the voice she heard was deep and male. "Jillian? Are you in there?"

It was coming from behind her, she realized, at the back door. She spun around and saw a shadow at the high window. The door handle rattled, but it seemed to be locked. "Jillian!"

"Here! I'm in here!" She knew she should run and open the door. Or go and find her mother. *Do something!* a voice in her head bellowed. But she was frozen in place, disoriented and growing faint from the expenditure of scant oxygen.

The door handle rattled once more and then the shadow at the window disappeared. A split second later, a gloved fist slammed through the glass. The smoke stirred, twisting and swirling toward this new escape outlet as a great, padded arm reached through, easily grabbing the inside knob and turning it. As the door flung wide, Jillian was knocked to her knees by the rush of superheated air coming from behind her. The fire, fanned by fresh oxygen, was on the move.

"Jillian!"

A pair of hands hooked under her armpits, yanking her upward, and she found herself looking into Nils Berglund's worried face. He was dressed in uniform, the fluorescent yellow stitching on his shoulder patches glowing in the dim light. His head was bare, and his cropped, snow-dusted hair sparkled in the flickering light as the flakes melted in the heat. He rose to his feet, lifting her easily along with him.

"What are you doing here? Where's your mother?"

Jillian's legs felt like rubber, and she was forced to wrap her fingers in the soft, padded bulk of his bomber jacket to keep herself from crumbling to the floor. "I don't know! I was out cold, and when I woke up..." Another painful spasm seized her lungs and she choked on the smoke once more.

"Come on, let's get you out of here!" Wrapping an arm around her, Berglund started for the door, half-dragging, half-carrying her with him, but after only a couple of steps, Jillian locked her knees and braced her feet—bare, she suddenly realized—on the hard tile floor.

"No, Nils! We have to find my mother!"

"I will, after I get you out of here!"

They were almost to the door, but she grabbed the rounded tile rim of the kitchen counter and steadied herself. "No, go now! I'll wait here."

"Outside, dammit!" he yelled, dragging her off the counter. He shoved her through the door and out onto the wide wooden back porch. "Get away from the house! The fire trucks are on the way. They'll give you a blanket. Go!"

Not waiting for an answer, he left her there and ran back into the house. "Mrs. Meade! Grace! Where are you?"

Jillian wrapped an arm around one of the porch's upright beams and drank a greedy gulp of fresh air, but it was too cold, too rich, and her lungs seized. Doubling over again, she coughed and hacked, gasping for air between each painful spasm that felt like a thousand tiny shards of glass slicing her lungs. Snow was falling around the house in great, feathery flakes, spinning and brilliant white against the black night. As Jillian struggled dizzily for air, the entire world seemed to be swirling.

Then, over the raspy sound of her own breathing, she thought she heard the faint wail of sirens. She pulled herself, hand-over-hand, along the freezing porch rail and looked out into the night through wind-whipped snow, ears straining. The half-acre lot on which the house sat was mostly wooded. At the far edge of the wood, as she searched for any sign of the fire trucks, she thought she saw something move—something or someone. But her eyes, smoke-stung and running with tears, couldn't make anything out. One of the Newkirks, maybe? Was it the neighbors who'd called in the alarm?

A bang sounded from behind her and she spun on her heel. The storm door was swinging on its hinges, buffeted by the pressurized air from inside the house, slamming against the stucco siding. She reached out and grabbed it on the next swing, peering into the kitchen, blinking as smoke and hot air poured out from the inside.

"Nils! Can you see her?"

The only answer was the splintering of glass as the window over the sink just a few feet away on her left shattered and sent glass shards tinkling across the wooden decking. She ignored the sting on her feet as the smoke inside cleared briefly in the newly formed vortex of air. Nils was standing at the framed archway that led to the front hall, but no sooner had she spotted him than he dropped, disappearing from her sight line behind the kitchen table.

"Are you all right?" she called.

"I found her!"

Jillian held on to the storm door while she waited for him to bring her mother out, ducking her head briefly once or twice for a gulp of fresh air. The sirens were unmistakable now, a panicky caterwaul that pierced the cold winter night. She glanced over her shoulder. Through the spruce trees at the bottom of the drive she spotted red lights winking as the trucks rounded the corner at the end of Lakeshore Road and turned up the street toward her mother's drive. Feeling was coming back into her legs, and the wooden planks were icy under her bare feet. She shivered, her jeans and black turtleneck sweater scant protection against the wicked night air.

Shifting her weight from one freezing foot to the other, she stuck her head around the door frame again. "Come on, Nils! Get out! The trucks are here!"

Silence.

"Nils?"

The smoke swirling under the ceiling was thick as soup now

and dropping fast. Jillian hesitated for a moment, then drew a deep breath and ducked low, trying to stay under the worst of it as she headed into the kitchen, across to where she'd last seen him. Rounding the oval oak table, she saw his back, POLICE stenciled on his jacket in large, reflective yellow letters. He was crouched on the floor, and to one side of him a pair of stockinged legs lay akimbo, splayed feet shod in familiar, tiny black pumps. The pose was uncharacteristically awkward, but Jillian would have recognized those legs anywhere—veinless, smooth and remarkably girlish for a woman of sixty. A source of great pride to her mother.

"Oh, God, Nils! Is she—"

His head snapped up at the sound of her voice. "Jill, no!" His arm shot out to hold her back.

Too late.

Jillian froze as his body shifted and she saw what it had been hiding. She dropped to the floor. "Oh, my God! No! Mother!"

Her mother lay on the tile floor, head tilted strangely to one side, intense blue eyes staring dully into space, half-hidden under heavy lids. Her silver-blond hair was tucked up as always into a chignon at the nape of her neck, virtually unruffled except for a single strand that had come loose and lay across her slack jaw. Her mouth was open, as if she'd been struck dumb in midprotest. Jillian's gaze dropped to the dark stain that had seeped across the front of her mother's pale cashmere sweater. All color was obscured by the strange tinge to the light flickering from the hall, but she knew the sweater set was robin's-egg blue, just like her mother's eyes. Grace had been wearing this sweater as she sat in her favorite wing chair in the front room.... When? Only moments ago, it seemed, sitting there, large as life, her spine ramrod straight, held away from the chair back, her hands clasped delicately in her lap, knees together, legs crossed demurely at the ankles. Always the picture of a lady. Now, the sweater was ruined. Her mother was lying sprawled on the floor, and the irrational thought crossed Jillian's mind that Grace Meade would be appalled to know she'd been found in such an ungraceful state.

"Let's get out of here!" Nils yelled over the roar of the fire and the wail of sirens that were right outside now. He coughed, drawing in air that was rapidly becoming completely unbreathable as he gathered the small, limp body into his arms.

Jillian stood and pressed herself against the wall, repelled by the burden in his arms, yet unable to look away. Her gaze rose with him as he struggled to his feet. He was huge, her mother's tiny form almost lost in the bulk of him.

He cocked his head toward the back door. "Get going! I'll follow you!"

He shifted the weight in his arms for a better grip, and as he did, her mother's head turned, those pale, dead eyes fixing Jillian with an accusatory glare. She recoiled, and as her knees buckled, she slid down the wall, landing with a thud on her backside.

"For Christ sake, get up!" Nils bellowed. "The fire's spreading! The whole place is going to go!"

She wanted to run but she was nailed in place by the judgment she saw in her mother's eyes. Nils hefted the body over one shoulder, freeing up a hand, and he used it to grip Jillian's upper arm. She shook him off and turned away, squeezing her eyes shut. Anything but to look at the stare of that monstrous thing that was—but couldn't be—her mother.

Mummy, no, please!

He grabbed her again, but she fought him off and scuttled down the hall, deeper into the house, moving toward the dull roar and the flickering light of flames that had now fully engulfed the living room.

"Jill! Get back here, dammit!"

Instead, she lay down on the threshold of the dining room, opposite the fire, pressing her cheek into its waxed and buffed cherry planks. The fire crackled in her ears, but beyond that sensation, which was more pressure than sound, she was aware of nothing. Her eyelids closed, and she gave herself over gratefully to whatever void she could find.

It wasn't to be. Something clamped on to her arms, and she was lifted in two sharp yanks, first to a sitting position, then to her feet. She opened her eyes. Nils held her by the elbows, both of his hands free now of that other load. He shook her once, then again, all will had drained out of her. Her head flopped, her body limp, joints unstrung.

"Dammit, Jill, come on! Do you want to die in here?"

A sweet lassitude overtook her. *Yes. Leave me alone.*

He caught her face and cupped it in his hands, his wide, worried face filling her field of vision.

"Jill, please!"

He leaned toward her until their foreheads were touching, and he held her close, thumbs stroking her face. Then his head tilted and he kissed her, hard. She felt his lips on hers, and for a moment, she was seventeen all over again. The intervening years faded away, and they were Nils and Jill, inseparable, deeply, obsessively in love, the way it only happens the first time, when every experience is new, every touch a revelation. It all came back to her—the smell of him, the taste of him, the safe refuge of him.

When he pulled back and looked at her again, his expression tortured, she nodded. He got to his feet and extended a hand, and she reached out, ready to take it, until she spotted the dark stain on the left shoulder of his jacket. Blood, she realized, soaked deep into the padding. Her mother's blood. She tried to push him away—push the blood away—only to realize that her own hands, too, were sticky and wet with it. She stared at them, horrified, and she screamed.

He grabbed her roughly. She fought him, scratching and kicking, but it was a hopeless mismatch. He was huge, well over six feet and even heavier now than he'd been in his high school linebacker days. He lifted her easily and was about to sling her over that same bloody shoulder when a lucky kick from her right foot connected with his groin. His grip weakened momentarily, and as he crumpled, Jillian pushed herself off his brawny frame and started to run. But before she'd gone more than a couple of steps, her bare heel hit a wet patch and skidded out from under her. She landed flat on her back on the hardwood floor, the wind knocked out of her.

She lay there for a moment, then rolled over—only to find herself right where Nils had laid down his bloody burden, face-to-face with her mother's dull, half-lidded stare. Unblinking, it cut through her like a judgment.

She was, indeed, in hell, Jillian thought. Exactly where she belonged.

CHAPTER 2

Washington, D.C.
Wednesday, January 10, 1979

Much later, when it was all over—and yet not really over because, as Alex Cruz knew, there were some events you never truly got over but only locked away in that dark recess of the mind where nightmares live—afterward, he did the calculations, backtracking, trying to figure out the exact sequence of events. Where he'd been the first time he'd heard the names Jillian and Grace Meade. Whether he'd had any premonition he was about to encounter a face of evil unlike anything he'd seen before in either his professional or personal life. Whether there'd been any warning sign that this would be the case to finally push him over the razor-thin line between the letter of the law he'd sworn to uphold and the rough justice of the vigilante; the line between his troubled past and the uncertain fate that lay ahead of him.

Even before he'd heard of these two women, Cruz had already witnessed more than his share of the horrors that human beings could unleash upon one another. He'd been a grunt in the jungles of Vietnam, then spent more than a decade as a U.S. Army criminal investigator, specializing in homicide, rape and other crimes of violence. Now, as a Special Agent with the Federal Bureau of Investigation, he spent his days tracking the worst of the worst—terrorists, kidnappers and serial killers who claimed the entire planet as their personal hunting ground.

At this point, there wasn't much he hadn't come across in the way of human depravity, but the events at the root of Grace Meade's murder and the others connected to it would forever stand alone in his mind, unequaled in terms of sheer cruelty. Did he have the slightest inkling of that the day the case first landed on his desk? One thing was reasonably certain: On the night Jillian Meade was trying to die in Minnesota, Cruz would have been eighteen hundred miles away and, taking into account time zone differences, already in bed. While the fire in Minnesota blazed, trapping mother and daughter, Cruz was struggling with the restless insomnia that had plagued him for almost as long as he could remember, part of the price he paid for past mistakes. If Jillian Meade was trying to die that night, Alex Cruz had long since resigned himself to the knowledge that he was condemned for his own sins to live.

The day after the fire, Cruz arrived at the office early. If he hadn't been trying to dodge Sean Finney, who worked in the next cubicle, he might have overlooked the notice regarding Jillian Meade, only one of at least a half-dozen pending cases sitting in his "In" basket. Given his already heavy caseload, he might have passed this one on to someone else, or at least delayed following up on it for a few days. But that morning, Cruz was determined to find a reason to get out of the office and avoid the loaded questions and broad hints Finney had been lobbing his way with increasing frequency of late. He needed a case that would take him on the road where he could slip back into comfortable anonymity.

Eleven months into a new job with the FBI, he was close to violating one of his cardinal rules: never blur the boundaries between the job and his private life. Maryanne Finney was Sean's cousin, and Cruz had met her at a New Year's Eve party hosted by his co-worker. An attractive redhead with hair that corkscrewed halfway down her back, Maryanne had an infectious smile that didn't take no for an answer, even from a taciturn newcomer who tried to telegraph he wasn't looking for romantic entanglements. Within hours of meeting her, Cruz had found himself accepting an invitation to a Sunday dinner at her parents' home in Bethesda, seduced by Maryanne's sweet Irish blarney when she'd assured him that it wouldn't be a formal date but that he'd be doing her a favor by going.

"They're a fine bunch, my family, but forever nagging me to settle down and produce a gaggle of little Finneys. They can't help themselves. It's a genetic defect—the Irish Catholic thing, you know. Last thing I'm interested in, believe me, after spending my days in a classroom riding herd on other people's rambunctious monsters. If a stranger's around, though, they'll be on their best behavior. Might actually stifle themselves about my pitiful life, at least for one day."

Like he himself wasn't the pitiful one, Cruz thought, an old stray taken in by a kindhearted woman. And so it had started, light and friendly, but in the usual way of these matters, one thing had led to another. Maryanne's enthusiasm in the bedroom, he'd discovered later that evening, was as cheerful and energetic as everything else about her. When she finally fell into sleep, it was deep and undisturbed, leaving him awake in the dark with only his guilty conscience for company. As he'd watched the pale luminous curve of her shoulder and neck in the soft glow of the candles she'd lit before they made love, he'd seen a Botticelli painting of uncomplicated virtues, a woman who, despite her protestations to the contrary, did seem to hanker after a man who'd stick around for the long haul.

He wasn't what a nice woman like that needed or wanted. After all these years, he was too wedded to his solitude and too addicted to the job. Sooner or later, every woman with whom he got involved came to the same conclusion, and the endings were always the same—tears, angry words and self-recrimination. So Cruz had done what seemed like the kindest thing—he called Maryanne the next day to apologize for letting things go further than they should have.

He'd been avoiding Sean Finney ever since. Like every matchmaker since the beginning of time, Finney took bumptious delight in the thought that his introduction of cousin and co-worker might bear fruit. As if that weren't bad enough, Sean was evidently plugged into some mysterious Finney family tom-tom network that seemed to have been vibrating since the moment Cruz's path had crossed Maryanne's, so that Sean spent half his time haunting Cruz's cubicle, fishing for details on what was transpiring between them. She deserved better than the both of them, Cruz thought guiltily, flipping through the papers on his desk.

He was assigned to the FBI's International Liaison Division, investigating a wide array of cross-border offenses—organized crime, kidnapping, terrorism, outlaw motorcycle gang activity, child abduction, art theft and violent crimes such as murder, rape and robbery—sifting through evidence, following up leads and liaising with law enforcement agencies domestically and internationally. During his Army career, Cruz had worked homicide cases all over the world, and the Bureau, desperate for experienced agents to help deal with the burgeoning of cross-border crime syndicates and international terrorism, had snapped him up as soon as he'd resigned his commission and his résumé had hit the street.

By 9:00 a.m., he'd narrowed down his day's work to the two or three cases that offered him the chance to get out in the field. Before the day was out, the Meade affair would push all the others aside. It wouldn't be long after that that he would be pursuing the elusive mystery of Jillian and Grace Meade with a single-mindedness bordering on obsession.

He was reaching for his coat when Sean Finney's rust-colored head and myopic gray eyes suddenly popped up over the beige fabric-covered divider that separated their desks. "Hey, Alex! What's cookin'? You comin' or goin'?"

"Going," Cruz replied, regretting that he hadn't moved a little faster. Engrossed in his review of background briefs, he hadn't even heard the voluble, heavyset Finney arrive. Yet there he was, larger than life, with his gravely smoker's voice and his unavoidable bonhomie.

"Where you headed?"

Cruz held up a blue sheet of paper, one of the stack of color-coded international alerts that crossed their desks daily. "Gotta track down a subject, try to take a statement."

The alerts, part of a global cooperative effort between various national law enforcement agencies, sought information and assistance in locating wanted persons. Red bulletins warned police and border checkpoints to be on the lookout for fugitives with outstanding arrest warrants. Green ones were for career criminals, like child molesters or pornographers, likely to commit repeat offenses in several countries. Yellow notices meant missing persons, gray ones detailed organized crime groups. The white notices, most often directed to Sean Finney's desk, provided details on stolen art and cultural objects. Black diffusions sought help in identifying dead bodies that had turned up with false or missing identification.

A blue alert like the one Cruz held in his hand was a request from a foreign police agency—in this case, Britain's Scotland Yard—to trace a witness to a crime. Many of these witnesses were actually suspects who, if the evidence panned out, would eventually be the subjects of red Fugitive Wanted notices. Once the suspect was located, an extradition request would be the next thing to come down the pipeline.

It was in this blue-printed notice that Cruz had spotted the Washington address of a witness wanted for questioning regarding two homicides that had gone down in Britain a couple of weeks earlier. One of the victims had been a seventy-one-year-old former civil servant by the name of Vivian Atwater, who'd been shot in her London apartment, which was subsequently torched. The other was a sixty-year-old spinster in Dover, England, and the murder of Margaret Entwistle appeared to have followed a similar M.O. Both women were somehow linked to an American whose address, conveniently, was right there in the capital, only a couple of miles from his office.

"Scotland Yard sent this over. They've had a couple of what they're calling 'elder murders' over the past couple of weeks," Cruz told Finney. "They're asking us to have a talk with a woman here in D.C. who knew both vics, see if she can shed some light."

"She? We got a female perp?"

"Don't know. Apparently she'd met with both victims a few days before they were killed. The fact that she called on one of the victims might be coincidence, but two starts to look a little hinky."

"You got that right. So you're gonna run her down?"

"Gonna try," Cruz said as he started to lock up his cabinets.

"Need some backup?"

"I think I can handle it."

"Oh." Finney sounded disappointed. Cruz felt the air move as he tossed his coat over the spare chair in his cubicle, then heard the hiss of a match as his neighbor lit the first of many cigarettes that fouled the air around his desk daily. All the more reason not to let the guy ride along in his car. Finney leaned over the divider. "If you change your mind and decide you could use some help—"

"You bet. I'll let you know." Cruz nodded and headed out of his cubicle. The squad room had filled by now, agents and analysts sifting paper, typing up case notes and working phones that never seemed to stop ringing.

Cruz made it as far as the elevator before his luck ran out. Finney's voice cut through the hum like a rusty hacksaw. "Hey, Alex, by the way—seen Maryanne lately?"

Caught in a trap of my own damn making, Cruz thought grimly, as heads popped up all around. Just then, the elevator door wheezed open. He leapt on, playing deaf and dumb as he hit the Close Door button.

* * *

According to the passport details supplied by Scotland Yard, the witness sought for questioning on the two open-book homicides in the U.K. possessed dual citizenship due to her parentage. Mother: English. Father: American. Date of birth: July 14, 1944. Place of birth: Drancy, France—which, technically, Cruz supposed, would make her a citizen of that country, too, if she ever cared to claim the right. A war baby, obviously. Thirty-five years old, born on the anniversary of the storming of the Bastille.

Cruz, too, had an historic birth date: December 7, 1941, the day of the surprise Japanese attack on Pearl Harbor. This coincidence might have seemed auspicious, had he thought about it at the time and been the type to find meaning in such things. If he had, perhaps he'd have been able to predict that, with such mutually bloody birth dates, he and this woman were bound to become the bitter adversaries they did.

The address supplied in the blue notice led him to a weathered, four-story brick apartment building near Dupont Circle in downtown Washington. On the intercom board between the building's open outer door and the locked inner door, Jillian Meade's name was listed next to 204. Cruz pressed the buzzer and waited, peering through the art deco stained glass windows of the inner door to a black and white tiled lobby. When there was no response after half a minute or so, he tried the buzzer again, then jiggled the handle on the lobby door. Locked. Turning back to the intercom, Cruz noticed a red plastic strip punched with the letters Super in white. He tried the buzzer next to it, with the same result as before. He had just about decided the trip had been a waste of time when he was startled by a crackled shout from the overhead speaker.

"I already called the cops, assholes!"

Taken aback, Cruz hesitated, then leaned toward the intercom grill. "Is this the building superintendent?"

"Who's this?"

"Federal agent. I'd like a word, please." Silence. "Sir?" When there was still no answer, Cruz rang again. Nothing. He was getting ready to lean on the buzzer for as long as it took when he heard a muffled but crotchety voice from the other side of the lobby door.

"Yeah, yeah, keep yer shirt on! I'm not jet-propelled, y'know."

Through the stained glass window, Cruz made out the image of a small, grizzled man in a dark jump suit limping across the lobby. The old man put one rheumy eye to the glass and hollered, "You're no cop!"

"Yes, sir, I am," Cruz said loudly, straining to be heard through the heavy door. "Sort of."

"What 'sort of'? Where's your damn uniform? Ya either are or you're not, fella, and if you're not, then I can tell you right now, the real ones are on the way."

"I'm a federal agent," Cruz said, pulling out a leather folder and slapping it up against the glass.

The old man peered at it, then pulled back, head shaking. "Well, that looks real official, I'm sure, but I'm damned if I can read it, 'specially without my glasses."

"I'm with the Federal Bureau of Investigation, sir."

"The whoosis? Who are they when they're at home?"

"FBI."

The old man cupped a hand behind his ear. "Who?"

"Sir, if you could open the door—"

"Wait, wait, lemme open the friggin' door." The super pushed it open a crack but stood barring the way with his bantam rooster frame. Cruz towered over him, looking down at the shine on the top of his bald head.

"Lemme see that," the caretaker said, waving a gnarled finger at Cruz's ID folder. "Oh, the FBI! Why didn't you say so? Jeez, Louise! I was figuring on the D.C. coppers."

"I don't know anything about that, sir. I'm just trying to locate one of your tenants."

"You didn't come on account of I called the police?"

"No, sir."

"Well that just friggin' figures, don't it?" The old man peered around Cruz toward the outer door and the street beyond.

"Called more'n three-quarters of an hour ago, but they never bloody show up when you need 'em."

"What did you call about?"

He waved an impatient hand. "Tenants were complainin' 'bout somebody hittin' the intercom buzzers. Then they go answer and nobody's there. Kids, prob'ly. It's happened before. You get these punks'll lean on all the buzzers, see. Chances are somebody upstairs is waitin' for pizza delivery or something, unlocks the door without checkin' who is it. Next thing I know, I got graffiti all over the hallways and units gettin' broke into. Real pain in the ass. One of the tenants says she saw some frizzle-headed guy wandering around a while ago, lookin' like he didn't know where he was going."

"Did she speak to him?"

"Nah. Said she figured he was there to visit somebody. Only mentioned it because when she came down here, she heard a couple of the neighbors complainin' 'bout gettin' buzzed. I woulda gone up to check it out myself, 'cept I got this hernia problem. Goin' in to get it fixed next week. Otherwise, I got no problem goin' after the little buggers myself and givin' 'em a rap upside the head so they don't come back here. Figured I better call the cops this time, though, let them do it. Only now," the old man added resentfully, "you tell me you're not even the cops."

"Sorry. I'm sure they're on the way if you called."

"Course I called. I said it, didn't I?"

"Yes, you did. Look, if you like, I can go up there with you to check it out."

The super looked him up and down for a moment, as though trying to decide whether or not Cruz made a suitable bodyguard. "Nah. It was over an hour ago already. If the guy was up to anything, he's been and gone already. I'll hear about it soon enough. So what about you? What do you want?"

"Like I said, I'm trying to locate someone who I understand lives in the building. A Jillian Meade?"

"Oh, yeah, sure, I know her."

"She around, do you know?"

The super hefted his thin, blue-clad shoulders. "I dunno. You buzz her?"

"Yes, but there was no answer."

"Then she's probably at work."

"Do you know where that is?" Cruz asked. "Where she works, I mean?" He was answered with another shrug. "How long has she been living here?"

"Oh, I dunno, couple, three years, at least. Yeah, at least that, come to think of it, 'cause she was here during the Bicentennial, I remember. She was one of the ones decked out her balcony in red, white and blue bunting."

"What kind of tenant is she?" Cruz asked, pulling a notebook out of his hip pocket and making notes.

"What can I say? Pays her rent on time, quiet."

"She's single? Lives alone?"

"Uh-huh. Kinda shy, but okay, you know. Goes to work early, comes home between, oh, six and seven most nights, I'd say. Never had any trouble outta her." The old man peered over Cruz's shoulder, trying to see if he was getting this all down in his notebook.

"Any friends you can point me to? A boyfriend, maybe?"

The super thought about it, his stained fingernails scratching across the stubble on his chin. "Not really. All the time she's been here, can't say I seen her go out on many dates. Now and then, there's this older guy comes around. Not that I'm spyin' twenty-four hours a day or nothin' like that, but my place is right down here on the ground floor, and I keep an eye on things. You gotta, in a city this size. Stuff goin' down all the time."

"Uh-huh. But this man who comes to see Miss Meade?" Cruz prodded. "You got a name, by chance?"

"Nah. Seen him come and go with her a few times, is all. Not a real social butterfly, is Miss Meade."

"And he's the only one?"

"Only one I ever seen. She ain't ugly, that's for sure, 'specially if you catch her without those glasses on. But she ain't no girl no more neither, know what I mean? I figure she's just another one of those career office gals this city's full of. But, hey! At least she don't make trouble, right? All my tenants should be so easy."

"Okay," Cruz said. "You say she gets home from work around six or so? But you don't know where she works?"

"Well, now, hang on a minute, lemme think about that." The old man's bristly eyebrows skidded together over his nose as he frowned, thinking hard. "I asked her that once, now you mention it. A few months back, it was. I was up in her apartment fixin' a leaky john. Just tryin' to make a little conversation, 'cause God knows, that woman hardly says 'boo' herself. And I did ask her what she did for a living. Now where did she say she worked? It was someplace, you know, like...oh, hey!" He snapped his fingers. "I remember. The Smithsonian. Yeah, that's it!"

Cruz's pen paused in midair over the notebook. "Like, at that big old castle, do you mean, or at one of the other related museums? 'Smithsonian' covers a lot of territory."

"Ah, well, now, that I can't tell you. Anyway, what does the FBI want with Miss Meade? She in some kind of trouble?"

"It's just a routine inquiry."

"I had a guy here once worked for the State Department. FBI came around, then, too, checkin' him out. For a security clearance, they said. That what this is about?"

"Something like that," Cruz said. A flash of light bounced off the stained glass of the lobby door, and both men turned to see a black and white cruiser pull up to the front of the building, cherry lights rotating. "Looks like the police finally made it."

"Well, it's about friggin' time."

"I'll leave you to deal with them, then, sir," Cruz said, pocketing his notebook. "I appreciate your help, Mr.—?"

"Ripkin. No problem. I run a nice quiet buildin', you know. Don't want any funny stuff here."

"Sure thing. Listen, Mr. Ripkin, I'm going to try to contact Miss Meade through her office, but if I miss her there, I'll check back here again this evening. If you see her or hear from her before then, though, I'd appreciate it if you wouldn't mention I came by." Cruz had no idea whether or not Jillian Meade presented a risk of flight, but there was no point taking unnecessary risks.

"Whatever," the super said distractedly, the glare returning to his beetle eyes as his attention shifted to the street, where two beefy D.C. patrolmen were lumbering up the building's front steps. "About bloody time you guys showed up!" he hollered as the front door opened.

Cruz gave the patrolmen a sympathetic nod and slipped out around them.

There was a drugstore at the corner of the street. Cruz ducked into it to use the pay phone and put in a call to the Smithsonian Institution main switchboard. The operator, after consulting a master directory, was able to tell him there was a Jillian Meade listed on staff at the National Museum of American History, one of several buildings scattered around the capital that fell under the Smithsonian's broad organizational umbrella.

The museum was located just across Constitution Avenue from the red-roofed buildings of the Federal Triangle. Its architecture was boxlike, a pink marble mausoleum that housed a vast collection of Americana, from the original star-spangled Banner that Francis Scott Key had seen "by the dawn's early light," to a pocket compass used by Lewis and Clark—a massive assemblage of memorabilia that ran the gamut from priceless national icons to sentimental kitsch.

In the main lobby, Cruz waited to ask the busy guard at the Information desk where he could find Jillian Meade's office. All around him, the halls echoed with the shouts and laughter of children, the hissing and shushing of their teachers, and the valiant efforts of docents to be heard above the din of young voices and feet tramping across Italian marble floors. Once he'd gotten directions, Cruz dodged kids careening up and down the stairs as he made his way to the third floor, where, according to the guard, he would find Miss Meade in a corner suite of administrative offices next to the military history display.

Most of the third floor was taken up with exhibits of ceramics, printing presses, money and medals, but on the far northeast side of the floor was the permanent exhibit on the history of the American armed forces. Passing through it to reach the admin offices, Cruz ran an uneasy gauntlet past mannequins dressed in U.S. military uniforms from down through the years, standing on sober guard. There were artifacts and photos linked to various conflicts, from the Civil War, the Spanish-American War, the First and Second World Wars and the UN action in Korea, all laid out in glass-covered display cases, a proud collection of weapons, tactical plans, strategic maps and portraits of victorious men and officers.

By contrast, Cruz noted, the exhibit on Vietnam was pitifully small, tucked away in the farthermost corner of the section. It was a case study in controversy avoidance, set up to carefully dodge the temptation to assign blame for the debacle that had taken fifty-eight thousand American lives in a war that couldn't be won. Five years after the fall of Saigon, emotions were still running too high for any kind of national consensus on that war, and the display reflected the national mood, treating the period like the historic equivalent of a drooling idiot relative whose embarrassing existence the family preferred to ignore. One day there would be a reckoning, Cruz thought. But not yet.

He was almost past the exhibit when a photograph in a case near the end of the display area caught his eye. He stopped and stared, his attention snagged not so much by the platoon of grunts in familiar jungle camouflage peering out at the camera, looking pitifully young in their face paint and false bravado, as by the buildings and hills behind them. He knew this place, he realized. Had stood on that very spot. It was a staging area outside Da Nang, a camp from which a small recon unit of seven men, himself included, had set out one day in 1966 under the command of an incompetent 1st Lieutenant named Darryl Houghton. A scared kid from Dayton, Ohio, Houghton had tried to cover his fear with bullying and intimidation, then issued one dumb order too many and never came back.

Cruz felt the air move and he looked nervously over his shoulder, but there was no one else around except for a uniformed guard standing watch over a Civil War cannon. For the moment, he was alone, falling through time and space. Logically, he knew the drumming sound in his ears was the rumble of kids' feet running up and down distant halls and not the drone of helicopter blades, but he couldn't explain why his nostrils had suddenly picked up the distinctive odor of heated gun oil—the familiar smell of petroleum steam that issued from the red-hot muzzle of an M-16 rifle after it had been fired. And there was something else: the sour stench of rotting plant material, the kind that always managed to work its way inside his clothes and ears and nose as he crawled on his belly on the jungle floor, trying to stay beneath the sight line of roving VC patrols. Worst of all, he was smelling black vinyl body bags, the way they got when they'd been filled and left out too long in the brutal heat.

An eruption of childish giggles brought him back to the present as a school group guided by a harassed docent spilled around the corner and spread out across the armed forces exhibit. Shaking ghosts off his back, Cruz moved on.

Passing through a door marked "Museum Staff Only," he found himself in the reception area of the corner suite of offices to which the Information guard had directed him. A woman sat at a secretarial desk, turned away from him so that he was out of her peripheral field of vision. Fingers flying over the keys of an IBM Selectric, she seemed not to notice the click of the door or the raucous group outside.

Approaching the desk, Cruz saw why. She was wearing a set

of headphones, half-hidden in the feathery, swept-back layers of her blond hair, connected to a Dictaphone machine on the desk beside her. Putting a hand to his mouth, he coughed once, then again, louder. She glanced up, then did a startled double take.

"Oh, my Lord! You scared the you-know-what out of me!" she cried, ripping off the headset with one hand as her other hand flew to her heart. Her chair swiveled around. Her eyes were heavily shaded with blue, her lashes blacker and thicker than Nature had ever been capable of producing without the help of the cosmetics industry. Early twenties, Cruz guessed.

"I'm really sorry," he said. "I tried to make as much noise as I could coming in."

She waved a dismissive hand. "Oh, it's okay. Never mind. Happens all the time. I just get so absorbed in what I'm doing, you know?" He nodded sympathetically and she gave him a smile. "What can I do for you?"

"I'm here to see Jillian Meade."

A perturbed crease marred the smooth expanse of her forehead. "Did you have an appointment?"

"No, but I was hoping to catch her in. It's important."

Deeply pink lips twisted in a grimace of regret. "You should've called ahead. Could've saved yourself the trip. She's not in."

"Will she be back later?"

"Unh-unh, not today, not tomorrow, either, I don't think. I was told she's out probably till the end of the week."

"Out where? I happen to know she's not at home."

"Are you a friend of hers?"

"No, this is official business. Is there someone who can tell me where I can find her?"

"I'm not really sure?" the woman replied, her voice rising uncertainly, as if posing unhelpful responses as questions might make them less irritating. "I'm just a temp? The girl who usually works here was in a car accident a couple of days ago and I was just called in to take her place while she's laid up."

"So, who would know?"

"Maybe you should talk to Mr. Twomey."

"And he would be who?"

"The boss here," she suggested, cocking her thumb at a set of double doors behind her. A brass plate at the side of the door noted the room number and the occupant: Haddon Twomey, Chief Curator. "Can you hang on a sec and I'll see if he's free?" When Cruz nodded, she rose, then seemed to have second thoughts. "Can I tell him who you are?"

"Special Agent Cruz with the Federal Bureau of Investigation."

"Whoa, FBI? Okay then, let me go ask."

She disappeared into the corner office. As murmuring voices sounded from behind the door, Cruz looked around the reception area. It was a study in beige, furnished entirely in plastic and steel. The tan walls were covered in brightly colored posters left over from the Bicentennial celebration. A half-dozen buff-colored, steel-framed chairs lined the walls, and back issues of the *Smithsonian Magazine* were splayed across beige plastic cubes that passed for tables. There were three other doors around the reception area besides the one he'd come in, all made of the same dark wood as the curator's, although these others were single rather than double openings. None had name plates. Maybe one of these was Jillian Meade's office.

Cruz heard the soft click of a door latch and turned as the receptionist came back and nodded, holding the door open for him. "You can go in now," she said, pressing herself against the door as he passed, then closing it behind her.

The office in which he found himself was markedly more luxurious than the utilitarian reception area. A massive desk the size of a dinghy took up nearly half the room, angled catty-corner against fully loaded bookshelves that covered two of the room's four walls. The desk, made of dark wood, was intricately carved with pillars and scrolls, and it looked very old—and, Cruz thought, very expensive. Several brightly colored area rugs covered the same nondescript carpet as in the reception area. The rugs, Cruz was reasonably certain, were genuine Navajo, and old ones, too. As for the rest of the pieces in the room, he suspected were rare antiques, as well.

Opposite the desk were two floor-to-ceiling windows set into the building's northeast corner, one on either side of the supporting corner block. Heavy silk panels in a rich shade of gold framed the windows, while the glass was covered with sheer gauzy material that did little to cut down the amount of light from the clear January day streaming in.

"Good afternoon...Agent Cruz, I believe?" The carefully modulated voice came from a silhouette that stood in front of the windows, back-lit so that Cruz found it impossible to tell whether the man was facing him or not.

"Yes, sir." Crossing the room, Cruz angled his approach so that he put the windows to one side, affording a better view of the other man. His eyes adjusted to the change in the light, and Twomey's features began to emerge from shadow.

He was tall, thin and patrician-looking, slightly stooped at the shoulder. Somewhere in his fifties, Cruz estimated by the mix of gray and white in his hair, which swept straight back off Twomey's high brow, waving slightly over his collar. His blue pin-striped shirt was open-necked under a crested navy blazer that seemed faintly nautical, although it probably reflected his status as an alumnus of some Ivy League school. Was this the older man the building super had said sometimes called on Jillian Meade? Cruz wondered. The man's eyebrows were tufted, his eyes half-lidded, as if he were bored or weary or both. His nose was long and prominent, with deep crevices running from either nostril to the edges of his plummy, turned-down lips, giving him the appearance of being permanently offended by the whiff of something malodorous in the air. Just the sight of him made every working class hackle on Cruz's neck stand up in protest.

"So, you're a junior G-man, are you?" Twomey asked, his hand dangling in Cruz's general direction.

Cruz shook it and found the skin icy to the touch and uncommonly smooth for a man. Like picking up a carp.

"We've had occasion to seek your people's assistance in the past," Twomey said. "An irreplaceable silver tea service manufactured by Paul Revere himself went missing from one of our exhibits some time back. The FBI said they had a lead to a New Orleans-based antique dealer of rather shady reputation. They suspected he'd secreted it out of the country, hidden in plain view in a shipment of English silver that an equally dubious but very wealthy client living in Barbados had bought at an auction around the same time. There'd been an export permit issued, but I suppose most government bureaucrats wouldn't know plate from pewter, much less Paul Revere, would they?"

Cruz opted not to speculate about which ignorant bureaucrats he was referring to. And while they were on the subject, wasn't Twomey on the government payroll, too? "Did you ever get it back?"

"No. Your people still haven't come through for us."

Cruz had the feeling he was supposed to feel guilty, but he was damned if he was going to apologize for not showing up with Twomey's missing teapot.

"I'm trying to get in touch with Miss Meade," he said.

"Yes, so the girl said. Jillian is one of my curatorial associates, but she's not in today. Is there something I can help you with?"

"Can you tell me where I might find her?"

"She's out of town."

"A business trip?"

"No, personal. What's this about?"

Cruz gave him the same stock answer he'd given the caretaker—the same answer he gave anyone with no need to know and without the sense to realize they *had* no need to know. "It's a routine matter. When do you expect her back at work?"

"I'm not sure. Friday, maybe? Monday, at the latest, she said."

"Where did she go?"

"To Minnesota to see her mother. I had the impression there was a problem at home, although Jillian didn't come right out and say, and I certainly wasn't about to pry."

"What kind of problem?"

Twomey moved to the desk and perched on the edge of it. "As I say, I didn't press her on it. I do know that her mother had a cancer scare last year, so perhaps there was a recurrence."

"Where in Minnesota, do you know?"

"A small town called Havenwood. It's about a hundred miles from Minneapolis, I think Jillian said. She grew up there."

"She wasn't born there," Cruz noted.

Twomey arched a brow, and the disapproving lines around his mouth deepened. "No, she wasn't, as a matter of fact. Been doing your homework, I see. She was born in France. Her mother was an English war bride, her father an American pilot with the OSS—the Office of Strategic Services. That's—"

"The forerunner of the CIA, yes, I know," Cruz said. He might not know plate from pewter but he wasn't a total idiot. "So the family came back to the States after the war?"

"Jillian and her mother did. Her father was killed in action over there. His parents invited Mrs. Meade to bring the baby— Jillian, that is—and come live with them. That's how she ended up out there, although Jillian left after high school. Attended Georgetown University, and then she came to work here."

"What does she do here? You said she's a curatorial associate. What does that mean, exactly?"

Twomey shrugged. "She puts together exhibits for our permanent and roving collections. Researches background materials, writes pamphlets and monographs. We have several different departments here, a couple of dozen researchers, but Jillian is really quite the best of the lot. Her specialty is the military and social history of World War II. She's been working on an oral history for the past four or five years, collecting interviews with people who were involved in various anti-Nazi operations in the European theater. It's fascinating work, you know. That generation isn't going to be around forever, and she's doing invaluable work, collecting their reminiscences. I've been encouraging her to develop it into a book or a doctoral thesis."

"She's been looking at operations in the European theater?" Cruz said, his interest piqued now.

"Yes. It started with recently declassified OSS files here in Washington that I'd arranged for her to have access to. Jillian began sifting through them and then got permission to follow up with some of the retired operatives. She's amassed quite an amount of interesting material. As I say, I think she has the makings of a book. Jillian's published several monographs and co-authored a couple of exhibit-related books under the auspices of our presses here, but I think this is going to be her breakout work."

"You seem very impressed with her."

"Absolutely. In the field of history, Agent Cruz, there are good researchers, good interviewers and good writers. Rarely, though, do you find all three in one person. Jillian is that rare exception. Unfortunately, unlike others of far lesser talent, she doesn't seem to realize her own gifts. I must confess, I despair sometimes of her reaching her full potential. It's a question of self-confidence, isn't it? But I'm trying to encourage her in any way I can."

"So, you're sort of Henry Higgins to her Eliza Doolittle?"

Twomey arched his brow slightly. "If I can mentor someone with Miss Meade's talents, Agent Cruz, then I am happy to do that."

Right, Cruz thought. The guy's in love with her. If she attracted a prig like this Twomey, he could just imagine the kind of dry, repressed, severe old maid this Jillian Meade was going to turn out to be. But that said, she hardly sounded like someone who'd be out creating mayhem and leaving dead bodies in her wake. "Had she been to Europe lately?"

"Yes. She was over in London and Paris last month. She's

working on a new exhibit we're pulling together here on American covert support to the French Resistance. We'd been offered access to some materials at the Imperial War Museum in London and the Quai d'Orsay. I sent Jillian over to take a look. She was obviously the best person for the job, but I was encouraging her while she was there to follow up on her own research, as well."

"What did she tell you about her trip? Anything unusual happen while she was over there?"

"Like what?"

Like, two people were murdered and she was among the last people to see them alive, Cruz was tempted to say. But he was there to get information, not offer it. "Anything unusual," he repeated, shrugging. "Anyone she met, or anything she might have seen that was out of the ordinary."

"I haven't really gotten the full rundown yet on how she made out over there. She just got back a few days before Christmas, and then she was leaving to spend the holidays with her mother. I was off with friends and then attending a symposium at Harvard last week. I'd no sooner gotten back into town than Jillian told me she had to go out to Minnesota and look in on her mother. Ships passing in the night, you see."

"The girl outside said she was due back Friday?"

"Or Monday," Twomey replied, nodding.

"Do you happen to have a number for her mother in Minnesota?" Cruz asked. Whatever else was going on, it was stretching credulity to think this Meade woman was going to be a murder suspect. Maybe this was one of those cases he could dispatch with a quick telephone interview, then move on to other, more pressing cases.

Twomey moved behind his desk, rummaging around in loose papers. "Yes, she did leave a number. She'd sent some new brochures off to the printer, and I wanted to be able to get in touch with her if there was any problem with them. Look, what is this about? Why is the FBI, for heaven sake, taking an interest in Jillian Meade?"

Cruz shrugged. "Just a routine inquiry, as I said."

"Aha, there it is!" Twomey spotted a scrap of paper taped to the corner of his telephone. Withdrawing a fountain pen from a burled walnut holder on his desk, he copied a number on a piece of paper and handed it to Cruz.

"Appreciate the information, Mr. Twomey."

"It's Dr. Twomey, actually."

"Right," Cruz said. He was already at the door with a hand on the knob, but he paused to examine a row of framed photographs and certificates he hadn't noticed on the back wall. Most seemed to feature Twomey himself, alone or in a group, standing at lecterns, or shaking hands with assorted dignitaries. "Is Jillian Meade in any of these?"

"I'm not sure. Let's see..." Twomey moved beside him to scan the collection. "No...no...yes, there she is. This was taken during the Bicentennial two years ago. There was a Smithsonian ball on the Fourth of July, and we all ended up on the roof watching the fireworks. That's Jillian right there, in the red dress."

Cruz leaned in to peer at the group Twomey indicated. He was a little surprised to find Jillian Meade not quite as homely as he'd been picturing her. She was one of a dozen men and women of various ages, the men in black tie, the women in gowns, caught by someone's camera as the fireworks exploded in the air behind them. She appeared to be slim and fairly tall, with long, dark hair tucked behind her ears and a soft fringe of bangs. She wore a simple red dress that rose high on her neck but was sliced away at the shoulders, halter-style. Like several others in the picture, she was holding up a glass of wine in an apparent toast to the nation's two hundredth birthday. But where other faces were laughing or animated, her expression was relatively sober as she stared, clear-eyed, at the camera, only a hint of a smile—superior? sardonic?—at the edge of her lips. Twomey was in the group, too, Cruz noted, holding his glass up distractedly to the camera, his gaze focused...where?

On Jillian Meade.

C H A P T E R 3

Montrose, Minnesota
Wednesday, January 10, 1979

Something clattered, faintly melodic, like wooden wind chimes or a handful of pencils dropped on a floor. The sound pulled her out of the drifting, soundless, seamless place in which she'd been floating. Jillian lay still, her senses on alert, afraid to open her eyes. She wanted to go back to that quiet place, but it was like trying to hold smoke in your hand. It slipped away on a wisp of air.

Whatever sound had awoken her was gone, too, before she could identify it. She heard only a low murmuring, like voices whispering from the bottom of a well, subdued and just beyond the range of the audible. She let the hum carry her along, until at last she felt herself floating again, drifting, back into the comfort of the white void. *Stay here,* the murmuring voices seemed to say. *Stay here with us where it's safe.*

Fine with her. There was nothing for her outside that formless place. She was content to drift there forever, a shade without substance. Anything else was too hard.

"Jillian?"

She felt a hand at her shoulder, and a jolt of adrenaline shot through her, as if she'd been touched by a cattle prod. Her body contorted, folding in on itself. The hand closed over her shoulder, a squeeze of reassurance, and then a light shake.

"It's time to wake up. Open your eyes now."

She was terrified, but she had no will of her own. The dead are like that, aren't they? Jillian thought.

She opened her eyes on horizontal bands of silver. She was supposed to be dead, but those looked like guardrails made of brushed steel, just inches from her face. They seemed very real. So did the wall beyond, solid-looking, a flat, dull green not found in nature. Her fingers slid tentatively across a field of bleached cotton to test the rails. Sure enough, they were hard and cold to the touch.

"How are you feeling, Jillian?" The voice came from behind her, a woman's voice, vaguely familiar and yet not. "I'm Dr. Kandinsky. I've been in to see you before. Do you remember?"

A doctor? And so...guardrails...a hospital bed. She was in a hospital bed. Was she sick? Or had she been in an accident? A car accident? When? How long had she been here? Obviously long enough, Jillian realized, for this doctor to have been to see her more than once. She stared at the wall, terrified to move. Terrified to breathe. If she didn't move, didn't breathe, she wouldn't feel pain.

But she *was* breathing and every inhalation hurt. She took a quick survey of the rest of her body. She could see, she could hear. She could smell—antiseptic, a plastic smell, and...smoke? She could feel air blowing gently into her nostrils. Could feel the soft mattress under the right side of her face, and a tiny, line-like hump along her cheekbone. A hose. She was hooked up to a thin plastic hose pumping air...no, oxygen, probably, into rasping lungs that hurt with every breath.

All right, she calculated, she was lying on her right side in a hospital bed looking through guardrails at a green wall, breathing air that hurt. What was wrong with her? She didn't feel particularly sick or feverish, though she was very groggy. Carefully, she flexed her muscles, group by group, without moving her limbs, an isometric test of a body that hadn't even seemed corporeal until just moments ago. All she wanted was to go back to that soft, quiet, safe place, but the voice wouldn't let her.

"Jillian? Come on now, it's time to wake up," it said again, kindly but firmly.

Arms, hands, legs, feet, neck, spine. Everything there, everything working. No pain, except for a dull headache and, when she inhaled, the sensation that her lungs were full of sand. She also had a sick, terrified feeling in the pit of her stomach that something was very, very wrong. She wasn't supposed to be there. If she could only go back to the quiet place.

Leave me alone!

"Jillian, how about if you roll over and sit up? Can you do that?"

The pressure increased on her shoulder, trying to force her onto her back, pulling her toward the voice.

No!

Jillian's left hand shot out, and she gripped the steel rail tightly, fighting to slow the spinning of her body and her mind. She felt a stinging pain in her left arm. She looked at it and froze. There was a bandage just inside the elbow, a thick white square of gauze anchored in place with adhesive tape that pulled at her skin. A small, red stain showed in the center of the gauze where blood had seeped through.

I thought I dreamt it....

Was it possible it had really happened? She'd had a dream about sirens and an ambulance, about being in an emergency room under blinding lights with people hovering and holding her down while she cried and tried to get away from them. She'd fought them, hard, until someone had stuck something into her right arm. She'd cried out—or maybe she only thought she had, because then everything had faded and she'd fallen into the quiet place.

Later, she dreamed she'd awakened and found herself lying on a gurney, only now there was no one around and the lights were dimmed. In the dream, she pulled herself groggily up to a sitting position, confused and frightened, because she knew there was somewhere else she needed to be. They'd taken her clothes, but she climbed off the gurney, anyway, naked except for the sheet she held around her, and started looking for something to put on so she could leave. That was when she found a drawer with paper-wrapped packages labeled Syringe. And suddenly, somehow, she'd known there was a faster way to get to where she needed to be.

She'd ripped open one of the packages and withdrawn a syringe, pulled back the plunger and slipped the plastic cap off the needle. The tip was in her arm and her thumb was on the plunger when the room had erupted in shouting and blinding light. Someone had knocked her to the ground and ripped the needle out of her arm. She'd cried out in pain, her blood streaming onto the floor as she fought them again, until finally, they'd stuck yet another needle into her and she'd tumbled into the quiet place once more.

She'd thought it was a dream, but that blood-stained bandage on her arm was only too real, and so she knew it was true. She had failed.

CHAPTER 4

Havenwood, Minnesota
Thursday, January 11, 1979

The billboard at the side of the highway was hand-painted with a lurid depiction of white-capped waves, a thick stand of towering evergreens, and some kind of huge fish devouring a lure.

WELCOME TO HAVENWOOD, ANGLING CAPITAL OF MINNESOTA! YOUR 4-SEASON PLAYGROUND!

What Cruz knew about fishing would fit on a toothpick wrapper, so he was in no position to argue with that municipal claim to fame. But he did wonder about those painted trees. For the entire eighty-mile drive from the airport, he'd seen nothing but rolling prairie landscape, bleak, barren and mostly snow-covered under a massive gray winter sky that stretched from horizon to horizon—scarcely a hill or a tree to be seen, except for the occasional spindly shelter belt planted by some farmer to keep the wind from carrying off all the rich agricultural topsoil.

He'd started out that morning with a sense of liberation, like a kid playing hooky. The feeling of well-being had lasted through his arrival in Minneapolis. But then, as he drove out of the city, northeast along an interstate that hugged the upper reaches of the Mississippi, the cold began to settle into his bones and the scenery grew monotonous, broken only by a few small, colorless towns with weathered grain elevators and balloon-shaped water towers. He asked himself why he couldn't have managed to wangle an assignment someplace a little more exciting and a whole lot warmer. Minnesota in January was nobody's idea of a holiday.

When he'd left Haddon Twomey's office at the National Museum of American History the previous afternoon, he'd had no intention of jumping on a plane and flying out to Minnesota in his quest to track down the elusive Jillian Meade. Instead, he'd returned to the office with little to show for his morning's efforts. The one good piece of news when he got back to the office was that Sean Finney, thankfully, had gotten off his duff for a change and gone out to do some actual legwork in the field. Cruz had settled in to enjoy an afternoon of relative peace at his desk, in spite of the jangling phones and noisy conversations all around him. Pulling out the list of interview questions that had come in with the blue alert from Scotland Yard, he'd put in a long-distance call to the Minnesota number Haddon Twomey had given him. If he couldn't find Jillian Meade in the flesh, he'd track her down by phone, ask her about her recent travels, and then decide whether to leave it at that or follow up with a more in-depth interview once she returned to the capital.

But three tries later, he was still receiving the same recorded message telling him the number was not in service. He'd called the long distance operator, who was able to confirm that the number he had was a good one, as far as she could tell from her listings, and was assigned to a party by the name of Meade, Grace S., residing at 34 Lakeshore Road in Havenwood, Minnesota.

The operator had tried to put the call through for him, but she'd had no more luck than Cruz. The line, she said, seemed to be down. Cruz asked if a winter storm was the problem, but the operator said no, she was right there in the Twin Cities, and the weather across the state was cold but sunny—had been all week, except for some light flurries, and as far as she knew, no other problems with phone lines had been reported in the vicinity of Havenwood. The problem seemed to be at that one location only.

Cruz's next move, after consulting his nationwide directory of local police forces, was to put in a call to the Havenwood Police Department. Chief Wilf Lunders came across as hearty and friendly, a relative old-timer by the sound of his voice, pleased to be of service, though a little mystified to be getting a call from the FBI. But he was a great admirer of the late J. Edgar Hoover, the chief said, so he'd be pleased to help out in any way he could.

"You say you're looking for Jillian Meade? Oh yeah, she's in town, all right."

"You're sure of that? You've seen her yourself?"

"Yep. Watched her being loaded into an ambulance last night. My own deputy pulled her out of her mom's house just before it burned to the ground."

Suddenly, Cruz felt every hair on the back of his neck standing on end. "Her mother's house burned down? How did that happen?"

"Well, now, I guess that would be the sixty-four-thousand-dollar question. Coulda been an electrical fire, I don't know, or it coulda been a problem with the gas lines. Our volunteer fire chief was heading over there to have a look-see by the light of day, along with my deputy and a couple of our men. Couldn't tell much last night. Fire wasn't even really burned out till around 3:00 or 4:00 a.m., by the time they gave everything a really good soaking. Make sure we didn't get another flare-up, you know."

"Chief Lunders? I don't want to tell you folks how to do your job there, sir, but I think you may have cause to suspect criminal arson."

"Well, as a matter of fact, you got that right. We do. But how would you know that, if you don't mind me asking?"

Instead of answering, Cruz sat back, pen tapping out a nervous beat on his knee. "What about the mother?"

"Well, now, as far as Grace goes, that's the real tragedy. I'm sorry to say she didn't make it. Sixty-years old and a real lady, she was. A pillar of the community, you know? Lord almighty, even as I'm telling you this, I can hardly believe it myself. You know, that family has had its share of sadness. And as for Grace...well, she will be sorely missed in this town, is all I can say."

"Has the body been taken out?"

"Yes, they went back in and located it this morning."

"There's going to be an autopsy, I hope, to determine the cause of death?"

"Oh, yeah, for sure. There has to be, naturally. Always have to have an autopsy when there's an unexplained death, don't you? Mind you, poor Grace's body was burned up real bad, so I'm not sure what the coroner's going to be able to determine from it. My deputy was able to confirm that she was already dead at the time the fire got out of control, though."

"She was dead how?"

Lunders started to answer but was overtaken by a sudden fit of coughing. He excused himself, half-choking, and seemed to set the phone aside for a few moments, but Cruz was able to hear the kind of wheezy, deep-chested congestion that told him the chief was probably a smoker, probably overweight, and probably moving slowly these days.

A mental image of his own father suddenly flashed through his mind: barrel-chested, gruff and stubbornly refusing to have anything to do with doctors. The old man was still laying bricks and tile in fancy new houses, any one of which probably cost more than he'd made in his entire lifetime. Cruz had seen the old man only briefly at Christmas, although he'd tried to spend a little more time with him last year after he'd resigned his

Army commission. He'd taken a few weeks off before starting the Bureau job and flown to California to pull his old Harley out from under its tarp in his father's garage in Santa Ana. See if the thing still had the muscle to make one more cross-country trip. See, too, if enough time had passed that he and his old man might actually be able to sit down over a beer and have something like a reasonable conversation. Neither of them was getting any younger, after all. Hadn't happened, though. His father had just shuffled around behind him for the entire three days he was there, grumbling and complaining and dogging his steps, like he thought his son had come back to steal the nonexistent family jewels. Finally, Cruz had given up, thrown the tarp back over the Harley, bought a plane ticket and headed for D.C.

Chief Lunders hawked wetly one last time, then came back on the line. "Sorry about that. Got this thing I just can't seem to shake. What were we saying?"

"You said your deputy found Mrs. Meade dead when he got to the house, and I was asking how she died."

"That's the thing. My guy wasn't sure. The place was full of smoke. He's a good man, is Nils, and when he found the body, he wanted to examine it in situ, as it were, see what he could tell based on where he found it and in what condition and all. But he said it was tough to see anything in all that smoke. All he really knew for sure is that she was dead and there was a fair amount of blood. Before he got a chance to figure out what the source of it was, though, Jillian, who he'd already gotten outta there once, came back in, took one look at her mom, dead like that, and went off the deep end. At that point, my guy's main worry was to get her out alive before the whole place went up. His hands were full, and by the time he got her squared away, there was no going back inside for Grace. The place was an inferno."

"So, what did the daughter say happened?"

"She hasn't said anything yet. We weren't able to get a statement out of her last night. She had real bad smoke inhalation.

A concussion, too, they said at the clinic. And then, of course, there was the emotional strain of seeing her mother dead like that. In the end, she had to be sedated. I'm sure she'll be okay, mind, once she's had a little time to get over the initial shock. Jillian's always been a very sensible young woman, so I'm sure she'll be able to give us a pretty good idea what happened there. Matter of fact, I was just getting ready to go over to the clinic and see if she was up to giving a statement when you called."

"You've got a hospital there in Havenwood? Is that where she is?"

"You betcha. It's just a little eight-bed job, mind you. Big cases go on over to Montrose, or into the Twin Cities, if it's real major. But for what Jillian had, they could handle her just fine right here."

"You mind if I come on up there and talk to her myself?" It was impulse more than rational decision-making, but Cruz's gut told him this was all far too coincidental. After more than a decade on a homicide beat, he always mistrusted coincidence, and he always listened to his gut. If nothing else, he wanted to see for himself this spinster bookworm with no apparent life outside the dusty back rooms of a museum who had, out of the blue, become the subject of an international police inquiry— only to have her own mother suddenly expire in a manner that bore an uncomfortable resemblance to the cases outlined in the British alert.

"What do you think of the idea that Jillian Meade killed her mother and then set the fire to cover her tracks?" he asked Chief Lunders.

"Jillian?" A snort of incredulity whistled down the line. "That girl grew up in this town, Agent Cruz. I've known her all her life, and so has everyone else around here. She's always been a quiet little thing. She's not hardly capable of something like this, believe me. It wouldn't be in her nature."

"That's probably what people said about Lizzie Borden, too."

"Well, now, I don't know about that, but I do know the Meade family. They've been living in this town for, oh, I don't know...several generations, anyway. Trust me, no daughter of Grace and Joe Meade would be capable of something like that. No, I'll tell you what I'm really thinking, just between you and me and the gate post. Don't want to say it too loud till we've gathered more evidence, but I'm thinking it was a break-in and attempted theft gone bad—somebody from away, you know. Some hippie probably drifted in off the interstate looking for quick cash to buy drugs down in Minneapolis. Grace's place is on the lake, a real nice spot—on the town side, whereas the summer places are over on the other side. But maybe this drifter saw it, figured it was empty. Or, even if he spotted Grace and Jill, maybe he figured two women like that, all alone in the house, he could overpower 'em, get what he wanted, then skedaddle."

"I don't know, Chief," Cruz said, head shaking.

"Look, keep in mind that Jillian got hurt, too. She had a concussion. Nils, my deputy, said she'd been knocked out, woke up on the kitchen floor. Who knows what might have happened if the neighbors hadn't called in the fire, and if my deputy hadn't gotten there fast as he did? She'd have died, too."

"Fair enough," Cruz conceded. There was no point in alienating a local police chief until he had more information. That said, he'd want a lot more information before he was prepared to rule out Jillian Meade as a suspect. "Chief Lunders, I'd like to make another request."

"What's that?"

"I'd like to ask you to seal off the scene. With all due respect to your volunteer fire chief and your men, sir, I think a professional arson team should go in and cover the ground with a fine-tooth comb. I can set it up through our regional office out there, if you wouldn't mind."

Of course, Cruz thought grimly, the local guys had already been tramping around in there when they went back to find the body, and who knew how many other pairs of boots had been in messing up the evidence since. But, with luck, the arson team would find enough of it intact to determine if the fire had had multiple start points or if accelerants had been used, either one a dead giveaway for criminal action.

"Well, no, I guess that might not be a bad idea at that," Lunders said. "Sure, you go ahead and do that. I'll get our boys to rope it off and make sure nobody goes in till your arson team gets here. But do you mind telling me what this is all about? Why are you folks taking an interest in this?"

"It's a little complicated to go into over the phone. How about if I make arrangements to get that arson investigation going, and then I'll get on a plane and be out there myself, tonight or tomorrow at the latest. I'll tell you as much as I can then about where we're coming from on this."

"If you think that's necessary..."

"Yes, sir, I do think it's very necessary."

Once past the garish billboard with the fish and the trees, Cruz drove up a small incline in the highway and found himself gazing down on a sweeping vista overlooking a picturesque little town that backed up against an evergreen forest, as advertised, one that extended right to the distant horizon. The town was wedged between the woods and a lake that bulged out from the western bank of the Mississippi, as if the river had sprung a leak in its headlong rush to reach the Gulf of Mexico. The map Cruz had picked up at the rent-a-car counter at the airport said this was Lost Arrow Lake. So maybe the angling claim on the billboard wasn't such a stretch, he thought. Unless he was up to a lesson in the finer points of ice-fishing, he'd have to take the boast at face value.

The official town marker appeared on the right shoulder of the road and declared his entry into Havenwood, population 2,012. Another blue sign beyond it directed him to take the next right for local police headquarters. His tires kicked up stones as he pulled into the gravel parking lot of the Havenwood Police Department a couple of minutes later. It was a squat, tan building with a prefab look, the kind of utilitarian structure thrown up by cost-conscious municipal councils all across the country. Cruz predicted a drafty squad room, a flimsy two-cell lock-up and a thin-walled office for the chief.

Parking next to a couple of black-and-white cruisers, he climbed out of the overheated rental, his lungs contracting in shock at the contact with air that was at least forty degrees colder than the balmy weather he'd left behind in D.C. Cruz flipped up the collar of his overcoat, wishing he'd remembered to put in the winter liner he scarcely used in Washington. His California-bred bones wondered, as they always did in places like this, what in hell possessed people to settle in such cold climates.

Inside the small lobby, a heavyset, gray-haired woman in a fuzzy pink cardigan sat behind a reception desk. She held a paperback novel in her hand, her arm extended across the black Formica countertop. As Cruz walked in, he saw her lick the tip of her forefinger, turn the page, then read on, her eyes furrowed in a deep squint. The wind whistled as he struggled to close the door behind him, and she glanced up at the sound, then did a double take.

"Hi, there!" Her face softened into a friendly smile as he crossed the speckled linoleum and came up to the counter. Squinting back at her book—a murder mystery, by the look of the cover—she folded over the corner of the page to mark her place, then closed it. "Can I help you?"

Cruz reached into his inside pocket and withdrew the leather case containing his identification badge and photo. "I'm Special Agent Cruz with the Federal Bureau of Investigation," he said. "Chief Lunders is expecting me."

The woman set the book aside and took his ID, extending her arm back and forth until she found a comfortable focal length. "Forgot my darn reading glasses on the kitchen table this morning," she said, shooting an embarrassed glance in his direction. "Let's see now...Alejandro Cruz."

"You speak Spanish," he said. Her pronunciation was pretty near dead-on, including substituting an aspirated "h" for the "j," instead of the soft "g" that had long ago made him abandon "Alejandro" for "Alex."

She blushed. "Oh, no, hon, not a word, unless you count 'una margarita, por favor.' I got that one pretty much down pat when I won a trip to Acapulco few years back."

He smiled. "Well, that's an important phrase to know."

"I'm Verna Rasmussen," she said, extending her hand. "Just call me Verna."

"Nice to met you, Verna. And you did say the name exactly right, by the way."

"Well, good. I try. I figure a person's name is special, so we should make a little effort to get it right, don't you think? My dad was a 'Bjorn', and he got so fed up with people calling him 'Ba-jorn' that he gave up and went by 'Bub,' if you can believe it. And, anyway, Alejandro's an easy one. Like Alejandro Rey, the actor. Right?"

He nodded. "I guess so. Most people call me Alex. And as I say, the chief's expecting me. Could you tell him I'm here?"

Her gray pin curls gave a regretful shake as she handed him back the ID. "'Fraid he's not in today, hon."

"I spoke to him by phone just yesterday afternoon. He knew I was coming."

"You came out from Minneapolis?"

"No, ma'am, from Washington."

"D.C.?"

"That's right."

"Oh, my, all the way from Washington, D.C."

Cruz tucked the ID away. "So, what do you think, Verna? Could you give him a call, remind him I'm here?"

"Well, I would, but there's just no way. Chief Lunders is in the hospital, and he's not going to be back for a while, I don't think." One of her eyebrows rose.

That and her grimace told Cruz there was a long story there that Verna was probably quite prepared to tell him if given half a chance. But, he noted, glancing at his watch, it was past noon. In another couple of hours, the winter sun would start sinking fast before he'd had a chance to get a look at the site of the fire. The arson team was supposed to have gone over the ground this morning and were to have left their initial findings with the chief, but Cruz wanted his own clear picture to go with the team's findings.

He glanced over Verna's head to the glass window behind her. It opened into what appeared to be the squad room, with four steel desks facing one another in the center and a bank of file cabinets on the far wall. There was only one officer inside, as far as he could see from his vantage point. A khaki-uniformed officer, with buzzed hair nearly as white as the paper in his typewriter, sat at one of desks, and he appeared to be engaged in the familiar, endless and thankless task of typing up police reports on the ancient Olivetti in front of him. He looked too young to be out of high school.

"Who's in command while Chief Lunders is laid up?"

"That'd be Nils Berglund, the deputy chief."

"Could you—"

"—but he's out on a call right now."

"Can you get in touch with him?"

"Oh, sure thing!" she said, brightening. She cocked her thumb at the dispatch unit behind her. "I can call him up on the car radio."

"Would you do that?"

"Sure. Why don't you have a seat?" She pointed to a row of padded arm chars hugging one wall. "Oh! And here," she added, pulling out a Tupperware box from a ledge behind her chair and peeling back the plastic lid. "Have a Toll House cookie while you're waiting. I baked these myself for the guys. Forgot to put 'em in the squad room."

Cruz took one of her cookies, then headed over to the waiting area while she put out the call. Instead of sitting, something he'd already spent far too much time doing that day, he headed for the bulletin board on the wall opposite, opening his overcoat which suddenly felt oppressively heavy in the heated building. Hot and cold, hot and cold.

He made short work of Verna's cookie as he scanned the notices on the cork board. In one corner hung a familiar notice, the FBI Ten Most Wanted list, a gimmick J. Edgar Hoover had dreamed up in one of his more creative PR moments back in his early days as Director. Now, the list hung in half the federal, state and municipal offices in the country. Mostly, though, the bulletin board featured local notices about septic tanks, fishing and boating licenses, and the burning of household trash. A clipboard hanging on a peg contained minutes of town council meetings, while a hand-drawn sign down in one corner of the board, covered in turquoise rabbits and colorful eggs, asked for volunteers to help organize the 1979 Havenwood Easter Parade and Egg Roll.

Cruz heard Verna put out the call over the radio to the deputy chief, and a deep voice, broken by static, came back in response. He was just turning to eavesdrop when the last line on the Easter announcement caught his eye.

For more information, please contact:
Grace Meade
Chairlady, Havenwood Easter Parade Committee

Grace Meade, recently deceased pillar of the community and mother of his quarry, Jillian Meade. Now who would the town turn to organize its official Easter celebration? Cruz wondered, as behind him, the deputy's crackled, baritone voice announced over the radio that he was on his way in.

CHAPTER 5

Montrose, Minnesota
Thursday, January 11, 1979

It was that woman's voice again, firm but friendly—the kind of voice that wants you to know it intends no threat, but which commands your attention, nevertheless. Jillian lay still, feigning sleep—which wasn't hard because sleep was never very far away. Hoping it would be enough to discourage the voice. Willing it to just leave her alone.

"It's Dr. Kandinsky, Jillian. Do you remember? I was in to see you a couple of times yesterday and then again last night."

Yesterday? Last night? What time was it? What day was it? When she'd opened her eyes a while back—when was that?— Jillian had noticed her watch was missing, taken along with the rest of her things, she supposed. The windows in the room were high and small, and all she'd been able to see out of them was a pale sliver of frigid-looking sky. There'd been daylight, but the shadows were long and blue-tinged, the way they get on cold winter days when the sun over the prairie is brilliant but without any heat in it.

"How are you feeling today?" the voice asked. "You're looking a little better."

Better than what? How long had she been there? If this doctor said she'd been in last night...well, fine. It could have been last week or last month for all Jillian knew. She did remember that voice, though, warm and reassuring. Seductive, like a promise of mercy. Or absolution, maybe, for what she'd done.

Her eyes snapped opened. The guardrails were still there, and the green wall. *What did I do?*

"You're safe now," the doctor said. "No one is going to hurt you here. I thought you might like to get cleaned up a little today. You'd feel much better if you did."

Cleaned up? What happened? She stared at her hand lying outstretched on the crisp white mattress. She recalled someone washing blood off her when she was first brought in, but there was still some under her bitten nails, crusted, brown and guilty looking. She must look godawful, Jillian thought. Her hair was hanging loose and unbrushed, sticky mats clinging to her cheeks and neck and shoulders, and the long bangs flicking against her lashes felt bristled at the ends. Singed, she realized suddenly. Singed like her lungs, which hurt with every breath she took. And she could smell the sour, dusky odor of charred wood. It seemed permanently etched in her nasal passages....

And then, suddenly, it all came back. She remembered the fire. She remembered Nils, and the ambulance, and what had happened after they had examined her in the ER and left her sedated and alone to try to sleep off the shock of the fire. Of what she'd seen in her mother's house.

She pulled in her arm and curled into a tight ball. *Mother!* Her mother was dead. Why wasn't she dead, too? A clipped voice in her head snapped a reply: *Because you're weak!*

It was true. She was weak. Twice now, she'd gone to the

brink, only to let herself be pulled back. She should have died with her mother. She'd wanted to. She'd wanted to crouch down on the floor next to that small body, take it in her arms and hold it close to her breast, a full-circle reversal of their earliest roles— she and her mother alone at the end as they were at the beginning, finally at peace with one another and with the past, waiting for the purifying flames. But at the last minute, she'd allowed herself to be saved. She'd never had her mother's iron will.

And then, in the ER...she'd been so close! The needle had been in her arm. All she'd had to do was push down on the plunger and let herself be swept to freedom on a tiny, merciful bubble of air. This could all have been over by now, but instead, she'd hesitated a split second too long and the decision had been taken out of her hands.

Now, here she was...where? Not on the emergency room gurney anymore, that much was certain. Lying in a bed, after having been moved to one of the wards probably. How long had she been here? She vaguely recalled they'd given her something after her stunt with the hypodermic, another tranquilizer, much stronger than the first, which had obviously kept her heavily sedated. For how long she didn't know, but long enough that she had no memory of being moved to this room. It was obvious she had no tolerance for drugs. Not surprising, she thought grimly. Even in college, at the height of the psychedelic Sixties, she'd never taken anything stronger than an aspirin. The ever-well-behaved daughter of Grace Meade.

She closed her eyes, and immediately, gratefully, found herself sinking once more. The mattress seemed to be absorbing her like some great, downy mouth swallowing her whole. She was Jonah in the belly of a feather tick whale, floating on soft cotton waves, content to go where the flow carried her.

After her stunt in the ER she felt as if she had viscous muck flowing through her veins instead of blood. She didn't care, as long as she didn't have to think or remember. Maybe it was more than the drugs. Maybe it was some primitive instinct driving her to shut down rather than face the unbearable. Playing possum in the face of horror.

Her mother would be appalled to see her lying here like this, mute, stupid and filthy. Grace Meade was always at her best, turned out to perfection. In her entire life, she'd never so much as answered a knock at the door without first glancing in the mirror to check her lipstick, pat her hair and smooth down her dress. She'd tried to make her daughter into a miniature replica of herself, but it was hopeless, of course. Jillian had lost the genetic lottery. Had failed to inherit any of her mother's fine features: her golden hair, her striking blue eyes, or her peaches-and-cream English skin. She was olive-skinned and brunette, like her father, apparently, growing taller and bonier than her mother had ever been.

Still, Jillian thought, she would have given anything, just for once, not to hear the note of hopelessness that always accompanied her mother's chirpy words of encouragement. "Well, we just have to work with what we've been given, don't we, dear?"

"What do you think, Jillian? Wouldn't it feel good to get up and take a hot shower? Have a little lunch, maybe sit and talk awhile?"

It was the doctor again, Jillian realized with a start, not her mother. She opened her eyes. She was trying to please, but this was about as much as she could manage. Her mother would definitely have disapproved. Grace was unfailingly poised and polite in any public venue, no matter how trying the circumstances. She would have at least sat up when the doctor came in. But, frankly, Jillian thought, she just couldn't be bothered. She didn't mean to be rude, but she had nothing to say to this woman.

The doctor, in any case, seemed content to wait her out. The minutes ticked by. Jillian could feel her presence, but she remained silent—watching, perhaps. Observing. *And what does she see?* Jillian wondered. *What kind of monster is this before her?*

Suddenly, she felt the bed vibrate. She cringed as a hand reached across her, a hand at the end of a white sleeve. A soft gust of air brushed her cheek as the doctor laid something on the mattress next to her head. It was a notebook, Jillian saw. A thick notebook with a stiff, nubbled black cardboard cover. Then, the white-coated arm withdrew again and the bed was still.

"If you're not ready to talk yet, Jillian, it's all right. I'll be here when you are. But I'm told you're a writer and historian," the doctor added—unnecessarily, Jillian thought. She wasn't that far gone. She knew who she was. That was the problem, wasn't it? "You know how to arrange facts into an understandable flow. I know you feel confused right now, but maybe it would help to sort out your thoughts if you wrote down what's going through your mind."

Oh, God...what's going through my mind?

Jillian's eyes closed once more, shutting out the light, praying for a miracle to shut out the sound of that woman's voice and, mostly, to drown out the screaming of her own guilty thoughts.

What does she want me to say? That I'm haunted by the memory of my mother, her lifeless blue eyes staring up at me from the kitchen floor, as accusatory in death as they were in the moments before it arrived? That I don't want to be alive anymore? That I don't deserve to be? My mother won't let me be. Her beautiful, dreadful face is an image I'll carry to my death— which will come soon, if courage doesn't fail me again.

CHAPTER 6

Havenwood, Minnesota
Thursday, January 11, 1979

Deputy Chief of Police Nils Berglund turned out to be one of those massively built Scandinavians who makes every man around him feel puny. From the moment Berglund finally showed up at headquarters and extended a reluctant hand, Cruz felt inclined to keep his distance, less out of intimidation (he hoped) than for a clearer view of this human mountain. He himself was five-eleven, but Berglund both overshadowed and outweighed him by quite a bit. Nor did anything about the deputy's taciturn manner spell welcome, despite the easy goodwill Cruz had sensed over the phone from the chief of police. Berglund's square features seemed permanently corrugated into a frown, and his pale, icy eyes defied reading.

"Guess we'll use the chief's office," he grunted, directing Cruz around the reception desk and through the door that led into the squad room beyond.

"Verna here tells me he's in the hospital," Cruz said.

Berglund was holding the door open, but his gaze shifted to the reception desk, where Verna had gone back to squinting at her mystery novel. His frown deepened, and it was impossible to tell which annoyed him more, her on-the-job reading or the fact that she'd been gossiping with a stranger. Verna, in any case, seemed oblivious. Cruz had a feeling she was more than capable of handling Deputy Berglund and anything else that came her way.

The deputy waved him into a corner office, then shut the door behind them. Shrugging out of his green nylon bomber jacket, he flung it over a chair. "Take your coat?"

"I'm okay, thanks."

"Suit yourself. Have a seat." Berglund moved around behind the big steel desk and settled into a brown, imitation leather chair that squeaked in protest at the sudden load.

"What happened?" Cruz asked. "To the chief, I mean."

"He's been feeling rough for a while, having tests. Doc called him last night, told him to check into hospital first thing this morning."

"Which hospital?" Cruz asked, remembering how the chief had ranked the area's medical options according to the severity of the patient's condition.

"The Mayo Clinic in Minneapolis." From that news and from Berglund's tone, there wasn't much doubt the diagnosis was serious, the prognosis iffy, and the deputy looking at imminent promotion.

"Sorry to hear it," Cruz said. "He sounds like a good man."

"Yeah, he is. Anyway," Berglund said, "he told me you called. He also told me it was you who arranged for that arson team that's crawling around over there at the fire scene."

"They're in town right now?"

"Working the scene as we speak. That's where I was when Verna called up on the radio."

"Maybe we should head over," Cruz said. "I wouldn't mind

taking a look myself before I talk to Jillian Meade. I'd like to hear what those guys have to say about the cause of the fire."

"Just hold on a minute," Berglund said as Cruz made moves to get up. "We can do that, but first, I want to know why you called them in, to begin with, and why it is you flew out here all the way from Washington."

Cruz settled back into his chair. "I'd been trying to track down Jillian Meade back in D.C. when I heard she was here visiting her mother. I tried to phone but the line was down. That's when I put in the call to Chief Lunders."

"Who told you she was at her mother's?"

"Her boss at the Smithsonian."

"And why are you looking for her?"

"Her name came up in an alert from Scotland Yard. I work in a section of the Bureau that liaises with foreign police forces on cross-border criminal investigations."

"And...what? You think Jillian Meade's some kind of international jewel thief or something?" Berglund snorted. "Get serious."

"You know her well, do you?"

Berglund shrugged. "She grew up here. It's a small town. Everybody knows everybody. So what is Scotland Yard claiming she did?"

"I don't know that they necessarily think she's done anything at all. She was over in England last month around the time some stuff went down, and—"

"What kind of 'stuff'?" Berglund interrupted.

"A couple of homicides, as a matter of fact."

"And they think Jillian had something to do with them?" The deputy's expression was so incredulous that Cruz was beginning to feel a little foolish for even suggesting it, except that Jillian Meade's mother had now turned up dead, too. At the very least, the woman was in danger of turning into the human equivalent of the Black Death, given the pernicious effect she seemed to have on those she visited. Berglund appeared intent on giving her the benefit of the doubt, however, and Cruz decided he could do the same, at least until he'd gotten the lay of the land.

"They're not necessarily saying she had anything to do with the murders, but Miss Meade was in the vicinity at the time and had apparently been in contact with the victims. Scotland Yard was thinking she might have seen or heard something that would bear on their investigation. As far as I know, they simply see her as a potential witness at this point."

"So you're looking to ask her some questions, nothing more?"

"That's right."

"If that's the case, how come you arranged for this arson team to come out? And," Berglund added, "how come you asked Chief Lunders if he thought Jillian had murdered her mother?"

"I guess because it's in my nature to play devil's advocate. It may be coincidence, but there were fires set after those murders in the U.K., too. Look at it from my perspective. I talk to her boss, he tells me she's here in Havenwood, then I talk to your boss, and he tells me about the fire. It does tend to raise a few questions in a person's mind, you have to admit."

"Humph."

"So can you tell me exactly what happened here?"

Berglund threw open his hands in a 'why not' gesture. "Tuesday night, we got a call about a fire out at Grace Meade's place. I was the first to arrive on the scene, ahead of the fire trucks. The fire was going strong by then. I found Mrs. Meade and Jillian still inside the house, although Grace was already dead. I got Jillian out, but then the fire spread so fast we couldn't get her mother's body out till yesterday."

"The Chief said you examined Mrs. Meade's body at the scene before you took the daughter out."

"Uh-huh. I found it lying in the hall, just outside the kitchen."

"What did you see as far as signs of trauma, anything like that?"

"There was a fair amount of blood on the front of her sweater, but that was about it. No bruising or any other sign of battery that I could see, although it was pretty dark in there, so I wouldn't swear to anything. The only light I had to go by was the fire burning in the living room, which was pretty much out of control by then."

"What was the source of the blood?"

"It looked like she'd taken a wound to the chest. Like I say, it was dark, so I was going half by feel. I noticed her sweater had a tear in it, just here." Berglund put his fingertips to his furnace-sized chest, high and just off-center. "The tear was right in the middle of the blood stain, which I could see clearly because she had on a light-colored sweater and the blood showed up dark."

"So she was down for pretty much the whole time she bled," Cruz said, thinking aloud. "If she'd been upright, the entry wound, if that's what it was, would have been at the top of the stain and the blood would have run down. Was it an entry wound, by the way? Did you turn her over?"

Berglund nodded. "Sort of. The fire was spreading fast, and I knew I needed to get her out of there, so I picked her up and put her over my shoulder to carry her out. Her back was soaked with blood, and when I put my hand there to steady the body, it felt pretty pulpy. Her sweater back was also shredded." Berglund seemed to shudder at the memory.

Poor guy, Cruz thought. His actions had been pretty heroic, when you came down to it, going into the burning house like that to rescue the women. Like most heroes, he'd probably acted on sheer instinct and adrenaline, revulsion at the ugliness of what he'd found only hitting him afterward, when the initial shock wore off.

"Chief Lunders told me you weren't able to get the body out, in the end, though."

"No. I'd already left Jill on the porch when I went back inside to look for Grace. I was trying to get a closer look at the wound when I realized Jill was back and standing right behind me. I didn't want her to see her mother like that." Cruz was startled by

Berglund's fist suddenly smacking his thigh. "I had her, dammit! I'd picked her up and I had her. She was sixty-years old, for chrissake, and just a little thing. Even with Jillian to worry about, I could have gotten her out. I could have managed them both."

Cruz had no doubt the deputy could have easily carried two women out of a burning building. "So what happened?"

"Jillian wouldn't leave! I tried to drag her out with my free hand, but she kept fighting me. She was disoriented—she'd taken a blow to the head herself, we found out later. And she was half crazy with panic and grief, screaming for her mother."

"But the mother was definitely dead?"

"Yeah, I'm pretty sure she was. I didn't have time to try for a pulse before Jill came back in and flipped out on me, but by the way Grace looked..." His cropped blond head gave a grim shake. "As it was, I had to put her down again and leave her there while I dragged Jillian out a second time. By the time I handed her off to the paramedics, the fire had gotten out of control and I couldn't get back inside the house. It was only when the ashes finally cooled down that we were able to get in and locate the body. It was in the rubble just off the kitchen, right where I'd left her."

"Chief Lunders said there was going to be an autopsy."

Berglund nodded. "It was this morning. County coroner took the body over to Montrose yesterday, but given how badly charred it was, he decided to call in a medical examiner from the State Bureau of Investigation. They've got more experience dealing with cases like this."

"Were they able to determine a cause of death?"

Berglund shook his head. "Not with any degree of certainty. All the flesh and most of the organs were toast."

"What about all the blood you'd found, and the entry and exit wounds? That would suggest a gunshot wound, wouldn't it?"

"Yeah, although, like I said, the body was burned beyond recognition, and they couldn't find much trajectory evidence. A couple of the interior organs were partly intact—the collapse of the roof eventually smothered some of the fire—but it wasn't enough to get a clear picture of whether or not she'd been shot. We haven't found any bullets or spent cartridges at the scene, although your arson guys are keeping an eye out for them. The ME did find a fracture on the breastbone, though, and taken together with what I was able to tell them about the holes in her sweater, he thought it was consistent with the theory that she'd been shot, probably with a fairly large caliber weapon."

"That would also explain the injury on her back, larger than the entry, which is what you'd expect to find with an exit wound," Cruz pointed out.

Berglund nodded. "The medical examiner said the position of the fracture on her breastbone was such that the bullet probably hit her left lung, maybe even the heart, although I doubt it, personally."

"Why's that?"

"Because there was a hell of a lot of blood. I would have thought that if she'd taken it in the heart, it would have stopped pumping and she wouldn't have bled out like she did."

"Not necessarily," Cruz said. "It would depend on the damage. It might take a few seconds or even minutes for her heart to stop beating completely. And if a bullet's large caliber, it'll often make a bloody mess regardless of whether or not the victim dies instantly." He watched Berglund's dour expression as the deputy scraped a smear of mud off his pant leg. "Are you beating yourself up here because you think you could have saved Mrs. Meade?" Cruz asked him.

Berglund looked up, then away, self-consciously. "Yeah, maybe, although I guess I knew there wasn't really a hope in hell. At the autopsy, the ME found that part of the right lung was more or less intact, and he said there was no sign of smoke inhalation in the air sacs."

"All right then, that's something, isn't it? It means Grace Meade had drawn her last breath before the fire even started."

Berglund frowned. "Yeah, I suppose."

"And that being the case, it wouldn't have made any difference whether or not you'd gotten her out."

Berglund seemed unconvinced. "Maybe. But there's no saying how long she'd been down. Maybe she could've been revived...or something. I don't know. It just feels like I could've handled it better."

Cruz shifted forward in his seat, elbows on his knees. "Look, Deputy, it seems to me you did plenty. You went into that house and you saved Jillian Meade's life—not once, but twice. I think you should let yourself off the hook and just focus on your investigation. If Grace Meade was dead before the fire broke out, it means she was murdered and the fire was probably set to cover tracks. I imagine this has to be tough on a lot of people around here, but the evidence is what you need to be focusing on. And it's your investigation, obviously. I don't mean to come riding in like some bounty hunter, okay? I asked for the arson team to look things over to make sure there was no confusion about what went down, but I'm not here to step on your toes. All I really want to do is speak to Jillian Meade and clear up some questions about what happened while she was over in England. She gives me her statement, I'm outta here. I'll send it off to the Brits and that'll probably be that. Is that okay with you?"

Berglund nodded wearily, like a man who was both exhausted and in over his head. How many murder investigations had he even handled? Cruz wondered. In a town this size, it was a distinct possibility this was his first.

"Talking to Jillian, though," Berglund said, "that could be a problem."

"How so? She's in the hospital here in town, right?"

"Not anymore. They moved her to the regional hospital over in Montrose. The local clinic isn't equipped to handle a case like hers."

"I thought she wasn't that badly hurt."

"She had a concussion, like I said, but it wasn't too bad. Mostly it was smoke inhalation they were worried about, but they figured she'd recover fully from that, too. Her mental state is something else, though."

"What do you mean?"

"She tried to kill herself in the ER in Havenwood."

Cruz pulled up short. "Chief Lunders never mentioned that."

"He hadn't heard about it yet when you talked to him yesterday. Happened early Wednesday morning. The chief was under the weather, and he didn't get in till after noon. Jill had spent the night in the ER here so they could keep an eye on her breathing. I was there myself till around four in the morning, but she seemed to be resting comfortably. Sometime around dawn, though, when nobody was watching, she apparently woke up and found a syringe in a drawer or something. They said she had it in an artery with her thumb on the plunger when an orderly happened to walk by and spot her. The guy thought fast, luckily. If he hadn't tackled her, she'd be dead."

"And now?" Cruz asked.

Berglund's big hands rubbed his face wearily. "Now they've got her locked down on twenty-four-hour suicide watch in the psych ward at Montrose. They kept her heavily sedated for the first twenty-four hours, but they're trying to back her off the meds now. We can go over later, after we check back with the arson guys, but I wouldn't count on getting much out of her today if I were you. They say she hasn't said a word since all this happened."

Evil never sleeps. It creeps in the night, appearing where it's least expected, Cruz thought. There's no sanctuary behind locked doors or the solid edifice of the law. Sooner or later, it finds the vulnerability in any hiding place and worms its way in. All it takes is a small point of weakness, a tiny chink in the wall of social order, a minuscule tear in the fabric of human decency. Even in a small prairie town that dared to tempt the gods and call itself Havenwood, there was no refuge.

"This is it." Berglund rolled the police cruiser to a stop before the blackened remains of what must have been, if neighboring houses were any indication, a pleasant family home in an pretty neighborhood before it had been put to the torch two nights earlier. Another black-and-white cruiser and a beige Ford Fairlane with the Minnesota state crest on the door were parked in the wide, sweeping driveway.

"I don't know as you'll see much," Berglund said. "Things are pretty raked over by now, but this gives you an idea of how bad the fire was."

The sour odor of soot was already insinuating its way in through the car's air vents. Cruz climbed out of the cruiser, moving off to the side, out of the direct path of the sunlight to get a better view of the burned-out shell. He cupped a hand over his eyes, squinting against the sun that was beginning to sink toward the western horizon, setting up a blinding glare of ice and snow on Lost Arrow Lake. From this vantage point, he could see little except the uneven silhouette of what remained of the Meade home.

The scene looked as the fire had rendered it, for the most part, bordered and contained by a band of yellow plastic crime scene tape. The house had mostly collapsed in on itself. All that remained standing were the sooty red bricks of a large hearth and chimney, rising like a sentinel above the cracked and blackened cement foundation. A few charred timbers lay tipped at odd angles, crusted over with a thick layer of ice from the soaking of the fire hoses.

The yard sloped down to a wooden dock that extended out to the frozen lake. On the opposite shore, a few snow-capped cottages and a dense line of pine trees stood in stark relief against the brilliant sky. The view was impressive, Cruz thought, like a Currier and Ives Christmas fantasy. In summer, the place would no doubt be a water sport paradise. Right now, he could make out the tracks of dozens of skis and snowmobiles crisscrossing the lake's frozen surface. Out in the middle of it, narrow gray plumes rose from makeshift chimneys poking through the roofs of small plywood huts, evidence of heartier souls than he sport fishing through the thick ice.

The cruiser rocked as Berglund climbed out on his side and slammed the door. His green nylon police parka was unzipped, despite the frigid temperature, and the brass buttons of his khaki uniform strained across his chest as he came around the car to join Cruz. Like many very large men, Berglund moved slowly and with great precision, as if worried about accidentally bowling someone over.

Two men wearing orange coveralls over their clothing were poking around the site, taking measurements by the look of it. A couple of local cops in uniforms like Berglund's stood just outside the tape, watching them work and standing guard over a large, articulated metal toolbox and what looked to be a pile of plastic and paper evidence bags.

"Pretty bad," Cruz observed, as they watched the men working over the grim scene.

"Pretty bad," the deputy agreed—both of them masters at understatement.

A silence settled over them, a quiet more profound than any Cruz could remember for a very long time. There were no automobile noises, no commuter planes, no traffic helicopters droning overhead. No hum of the heavy machinery that is a city's living, beating heart. He might have expected a few chirping birds, at least, but any that were wintering here had obviously had the sense to flee this place of death.

Cruz would have welcomed the opportunity to fly away himself. His stomach turned at the acrid odor of wet, charred wood and the toxic stench of melted plastic, rubber and paint.

He took a step forward and heard a brittle crunching sound under his shoe. He looked down to see that he was standing on broken shards of glass, maybe a piece of shattered window pane. He kicked it aside, then stopped to pick out a small fragment that had become wedged into the hard rubber of his left heel.

"Winds were high the night of the fire," Berglund said. "Flames jumped from treetop to treetop, and it looked like they might cross the lot line. We were worried we'd lose half the street."

Cruz followed the direction of the burly man's cocked thumb to the white birch and silver maples standing between the destroyed house and the property to the north of it. Several were scorched and fire-capped. On the neighbor's garage, maybe sixty feet away, the wood siding was visibly blistered and peeling in a couple of spots, mute testimony to the intensity of the blaze.

"We've only got two pumper trucks," Berglund said. His deep voice doled out words sparingly, Cruz noted, like someone unaccustomed to strangers or long explanations. "It's just a volunteer force, and fighting the wind like we were..." The frown deepened on his square face and his white-blond eyebrows were almost linked now by the two vertical creases above his nose. "If it hadn't been for the wind, we might have been able to get it under control, save more evidence. Once we realized there was no way of saving the house or pulling Mrs. Meade out, though, we made the decision to save the neighbor's place."

He said it defensively, Cruz noted, like he thought this D.C. hotshot might be getting ready to ream out the locals for their ineptitude. "Makes sense," he agreed.

A cold wind blew up off the lake and Cruz felt the damp cut through him. He turned up the collar of his overcoat, wishing once again that he'd worn something warmer. Back in D.C., they were just weeks away from cherry blossom time, when the air would turn humid and ripe, but that kind of weather was a long way off here. There was no point in looking for warmth in these ice-crusted coals, either.

Suddenly, he recoiled, picking up a trace scent through the pervasive stink of charred wood, a smell that was both familiar and unforgettable—the terrifying odor of roasted human flesh. It was just his imagination messing with his head, he tried to tell himself. Grace Meade's charred body had long since been removed.

Logic carried no weight, however, because what he was seeing in his mind's eye was not this scene, but another fire long ago—another murder victim's body torched in a deliberate bid to destroy evidence, only this victim hadn't been a stranger, and Cruz hadn't been some impartial investigator arriving after the fact.

"You want to take a closer look?" Berglund asked, stepping up to the ribbon of yellow plastic crime scene tape that circumnavigated the lot. He reached out and lifted it, holding it up for Cruz to pass under. All the professional courtesies.

God almighty, no, he didn't want to get any closer, Cruz thought, revulsion springing from the deepest recesses of his brain, that primitive part that deals in instinctive fear and the impulse to flee. He managed to hold his ground—just.

"I can see all I need to from here," he said. "I'll just wait till those guys get done. I don't want to be trampling over evidence."

He turned his back to the site, looking up and down the road as if recreating in his mind the scenario as it had played out two nights earlier. All along the curving lakefront road, well-tended houses with two-car garages nestled into wooded lots that flowed, unfenced and unbroken, from one into the other. They were a custom-built mix of ranch-style bungalows, Cape Cod salt boxes and sprawling split-levels with sand-colored prairie limestone facades. The lots were large, none smaller than a half acre, Cruz estimated, space beyond the reach of all but the wealthiest of urban dwellers. Even in a small town, this had to be prime real estate. Cruz saw snowmobiles parked in several of the driveways, and a couple of tarp-covered powerboats jacked up on trailers for the winter.

When his heartbeat had finally slowed to a normal pace, he allowed himself to turn back toward the destroyed house, where the two jumpsuited investigators seemed to be finishing their work. They picked their way across the rubble, stopping to lay down a few evidence bags in the tool case. One of the men was carrying a long-handled spade, and he jammed it upright in a pile of ash. Clapping the dust off their hands, they ducked under the tape and walked over to where Cruz and Berglund were standing. One was gray-haired, balding, but fit-looking under his orange jumpsuit. The other was younger, heavyset and perspiring, despite the cold, so that his black-framed glasses kept slipping down the slick incline of his nose, which was black from the repetition of his sooty hand pushing them back.

"This is Agent Cruz from the FBI," Berglund told them.

They nodded, and the older of the two men held out a dirty hand. He then thought better of it and transformed the shake to a quick wave. "I don't think you want to touch this hand," he said. "I'm Don Beadle from the State Bureau of Investigation. This is Bill Oppenhalt from the Arson Investigation Unit. I guess it was you who originated the request for us to come out here and take a look, Agent Cruz?"

Cruz nodded. "That's right. Appreciate the cooperation."

"No problem. That's why we're here."

"So, how does it look? Do you think this was deliberately set?"

Beadle deferred to Oppenhalt, who pushed his heavy glasses up his nose once more and nodded. "Oh, yeah, not much question of that, I'd say. Things were a little stirred around before we got here, mind you, but we were able to spot a fair number of physical indicators just the same."

"Like what?" Berglund asked.

"Well, you got your multiple high burn points and several localized heavy burn patterns indicating that there was more than one point of origin. Some spalling in the concrete foundation, too, which some would say indicates an accelerant, although it's not a real reliable indicator, in my experience. We took some carpet and underpad samples, though, and those were a little more conclusive. I'll want to run them through a gas chromatograph back at the lab just to be sure, but in the end," he said, tapping the side of his blackened nose before pushing his glasses up yet again, "the nose knows."

"What do you mean?"

Oppenhalt grunted as he bent to scoop a sample of dirt, which he rubbed between his fingers, then held under his nostrils. "Gasoline," he said. "On a cold day like this, it's real easy to pick it up. You guys don't smell it? It's all over the place here."

Berglund shook his head. "I can't smell anything except charcoal, and that's been stuck in my nostrils since the night of the fire. And anyway," he added, nodding to the gravel driveway beneath their feet, "what you're smelling here is probably several years worth of dripping oil from all the cars that have been parked in this drive."

"Well, sure, but it's not just in the drive, Deputy," Beadle said, cocking his thumb back over his shoulder. "It's all over the scene. Really strong in the carpet samples we found, like Bill here said. Even I picked it up, and my nose isn't nearly as well trained as his is."

The broad shoulders of Berglund's green parka hefted, sending a shower of what looked at first glance to be dandruff flying to the ground, until Cruz realized it was actually a fine layer of ash that was still settling almost forty-eight hours after the blaze.

"You guys happen to come across any spent cartridges or slugs while you were sifting through the ash?" Cruz asked. "Deputy Berglund says the autopsy on the lady who died here indicates she may have taken a shot to the chest from a fairly large-caliber weapon, like maybe a forty-five or a nine millimeter."

Beadle shook his head. "No, we were on the lookout for it, but nothing showed up. If your killer was the careful sort, he might have picked up his spent cartridges before he left the scene."

"That would make him one very careful drug-crazed hippie drifter looking for a quick score," Cruz said dryly, glancing at Berglund.

"I never said that was the only explanation for what went down here," the deputy said irritably. "That was the chief's thought, and it's as good as any other at the moment. On the other hand, somebody that calculating..." His voice drifted off.

Berglund's face was drawn and showing signs of weariness and strain. It was obvious he was also ticked off at being second-guessed by meddling strangers. Fair enough, Cruz thought. If it was him in the deputy's place and some stranger had dropped into the middle of one if his cases, pulling rank and calling in outside investigators, he'd probably be just as pissed. But that didn't change the fact that, frankly, the guy needed the help.

"You seen all you need to here?" Berglund asked.

Cruz glanced back at the rubble and nodded. "I guess I have. You guys?"

Beadle also nodded. "We'll get our preliminary report out to you both within a couple of days. Final has to wait for the chemical tests on the samples we took, but like Bill said, our view is that you've definitely got an arson case on your hands here, guys, so you'll want to bear that in mind as your investigation proceeds. Anything else you need from us?"

"Not for now. I'll let you know if I do," Berglund said glumly.

CHAPTER 7

That doctor stopped by to see me again—a couple of hours ago, I think. I wasn't quite as doped up as I've been the last few times she was in. (And how many times is that, I wonder? I have no idea.) But it's quiet now. No one has been in for quite a while. They seem to have decided to leave me with nothing but this notebook for company. That's fine with me. I just want to be left alone.

I hear the murmur of voices out in the hall, sounding low and disapproving as they pause occasionally at the window of this room. They consider me stark raving mad, I suppose, and dangerous to boot.

The doctor never actually came out and said so, but I suspect she's a psychiatrist. It makes sense, after what I tried to do in the ER—after everything else, too. Maybe she really does want to help. But it's more likely, I think, that this is part of the process they're going through now—determining my competency before they decide what to do with me. I'm beyond help, in any case. Though I'm sure I will be judged, it won't be in this lifetime.

I never even looked at the doctor, although she did her best to engage me in conversation. She's good, too. Pulled out all the tricks—open-ended questions. Empathy. Those long, pregnant silences that normal people feel obliged to fill with nervous chatter. She seemed disappointed when I didn't respond.

"Perhaps you'll feel like talking tomorrow, Jillian," she said just before she left.

Well, no, I could have told her, I won't. It may be her business, if she is a shrink, to get people to talk about their deepest feelings, but I can't do that. She's a stranger to me. I'm not the kind of person who confides, even to people I've known for many years. I never was. I know there are those who see it as evidence that I feel somehow superior, but the truth is just the opposite. I've always been embarrassed to talk about myself. I can't imagine a duller subject, or why anyone would be interested. I'm a good listener, though. I suppose it's why I chose to do the work I do, gathering oral histories, recording the reminiscences of mostly older people about the great events they've lived through. Their lives are so much more exciting than mine.

This doctor is stubborn, though. I can tell. I know she'll be back. To be honest, she seems like a very nice person. I feel guilty about ignoring her, but I simply don't want what she has to offer. How can I convince her I'm a waste of her time and skills? That she'd be better served expending her energies elsewhere, on someone who wants—deserves—to be saved? That I am beyond redemption?

She was careful before she went out to catch the door before it slammed, easing it gently shut. Still, there was no mistaking the sound of the dead bolt ramming home. Obviously, they're taking no more chances with me. Maybe they think I'll try to run, but what would be the point, when my thoughts would only come along for the ride?

No, there's only one escape for me.

In any event, even if I did want to walk out of here, they've taken my clothes—destroyed them, I suppose, since they'd have been ruined, what with all the blood, and then blackened from the fire....

Oh, Jillian! What are you thinking? Of course they wouldn't destroy them. Far from it. Every item would have been painstakingly preserved. Some criminal investigator is no doubt examining them at this very moment, lifting hairs, microscopic bits of lint and drops of my mother's blood, accumulating the mountain of evidence they'll be building against me. But that, too, is a waste of time and resources.

In place of my ruined things, they've given me a short blue hospital gown and white cotton socks. There's also a terry robe lying at the end of the bed—beltless. I've already checked. Nor is there anything else in here remotely long enough to be used as a rope, not even a sheet on the mattress. There's just a quilted pad and a thick down duvet to keep me warm. It hardly matters. Even if there were something to make into a noose, there's no place to hang it. The half-globe light fixture seems firmly anchored to the ceiling, and there are no convenient bars on those high windows. That mesh-reinforced glass looks unbreakable, too, and the room is devoid of any other sharp objects. Even the food trays they bring in and carry out, untouched, hold only round, stainless steel spoons and melamine plates and cups. No breakable plastic or lovely glass shards with which to slash those wrists today, dearie!

Amazing how they think of everything.

The doctor left another parting gift along with this notebook— a box of fine-tipped colored markers. I almost smiled. She's no fool, this woman. There's no chance she'd leave me sharp lead pencils or ball point steel suitable for ramming into eager arteries. It's pretty hard to kill yourself with fuzzy felt Crayolas.

She wants me to write down my thoughts. How cruel is that? My mind wanders between stupor, rage and grief, and sometimes, for a few minutes, I forget. Then suddenly it comes back, slamming into the center of my chest like a sledgehammer—these awful, monstrous memories clawing at my brain—and I remember where I am and why I'm here.

I can hardly bring myself to believe it—my mother is dead....

My mother is dead and I have no business being alive. That's the fundamental truth here. But maybe it's not too late. Maybe I have inherited just a tiny measure of her indomitable willpower, after all.

It occurs to me, though, that perhaps I owe society an explanation. If I do that, will I find the courage then to do what I have to do?

I know there are those who will resent justice being cheated in this way. All I can say to them is that I don't want or expect forgiveness. It's not even that I'm afraid to face the consequences of what I might have done. I just can't live with the knowledge of what I am.

They say confession is good for the soul, but I don't believe it for a minute. Nothing will take away this burden of guilt and shame. And the idea that people will look on me as an object of curiosity, disgust or (God forbid) pity is so insufferable that it gives me pause even now. It's horrible enough to have the truth here inside me, eating at my soul like a malignancy, but to bring it out into the open for all the world to see? Why would I do that, when it would be so easy to let this all die with my mother—with us both?

Except, what have I learned in my life, and my work, if not that we human beings are doomed to repeat those atrocities we don't take the time to understand? But before there can be understanding, someone has to bear witness. The innocent deserve that.

Oh, yes, there are innocents in this tale. Maybe I owe it to them to tell this story. For their sake, then, I should set the record down now while I can—while these people are leaving me in peace. I can't imagine it will last for long. The authorities are bound to show up with their questions sooner or later, and I'll probably be arrested as soon as I'm deemed fit to walk out of here. But if I can lull this doctor into believing I'm making some sort of therapeutic progress with this notebook, maybe she'll hold them at bay long enough for me to get it all down.

These gifts of hers—this notebook, this quiet time, and these markers in their ridiculously cheerful hues of wild cherry, magenta and indigo—maybe they're Fate's way of offering me a chance to atone for my sins. Mine and my mother's. We owe a vast debt, she and I, and while nothing can ever repay it, a full confession is the very least we can offer.

Then, once I've finished, I'll look for my chance. Because it's a sure bet that, sooner or later, the attention of these caretakers will flag, however briefly. And when it does, I'll seize the opportunity to end a life that never should have been and submit to whatever judgment lies waiting for me in the next.

CHAPTER 8

Montrose, Minnesota
Thursday, January 11, 1979

Cruz and Berglund pulled into the parking lot of the Montrose Regional Hospital, sixteen miles northwest of Havenwood. In an area reserved for official vehicles, Berglund nestled the black-and-white cruiser into a parking spot just opposite the emergency entrance ramp.

The three-story hospital looked new, with fresh, brightly painted signs in orange and blue, and sidewalks and roadways still untouched by the frost heave of unrelenting winters that turned every paved surface into a spiderweb of cracks, fissures and potholes. But, Cruz thought, the hospital could have been in Tallahassee, Florida or Missoula, Montana, for all the uniqueness of its institutional tan and stucco exterior.

"Do you really think Jillian Meade intended to kill herself?" he asked, as he and Berglund climbed out of the cruiser and headed up the walkway.

"No question. They said she had that needle in her arm, and

that she fought like hell with the orderly who tackled her, just like she fought me when I wouldn't let her stay in that burning house. They doubled up on her tranquilizers after that. Even then, the doc on call said he thought she was serious enough about doing herself in that he had her put in full restraints before they transferred her over here to the psych ward."

Cruz said nothing, but the cynic in him had his doubts. Just because the woman was in the loony bin didn't mean she wasn't crazy like a fox.

He drew a deep breath of piney air just before they passed through the sliding glass front doors, girding himself. He'd visited more than his share of psychiatric units. In the course of eleven years as a U.S. Army criminal investigator, he'd run into every conceivable mental quirk, malady and trauma that could erupt in violence. He'd personally witnessed his first murder on June 11, 1965, a day that had changed the course of his life forever. Since then, he'd investigated more than three hundred others. Most of them had sprung from stupid rage and momentary loss of self-control, senseless acts committed in a blur of drugs or booze. A few had been meticulously planned, the murder itself secondary to an insatiable desire for something else—money, a woman, revenge.

And then, there were the tragedies, pure and simple. Even normally decent, sane people had their triggers, and under the right amount of pressure, anyone could buckle. Cruz had seen that fourteen years earlier, on a June day out in a swampy delta north of Da Nang. His faith in humanity had been on shaky ground ever since.

Berglund looked grim, as if he was dreading this as much as Cruz was. "Ready?"

Cruz nodded.

So what was Jillian Meade's story? How coincidental was it that three women linked to her had now died under suspicious circumstances within the span of a month? Was she some kind of uncontrolled psychopath, or a smart faker with some obscure and twisted motive? If the latter, they weren't going to do anything for her in here. Drugs and therapy might unkink a mildly bent psyche, but there was no curing a killer who was genuinely psychotic or very clever—and they were often one and the same. He'd seen thieves, rapists and serial killers who could mimic an entire catalogue of clinical symptoms in a bid to dodge criminal responsibility for their acts, trying to cop a "not guilty by reason of insanity" plea. Was that Jillian Meade's game?

Inside, the hospital had the cookie-cutter look of medical institutes all over the country, with scrubbable white walls, industrial carpeted floors, and utilitarian, charm-free furnishings. A few garish splashes had been added in the form of wide racing stripes in the hallways, but even these were resolutely functional, color-coded by department. Cruz and Berglund followed a blue stripe to the main reception, where the deputy approached the desk to ask for directions. The stripes leading back to the ER were red, Cruz noted. Green was apparently for obstetrics, orange for pediatrics. And the psych ward?

Berglund turned to him and nodded at the bank of elevators on the opposite wall. "She says go to three, then follow the purple stripe."

At the elevator doors, as they stood in silence watching the lights overhead dance down to one, Cruz thought about possible links between Grace Meade and the other victims. Mrs. Meade had been English by birth, so maybe the two female victims in Britain had been friends of hers, which might explain Jillian Meade's calling on them. One of the women had been a semi-retired civil servant of some sort, his Scotland Yard contact had said. The other, a retired hospital "tea cart lady." Both of them elderly, both of them living alone when they died, brutally attacked and killed in their homes, which had subsequently been torched. Why?

Both of them visited by Jillian Meade only a short time earlier. Why?

At the third floor, Cruz followed Berglund to a thick glass window under a plaque that read: "Reception—Please Sign In." On the other side of the glass, a guy in green scrubs sat in a swivel chair with his back to the window, his white sneakers propped on a credenza behind. Coffee cup in one hand, he was reading a newspaper that he held awkwardly folded in his free hand, shaking it back open from time to time when it occasionally collapsed on itself. The comics page, Cruz noted, peering over his shoulder.

Berglund tapped on the window and he started, splashing coffee on his pants, the paper and his arm. A muffled curse sounded through the double-plate glass as his feet dropped to the floor. The chair pivoted and he looked up, peeved, but at the sight of the burly man in uniform bearing down on him, he prudently swallowed his protest.

"Help you?" he asked, shaking splattered coffee from his hands. His voice came out of a round, slatted steel disc in the glass sounding tinny and crackled, like every drive-in movie speaker Cruz had ever encountered in his misspent youth.

Berglund planted his hands on the counter. "I'm Deputy Chief of Police Berglund with the Havenwood Police Department. This is Federal Agent Cruz. We're here to speak to Jillian Meade."

"I'm just an orderly. I'm filling in while the head nurse is on her coffee break, but lemme see..." He slid a clipboard in front of him and ran a finger down the page. "Meade, Meade...nope. Can't help you right now."

"What do you mean? I just spoke to the front office by phone a couple of hours ago. I know she's here."

"Oh, yeah, she's here all right, but she's still being evaluated. No visitors."

"This is official business."

The orderly shrugged. "Her doctor would have to clear it."

"Fine," Berglund said, "we'd like to speak to him."

The reply was a one-syllable pop.

"Pardon?" Berglund asked.

"Her," the orderly replied. "The psychiatrist is a woman, Dr. Kandinsky."

"Her, then. Could you get her, please?"

The speaker crackled once more. "I think she was on the ward a while back, but I'm not sure if she's still there. Take a seat. I'll page her."

Cruz had already moved over to a window that overlooked the parking lot and the broad, frozen prairie beyond. The hospital stood at the very edge of the town of Montrose. Beyond was a flat expanse of open farmland broken only by a grid of shelterbelts, poplar and spruce mostly. The fields were dark and dead-looking, blackened by stubble burned off after the harvest, only occasional patches of snow here and there. What snow there was had piled up in drifts that littered the shade of the shelterbelts, like beach debris left behind after a receding tide. Cruz had seen places like this at the height of the growing season, though, when they were transformed into a vast, swaying sea of golden wheat. During those restless months after his first tour of duty in Vietnam, before he'd decided to re-up and go back, he'd ridden his old Harley down back roads from one end of the country to the other, drifting aimlessly, keeping mostly to himself. Trying to come to terms with what he'd seen and done over there. Trying to come to terms with himself.

Berglund's massive frame moved beside him. The deputy gave the view out the window a glance, but it was probably as familiar to him as his own face in the bathroom mirror. He turned back to the waiting room, hooking his thumbs in his belt as he leaned against the window ledge, the typical stance of a brawny man unconsciously compensating for the unfortunate tendency of his arms to swing, gorilla-like, away from his overbuilt body.

"Let's hope this lady shrink's around, or we've made the drive for nothing," Berglund said, his fingers drumming against his thick leather gun belt as they listened to the soft hum of the building, the ping of the elevators, and the sing-song tone of pages going out over the hospital's PA system. "Not much snow out there," he added conversationally, giving the view behind them another glance. "Almanac says it's going to be a hot, dry summer."

"Guess the farmers won't like that."

"No. It's typical, though. Feast or famine. Last spring, the fields were so saturated it was nearly June before we could get machinery out onto them. Finally get a crop in, and the next thing you know, summer drought sets in and the ground dries up harder than cement."

Cruz gave him a sideways look. "You farm yourself?"

Berglund shrugged. "A little. Work my father-in-law's old place. Got a few fields in barley and winter wheat."

"Must keep you pretty busy, between that and the police work."

"It can get hectic. Summertime's when the town fills up with tourists and cottage people. Population jumps from a couple thousand to nearly ten."

"You're going to be really stretched this year if your chief's still off the board."

Berglund paused, as if that realization were just sinking in, and he passed a weary hand over his square, lined face—a man with too much to do and not enough to do it with. "I guess we will. What about you? You live in Washington?"

"These days, yeah, since I took this Bureau job."

"Wouldn't be my cup of tea, living in a big city like that. Where were you before the Bureau?"

"All over the place. Thailand, the Philippines, England, Germany. A tour in the Pentagon, a stint at Fort Gordon, Georgia."

"Military, huh? Air force?"

"Army."

"That a fact?"

They stopped, listening, as a page for Dr. Kandinsky finally went out over the PA system.

Berglund turned back to Cruz. "So where's home?"

"Southern California. Santa Ana."

"Oh, yeah. I know where that is. Near Disneyland, right? Wife and I took the kids there a couple of years ago. 'Happiest Place on Earth.'"

Cruz nodded. "So they say. Haven't lived there myself since the draft, back in '65."

Berglund glanced around, but the waiting room was empty. "Were you in 'Nam?" he asked quietly.

That was how vets talked amongst themselves these days, Cruz reflected grimly—in low voices and in safe places. Nobody spat at them and called them "baby-killers" anymore, but nobody wanted to hear about what happened to them, either. How kids got sent to fight an enemy they couldn't see for a cause nobody believed in. How it messed with their heads, turning too many of them into burnout cases. "I did two tours," he told Berglund.

"Two? Christ, one was enough for me. Why'd you go back?"

"Unfinished business. Then the Army turned into a career. What about you? Ex-grunt?"

"No, Navy man. Crazy, huh? Landlocked guy like me, ends up swabbing a deck? I didn't even wait for my letter from the draft. Figured they were going to get me, anyway, so I volunteered to have my pick of services. Coming from a dust bowl like this, the idea of the ocean just appealed, you know?"

"Yeah, I guess I can see that."

"So, you reenlisted, then stayed on? What kind of work did you do?"

Cruz hesitated, loathe to give details. He'd re-upped as penance for his sins, and penance it had turned out to be when word leaked out that he'd testified against those involved in a murder and subsequent cover-up conspiracy in his old unit. Being the guy who sent four former buddies to Leavenworth had earned him no points with his new outfit. On the contrary. He'd already endured two savage beatings he refused to talk about by the time the Criminal Investigation Division finally moved in and yanked him out of there. When they'd seen he'd taken a couple of criminology courses during his college days, they'd offered to train him as a professional investigator. It had been an offer he knew he couldn't refuse. The only alternative was to return to a front-line unit and the near certainty of being taken out sooner or later by some hothead's "friendly fire."

He wasn't about to tell Berglund that, though, and not just because the deputy, like so many others, would probably think he should have kept his mouth shut and not testified. No one in the service liked the CID, just like no city cop had anything good to say about internal affairs divisions. Cops who policed other cops and soldiers who investigated other soldiers learned to stick to their own kind and watch their backs.

"It was mostly field work I did," he told Berglund. "Army life appealed, I guess."

"Humph. Well, you've seen some places, I guess. Me, I did the run between San Diego and Cam Ranh Bay when I was in the Navy. Had a furlough in Bangkok once, attended police academy in St. Paul. Took that vacation in California with the wife and kids. Period. Rest of the time, I've been right here."

"Havenwood seems like a nice town."

"Yeah, it is. Some people might find it a little slow-moving for their taste, but I never wanted to live anywhere else." He paused for a moment, as something flashed across his features, like a bad memory or an image of ghosts walking on his grave. "This thing with Grace Meade and the fire and all, though...stuff like that doesn't happen around here, you know? You get your Saturday night bar fights and too many drunk kids wiping themselves out on the highway every year, but a murder...."

It happened everywhere, Cruz wanted to tell him, but he just nodded.

"How long are you planning to stick around?" Berglund asked.

"Only as long as it takes."

"You just need a statement from Jillian, right."

"Pretty much. I wouldn't mind talking to a few people who

know her, too, just to round out the report I have to make back to Scotland Yard. You know, the usual background stuff. Can you suggest some names?"

Berglund seemed non-committal. "I can't think who, at this point. She's been gone a long time. She left right after high school. Went to college out east and hasn't been back here much since. Drops in to see her mother once in a while, that's about it."

"What about family and friends?"

"Her mother was the last of her family. Jillian was an only child. Her grandparents helped raise her, but they've been gone for years. As for friends..." Berglund shrugged. "You know how it is. You lose touch. Seventeen years is a long time."

A long time, Cruz noted, but a very precise number—one that Berglund hadn't even paused to calculate. Was that only because Jillian's whereabouts had been on his mind since this business with the fire and her mother's death? Or was there more to it than that? He studied the deputy out of the corner of his eye. Berglund couldn't be much older than Jillian Meade, and like the man said, it was a small town. They had to have known each other since they were kids. How well? Obviously well enough for Berglund to have counted every year since she'd been gone.

"What about her father?" he asked.

"She never knew him. He was a flyer, killed during the war. Her mother was English. They met over there. Apparently she was working for British special ops, and Joe Meade was flying for the OSS. You know what that was?"

Cruz nodded. "The Office of Strategic Services, forerunner of the CIA."

"That's the one. They say Grace was quite the bombshell in those days, like some kind of Mata Hari, I guess. I don't know. Anyway, the Brits had sent her behind the lines into France, and Joe was flying secret supply missions to the Resistance. His plane got shot down and the Resistance hid him from the Germans for a couple of months or so while they looked for an opportunity to smuggle him out of the country. That's how the two of them met. Kinda like a movie, you know. Got married in secret by a French priest and were together long enough that Grace got pregnant, but then they were separated. Joe Meade was killed trying to get back to England, and Grace got stuck in France till the end of the war."

"So that's how Jillian ended up being born there," Cruz said. When Berglund gave him a curious look, he explained, "I saw it on the passport details that were sent over to the Bureau."

"Oh, right. Anyway, that's about it. Joe's folks sent for Grace and the baby after the war, invited them to come and live here in Havenwood with them."

"And Mrs. Meade never remarried?"

Berglund shook his head.

"You sure know a lot about the family's history," Cruz noted.

"Everybody in Havenwood knows that story. Joe Meade's a local war hero. My kids go to Joseph Meade Elementary School. So did I, for that matter. As for Grace, well, she made her own mark on the town. It can't have been easy for her, I guess, leaving everything and everyone she knew and coming out here to live. But by the time she died, there wasn't a thing went on here she didn't have a hand in. Ran half the town, for that matter. Her funeral's probably going to be the biggest one the town's ever seen. I can't imagine many who won't be there."

Except her daughter, Cruz thought.

Muffled voices sounded behind the glassed-in reception area, and they looked over to see an older woman speaking to the orderly.

"This must be the psychiatrist," Berglund said, pushing himself off the window ledge.

Cruz had to agree. The woman wore no white coat, just a long, belted navy cardigan and slacks, but there was no mistaking the authoritative bearing of someone used to having her way. Sure enough, the orderly nodded in the direction of the two men in the waiting room. The woman disappeared behind a partition, then reappeared, frowning and pushing her way though the heavy door that separated the waiting area from the ward beyond.

Tall and heavyset, she had frizzled, steel-gray hair coiled in a knot on top of her head. A pair of gold-rimmed eyeglasses dangled from a chain slung around the collar of the brightly colored blouse she wore under the navy cardigan, a riotous Rorschach test pattern of pinks, white and oranges. As she strode toward them, hands jammed in the pockets of her sweater, the crepe soles of her brown Hush Puppies squeaked on the tiled floor.

"I'm Dr. Helen Kandinsky. What can I do for you gentlemen?"

Her irritable expression put Cruz in mind of Miss Nugent, his junior high English teacher, whose habit it was to send all the "Mexicans" in her classes to seats at the back of the room. They could do what they wanted back there, she said, as long as they kept quiet, because she had no intention of wasting her time on bean pickers. Somewhere in America, people were marching for civil rights, but Miss Nugent obviously hadn't heard the news. The fact that Cruz's family had been in California nearly two hundred years cut no ice with her, either. No amount of effort ever earned him more than the standard "C" she handed out to every student with a Spanish-sounding last name, the minimum required to ensure that there would be no repeat appearances in her class.

Berglund introduced himself and Cruz, explaining why they were there. The doctor pulled her hands out of her pockets to shake theirs in turn. When she turned her clear-eyed gaze on Cruz, she held on to his hand for an extended moment, her expression softening, less irritated now than curious. In that split second, Cruz saw Miss Nugent slink away into that dank mental corner where all his anger and self-doubt lived and festered.

"An FBI agent?" she said. "I can see why the deputy here

would need to speak to my patient, but why would you people be taking an interest in a local tragedy like this?"

"I'm working on another case where Miss Meade may be a material witness," he told her. "I'd been trying to track her down in Washington, and when I heard what had happened here, I decided to fly out."

"I see. Well, I'm sorry to say you've probably made a trip for nothing. I doubt Jillian's going to be in a position to answer your questions anytime soon. I'm trying to get her to open up and talk about what happened to her mother, but it's slow going, and I think it could take a while."

"Has she said anything at all about what happened that night?" Berglund asked.

"She hasn't uttered a single word since being brought in, not about that or anything else. Mind you, she was heavily sedated for the first twenty-four hours. I've backed her off the meds today, but she's still largely unresponsive. She seems to be in shock."

"She hasn't tried...you know, to hurt herself again or anything, has she?" Berglund asked.

"No. We're monitoring her very closely, mind you, but she's been quiet. Too quiet, in fact. I'm getting concerned about the fact that she's not eating or drinking. If she doesn't start taking something in the next few hours, I may have to put her on an intravenous line. I'm hoping to avoid that, because it's bound to upset her. If she resists and has to be restrained, physically or chemically, then we're going to end up right back at square one."

"Are you saying she has made some progress since coming in?" Cruz asked.

"Maybe just a little. She was completely unresponsive at first. A lot of that was the drugs, of course. And while she still hasn't spoken, she has taken a tentative step out of her self-isolation."

"How so?"

"I was in to see her a little while ago. She's still not talking, but she's listening, I can tell. I left her with a notebook and some markers. It seemed like a worthwhile gambit. I was told she's a historian by profession and that she's written for publication. Some writers can't resist a blank page."

"And that worked?"

The doctor nodded. "I think so. Sure enough, when I peeked in on her just a few minutes ago, she was writing feverishly. It's very strange. It almost looks as if she were undergoing some kind of exorcism. Frankly, though, it's an encouraging sign. Something is bothering her deeply, and she's trying to communicate in the way she's most comfortable. If that's all she can manage for now, it's fine with me."

"So, what's she writing?" Cruz asked.

Dr. Kandinsky's lower lip jutted as she lifted her shoulders in a shrug. "I have no idea."

"You haven't read it?"

"No, I promised her privacy."

"Then how do you know she's not writing gibberish?"

"I don't. But even if she is, it says something about her mental state. In the meantime, as long as she's involved in some kind of external activity, she's not trying to kill herself."

"I'd like to try talking to her, Doctor," Berglund said. "She and I..." He hesitated. "Jillian's known me her whole life, that's all, and she could probably use a familiar face right about now."

The doctor studied him for a moment as she considered the request, but then shook her head. "I'm sorry, I have to say no. Not today, anyway. She's at a very tricky juncture right now. She's been severely traumatized, and in my professional opinion, she's right on the cusp of total withdrawal." Berglund started to protest but she held up a hand. "I have no doubt you mean well, Deputy, but to walk in now, wearing that uniform and asking questions about the fire and her mother's death...well, it's premature, I'm afraid."

Berglund nodded, obviously resigned to wait, but Cruz shifted his weight from one foot to the other.

"With all due respect, Doctor, I'm a little skeptical about how traumatized she really is. There's some evidence Miss Meade may have pertinent knowledge on at least two other recent homicides—and her mother was murdered, by the way, in case you weren't aware."

"Is that true?" Dr. Kandinsky asked, turning to Berglund. He nodded.

"So that being the case," Cruz went on, "I think we need to consider the possibility that she could be faking these symptoms of hers."

"She wanted to die in that fire," Berglund said. "I know. I was there. I practically had to coldcock her before I could carry her out of there."

"And then there was the second suicide attempt in the Havenwood ER," Dr. Kandinsky pointed out.

"Conveniently unsuccessful once more," Cruz said. "Look, you have to admit, Doctor, there are clever people who sometimes act crazy in order to throw up a smoke screen to cover their actions. I know—I've seen it before."

"I'm not saying it's impossible, but I doubt it, in this case. And if you're wrong and we push her too hard prematurely, Agent Cruz, we could very well do permanent damage. She could shut down for good, and then she might well succeed at her next attempt at suicide. Because make no mistake about it, gentlemen, the opportunity will arise sooner or later, and that wouldn't suit your purposes or mine."

Cruz was ready to argue it further, but her fighter's stance and the shake of her gray head made it clear she was not about to back down.

"No. You can come back tomorrow and we'll see where we're at then. For now, my medical order stands—Jillian Meade is not to be disturbed. You can try for a court order, if you want, but I warn you, I'll oppose it vigorously."

Cruz would have been willing to take his chances with a

judge, but Berglund's set expression told him he'd be on his own. "One more day isn't going to make any difference," the deputy said. "We'll wait."

Kandinsky nodded. "I think that's the best course."

"Could we at least see her?" Berglund asked.

"I suppose that would be all right. I don't see what harm it would do for you simply to look at her—from a distance, you understand. There's a one-way observation window in her room. You can see her from there."

They followed her over to the solid steel door next to the reception window and waited while the orderly at the desk buzzed them through. Dr. Kandinsky led them past a large common room just behind the reception desk, where eight or ten people in robes and hospital gowns, elderly for the most part, were sitting around card tables, or in recliners or wheelchairs arranged in a circle in front of a television set.

"Our geriatric cases," the doctor told them. "Dementia, mostly. We give them a little occupational therapy, but there's not much potential for happy endings there."

They continued down a long narrow hall, past rooms with heavy doors that stood open now, each room with a rectangular observation port, about two feet by three, set into the wall to allow a view of the inside. By the faintly shadowed look of the windows, Cruz knew they were mirrored on the other side, like the observation windows of the countless interrogation rooms in which he'd worked witnesses over the years. Most of the rooms were empty now, their occupants obviously those geriatric cases down the hall, but they passed one closed door, and through the observation window, they saw a lanky, long-haired boy lying in a knot of covers, his body twitching as if in response to a thousand small electric shocks.

"Drug overdose," Kandinsky said, frowning at the boy's spasms. "Sixteen years old. He's three days into detox. This is his third time trying to get clean, and if he doesn't straighten up and fly right this time, I don't think he's going to see seventeen." She shook her head wearily. "A nice kid from a good home. Such a stupid, bloody waste. He's the only other patient on total lock-down and round-the-clock watch."

They moved on to the last room in the hall, and the doctor's voice dropped to a murmur. "There she is."

"Oh, Jesus!" Berglund breathed, his pale eyes gone wide.

Cruz turned to the window. He, too, was taken aback. He had Jillian Meade's passport details, and from them, he'd begun to form a mental picture of her. Hair: brown. Eyes: brown. Height: 5'5". Weight: 110 pounds. Place of birth: Drancy, France, July 14, 1944.

All this information was contained in his battered briefcase in the trunk of the rental car, which was still parked back at Havenwood police headquarters. He'd also seen her in the Bi-centennial group photograph hanging on Haddon Twomey's wall, and there was another photo in his briefcase, as well, clipped to the corner of her file. The State Department had sent over a grainy copy of her passport photo, but it was clear enough to put some flesh on the bones of the other details he'd gathered. Hair not just brown, but very dark; long, below her shoulders at least, although she'd worn it center-parted and tied back con-servatively for her passport picture. A wisp of long bangs, like a curtain, half concealing eyes that were large and slightly al-mond shaped. Her expression sober, chin tilted up slightly, as if she'd instinctively recoiled from the intrusive stare of the lens, the angle leaving the impression of someone looking down a nose that was unremarkable, neither too large nor too small. Her unsmiling mouth had been full, deeply colored, probably from lipstick, although it was hard to tell, since the picture was black and white. She wore small gold earrings and a simple gold neck-lace against a plain, rounded black neckline.

From those details and from the other information Cruz had gathered about her yesterday, as he'd gone from her apartment building to her workplace, he'd formed an image of a woman who was quiet, intellectual, buttoned-down and caught up in her work. Not unpleasant, but the kind who, as she approached middle age, rarely made eye contact, as if afraid of catching some fatal disease through the osmosis of social intercourse. A woman who might smile out of manners or nervousness, but who rarely laughed out loud. A thin woman with pale hands that never got dirty. A woman who haunted library stacks and hurried home each night from her museum job to a quiet, tidy apartment where she survived on yogurt, apples and three good books a week.

The problem was, that image didn't mesh with the reality of a woman linked to three violent deaths. And it certainly didn't fit with the image in the viewing port in front of them.

The room was painted a dull green color, furnished with a hospital bed, a steel chair and a rolling side table. Nothing more. The foot of the bed faced the window, so that although the woman lay on her side, propped on one elbow, they could see her in profile. She was wearing an oxygen feeder tube, and her breathing seemed raspy and labored. Her long legs were bare and bruised, tangled in the quilt but folded up in a near fetal position making her seem small, childlike and lost in the big institutional bed. Her face was strained and pale, eyes puffy, skin smeared with traces of soot. Her long hair was tangled and falling unheeded in her eyes. Thin arms poked from the short sleeves of a blue cotton hospital gown; like her legs, they seemed covered with bruises—although maybe, Cruz thought, it was only soot. There was, however, no mistaking the thick, gauze bandage on her left arm, just below the elbow, the aftermath, he presumed, of the incident with the air-filled hypodermic syringe.

Scattered on the mattress beside her were the spilled contents of a box of felt markers. Her right hand clenched one of the markers as she scribbled, rapidly and frantically, in a thick notebook, pausing only to flip pages. She was supporting herself on her left elbow as she lay on the bed, and that hand was compulsively kneading a corner of the quilt. Cruz watched the counterpoint movements, mesmerized by her left hand clawing at the covers while her right went on, scribbling and scribbling—down the notebook's left-hand page, then flying to the top of the right, madly filling that one, and then flipping to the next. She worked with a frenzy that left him inclined to believe she was truly insane. And at that speed, he thought, she had to be writing gibberish.

So was she mad? Or too clever by half?

"She looks awful," Berglund muttered. "Locked up in there, all alone. Isn't there something...?"

"We're doing all we can for her right now," Kandinsky said. "At this point, the most important thing seems to be that she get down in that notebook whatever it is that she seems driven to put there. That and, hopefully, for her to sleep, and also to eat something. I might see if we can get her into a shower eventually, too. I know that would make her feel better. But right now," she added, "this is what she needs to be doing."

Berglund couldn't seem to take his eyes off the crumpled figure on the bed. The doctor watched him for a moment, her face shifting to a puzzled frown, and then she reached out to touch him on the arm. "Deputy? Why don't you and Agent Cruz go now? You can come back tomorrow and we'll see where we stand then. She's not going anywhere, and I'm sure you'll find her much improved after a night's sleep."

Berglund snapped back to attention, pulling his gaze away from the window. "Right, that's what we'll do. I'd like to know right away if her condition changes, though," he added, pulling out a business card, and then a pen that he used to scribble a number on the back. "These are my office and home telephone numbers. Would you tell her I was here, if you get a chance? And if she wants to talk, any time, no matter how late, call me?"

Kandinsky took the card he held, looked it over, and then slipped it into her sweater pocket. "I will, I promise."

Berglund studied her for a second, then turned on his heel and headed up the hall without a backward glance.

Cruz took one last look at the figure on the other side of the glass. Jillian Meade's one hand continued its frantic kneading of the bedclothes while, clenched in her other, the turquoise marker flew across the notebook pages.

CHAPTER 9

I don't know where to begin to tell this story. I lie here, searching for meaning in what happened, finding none that makes any sense. At the very least, I need to lay this out in a logical sequence of events, but I'm so confused by guilt and anger I can hardly think straight.

How do I do this? How do I explain why a woman as admired as my mother had to come to the end she did? And how do I account for the sick, twisted fate that forced me, a daughter as fatally flawed as she was, to sit in judgment over her?

I want to scream out at the unfairness of it. My throat and chest ache with the pressure of unshed tears, the way a dam must ache as it holds back a flood. But I can't indulge myself. I haven't earned the right to cry.

One thing seems clear: if I'm going to get this all down, I'm going to have to try to muster up some kind of detachment. Treat Grace Meade as just another one of my research subjects, a minor historical figure upon whom a handful of fates turned. Ignore the emo-

tion-laden tie that binds us even now—that soft, invisible umbil-
ical cord that's been wrapped around my neck since the day I was
born, slowly strangling the life out of me.

And who knows? Maybe it strangled both of us. For years now,
I've harbored the guilty feeling that my mother would have been
happier if I'd never been born. That the burden of my childish needs
forced her to abandon any thought of pursuing her own. That ensuring my security destroyed any chance she might have had to
find a little happiness of her own.

She left her country and the life she knew to bring me here to
live with my father's parents. I can't remember a time when my
grandparents weren't the most loving influence on my life, and I
will always be grateful for the safe cocoon of their warmth. I'm certainly glad they're not alive now to see how I've ended up.

In spite of my grandparents' unswerving love and support,
though, there was a sadness that permeated our home like a layer
of fine dust. Now and then, it lifted a little, but inevitably it would
soon settle back over us all.

My late father was Nana's and Grandpa's only child, and of
course, no worse tragedy can befall a parent than to lose a child.
Now, as I look back through adult eyes, I can see how my young
life was marked by the faint shadow of grief behind their encouraging smiles. Every milestone I passed successfully must
have reminded them of that other child they'd nurtured safely
through the pitfalls of childhood, only to have him perish alone
in a foreign land.

And my mother? His shadow seemed to hang over her, too, and
I sometimes felt she could barely make me out in the gloom of those
memories. When I was little, there were moments when I wanted
to fly into a room and just crash into her—anything to break
through, to get her to notice me. But fear or training or both held
me back. I waited, watching and hoping she would turn on me the
radiant, incredible smile that she bestowed like a blessing on so
many others who came to love and admire her. She never did—at

least, not when we were by ourselves and I could be absolutely certain that she meant it for me and me alone.

For years, I thought the problem was that I reminded her too much of my father, whose silver-framed photograph smiled down on us from the living room mantle. That my existence was a constant, aching reminder of his absence. In recent years, though, I resigned myself to the possibility that she might simply have been one of those women who didn't enjoy motherhood. I even wonder whether she'd ever really wanted a child. She never said, but I can't help thinking that I was an accident with which she simply coped, just as she coped with all the other setbacks and tragedies in her life. There is nothing worse than thinking your very existence is a mistake.

Mind you, I'm sure all of Havenwood would testify that she was a model parent, utterly conscientious. As a child, I adored her and lived in terror of losing her. But as I grew older, I began to realize that her life might have been so much more had she not sacrificed herself for my sake—buried herself alive in this tiny prairie town where her experience and skills would always be underutilized, her past little understood, no matter how much she was admired.

I knew—everyone knew, vaguely—how her life before coming to this country had been full of action, danger and passion, like something out of great fiction or the movies. Living on the front lines of World War II, plunged right into the action, she'd been part of one of the greatest struggles between good and evil the world has ever known. Lines were clearly drawn then, more so than at any time before or since. For my mother's generation, there was the evil of fascism on one side and all those who opposed it on the other. As a partisan, she led a life of action and passion—and unthinkable tragedy. But when the battle for freedom was won, she retired with me, her infant daughter, to a remote and foreign place, the small hometown of the husband she'd found, then lost in the midst of that great struggle.

I can't believe she wasn't sometimes bored to utter despair here. Bored and lonely. And yet, to my knowledge, she never considered packing up and moving someplace else where she might at least attend a concert or a stage play from time to time, perhaps find someone—a friend, lover, or new husband—whose interests went beyond grain prices, TV shows, local gossip and the winter wind-chill factor. Someone to understand her and share her life.

I remember the first time it really dawned on me that my mother had once had a life beyond Havenwood. It was after both my grandparents had died; I must have been twelve or thirteen at the time. My mother and I were at home one evening, watching an old movie on television. I don't remember which one. All I know is that it was set on one of those elegant British estates that hardly exist anymore and that the entire cast spoke like my mother. And it suddenly struck me there might actually be a place on this earth where Grace Meade didn't stand out like a mink coat at Woolworth's.

I remember, too, glancing over at her and being thunderstruck by the realization that she could cry.

"Mum? What's wrong?" I asked her—panicked really, because this was so unlike her.

Her ivory linen handkerchief fluttered in an embarrassed little wave. "Oh, nothing, darling. I'm sorry. I don't know what's come over me."

"What do you mean? What's wrong?"

She hesitated, glancing at the television, but Deborah Kerr (I think that's who it was) had given way to Tony the Tiger and a Frosted Flakes commercial. My mother's porcelain blue eyes, brimming with tears, turned back to me, two points of color standing out on her cheekbones, which were high and smoothly defined. Although her face became a little softer and rounder as she aged, she was beautiful right up to the day she died.

"It's silly, really," she said. "I suppose I was just feeling a little homesick."

"Homesick? You were?"

I was dumbstruck. The thought had never occurred to me that

she might wish to be anywhere but where we were. She did have an airmail subscription to the *Daily Mail* and the *Times of London,* of course, and she kept a short-wave radio in her bedroom so that she could listen to the BBC. We had a tradition in our house that on December 25, we had to wait until after the Queen's Christmas message before my mother would come out and join my grandparents and me in opening our gifts around the tree.

But those were just my mother's strange little quirks. I'd never thought of her as a particularly sentimental person. She almost never spoke of her life before coming to Minnesota. Like most overconfident Americans, I simply assumed that she was thrilled to be here.

As I grew older, though, it dawned on me that her reluctance to revisit the past mightn't be lack of sentimentality as much as her way of coping. After all, she'd endured terrible losses in those years before I was born—her parents, a fiancé, my father, her home, not to mention God knows how many friends and comrades from her period of war service.

Was it any wonder, then, that the subject of the past would be painful for her.

"Do you miss England, Mum?"

"Sometimes, yes, I suppose I do," she confessed.

"Are you sorry you left?"

"No, not really. There'd be no point in being sorry, would there? Always remember, Jillian, once you make a decision, you must never look back."

"You could have stayed there," I pointed out, intrigued at the idea that I might have had an entirely different life, one in which I went to a school that looked like an old castle and wore a school uniform with a kilt, knee socks and a crested blazer. Mentally, I tried on an English accent, picturing myself as a more gangly, less pretty (obviously) version of Elizabeth Taylor in *National Velvet.*

But my mother's head gave a firm shake. "No, darling. Coming here was the best option at the time. Things were terribly difficult at home when the war ended. You were a tiny baby, so you can't remember what it was like, but I remember it very well, indeed. We were living in one cramped little room in an old house outside London. It was hardly big enough for a bed and a small table. Your cradle was an old bureau drawer. We needed a flat desperately, but there were simply none to be had. So many houses had been bombed by the Germans, and with all the men coming back from the front after 1945, there was a dreadful shortage of housing. Naturally, war veterans were at the top of the waiting list, so there was no telling how long we would have to live like that. It was no way to raise a child."

"But that's not fair! You should have been at the top of the list, too. You served in the war. So did my father."

"Yes, but Daddy was an American, wasn't he?"

"That shouldn't have made any difference. We were allies and everybody was fighting for the same side. And what about you? You fought for England behind the lines in France just the same as if you'd been in a uniform. You should have gotten the same treatment as the soldiers coming back."

"Well, perhaps, in theory. In practice, though, it wasn't that simple. I'd worked for a very small, very secret part of the government. Even now, you know, Whitehall never publicly acknowledges the special services, even though everyone knows they exist. In any case, dear, we were a very few, and there were so many other needs to fill. They had to establish priorities somehow, and British servicemen and their families simply came first."

I started to renew my protest against the unfairness of it all, but my mother held up her hand. "It wasn't only the billeting problem. Food and clothing were in short supply, too. Rationing was still in force. You needed formula, nappies and, oh, so many things that just weren't to be had. Really, darling, when your grandparents wrote and invited us to come and live with them here, I knew it was for the best. As for this..." She waved a neat, manicured hand at the TV screen, where Deborah Kerr had returned, dressed in a simple but elegant little black dress very much like one my mother owned. "...this is just Mummy being very silly, that's all."

In my heart of hearts, I was glad she had taken up my grand-parents' offer. They'd been wonderful, loving people, and through their stories and those of so many old friends and neighbors in Havenwood, I grew up feeling linked to a father I'd never known—a father about whom my mother, frankly, could tell me frustrat-ingly little, so short had been their time together before he was killed.

That evening, though, I began to see my mother in a whole new light. To me then, a young girl on the brink of womanhood, there was great melodrama in the notion of this brave young English widow, a war heroine in her own right, clutching a tiny baby to her bosom as she hurried from one government office to another under a relentless English rain, pleading with harried and un-sympathetic clerks for lodgings that just weren't to be had.

"What about now?" I pressed.

"What do you mean?"

"Do you ever think of going back?"

"To England? And leave you here all alone? What an absurd idea!"

"No, I mean we could both go. It'd be neat. I could see where you grew up, and where you met Dad."

"Oh, I don't know about that, Jillian. It's such a long trip, you have no idea."

"We'd fly over."

"That would be terribly expensive. And not at all feasible. The school systems are very different and..."

"Not for good. Just for a visit. Summer vacation, maybe. You could see old friends, take me to the white cliffs of Dover. Maybe we could go to France, too, look up those cousins."

My mother had been born in Dover to an English father and a French mother. It was that combined heritage that had made her such a prize to the British secret service when the war broke out and finally landed her behind the lines in occupied France. But that night in front of the television, she displayed no interest whatsoever in a return visit.

"It would all be very different now, Jillian. So many places were bombed during the war, including the house I grew up in and my father's print shop. Everything's been rebuilt and changed, I'm sure. I don't think I should enjoy seeing that. I'd rather remember it as it was."

"What about people?"

"People?"

"Family, say? On your father's side—or your mother's?"

On her bedroom bureau she had a small, pewter-framed photo of her own mother, whose beauty she'd inherited. British sapper Albert Wickham had met young Sylvie Fournier in Normandy during the First World War and had utterly lost his heart to her. They'd married after the war, but sadly, my grandmother had died in an influenza epidemic when my mother was just a toddler. My mother, like me, had grown up an only child.

"There's no one left to speak of on my father's side," she said. "He only had one sister, and she died years ago, never married. On the other side—your *grandmaman's* family—well, there were the uncles in France, of course, but they're gone now. As for *les cousins*," she added, her French pronunciation flawless, her nose wrinkled in distaste, "I made very sure to lose touch with them the moment I grew up. A right obnoxious bunch, they were."

I smiled. She'd told me once about the awful teasing she'd suffered at the hands of the horrible Norman cousins with whom she'd spent her summers as a child. They were the reason my mother spoke fluent French, however, heard first at her doomed mother's breast, then fine-tuned during those childhood summers spent with the uncles and their families. And years later, in fact, when she was sent back into France to work with the Resistance, my mother adopted Grandmaman's name, Sylvie Fournier, as her nom de guerre.

"What about old friends?" I pressed.

A small crease appeared on her high forehead. Her hair was probably already in the process of turning from its original honey-blond to silver-white at this period of her life, although I can't remember clearly. But that evening, I'm sure, she would have been wearing it as she invariably did, smoothed back from her face and rolled into a neat chignon at the base of her skull. When she rose in the morning, it flowed like a soft, golden storm halfway down her back, but she would never have thought of leaving it down during the day.

Her tiny pearl stud earrings matched the single strand at her neck, and she was wearing a peach twin set, I remember, the cardigan draped around her shoulders, cape style. As she pondered my question, she crossed her wrists over her chest and tugged the cardigan closer, as if she'd felt a sudden chill. As the air between us shifted with her movement, I remember, a subtle hint of her perfume, Ma Griffe, wafted from her chair to my corner of the living room sofa.

"It's been a long time, dear," she said finally. "The war changed everything and there's no going back. It's better to leave some things locked away in memories."

In my mother's voice that night, I imagined I heard the whispering ghosts of all the people she'd lost to the war. Her beloved father, of course, killed in 1941 by the German bomb that destroyed his printing press in Dover. I also knew, because I'd only recently dragged it out of her, that she'd once been engaged to another man, long before she met my father—long before the U.S. had even entered the war. He'd been a British naval lieutenant, but he had died early on in the war.

There had to have been countless other friends and comrades, too, from her youth and from those nearly five long years of war, most of which she'd spent working as a British special agent, first in England, then in France. English spies. French Resistants. And, of course, Joe Meade, the dashing American flyer with whom she'd fallen in love, married and conceived a child, and then lost just weeks before I was born.

I can only imagine that the spirits of all those departed souls haunted my mother—that night and to the end of her days.

CHAPTER 10

Havenwood, Minnesota
Thursday, January 11, 1979

Cruz knew a brush-off when he heard one. He and Berglund were at the Havenwood police headquarters, standing outside the low-slung stucco building. Cruz was hungry and tired, and his feet and hands were freezing. The sun had set while they were inside the hospital at Montrose and now, a bitterly cold night wind was whistling through the empty baseball diamond across the road. Under his shoe, Cruz felt the crackle of thin ice on the asphalt lot, which was empty, except for one other police cruiser besides Berglund's.

"Why don't you leave it with me?" Berglund told him. "Once Jillian's back on her feet, I'll ask her about that visit she made to England—who she talked to over there, whether she noticed anything out of the ordinary. Whatever. You can leave me a list of questions, if you want, and I'll get back to you on it. God only knows when that'll be, mind you, the way she looks now. Meantime, seems to me there's not much point in you wasting your time hanging around here."

Cruz studied the ground as he kicked tiny fragments of ice and sent them skidding across the parking spaces. They had driven back from Montrose along a rural secondary road—a shortcut, Berglund said, although to Cruz, the black void they'd traversed had seemed grim, forbidding and endless. For the entire length of the trip, they'd seen exactly one other vehicle, a pickup traveling in the opposite direction. No one else. No roadside service stations, no call boxes, no lonely farmhouses. After the first few minutes of passing nothing but pale, twin slivers of potholed road flying by on either side, dimly lit by headlights that obviously needed cleaning, Cruz had had the anxious sense he was losing his eyesight.

Berglund had uttered hardly a word since leaving the psychiatric ward. Now, the two men stood face-to-face in the parking lot, illuminated by a single sodium floodlight mounted high on a weathered pole that threw long shadows and cast a jaundiced light on the deputy's broad face. His breath plumed around his head in the cold night air like smoke from a locomotive getting ready to shove off. Clearly, Cruz thought, there would be no invitation to come inside. Berglund was done playing host.

"I'll give it some thought," Cruz told him. "I might end up leaving those questions with you at that, but we'll see how things go. Meantime, don't let me hold you up. I'm sure you've got plenty to do without having to baby-sit me."

Berglund cocked a thumb at the low stucco building. "Got a ton of paperwork to do before I can get out of here."

Cruz nodded. "You go ahead. Thanks for taking me around."

"No problem. Are you going to catch a flight back tonight?"

"I doubt it. The last flight to D.C. is around seven-thirty, and there's no way I'd make it, especially with a rental car to return."

"Maybe an early-morning connection. Return your car tonight, stay at one of the Minneapolis airport hotels."

"I could do that, but actually, I was thinking I might stick around here for another day. See how Miss Meade's doing tomorrow."

Berglund paused. Lost in shadow under the prominent ridge of his brow, his eyes were totally unreadable. "Suit yourself," he said finally.

"Can you recommend a hotel?"

"Only two places open this time of year," Berglund said. "Lakeside Inn and the Whispering Pines."

"Which is better?"

"Lakeside's got bigger rooms and a better view, not that it makes much difference at night. It'll be noisy, though. There's a steak pit and pub downstairs. Real good rib-eye, if that appeals. The Whispering Pines Motel is attached to that Chevron station half a mile back down the highway, the way you came into town. Rooms are pretty basic, but they're clean and it's quieter out there, especially at this time of year. Plus, if you want a decent breakfast for a good price, the café there's the place. All the truckers make a point of stopping there on their way through these parts."

"Sounds like it might be the best bet," Cruz said. "What about you? You interested in grabbing a bite later? Buy you a beer?"

Berglund shifted his bulk from one big leather boot to the other. "Don't think I can make it. I got that paperwork to do, and then I want to check with the chief's wife, see how he made out today. And—" He straightened suddenly and pushed his padded nylon jacket sleeve up his arm to check his watch. "Oh, shit! I didn't realize how late it was. My kid's got hockey practice in half an hour. I coach his team. Sorry," he said, shoving out his hand, "I'm gonna have to leave you to your own devices."

"It's no problem, I'll manage fine," Cruz said as his hand disappeared in the deputy's maw. "Thanks again. What time are you figuring on heading back over the hospital tomorrow?"

"I don't know. Hard to say. Depends what else is going on around here."

"Sure, you've got a lot going on. I'll probably just head over there on my own. Maybe we'll meet up."

Berglund was making ready to go inside, but he paused, the shadows on his face spreading as his frown deepened. "Understand, Cruz, our first priority here is to find out what Jillian can tell us about the fire and her mother's death. Even assuming the doc lets us—lets *me*—in tomorrow, and that she's ready to talk, this investigation of yours has to take a back seat right now. That's why I'm saying you might be better off to leave your information with me, let me get back to you on it."

"Like I said, it could come down to that," Cruz conceded. "How about we wait and see what happens tomorrow?"

"She's going to have a hard enough time dealing with what went down here. I'm going to have to ask you not to distract her with any other outside matters right now. I mean that."

Cruz nodded. "I understand you're under a lot of pressure to come up with some answers here, Deputy."

"That's right, I am. And who knows how long that's going to take? The last thing I need is some federal hotshot breathing down my neck while—" Berglund's frame had shifted until he was looming over Cruz, but he caught himself suddenly and pulled back, exhaling heavily. "Never mind. Sorry. It's been a rough couple of days. And look, I know you've got a job to do, too, but I just can't be concerned about that right now, you understand?"

"Sure, I understand. No offense taken."

"I appreciate it. I just hate to think about you hanging around here, wasting your time. I'm sure you've got other things to be doing, too."

"I've got a pretty full caseload," Cruz admitted. "On the other hand, this is what's on my plate right now, and as long as I'm here, I guess I'll just push it around a little. But I appreciate your concern for my busy schedule."

"Suit yourself," Berglund said. "Let's just get one thing straight, though—I don't want you bothering Jillian Meade right now. Clear?" Without waiting for an answer, he turned on his heel and headed up the walk and into the building.

Left alone in the parking lot, Cruz climbed into his rented Buick and started the engine, cranking the heater dial up to full blast. His shoulders, arms and legs, every muscle in his body, felt as if they were locking up in protest against the cold. He hunkered down in the front seat, massaging his arms and watching the building as he waited for the heater to kick in.

To the right of the glass front door was the window of the chief's office where he and Berglund had first talked. The lights were off, but the office door was open and through it, Cruz could see the brightly lit squad room beyond. Berglund was in there now, talking to one of his men, the white-haired uniform Cruz had spotted typing reports when he'd arrived. Suddenly, the guy rose and reached for the parka slung over the back of his desk chair.

The deputy chief looked somber as he turned and headed toward the office. He was the very picture of a straight shooter, Cruz thought, a decent if inexperienced small-town cop burdened with the unexpected double load of a murder and the responsibility of command. But if Berglund was as clean as he seemed, why was this knot of suspicion hardening in his gut? Was it Berglund, or was the problem his own, a reaction caused by too many years of looking for and finding corruption behind a uniform? He watched as Berglund flicked on the office lights and closed the door behind him, throwing his coat aside as he reached for the phone.

Movement in the reception area, meantime, drew Cruz's attention toward the front door. The white-haired cop appeared. Slapping on a police cap, he waved back to someone at the front desk—still the mystery-loving Verna? Cruz wondered, or would she have gone home by now? Outside on the front step, the cop paused at the sight of Cruz's Buick sitting in the parking lot with its engine running.

It was time to move. Cruz put the car in gear, feeling eyes on

him as he pulled out of the lot. At the edge of the roadway, just
before turning, he glanced in his the rearview mirror. The uniform was climbing into the other black and white next to
Berglund's. Cruz kept his pace leisurely as he headed down the
deserted highway, looking for the Chevron station and attached
motel that Berglund had recommended. Watching, too, for the
car that he suspected would be on his tail momentarily. Sure
enough, a pair of headlights swung out onto the highway a moment later, heading in the same direction he was moving, away
from town. In a place this small, there'd be no hiding if Berglund
decided he bore watching. All he could do was make the surveillance as dull as possible.

The Whispering Pines Motel, as advertised, stood about a mile
outside of town. Cruz pulled into the lot, grateful to be off the
highway, where visibility was dropping fast. The weather had
taken a turn for the worse in the last while, and icy sleet was
whipping across the pavement, accumulating in little drifts
wherever it encountered an obstacle like a curb or the base of a
tree. The night was dark, the space beyond the service center
transformed into a black void, but the lot itself was illuminated
by floodlights mounted on tall poles affixed to the roof at either
end of the long, low building. Gusting snow performed under
the spotlights, spinning an energetic dance in midair. Pretty to
look at, Cruz thought, but nasty weather to be stranded in.

All the rooms of the motel fronted onto the parking lot, lined
up behind a homey-looking café. The Chevron service station attached to it had a couple of open service bays and was connected
to the café by an adjoining office that seemed to do double duty
for the garage and the motel behind it. A red neon Vacancy light
was lit next to the front door. A couple of big rigs were lined up
in a side lot and the café looked moderately busy, but the parking spaces in front of the motel rooms were all unoccupied.

A bell over the door tinkled as Cruz walked into the office.

The place smelled of machine oil, French fries and coffee, the latter scents drifting in from the café through an open inner connecting door between restaurant and office. Cruz saw a solidly built, middle-aged waitress balancing three plates on one arm, her free hand gripping the handles of three white ironstone mugs as she headed for a trio of men sitting at a corner table. Cruz's stomach grumbled. He hadn't eaten a thing except Verna's cookie since the rubbery eggs and rock-hard roll served on his flight from D.C. that morning.

"Evening," a voice behind him called.

He turned to see an older man with a thick head of slick-backed hair and wearing a grease-stained blue jumpsuit leaning on the office counter, gnawing thoughtfully on a yellow wood pencil. An old-timer in a red plaid jacket and green John Deere cap stood across the counter from him. The two had been shooting the breeze when Cruz walked in, but they paused now to study the newcomer, taking his measure. The blue jumpsuit—the owner, Cruz guessed—pulled the pencil out of his mouth and nodded a welcome, but the grizzled old guy turned away, ignoring Cruz as he resumed their conversation.

"You gotta wonder what she needed it for, is all I'm saying."

"Be with you in a minute," the man behind the counter called over the old guy's head to Cruz, before turning back to his customer. The red-trimmed oval at the breast of his jumpsuit read "Norbert." "Uh-huh," he told the old-timer, although whether he agreed or was just filling dead air was hard to say. He reached for a pile of invoices and started flipping through them, then withdrew one and ran an oil-encrusted index finger down the page. "Anyway, Henry, I replaced her muffler and wheel rim right enough. Had to order a replacement for that tail pipe bracket, though. Kind of jury-rigged the old one so it'll hold you for now, but a guy wouldn't want to give odds on how long she'll last."

"So I gotta bring her back in, then?"

"You bet. We don't change out the bracket, she'll be draggin' her ass inside a coupla weeks—especially the way you drive," he added, grinning and throwing a wink in Cruz's direction.

The old guy, Henry, ignored the gibe. "How long's it gonna take to get here, then?"

"Week, ten days. Won't take long to weld her on, though."

"Humph! So what's this gonna set me back?" He pulled a bulging, worn leather billfold out of the back pocket of his rumpled green work pants.

"Call it a eighty bucks."

"Includin' the bracket?"

"No, not includin' the bracket, but I threw in the tow. Bracket's gonna set you back another ten or twelve—say, twenty with the labor, but we'll wait on that till it gets here."

"Geez, Norbert, you're killin' me!"

As reluctantly as if it were a layer of his own skin, the geezer peeled a bill from a fat wad in the wallet. He slapped the bill down on the counter, and Cruz saw Ben Franklin's features on its worn, wrinkled face. Like Cruz's own father, Henry here obviously distrusted banks, preferring to guard his money himself.

"I told you not to take that old beater off-road, didn't I?" the garage owner said as he palmed the bill and rang up the sale on an ancient cash register. "You're lucky you didn't rip off the whole underside." The register pealed and the cash drawer popped open.

Henry waved a dismissive hand. "She's got plenty of life in her yet."

The mechanic lifted the pile of twenties and slid the hundred underneath, then pulled a twenty-dollar bill off the top of the pile. "Sure she does, Henry," he said, grinning as he slammed the drawer shut and handed over the change. "You just keep tellin' yourself that. It's good for business."

The old man scowled and snapped the twenty between his thumb and forefinger before jamming it into the overstuffed billfold. "Anyway," he said, returning to their interrupted conversation, "you gotta wonder what she wanted it for, dontcha think? Not like the grass needs trimmin' these days, know what I'm sayin'?"

"Yeah, you got that right, I guess."

"The wife'd seen Grace that afternoon, you know. Over to the Set 'n Style it was."

"Oh, yeah?"

"Uh-huh. She was sittin' in the next chair, the wife said, tellin' the girl doin' her that Jill had just shown up, right out of the blue. The wife said Grace had no idea she was gonna be in town."

Cruz had been studying the postcards on a rack near the desk—summer scenes of power boats and water skiers on Lost Arrow Lake, grinning fishermen holding up their day's catch, and picturesque shots of the sun setting behind the trees across the lake, which was stained bloodred from the sky's reflection. There were also a couple of shots of racing snowmobiles and the kind of winter wonderland scenes that Cruz had seen out at the Meade place as he gazed across the frozen lake, but summer was obviously the high point of the tourist year. His ears perked up, though, as he realized the two men were discussing the Meades.

"Grace didn't know she was coming?" the mechanic asked as he ripped off the carbon copy of the old man's invoice and handed it over. He folded his arms and leaned against a glass display case behind the counter that held a eclectic variety of sundries—aspirin, razor blades, pocket packs of tissue, and a selection of brightly colored fishing lures and nylon line.

"No idea at all," the old man said. "So, you gotta just wonder, don't you?"

"Well, yeah, you got that right. Anyway, Henry, I'll give you a shout soon as that bracket comes in."

Henry folded the invoice and crammed it into the back hip pocket of his sagging work pants. "You bet." He hesitated, clearly wanting to continue the conversation, but the mechanic's crossed arms sent an unmistakable negative message. Old Henry gave Cruz another none-too-subtle once-over and headed for the door, pausing to call back over his shoulder, "You goin' to the smoker Saturday night, Norbert?"

"Oh, yeah, you betcha."

"Well, okay then. We'll see you."

"I'll call you on that bracket."

"Whatever." The bell over the door tinkled as the old man went out.

The mechanic shook his head, smiling wryly, then turned to Cruz. "The guy's something. Decided to try a shortcut home from the beer parlor the other night. Took his '57 Ford straight across an open field. Only made it about a hundred yards before he got hung up on a stump."

Cruz returned his grin. "Well, like you said, it's good for business."

"That's a fact. So, what can I do for you?"

"I need a room. I was told yours were about the best around."

The other man shrugged modestly. "A guy could do worse, I guess. So who was it recommended us, then?"

"Deputy Berglund."

"Nils did, eh? Well, sure, that's no problem. Not too busy this time of year. You can have your pick, matter of fact."

"Maybe you could let me have the room down at the end, farthest from the gas pumps?"

"You bet." He pulled a large binder out from under the counter and opened it to the last page that had writing on it. "How many nights are you going to be staying, then?" he asked.

"I'm not sure. One, maybe two. Depends."

There was a wall calendar from a feed grain company hanging on the wall behind the desk. The man turned to check the date, then noted it and the room number in the register before turning it around on the counter to face Cruz. "You here on business, are you?"

"That's right," Cruz said, taking the pen and leaning to fill in his name and D.C. address.

The owner nodded at Cruz's coat and tie. "Didn't figure you were here for the ice-fishing derby."

"No, I guess not." Cruz craned his head to see out the plate glass window to his rental parked in front of the building, then turned back to the register and wrote down the license plate number.

"That's twenty dollars a night," the manager said, taking the register back and studying the entry. "Local phone calls are on the house, but long distance is extra." Cruz nodded. "You're from Washington, are you? Long way from home, then."

"That's a fact. Can I ask you something?"

"What's that?"

Cruz cocked his thumb toward the door. "The old fella who was just in here, was that Grace Meade and her daughter he was talking about?"

"You a reporter?"

"No, not exactly." When it became obvious the owner was waiting for more, Cruz added, "I'm an investigator."

"So that's why you've been talking to Nils Berglund. A fire investigator, is it? I heard there was an arson team over at Grace's, lookin' things over."

"I'm with the Federal Bureau of Investigation."

"A. Cruz," the owner read out of the register. He looked up. "FBI, you said?"

"That's right," Cruz said. "Special Agent Alex Cruz. I just got in this afternoon. And you're...?"

"Norbert Jorgenson. I own this place," he said. He tucked the register under the desk. "I'm also the deputy mayor of Havenwood. Folks around here are pretty shook up about this business, I can tell you."

"I can imagine."

"Uh-huh. It's a terrible thing, this fire. Mrs. Meade was real active in the town. A lot of people are going to miss her. But even so, I'm a little surprised the FBI would send out an arson investigator."

"No, I'm not with the arson team. I'm here on another matter altogether. It was only after I tracked Jillian Meade here that I found out about the fire and her mother's death."

"You were looking for Jillian?" Jorgenson leaned against the counter, crossing his arms affably in front of him. "So, what's that all about, you don't mind me asking?"

"It's a routine matter. This business with the fire has complicated things a little, though. What was that old fellow saying a minute ago? About Mrs. Meade, and before that, something about cutting grass?"

"Oh, Henry was in here a couple of days ago, and as it happened, I was out at the pumps when he pulled in, filling a jerry can for Jill Meade."

Cruz felt his jaw dropping. "Jillian Meade came in here to fill a jerry can with gasoline? Was that the day of the fire?"

"Yeah, day before yesterday, I think it was."

"She say why she needed it?"

"Well, that's the thing. I was surprised to even see her. Been a couple, three years at least. She and our daughter used to be friends in high school, so the wife and I got to know Jill pretty good," Jorgenson said, cocking his head toward the café, where his wife was wiping down a table. "Our daughter's married, lives out in Seattle now, so we all kind of lost touch. Grace said Jill didn't come home too much, though. Wasn't here for Christmas, I know, because Grace spent it with the Newkirks. They're neighbors, see. Tom Newkirk's the mayor, actually, and he and I had a drink together the afternoon of Christmas Eve. He's the one told me Grace was on her own over the holidays and was going to come over for turkey with him and Sybil and their gang.

"Anyway," Jorgenson added, apparently realizing he'd drifted from the original question, "all of a sudden, couple of days ago, like I say, Jillian shows up out the blue, looking to buy some gas.

I was real surprised to see her. Told her she'd been missed over the Christmas holidays."

"Did she say why she didn't come?" Cruz asked, thinking back to his conversation with her boss. According to U.S. Customs, Jillian Meade had returned from her trip to Europe on December twentieth. Haddon Twomey had said the two of them hadn't had much chance to discuss what she'd done in England and France because they'd both been getting ready to leave again on Christmas holidays, Jillian to her mother's, Twomey to spend them with friends. So why hadn't she come, after all, as she'd told her boss? Had she decided to stay back and hold the fort at work while Twomey was gone? Or maybe to catch up on missed work? Cruz made a mental note to try to clear up that point, either with her or through a return visit to Twomey.

Jorgenson, obviously, didn't have the answer. "She just said she wasn't able to come at Christmas. She's still single, of course, so I wondered if maybe she had somebody special she was spending the holidays with, instead, but Jillian wasn't volunteering, so I didn't want to ask. Years ago, I might have teased it out of her, you know, but she's not a young kid anymore and we don't know her like we used to, so..." Jorgenson flung out his hands, palms up, in a "whaddya gonna do?" gesture.

"And the gasoline? What did she say about that?"

"She didn't say and I didn't ask, to tell you the truth. Didn't figure it was any of my business."

Cruz glanced outside, where the wind had picked up and was blowing sleety snow across the wide-open expanse of the parking lot, tattooing the window with a sound like someone spitting sand. "But at the time, you didn't think anything of it?"

"Not at the time, no. People out here are filling up jerry cans all the time for one thing or another. It was only after I heard from Nils Berglund that an arson team had been out, and then Henry there reminded me Jillian had been here that afternoon." Jorgenson shrugged. "What did the arson team say, do you know?"

"They won't issue a final report for a while," Cruz said. "Have you told Nils Berglund about the business with the jerry can?"

"No, I haven't gotten around to it yet. Like I say, it only just occurred to me when Henry there came in. I'm sure to see Nils around in the next day or so, though. I guess I could mention it."

A bell dinged once, then again, and both men's gazes shifted outside to where an old VW van with more rust than steel on its undercarriage was pulling up to the gas pumps. Jorgenson walked over to a pegboard behind him where a series of keys hung on cup hooks, each attached to a bright green plastic fob in the shape of an evergreen tree. He pulled down one with a large, white number eight on it and handed it across the counter to Cruz. "There you go. That's right down at the end of the row."

Cruz took the key, but made no move to leave. "Can you think of any reason why Jillian Meade might have set that fire?"

The other man's response was immediate. "Jillian? Not hardly likely. She's a nice, quiet girl, and the Meades are real good people. Jillian grew up here, for Pete's sake. There's just no way she'd do something like that."

Cruz was beginning to suspect that if he could collect a buck for every time someone suggested that growing up in Havenwood was an indicator of innocence, he'd be—well, not rich, maybe, but at least flush enough to swing one of those rib-eye dinners Berglund had mentioned, the thought of which reminded him yet again he hadn't had a meal since breakfast.

The Volkswagen outside gave a toot of its horn, and Jorgenson started around the counter. "I gotta go take care of these folks, but you need anything, Mr....uh..."

"Cruz."

"Right. You need anything, you just pick up the phone in your room and call on down here to the office. If I'm not here, the missus is there in the restaurant and she'll pick up, make sure you get whatever you need."

CHAPTER 11

Now I've gone and cried. The page I was writing on is soaked, and the fuchsia ink from this ridiculous marker has smeared. Worse than that, I've wasted time, when it's obvious I don't have much. Nils Berglund has been here. I heard voices out in the hall, and I'm almost certain his was one of them. No one came in, though. I think that doctor was there, too. She must be holding back visitors. It's the only explanation I can imagine for why they haven't come for me yet.

When I heard them out there, though, I suddenly remembered that it was Nils who pulled me out of the fire. Has he gotten stuck with this investigation? He must be involved in it, at the very least. There are only five or six men on the Havenwood force, after all, and somehow, I can't picture old Chief Lunders managing anything as serious as a murder investigation.

I'm not even sure there's ever been a murder in Havenwood before. Accidental hunting and boating deaths, of course, and more than a few drunken car wrecks—including four of our friends, who were killed after senior prom. But I don't recall ever hearing of a homicide. Nils is conscientious, though. He'll do a thorough job—run it by the book, regardless of personal considerations.

Will he be the one to lead me out of here in handcuffs? Poor Nils! I'm so sorry, for this and for everything. I keep messing up your life, don't I? It's small comfort, I'm sure, but I never meant to. And whatever you have to do now, I want you to know I don't hold it against you. I'm only sorry to have put you in such an awkward position.

This record should make things a little easier, and help explain what went wrong. I'm still a little vague on some of the details, and my mind keeps drifting. I'm trying to keep it all straight so I can set it down in some sort of coherent way—why I came out here this week, and what happened after I got here. If I can only stay detached and keep my wits about me long enough to get it all down.

How did things end up this way?

I never meant to hurt my mother. I loved her, I really did, even if she and I saw little of one another in recent years. If truth be told, I always felt I wasn't the child she might have wished for—if, indeed, she'd even wanted a child. Over time, guilt about my inadequacy twisted back on itself until I ended up resenting her, as if her very presence were a reproach for my own inadequacies.

Lately, though, it dawned on me that my mother was getting older (she turned sixty on her last birthday), and I found myself approaching the middle of my own life, too. Maybe I finally grew up, because I began to see how pointless it was to hold her responsible for everything that had ever gone wrong in my life. Suddenly, I regretted the time that had been wasted. She was my mother, after all. I wanted to know her better and to make amends for the misunderstandings we'd had over the years.

How could it all have gone so wrong?

Most people in town, of course, would roll their eyes at any declaration of love from me, especially now. I think they consider me a pretty poor excuse for a daughter. On the rare occasions I've run into my mother's friends during my infrequent visits home, I could feel the disapproval in their cool questions about how I was getting on in Washington. The last time I was here, Sybil Newkirk, our neighbor and probably my mother's closest friend, scolded me outright for neglecting her.

"She deserves better, Jillian. She's an amazing woman, but she's getting on, like the rest of us. You're the only family she has, but you're so far away. Grace says you hardly ever call. It isn't right, after everything she went through—losing so much, then uprooting herself so you could have a good home."

Thank you, Mrs. Newkirk. As if I didn't already feel guilty enough.

Everyone around here knows the story of Grace and Joe Meade, of course: how the handsome ex-quarterback for Havenwood High went off to war and ended up flying secret supply missions to the French Resistance. How he became trapped behind enemy lines, where he fell in love with a beautiful young English woman working undercover with the Maquis. How they were married in a secret ceremony right under the Gestapo's nose, only for Joe to be captured during an attempt to escape occupied France. How Joe was shot and killed without ever seeing their child (me), born just weeks before the Liberation. How Helen and Arthur Meade wrote to their son's bride after the war, inviting her to bring her baby and come live in Havenwood with them.

It was the stuff of Hollywood movies, and Havenwood embraced Grace, its heroine, with all the protective love and loyalty a small town could offer. Even my teachers at Joseph Meade Elementary School drummed into me the importance of making my life worthy of my parents' sacrifices.

So it's probably inevitable that I'll come out the villain in this piece. And what does it matter, really? Nothing is going to undo what's happened. I can't offer excuses for my actions and no one would want to hear them, anyway. All I can offer is an explanation—knowing full well I'm going to come out looking even worse than I already do. At this point, I'm past caring. I just want it all to be over.

* * *

For as long as I can remember, people have studied me, looking for some trace of Grace's beauty and courage. They weren't the only ones disappointed not to find any evidence of it. My own sense of inadequacy next to her was probably part of the problem between us. I wanted so much to be like her. She was afraid of nothing; I was afraid of everything. She was universally admired; I was universally overlooked. She excelled at anything she put her hand to; I was strictly average in all areas except academics, where the sheer amount of time I spent hiding behind the cover of a book meant that I usually managed to do well. Jillian Meade, slogger first class: that would be me.

But like most paragons, my mother was not always easy to live with. She could be demanding and found it difficult to accept that not everyone was as certain of themselves as she was. After we'd all put her on such a pedestal, though, it came as a shock to me to realize as I grew older that she wasn't really perfect, either. When she made mistakes, as she ultimately did, they were as outsized as her virtues.

The strain between us had already been building during the last couple of years I lived at home. Much of it was probably the normal tension between a strong-willed mother and a daughter beginning to feel her oats. I was trying, in my typically feeble way, to stand on my own two feet. At the same time, I desperately wanted to please her and win her approval. She, like most mothers, hadn't yet accepted that her days of trying to mold me were pretty much over; that whatever she hadn't accomplished by then was never going to happen. By my senior year of high school, I was chafing under the contradictions of trying to please her and still be my own person. She was such an overpowering presence that I knew if I didn't make a break, I'd spend the rest of my life in her shadow, living under her influence, if not under her roof, dressing the way she thought I should, living my life according to her prescription, trotting behind as her spear carrier while she ran half of what went on in this town.

So I applied to colleges as far from Havenwood as possible, but even after I was accepted at Georgetown, I wasn't sure I had the nerve to cut the cord. Then, not long before I was to leave, we had a horrible falling out. The incident that sparked it seems surreal and unbelievable now, viewed from this distance. I'm sure we wished it had never happened. Certainly, neither of us has ever dared mention it since. But at the time, it was more than enough to drive me away, vowing never to return.

I did return, of course, however infrequently. I was too ruled by convention to make so grand a gesture as disowning a mother. In the last seventeen years, though, I don't think I've been home much more than a dozen times, and when I have come, my visits have been as short as I could make them.

Then, last summer, my mother had a cancer scare. It turned out that the tumor on her kidney was benign, but afterward, I realized I might have lost her without us ever having fully reconciled. And after having been out on my own for as long as I had, leading a life far simpler than hers had been, I started to really appreciate how hard her life must have been. It was time to forgive her for not being the superwoman I'd childishly expected her to be.

It was about that time that Haddon Twomey, curator of the museum where I work, approached me about pulling together an exhibit based on newly released information concerning secret American support to the French Resistance during World War II. Haddon knew a little of my parents' story. I think that's why he chose me to go to England and France to gather artifacts for the exhibit. As soon as he mentioned it, I knew I was being been handed a gift—a heaven-sent chance to learn more about my parents and understand a little better what made my mother tick.

I decided then and there that I would do more than just sift through old files and photos to pull together material for this exhibit. I'd use the opportunity to prepare a more personal history, as well. I'd track down as many of my mother's old friends and colleagues as I could; interview them for their memories of her and the times they'd lived through; take pictures of places she'd lived and worked before coming to the States. Put it all together in an album and make her a gift of her past.

And then, I thought, I would present the album to her for Christmas, and I would tell her at last how very proud I was to be her daughter.

Now, knowing what I do, it all seems horribly twisted and ironic. Enough to make the gods laugh—or weep bitter tears.

CHAPTER 12

Havenwood, Minnesota
Thursday, January 11, 1979

Cruz moved his car in front of Unit 8 at the end of the row of rooms. Grabbing his briefcase off the front passenger seat, he climbed out wearily. From the trunk he withdrew the small duffel bag into which he'd stuffed a change of clothes and his shaving gear before heading to the airport that morning, hoping he'd be on his way back to D.C. before nightfall and not have any need of them. No such luck.

Each of the motel units had a outer screen-and-glass storm door and an inner one of wood. With the briefcase under his left arm and grasping the duffel in that hand, Cruz yanked open the storm door at Number 8, propped it with one foot, turned the key on the inside lock and managed to wrestle open the other door. Both were on pneumatic hinges, and they were working hard to shut again, with Cruz wedged between like a rat in a trap. The room inside was pitch-black, the curtains drawn against the invasive lights of the parking lot. Before he'd walk into any unknown space, Cruz wanted to see what he was getting into. Force of habit.

He wedged a hip against one door and a foot against the other, struggling to keep them apart while his hand fumbled along the wall to find a light switch. When his frozen fingers finally landed on it, the room exploded in a riot of color. Cruz squinted, rapidly taking in the layout of the place. Then, in spite of his weariness, he felt a small grin pull at the corners of his mouth.

He was suddenly back in his old room at his aunt Luisa's— not the way it had been when he'd lived in it, but as he'd found it redecorated a couple of weeks earlier, when he'd gone to stay with her over Christmas and, incidentally, check in on his father.

"This is always your room, Alejandro," she'd told him, "but it was time to update it, no? And these colors are the very latest style, you know. I read that Mrs. Carter's living room in Plains, Georgia is done in this same harvest-gold and avocado-green. Me and the First Lady, we have the same taste."

"I always knew you had good taste, Aunt Lu," Cruz told her, nestling her round little body under his arm. She'd blushed happily as he kissed the top of her head.

He'd lived with her from the age of thirteen until the draft board finally caught up with him. The first time he'd gone to stay with her was when his father had locked him out of the house for missing a curfew. He'd returned home a day or two later, after the old man cooled down, but the move to his widowed aunt's home became permanent a few weeks later, when his father once again threw himself into a blind fury over some stupid incident Cruz couldn't even recall anymore. He only remembered the humiliation of being chased down the street, dodging blows from the baseball bat his father had grabbed, running until the cops showed up after having been called by some busybody neighbor.

Social Services had stepped in then, taken one look at the bruises covering Cruz's face and body—some new, most of them old and nearly healed—and threatened to remove him to a foster home. Cruz had been as outraged as his father at the notion he needed to be removed for his own protection. He could take care of himself. He already outweighed the old man by twenty pounds and towered over him. The only reason he hadn't coldcocked him long ago was that he knew the real reason for his father's rages was grief over his dead wife and shame at his helplessness to do anything about the cancer that had tortured her for three long years before finally killing her. Cruz hadn't enjoyed playing whipping boy to the old man's impotent wrath, but that didn't mean he wanted to live with strangers, either.

There was no question of counseling, though. In the first place, Cruz thought, that kind of help probably wasn't even available back then for an itinerant bricklayer whose command of English was sometimes as shaky as his control over his temper. And even if it had been, his father would never have agreed to go, since the only problem he had, as far as he cold see, was a defiant son who refused to show the proper respect.

But the Social Service case worker had turned out to be as stubborn as old Vicente Cruz, and in the end, the man had been forced to accept the indignity of having his son live in his sister's spare room. It was either that or lose him altogether—a total destruction of *la familia,* Aunt Luisa told her brother, which would mean that the disease had beaten him, after all. Had beaten them all.

Cruz tossed his duffel bag on a chair upholstered in bright gold that matched the gold-and-green jungle print on the double bed and on the window curtains. The walls were papered in some kind of textured stuff that looked like bamboo, and the green shag carpet covering the floor from wall to wall reminded him of nothing so much as early spring swamp grass. But the room seemed clean enough, as Deputy Berglund had assured him it would be, if a little on the cold side.

He cranked up the thermostat to take the chill off the air, then went to check out the bathroom. A couple of paper-wrapped glasses were lined up over the sink and a good supply of fluffy towels hung on a rack. Back in the room, he lifted the edge of the jungle print bedspread and found sheets that seemed well bleached and freshly made up. Without bothering to remove his coat, he turned and collapsed wearily on top of the bed, leaving his legs to dangle over the end. The mattress bounced once, but it was firm, comfortable. Cruz closed his eyes, ignoring the hollow feeling in his stomach after the teasing smell of onions and fries back in the motel office.

He'd rest his eyes for just a minute, then head back over to the café....

A sudden bang woke him with a start some time later, and raw instinct kicked in. Cruz rolled to one side of the mattress and dropped to the floor, hand fumbling under his tangled coat for the gun holstered at his waist. His eyes scanned the room and his ears listened for clues even as his disoriented brain struggled to remember exactly where he was. A hotel room, obviously. Where was he again?

Another whumpf sounded from outside. A car door closing, he decided, as his mind finally replayed for him the layout of the Whispering Pines Motel.

Releasing the breath he hadn't realized he was holding, he rose cautiously to his feet. Moving to the window, he held himself to one side and peered out through a crack in the curtains. Across the parking lot, in front of the café, the back lights of a pickup glowed bright as the engine roared. A moment later, the truck caromed out of its parking space and headed for the highway. The gas pump island in the middle of the yard was brightly lit but unoccupied. Through the café's broad glass windows he saw it was empty, even though the place had been jumping when he'd arrived. Only the guy in the blue jumpsuit who'd checked him in was there, elbows sprawled on the counter as he hunched over a plate of food. His wife was moving around the café, clearing and wiping tables.

Cruz let the curtain swing back into place and turned to the jungle-printed room and reholstered his gun. The red glow of a clock radio on a table next to the bed told him it was 7:44 p.m. and that he'd slept for over an hour. His eyes felt gritty and his spine ached from the awkward position in which he'd been lying, legs draped over the side of the mattress, deadweight dragging on the muscles of his back. The room had grown hot and stuffy while he slept, and it hadn't helped that he'd conked out still wearing his overcoat. However inadequate it might be against the bite of a prairie winter wind, it was too damned hot for indoor wear.

Cruz shrugged out of it and out of his suit jacket, as well, then ripped off his tie and tossed it aside. Undoing the cuffs and top couple of buttons on his white cotton shirt, he grabbed it by the back of the collar, pulled it over his head and threw it on the back of a chair. In the bathroom, he filled the sink with cold water and then pushed his face down into it.

After drying off he glanced at himself in the mirror. His cheeks were blue-tinged with a half-day's growth of beard and his black eyes looked shadowed, sunken with fatigue. A stranger might put it down to travel weariness, but Cruz knew those dark circles were there more often than not, an inevitable result of chronic inadequate sleep.

It had been like that since his first tour of duty. A shrink had later told him it was his subconscious that kept him on the prowl, his mind loath to slip into the realm of unconsciousness, where too many memories of death ran unchecked. It wouldn't get better, the shrink had said, until those memories were brought out in the open, examined and accepted for what they were—pieces of brutal history Cruz couldn't undo, could only learn to move beyond. But talking about it, which the shrink had insisted was the first step, wasn't for him. He'd tried drinking himself into oblivion for a while, but that only made the dreams more vivid. In the end, he'd decided to reenlist, go back to the scene of the crime. Dare the fates to kill him this time, as they hadn't managed to do the first time around. Things hadn't worked out that simply, but in his own way, he had moved on. And if he rarely slept a full night? Well, maybe it was only babes and innocents who were meant to do that.

He ran a hand through his hair to smooth it down a little. It was thick and wavy, showing no sign of receding even as middle age loomed on the horizon. But the black was slowly, imperceptibly, giving way to gray. It had started to show up, like the sleeplessness, after that first tour. Now, his temples were shot through with strands of silver. His hair curled over his ears and neck, disheveled in a way it had never been all the years he'd worn an army buzz. It was still too short to be fashionable in the civilian world, but it wasn't like he cared.

He tossed the towel over the side of the tub and headed back into the room, rummaging in the duffel bag for the black woolen turtleneck he'd thrown in that morning. He pulled it on over his head and refastened the safety strap on his waist holster, then he slapped his hip pocket to be sure his wallet hadn't fallen out. Grabbing his overcoat and the room key, he headed out, giving the parking lot another quick once-over before pulling the door shut behind him. Empty. He yanked the door and rattled the knob to be sure it was locked.

He wanted food and he wanted a beer. Berglund had said something about a hotel in town with a pub and a steak pit. The name of the place escaped him, but Cruz doubted he'd have any trouble finding it in a town this small. As he made his way back down the highway, he glanced in the rearview mirror occasionally, looking for the giveaway sign of tailing headlights, but there wasn't another soul on the road until he hit the main drag. If Berglund had put a tail on him earlier, the guy had apparently checked out for the night. Cruz doubted Berglund had the resources to assign a round-the-clock watch, and when it came right down to it, why should he? There was no reason Cruz could think of, and yet, there was also no doubt in his mind that the deputy had sent a cop out after him the minute the two of them had separated. Why? Havenwood appeared clean as the driven snow that was scouring it even now. But lift that spotless carpet and what rot lay underneath? Cruz wondered.

The Lakeside Inn was on the town's main street, opposite what looked to be a downtown park. They both fronted, as the hotel's name suggested, the lake that gave the town its recreational economy. The park opposite the hotel ran down to the shoreline, with a long wooden dock stretching fifty or sixty feet out onto the water, with boat slips on either side that were half-buried now in snow and ice.

Most of the parking lot directly in front of the hotel was taken up by snowmobiles, so Cruz pulled his car into the one of the diagonal parking spots on the other side of the street. As he killed the motor and cut his lights, he was startled by a pair of snowmobiles roaring by on his left. They bombed out onto the dock, and just as Cruz thought they were going to fall off the far end, they disappeared down a boat ramp he hadn't noticed, then careened out onto the frozen lake. Cruz saw a dozen or more other headlights moving up and down the ice, and in their glow, he made out the scattered, square forms of several small plywood structures.

He climbed out the car, the wind biting into his face as the high-pitched whine of two-stroke engines drifted toward him across the lake. A four-season playground, indeed. Give him Bermuda any day.

As he made his way across the road, he could hear laughter and music coming from the hotel. He also picked up the inviting odor of seared beef. Inside, the place was dimly lit, but noisy and surprisingly busy for a Thursday night. The crowd seemed to be a mix of under-thirties in party mode and red-nosed old-timers hunched over round tables laden with beer bottles. At least half the people in the room were dressed in heavy sweaters, thick boots and the padded nylon snow pants that obviously went with the snowmobiles parked outside the door. The smells made Cruz's mouth water—yeasty beer and prime beef almost overpowering the stink of cigarette smoke that wafted along the ceiling like a canopy of dirty gray gauze. Neon advertisements for Miller High Life, Schlitz and Bud adorned the wood-paneled walls, casting a warm glow over faces already flushed from the effects of the booze and the cold outside.

A long oak bar ran across the far wall of the room, and behind it, Cruz saw the flames of an open fire pit reflected in the shining face of a cook expertly flipping huge slabs of beef on a grill. In another corner, a rainbow-colored Wurlitzer vibrated to the beat of the Bee Gees. Half a dozen pinball machines were lined up beyond that, all of them clanging noisily, adding to the general din. On a small open area of hardwood floor near the jukebox, some overweight, red-faced guy with an obvious load on was doing a *Saturday Night Fever* routine, complete with thumb hooked in the waistband of his blue nylon ski pants, gyrating hips, and index finger jabbing the air overhead.

"Stayin' alive! Stayin' alive!" he bellowed along with the Wurlitzer.

A low button popped on his shirt, prompting a chorus of hoots from a group of women at a nearby table as his hairy belly winked at the room with every movement. "You go, Ed!"

Cruz stood uncertainly in the entrance, trying to decide whether to pass on the raucous place or give in to the seduction of the food. Just then, a waitress came by, balancing a trayload of beer on one arm. She paused in front of him.

"You looking for someone?"

"Just hoping to get some dinner. Are you still serving?"

"You bet. Steak pit's on till ten."

"Pretty busy place."

"You got that right. Whyn't you grab yourself a table if you can find one? I'll be over in a minute and take your order."

Cruz pointed to the bottles on her tray. "I'll take one of those when you get around to it. Make it a Bud."

"You bet," she said again, raising the tray overhead as she wound her way in the narrow space between tables.

Cruz searched for a vacant table, but they were nearly all taken. He spotted one in the center of the room, next to the dance floor and the oversized Travolta wannabe, but then his eye landed on another in a far corner where he could sit with his back to a wall and his eye on both the room and the door. As he moved toward it there was an almost imperceptible shift in the noise level, and he felt eyes watching him. He tossed his coat on an empty chair, thankful he'd at least ditched the shirt and tie. But as he settled with his back to the wall and glanced around again, he knew he'd have stood out like a sore thumb no matter what he was wearing. Most of the faces in the room were broad, fair and Scandinavian-looking, and confronted with such an abundance of flaxen hair and pale eyes, he felt like the Frito Bandito stumbled onto an Ingmar Bergman film set.

The music downshifted to a slower pace as someone dropped a couple of quarters into the Wurlitzer and pulled up Harry Chapin. The sweating dance king fell into a chair, looking relieved to have dodged the coronary he'd have been risking if he'd kept up that kind of nonsense much longer. A buddy pushed a mug of beer across the table toward him and Disco Ed downed it gratefully in one long swallow.

A bottle of Budweiser and a glass appeared in front of Cruz, as well, and he looked up at the blond—what else?—waitress who'd spotted him at the door. "Here you go," she said. With translucent skin and wide blue eyes, she looked all of sixteen. "So, can I get you a menu then?"

"I was told you serve a mean rib-eye here."

"For sure. Comes with a salad, roll and baked potato. Six ninety-five plus tax."

"Sold."

"Well, okay, then, that was easy. It'll be out in just a few minutes. Anything else in the meantime?"

"Just another one of these," Cruz said, raising the bottle.

"You bet. How do you like your steak cooked?"

"Medium rare, please."

The girl nodded, then moved off. Ignoring the glass she'd left on the table, Cruz lifted the Bud to his lips and took a long pull, trying to quell the lonely ache that had suddenly clamped on to his gut. It was obvious by the shouted conversations and table-hopping going on that pretty much everyone in here knew everyone else. What must that be like, he wondered, spending your whole life in a place where everyone knew you? Who you were related to, what you did for a living, who you'd slept with, and how much of an ass you'd made of yourself on how many public occasions.

Come to think of it, it wasn't all that different from where he'd grown up, part of a small community inside the urban sprawl of the Los Angeles basin. Guys he'd gone to school with still lived within a block or two of the houses they'd grown up in, married to neighborhood girls, half of them little sisters of buddies they'd been hanging out with since taking their first communions together. He'd been the only surviving child of hardworking parents living in a close-knit community slogging its way toward the American dream. He'd had one sister named Pilar, born when he was three, but she'd died of meningitis at five years of age. His mother had miscarried two other babies, one between him and Pilar and one after. Then she'd been diagnosed with cervical cancer. His father had had dreams of owning his own construction company someday, but the dream had died along with his wife and the babies, and Vicente Cruz had ended up a bitter man, old before his time, living an isolated, angry life while he left the job of watching over his son to his sister. Cruz's aunt Luisa, too, had been widowed young and left childless, when her husband was killed in an industrial accident. She could easily have remarried, Cruz often thought. She was an attractive woman with a warm and giving nature, and there was no shortage of lonely men around them, many of them immigrants separated from family and friends back in Mexico as they worked to build a better future in *El Norte*. Several had come courting, but when they or her nephew pressed her on why she didn't offer them any encouragement, Aunt Luisa only shook her head.

"There is no one for me but my César," she said. "If I cannot have him, I would rather be alone."

His father had been just as single-minded, come to think of it. That must make them a one-love-to-a-customer kind of family, Cruz thought. The mistake of his own brief marriage notwithstanding, he didn't think he'd yet met his woman of a lifetime. Or maybe he had, but his head had been too buried in case files for him to notice.

The waitress reappeared at his table in short order and set down a heavy white platter loaded with the largest steak he'd ever seen, seared nearly black on the outside but running with fragrant pink juices. Next to it sat a huge, foil-wrapped potato, cut in half and smothered with sour cream, chives and butter. The girl set a salad bowl on the table next to the plate, a basket of crusty rolls and butter pats, and a set of cutlery wrapped in a paper napkin.

"And another Bud," she added, lifting a fresh bottle from the tray and setting it down in front of Cruz.

"This looks great. Thanks," he told her.

"You bet." She rested the tray on her hip. "So, are you in town for the ice-fishing derby then?"

"There's an ice-fishing derby?"

"A derby and a smoker. It kicks off tomorrow night, but half these guys are getting a head start on the fun," she said. "Been out setting up their shacks."

"That explains all the traffic out on the lake."

"There you go. So you going to give it a shot? There's a hundred-dollar-a-pound grand prize for the biggest fish."

"No, I'm afraid not. I'm just passing through."

The girl lingered, obviously curious but too polite to press the issue. "You've got all your condiments on the table there. Anything else you might be needing?" Cruz shook his head. "Well, you just holler if you do need anything, okay?"

"Will do."

Cruz watched her go, then lit into the steak. It was tender and flavorful, the potato in its foil wrapper dripping with butter and sour cream. Starving, he made short work of it, then sat back and nursed his second beer, sated and content now to watch the dynamic of the crowd, the alcohol numbing his uneasiness at being the loner in the room.

Even as a kid, he'd always felt as if he were standing outside the big picture window looking in, his family unlike others around them. His friends' families were large and interrelated by a network of marriages, whereas his had withered and drawn into itself. By the time he hit his teens, Cruz had been restless, itching to escape a community whose vibrancy seemed like a reproach to his own family's failure to thrive. It had probably been his aunt Luisa who'd first given him the idea that education would be his ticket out, urging him to pursue a college degree. A young Cruz had taken the message to heart—at least, until the draft board caught up with him.

"Excuse me?"

Cruz looked up to find an Amazon standing next to his table, a woman who might be anywhere between twenty-five and thirty-five, tall and heavyset but pretty enough, with a Farrah Fawcett mass of feathery hair and darkly lined hazel eyes.

"Sorry to bother you," she said, "but my friends and I couldn't help noticing that you were on your own here." She indicated a table a few feet away, where two other women were watching. They waved sheepishly. "We were wondering if you'd like to play shuffleboard with us. We need a fourth."

Cruz had noticed them looking his way earlier—although, so,

it seemed, had everyone else in the room at one point or another. Some kind of girls' night out, he guessed. He leaned back to take in the full height of her. "I don't know," he said. "I'm just about done here and I've had a pretty long day. And, anyway, I've never played shuffleboard before."

"Oh, it's real easy. We can show you. We play two to a team. You can play with my friend Shelli, there. We'll explain the rules as we go."

Cruz looked over to where one of the women, wearing a red sweatshirt with a Disneyworld logo, waved again. Shelli, he guessed. The other woman at her side, very pretty, pressed her lips together and looked down into her glass, whether from shyness or embarrassment, Cruz wasn't sure. Back at the empty motel room, he knew he faced a long night with no one but the *Tonight Show* for company. He could sit here alone, downing one beer after another until closing, but if he did that, he'd pay the price tomorrow. Or he could play shuffleboard with these three ladies.

"Sure, I guess I could. Why not?"

"Great! You wanna bring your beer over and join us, then? The shuffleboard table should be free in a few minutes."

Cruz hooked a finger around the neck of his bottle, got to his feet and grabbed his coat before following her over. The woman in the Disneyland sweatshirt pushed a chair toward him.

"My name's Carla, by the way," the Amazon said. She nodded at the shy, pretty girl across the table, and then at the one favoring the Disney mouse. "That's Lydia, and this is Shelli."

"Alex Cruz," he said, shaking hands all around, then settling into the empty chair, trying to keep the names separate in his mind. Lydia was the petite one with eyelashes so long they almost hid her blue eyes, fixed shyly on the table in front of her. On her left hand she wore a thin silver band with a small blue stone in it, a ring that might or might not be a wedding or engagement band.

"Nice to meet you, Alex," the one named Shelli said. He pulled his gaze away from the lovely Lydia. This other one was pleasant-looking, too, but the ring on her left hand was un-equivocally marital. "You're not here for the ice-fishing derby, are you?" Shelli added.

"How'd you guess?"

"Well, you've got the wrong clothes, for one thing. But as I was just telling Lydia here, I bet I know who you are."

Cruz glanced again at the pretty woman to Shelli's left, whose eyes immediately dropped and whose cheeks flushed at having been caught staring. "You know who I am?" he said, turning back to her friend.

"You do?" Carla the Amazon echoed.

Shelli nodded. "Yup, I think so. You're a G-man, am I right?"

"Run that by me again, Shell?" Carla said.

"I just figured it out after you got up to go over to his table," Shelli told her. "I'm guessing Alex here is from the FBI in Washington, D.C., and that he's come about the fire at Grace Meade's. I heard Nils took him over this afternoon, and then to the hospital in Montrose to see Jillian. I also heard this agent was planning to stay on for at least another day, and it makes sense he'd show up here for dinner. So, am I right?"

What were the odds? Cruz wondered. Admittedly, it was a small town, but even so, he'd been there less than six hours, and Berglund was the only person he'd spoken to, aside from Verna, the arson investigators and the owner of the Whispering Pines. "How do you know all that?"

Shelli smiled mysteriously, but Carla rolled her eyes. "No big whoop there. Nils is her brother-in-law. He's married to Shelli's sister, Sharon. She was supposed to come out with us tonight, only she couldn't, 'cause Nils was tied up."

Shelli nodded. "I went over there to pick her up, but Sharon said she'd better stay home. Nils was still out with their boys at hockey practice. He was supposed to be back any minute, but she said he was figuring he'd have to go back into work tonight, and Sharon didn't think she could get a sitter at the last minute, seeing it's a school night and all. Anyway, she's the one told me Nils wasted his whole...oops, sorry! I mean spent his afternoon with some FBI guy who'd showed up out of the blue. Process of elimination, when we saw you sitting over there, I figured that had to be you."

"Shelli's a schoolteacher," Lydia piped up, her voice as tiny as she was.

Cruz turned and gave her a smile. "I guess that accounts for her amazing deductive powers. What about you?"

"Me?"

He nodded. "What do you do?" Was it the beer or the change of scene? Was he flirting, for God's sake? Maybe it was just the thought of that cold, empty bed back at the motel.

"Oh, I work over at the hospital in Admissions," Lydia said shyly, adding, "the hospital here in town, I mean, not the one over to Montrose where Jillian is." Her long lashes dropped again, as if the exertion of this much eye contact and this much speech had overwhelmed her. The other two women had green Heineken bottles on the table in front of them, but she was drinking something pink that came in a tall glass with a thin red straw. She lifted the straw to her lips and took a tiny sip, then glanced up and blushed when she realized Cruz was still watching her. "Singapore Sling," she told him, with a small shrug of her shoulders. "I'm not much of a drinker."

Carla leaned toward Cruz, interposing herself between them. "I'm a hairdresser myself," she said. "A stylist, actually. I'm almost accredited by Vidal Sassoon. I've been taking weekend seminars in Minneapolis."

"No kidding. Vidal Sassoon, huh?" Cruz took a pull of his beer.

Carla crossed her arms on the table and leaned eagerly toward him. "So, Alex, are you really an FBI agent?"

"Guilty as charged."

"So what's the deal? What brings you all the way from Washington, D.C.?"

"Just some routine casework."

"Are you sure you're not CIA?" Carla pressed, her tone unmistakably coquettish. "After all, everybody knows Grace Meade was some kind of spy in the war and all that."

"No, definitely not," Cruz said. The shuffleboard table was in the process of being vacated. "Didn't you say something about a game? I think it's free now."

Carla leapt to her feet with a speed that was amazing for a woman of her size. "Come on, let's get dibs on it before some of these other bozos do." She barreled across the room and planted herself at one end of the table, shaking off an offer from a couple of snowsuit-clad boys to team up with her and her friends. Cruz rose and stepped back to let the other two women pass. As Lydia slipped by him in the narrow space, he smelled something floral—lavender, maybe. Her soft blue mohair sweater brushed against the back of his hand, and the urge to reach out and touch her was almost irresistible.

"I really can't stay long," she called ahead to Shelli. "Brad gets off work at ten and I need to be home before then to get his dinner on the table. That's my fiancé," she added, looking back to Cruz. "He works over at the hospital, too. He's an orderly there, but he's taking classes part-time. In nine more months, he'll have his R.N."

"Wow, that's great," Cruz said, smiling gamely. *Damn.*

When they got to the shuffleboard table, he realized that, although Shelli was to be his partner as Carla had first suggested, the teams were split, with one member of each team at either end of the waist-high table. Carla directed her own partner, the lovely Lydia, down toward Shelli's end, which allowed her to remain at Cruz's side. As they waited for Lydia and Shelli to make their shots from the opposite end, Carla returned to the charge. "So why is the FBI interested in a house fire way out here in Havenwood?"

"I didn't say it was."

"But you're here."

"Here we go, I think it's our turn to shoot."

"Go ahead, you shoot first on this round."

Cruz took up a disc and concentrated on propelling it hard enough that it would cross the score line at the other end, but not so hard that it would shoot right off the end of the lane and into the trough that rimmed the table. The woman at his side left him in peace for a while as she, too, frowned and took her best shots. But when the round was over and the play passed again to the other end, she was back for more.

"So?"

"So what?"

"So is it Grace or Jillian you're investigating?"

"You know, Carla, I just came in tonight for a beer and a bite to eat. I'm really not supposed to be talking about the job, if you know what I mean."

"Oh, top secret, huh? Well, okay, sorry about that. I didn't mean to be pushy or anything. No offense?"

"No, absolutely not. None taken. And it's not top secret, or even all that interesting, really."

"Oh, sure, I get you. But it's still kind of curious, that's all. You being here, I mean, after what I heard at work today."

Cruz sighed. "And what was that?"

"That there'd been some arson investigators out to look into the fire, like maybe the cops thought it was deliberately set. And on top of that, one of the ladies who came into the Set 'n Style today—that's the salon where I work," she added by way of explanation. "Anyway, Olive, this lady who was in? She told us Jill was seen filling a gas can over to the Chevron that very same day the fire broke out. That's a little coincidental, don't you think?"

"How well do you know Jillian Meade?"

"Oh, I know her to say hi and all, but not real well. We were in high school at the same time, but she was a couple of years ahead of me. I think she was a senior when I was a freshman. She went off to college and she hasn't really lived in Havenwood since. But everybody knows the Meades, especially Grace Meade, so of course, it's quite a topic of conversation when somebody like her up and dies like that." Her broad forehead creased. "And you know what else? I actually saw Mrs. Meade just a few hours before she died. She was in having her hair done that afternoon. She came in once a week. It's kinda spooky, you know what I mean? Has that ever happened to you? Somebody dies, and then suddenly you can't stop thinking about the last time you saw them? Like, even if you talked about something really ordinary, once they're gone, you go, 'Those were the very last words I ever heard that person say,' and they seem, I don't know, a lot heavier than you thought at the time?"

Cruz nodded. It had happened to him more times than he cared to remember. "Don't forget to go over and see if Aunt Luisa needs her grass cut." Those were his mother's last words to him when he was leaving the hospital the afternoon before she died. And then, there were the last words of false bravado he ever heard muttered by 1st Lt. Darryl Houghton, just before Cruz set off alone with his M-16 to scout the sniper-thick jungle trail Houghton was insisting they follow. "You go on ahead and check it out, Cruz, while I baby-sit these scared little girls here." Of course the guy had been an idiot, Cruz thought, but that didn't mean he'd deserved to die the way he did.

But before Carla could tell him about Grace Meade's last words to her, it was their turn to shoot again. She turned her concentration back to the game, and the subject of Grace Meade and the fire wasn't mentioned again as they finished it out. It was a close match, but in spite of the fact that he was a rank beginner, Cruz managed a credible showing, and he and Shelli won by two points. Carla seemed miffed when they sat down again for one last drink. He felt a little guilty. It had turned out to be a better evening than he'd expected, all things considered. It was only fair to appease the instigator of this unexpected invitation. At this point, he was also curious to know what these women could tell him about Grace and Jillian Meade.

"So, did you do Mrs. Meade's hair when she came into the salon that last time, Carla?" he asked, as he ordered them all another round of drinks.

"Not usually. I'd done it once or twice when the owner was sick or on vacation, that's about it. Mrs. Meade was real particular. She's known me since I was a kid, which didn't help." She grimaced. "Actually, my mom used to clean her house. I sometimes used to go over at the Meades' when I was on my way home from school. And then, Mrs. Meade knew me when I was just starting out in the business, too, so naturally, she never really trusted me to do her up the way she wanted, no matter how much training I had. But a person could do worse than trying a new style once in a while, don't you think?"

"Makes sense."

"Yeah, it does to me, too, but not to Grace Meade."

"She was a tough customer, was she?"

"Let's just say she thought of herself as the queen bee."

"So did half the town," Shelli pointed out. "There wasn't anything that happened around here she didn't have a hand in. She headed up the Christmas and Easter and Fourth of July celebration committees. She was President of the Lions ladies' auxiliary. She was active in her church. And if you take a look at the *Havenwood Herald*—that's the local paper," she added for Cruz's benefit, "you'd see Grace wrote most of the columns."

"Did you like her?"

Carla grimaced, but Shelli frowned thoughtfully. "Be fair, Carla. Considering she wasn't even from here, she contributed a lot to this town. You had to admire that. As for liking her, well, she was different, you know. Maybe it was that class thing that came from her being English."

"Yeah, so you can imagine how much time she had for her cleaning lady's daughter," Carla said grimly.

"We were too young to move in the same circles she did, that's all," Shelli said. "I worked with her on the Easter Parade committee this year, though, and she was very nice to me."

"Yeah, well, she would be, wouldn't she, Nils being your brother-in-law, and all?"

Shelli bristled. "What's that supposed to mean?"

Carla seemed to be on the verge of blurting something, but she hesitated, then shrugged. "Nothing. Never mind."

"No, Carla, come on. You started it, so finish it," Shelli insisted. "What are you getting at?"

"Well, it's just that Nils is probably going to be the next chief of police, is all I meant. He's getting to be an important guy in this town, and God knows, Mrs. Meade only hobnobbed with the important people."

Shelli frowned, and Cruz had the impression there were volumes of subtext here he couldn't begin to understand, but no one seemed prepared to elaborate. "What about Jillian?" he asked, hoping to break the tension. Unfortunately, it was exactly the wrong question.

Shelli glanced at him sharply, and then at Carla. "What did you tell him about that?"

Carla held up her hands defensively. "Nothing. I didn't say a word, I swear." She turned to Cruz. "Like I said, Jillian was a couple of years older than us, so we didn't know her real well. Anyway, she's been gone a long time now."

"I always thought she was nice," Lydia said.

Cruz looked over at her. It was the first time she'd spoken since they'd sat down again. Her cheeks flushed anew under his gaze, but she went on.

"Jill used to baby-sit me and my sister. We loved it when she came over. She was really smart, and she brought over great stories to read to us. King Arthur and Guinevere and the knights of the round table. And *Jane Eyre*. She read that whole book to us one winter when my dad was away working on a highway project down south and my mom was working nights at the hospital. It was such a great story." Lydia smiled, then looked up, startled, as if remembering the center of attention was her least favorite place to be. She picked up her tall glass and moved the umbrella aside so she could take a nervous sip, then turned her attention to the thin red straw. "Anyway," she added, her voice trailing off, "I really liked Jillian."

Carla drained her own glass, then smacked it down on the table. "Personally, I always thought Jillian Meade had a big, fat stick up her behind."

"Carla!" the other two women exclaimed in unison.

"Well, excuse me, but you have to admit, she's always been pretty full of herself."

"That's not true," Shelli said. "She was just shy, that's all. It can't have been easy for her, living with someone as...um..."

"Pushy?" Carla suggested.

"No, 'accomplished' is what I was going to say. It couldn't have been easy living under the shadow of someone as accomplished as Mrs. Meade, I wouldn't think."

"You wouldn't think?" Carla's plucked eyebrows rose in a sarcastic arch. "Is that your opinion? Or is that what Nils says? Because everyone knows, Shelli, that Grace Meade was not one of Nils's favorite people."

"No, Carla, that's not what Nils says. As a matter of fact, he's never even mentioned Grace or Jillian in my presence."

"Humph! Well, I still don't know why you'd stick up for either of them. If it was my sister..."

Cruz frowned. "Hey, ladies? What am I missing here?"

Shelli waved an impatient hand. "Nothing. You're not missing a thing." She cast a withering look in Carla's direction, then turned back to him with a sigh. "Nils and Jillian Meade used to go together when they were in high school, that's all. They broke up around the time he went into the service, and then Jillian went off to college. They were history long before he and my sister ever got together, so it's not like Sharon and Jill were rivals or anything. Honestly, Carla!" she added, exasperated.

"Well, ex-cuse me! But Nils and Jill were engaged, for chrissake! And everyone knows that Nils was still carrying a torch for her long after she left town. Okay, so maybe not anymore, but on the other hand, who knows? At the very least, Shell, you have to admit, it's a little awkward. There's Jillian, locked up in the loony bin over in Montrose, looking like a prime suspect if those arson guys find out that fire was deliberately set. And who's supposed to be investigating all this, I ask you?" She gave a shrug of her shoulders, as if the whole problem were self-evident. "If it were up to Nils—"

"If it were up to Nils, what?" A voice sounded, low and dangerous, from over Cruz's shoulder.

All three women looked up and paled. Cruz turned to find Berglund looming over them, his scowl fixed on the hairdresser. He was out of uniform, hatless, wearing a blue parka with a Minnesota Vikings logo on the left breast.

"If it were up to Nils, what, Carla?" he repeated.

"Nothing. Not a blessed thing." She waved a hand and picked up her glass, then looked irritated when she realized it was already empty.

"What are you guys up to?"

"We were just having a couple of drinks, Nils, that's all," Shelli said.

"And you?" Berglund asked Cruz. "What are you doing here?"

"You told me it was a good place to get a steak. You were right. Thanks for the tip."

"We invited him over to play a game of shuffleboard," Shelli added nervously.

Lydia, meantime, was checking her watch. "Oh, jeez, look at the time! I really have to get going. Brad'll be home soon." She scrambled to her feet and grabbed her jacket from the back of her chair. "See you guys later. It was nice meeting you, Alex," she added, blushing but not meeting his gaze.

He rose to help her as she fumbled to get the jacket on. "It was nice to meet you, too, Lydia."

"I'd better be off, too," Shelli said. "I told Ben I wouldn't be late. You coming, Carla?"

The other woman, however, seemed reluctant to call it a night. "I'm in no rush. I'd stay for another round if you wanted to, Alex."

Berglund lifted her coat off the back of her chair and held it up. "I think you've had enough for tonight, Carla. Unless, that is, you want to take your chances on me running you in for DUI."

She rose and snatched her coat out of his hand. When she glared at him, they were nearly eye to eye. "God! You can be a real party-pooper, you know that, Nils Berglund?"

"Just get on home before I take away your car keys."

She continued to grumble, but then smiled as Cruz helped her into her coat. "Thank you very much, Alex. It's a real pleasure to meet a gentleman—for a change," she added scathingly to Berglund. She turned back to Cruz. "Did you say you're going to be around town for a few days, Alex? Because if you'd like a home-cooked meal—"

"I'm probably heading out tomorrow. I appreciate the offer, though."

"Well, if you change your mind, I'm at the Set 'n Style all day. You can drop in anytime. That's just down the street. You can't miss it."

Cruz gave a noncommittal nod, then said goodbye as well to Shelli. He and Berglund stood and watched the two women leave, and then he turned to the deputy. "Buy you a beer?"

"No, thanks, I have to be getting home."

"Yeah, well, I guess I've probably had enough, too."

"Good."

"I'm going to head back over to the hospital tomorrow. I am going to try to talk to Miss Meade," Cruz warned him as they headed out the door and into the cold night air. "I promise you, though, I'll keep it as low-key as I can."

"Well, I guess I can't stop you. Frankly, though, I doubt you'll get past that psychiatrist."

"Maybe not. Just thought I'd tell you."

"Fine. Meantime, you should watch yourself out there on the highway driving back. That last curve before the motel can get slippery in this kind of weather."

So Berglund *did* know he'd opted to stay at the Whispering Pines rather than upstairs at the Lakeside Inn, Cruz thought. Why was he not surprised? "Hey, Berglund?" he called to the deputy's back, since the other man was already walking away.

"What?"

"Did you hear that Jillian Meade filled up a jerry can with gasoline at the Chevron station the afternoon of the fire?"

Berglund's features darkened. "Who told you that?"

"The owner of the place. Did you know?"

"Yeah, I guess I heard that."

"So?"

"So what? So she filled a gas can. Doesn't mean she used it. Anybody could have found it in the garage that night, made the decision to set a fire to cover up their trail."

"But why would she be filling a jerry can at this time of year? It's too early for lawn mowers, and I can't imagine she or her mother would be needing it for a chain saw or anything else like that. You're not going to tell me one of those women was planning to enter the ice-fishing derby, I hope."

Berglund turned and walked back over to Cruz, coming a little closer than polite intercourse required. "I don't know what she might have wanted it for, but I'll be sure to look into it. Okay? Anything else?"

"Did Grace Meade have any enemies in town?"

Berglund shook his head. "Not that I know of. She was a pillar of the community."

"Even pillars of the community have enemies."

"Where? In her church? Somebody else wanted to take over the ladies' auxiliary? Somebody upset that her petunias beat theirs in the annual flower show? Somebody wanted to take over the running of the Easter Egg Roll? Come on, get serious." He snorted.

"What about her property? It looked to me like a prime piece of land. Could somebody have wanted it, maybe bad enough to burn her out?"

"Look around you, Cruz. This is a small town, more empty land than not around here. There's dozens of river and lakefront lots available if somebody wants to develop 'em."

Cruz knew he was reaching, but he had to eliminate simple explanations. It made no sense that something like this should have happened here. "So if Mrs. Meade wasn't the target, can you think of anyone who might have wanted to hurt her daughter?"

"No. Jillian's been away for years. I doubt many people even knew she was back in town this week. But obviously," Berglund added, "we're looking into all the possibilities."

Again, Cruz detected the defensiveness of the small-town cop. He debated letting it go at that, but it just wasn't in his nature to walk away, no matter how unpopular he was about to make himself. "Is it true?"

"Is what true?"

"That you and Jillian Meade were once engaged to be married?"

Berglund hesitated, but only for a moment. "That's no big secret. So?"

"Carla says—"

"Carla's a gossip."

"Carla says you weren't fond of Grace Meade. What was that all about? Didn't she think you were good enough for her daughter? Is she the reason you and Jillian broke up?"

"Jillian and I broke up seventeen years ago, for chrissake! You got no old girlfriends in your past, Cruz? Just what the hell are you suggesting?"

"I'm just wondering if your personal history doesn't put you in a bit of a conflict of interest where this investigation is concerned."

This time, Berglund stared him down for a long time before answering. "You don't know the first thing about my personal history, buster. But let me tell you this—I may be a small-town hick, but I'm a sworn officer of the law, the same as you. I'm also the acting chief of police here, and I take that responsibility very seriously. I'll take this investigation where I think it needs to go. As for you, from what you've told me, Grace Meade's death has little or nothing to do with the business that brought you to town—whatever the hell that really is. I'd suggest you do your job and I'll do mine as I see fit. Does that work for you?"

Cruz shrugged. "Sounds like a plan."

"Good. And like I said, you wanna watch yourself out there." With that, Berglund turned on his heel and strode off.

CHAPTER 13

I think the drugs are still working their way out of my system. I find myself drifting, caught in a half-world somewhere between catatonic and hyper-alert, stupidity and sentience—thinking of either nothing at all, or of airy philosophical concepts like fate, destiny and retributive justice.

I've tried to tell myself that it was *her* fault, *her* secrets that destroyed us in the end—that set in motion the wheel of events that ran over us both. But that's cowardly. She was what she was, but who am I to claim the moral high ground? What kind of child destroys its mother? I'll tell you what kind: a monster.

But what about her? Was she destined from the outset to suffer the ugly fate she did? I find that hard to believe. There must have been a time when she was as sweet and pure on the inside as she was on the outside. We want to believe that, don't we, of someone so beautiful?

People who didn't know her when she was young can't imagine how exquisite she really was. She was already twenty-six when she came to this country, and by that point, she'd already lived through five long years of war. Been bombed, lost friends and family, including her beloved father and the man she'd been engaged to marry long before she ever met Joe Meade. In addition, she'd spent fourteen months working underground with the French Resistance, living in daily terror for her life. As if that weren't enough, she'd found and lost a great love, and had given birth to a child. All those things had to have taken their toll on her appearance, and yet she was still the most beautiful woman ever to set foot in Havenwood.

We can only imagine what she must have been like as a carefree girl. But it was with the intent to remind her of the spirit that had animated that younger version of herself that I had set out to create my gift of her past.

Last month, I finally made it to Dover, England, where my mother was born. Once I'd decided to put together this Christmas gift for her, it seemed logical to start there, and so I made my way down on my first free day after finishing up my appointments and research at the Imperial War Museum.

Dover is an uninteresting town for the most part, the kind of place people pass through on their way to somewhere else. A working-class town, it features row after row of brick flats housing a population that seems to be either on the dole—especially now, with the British economy in such dire straits—or employed in menial jobs in the port and on the ferries and railways that bring people to and through that restless town at the end of the "green and sceptered isle."

But high above the town rises Dover Castle, a medieval fortress that has stood for almost a millennium as a symbol of British resistance to invasion from the continent. While I was there, I stood on the castle ramparts and was able to look down on the stony beaches where my mother would have played as a child. Beyond the beaches and across the English Channel, away on the distant horizon, I could just make out the ghostly outline of France through the fog, twenty-one miles away—the land of my grandmother's birth.

Standing on those ramparts, I wished that my mother were with me. I tried to imagine how she would have felt after all these years, looking out on that view of the French coastline. It would have evoked intense memories, I'm sure, of childhood summers spent with the uncles and her awful cousins. And, of course, she would have thought back to the fourteen months she'd spent in and around Paris, living under her mother's name, "Sylvie Fournier," working with the Resistance.

As I looked out over those famous chalk cliffs, that old wartime song kept running through my head: "There'll be bluebirds over the white cliffs of Dover...." I didn't see any bluebirds, but it was December, cold and dreary gray, and the bluebirds had no doubt migrated to wherever it is they go in winter. There must have been bluebirds when my mother was growing up, though. They're a symbol of happiness, after all, and I think those were the happiest years of her life. Certainly her face always glowed when she talked about her childhood in Dover, the only part of her past that she was ever comfortable discussing. The rest, from 1940 until her arrival in America in 1945, seemed too painful for her to think about. What little I knew about that later period had come from offhand comments she'd made over the years, little threads of information that I'd hoarded and strung together until they formed a golden chain that I treasured and guarded jealously.

I wonder even now whether my impressive, elusive mother had any idea how eager I was to know everything there was to know about her. How desperately I wanted to be just like her.

England was bathed in a dull wash of gray for the entire ten days I spent there. Frankly, I liked it that way. It seemed appropriate, somehow, as I searched for my mother's past—like moving inside the old black and white newsreel footage that seems to define my mental image of her home and her life before she came to this country. The country still bears wartime scars, empty lots of rubble that even now haven't been cleared, thirty-five years after the last German bomb fell. Elsewhere, ugly, nondescript modern buildings stand on the sites of older buildings that were there before the Blitz—buildings that were possibly no less ugly, although we always like to think that they did things better in the past.

I knew my grandfather's print shop in Dover would be long gone. A German bomb fell on it at the height of the Battle of Britain, when England's ports and industrial centers were being subjected to night after night of punishing air attacks intended to destroy the country's resistance and the people's morale in preparation for German invasion. On the lot where Wickham Press had once stood, according to the old town maps I found in the public archives, there was now a four-story brick building of modern design housing an estate agent's office on the ground floor and a variety of law and accounting offices on the floors above. I was going to take a picture, but I felt sure it would break my mother's heart to see it.

At the local library, though, I found dozens of copies of items that had been printed by Wickham Press before it was destroyed, including wartime propaganda posters exhorting Britons to Make Do And Mend! Lend A Hand On The Land! Turn Scrap Materials Into War Materials! I made copies of some of those to include in her memory album.

It was also at the Dover public library that I consulted a local telephone directory, looking for the name "Entwistle." After only two calls, I managed to locate a woman my mother had mentioned as a friend of her youth, one of those treasured threads of information from which I had spun the whole, wonderful cloth of her early life as I imagined it. As luck would have it, Nellie Entwistle had never married and still bore that unforgettable name.

"You're the daughter of who, dear?" she said over the phone, sounding very confused by this sudden communication from an unknown Yank.

"Grace Meade—Grace Wickham, as you would have known her. I'm Jillian Meade, her daughter."

"You're Grace's daughter? Good heavens! And you've come from America, you say? How is Grace? She's not...?"

"She was just fine, last time I spoke to her."

"She's not here with you, then?"

"No, I'm afraid not. She lives in Minnesota."

"Minnesota? Fancy! I always wondered what had happened to her."

"She's often spoken of you. I gather the two of you grew up together?"

"Oh, yes," Miss Entwistle said, warming now that the connection was made. "Together right from primary, we were. We were ever such good chums."

"I'm over here on business, Miss Entwistle, and while I'm here, I decided to visit some of my mother's old haunts and take her back a few souvenirs. I remembered your name, and it occurred to me to try to look you up while I was in Dover. I know my mother would be delighted to have news of you—if you don't mind," I added hastily.

My mother and this woman had obviously not seen or spoken to each other in years, however close they may have been as children. I had no way of knowing the circumstances under which they might have parted, and since they'd obviously not kept in touch, maybe they had quarreled.

But now that she'd gotten over her surprise at who it was at the other end of the line, Miss Entwistle seemed eager to meet me. She invited me to tea that very afternoon.

She lived in a small white cottage just off the Canterbury Road, a little house with black half timbers under an authentic thatched roof. The white stuccoed sides of the house were covered with rose vines that wound around leaded, mullioned windows and over the arched green door. The climbers were dormant at that time of year, of course, but I could imagine how pretty the place would look when the roses were in bloom. It was something out of a fairy tale, like the Seven Dwarfs' cottage.

Her green wooden front door opened just as my hand reached to unlatch the low gate at the bottom of the garden, and a round figure with rimless spectacles and snow-white hair appeared in the entrance. Rain was pouring down.

"Come in, come in, love!" she called. "What a dreadful day, after you've come all this way, poor thing!"

I smiled as I stepped inside the cottage, pausing at the threshold to shake the water from my umbrella before collapsing it and propping it into a rack by the door. The rack held just one other umbrella, bright red with a knobbed wood handle. The house smelled of lamb and lavender, and the faint odor of mustiness that seems to permeate everything in that beautiful but damp country.

"My goodness, I can hardly believe my eyes," Miss Entwistle said, her glasses slipping down her nose as she peered up at me. She was wearing a floral print dress with a high collar and an old-fashioned cameo brooch at the neck, a white woolen cardigan slung over her shoulders. "Are you really Grace's daughter, then?"

"Yes, I'm Jillian, Miss Entwistle. Jillian Meade."

"Fancy! All the way from America! This is ever such a surprise. Come and let me take your coat, dear, and we'll have a nice cup of tea. It's all ready."

She was shaped like a little teapot herself, and she had to rise on the tips of her toes to lift my trench coat off my shoulders. She was my mother's age, but unlike Mother, Nellie Entwistle showed every one of her sixty years and then some, with a soft white helmet of hair done up in an old-fashioned pin curled style and skin that seemed soft and puffed as pastry dough. She glanced back at me as she hung my coat on a hook under the hall stairs. By the small crease that appeared on her forehead, I knew she was searching in vain for some hint of her old school chum in me.

"I'm not what you expected, am I?" I asked, feeling every inch of my awkward height and plain brown features.

She blushed. "Oh, I'm sorry, dear. I didn't mean to stare. But, yes, I suppose I was looking for something of Grace. You don't seem to favor her, I must say."

"People say I look like my father's side, if anything. He was dark-haired and tall, too."

"That must be it. Grace was ever so lovely. Not that you aren't," she added hastily. "You're very striking, indeed. It's just..."

"No need to apologize, Miss Entwistle. I understand."

"Oh, dear. Well, come into the parlor, love. The tea's just steeping."

She showed me into a tiny room off the front hall that seemed to have been the target of a floral bomb. There were flowers everywhere: on the wallpaper, the curtains, the tapestry covered chairs, the cushions, and the embroidered linen table cloth laid out over the small gate-leg table. We settled on either side of the table. An ornate silver tea service was set out, and china plates held cold cuts, cheese, Hovis bread, and an assortment of the same Peak Frean biscuits that Arneson's Grocery in Havenwood always kept in stock especially for my mother. It was clear Miss Entwistle had gone to some effort, and I was flattered to be made such a fuss of, especially at such short notice.

"This looks lovely," I said. "Thank you for agreeing to see me, Miss Entwistle."

"Oh, it's my pleasure, dear. It was such a surprise to get your call. I often think of your mum, you know. I haven't heard from her since the war. She's well, is she?"

"Yes, quite well. I live in Washington, D.C., myself, but I'm expecting to see her at Christmas. I spoke to her on the phone just last week. She seemed fine, busy as always. She writes a community events column for the *Havenwood Herald*—that's the local newspaper—and she's chairwoman of the town social committee and her church ladies' auxiliary, so there's always something requiring her attention. I think the town would have to roll up its sidewalks and shut down if anything ever happened to her."

Miss Entwistle smiled. "She always did keep busy. She used to do a column in the newspaper here, too, you know. Mr. Wickham—Grace's dad, bless 'im—he used to put it the paper. He'd a print shop here in town before the war, you know." I nodded. "Grace used to write a column called 'Dover Delights,' all about what was showing at the cinema and who was going to be playing at the dances and all. Of course, she was the best person to do it. There wasn't anything going on that your mum wasn't in the middle of."

"Quite the social butterfly, was she?"

"Oh, my, yes! She was in great demand. Had ever so many young men wanting to take her to the pictures, and queuing up to dance with her on Saturday nights." Miss Entwistle blushed. "Oh, dear, I don't mean to make her out to have been loose, you know. Oh, no, not at all. She was very particular about who she'd step out with, and rightly so, a lovely thing like her. Had very high standards, our Grace did. But we were young, and we did like to have our fun. Even after the war started, I'd have to say it all seemed a bit of lark—in the beginning, at least," she added, her expression growing more serious.

She paused to pour tea into our cups, hot and milky.

"I imagine that emotions would have been running high," I said, as she handed me a cup and saucer. "To young people, it probably all seemed some great adventure."

"Oh, yes, it was, ever so much." She passed over a plate and urged me to help myself to some of the bread and cold cuts. "There was a roller skating rink down next to the Grand Hotel, you know, right on the waterfront, and we'd all go there of an evening. Even after the fighting had started, they'd play the gramophone ever so loud. They say the music could be heard right across the Channel. After France fell to the Nazis, of course, it was the Germans over there listening to us having a grand old time—our way of cocking a snoot at them, you see, just to show they couldn't dampen our spirits."

I smiled at the gritty John Bull stubbornness that still animated those watery old eyes.

"We'd keep one eye on the castle, mind," she continued. "When the red flag went up over the ramparts, it meant the bombers were on their way. The gramophone would be shut off, then, and it would be ever so still, until suddenly, off in the distance, we'd see the Luftwaffe planes coming in low over the water, like a swarm of insects. Small boys had plane spotter cards, and they'd make a game of how many of each kind they could spot—Messerschmitts or Junkers or Heinkels or what have you. And then, from behind us, we'd hear our own RAF boys coming up to meet the Luftwaffe over the Channel. People used to climb up to the top of Shakespeare Cliff to get a better view of the air battle. It was terrible, you know, watching them engage, plane after plane being shot down into the water. Terrible, and yet so exciting, too."

I took a sip of my tea. "Did you ever meet my father, Miss Entwistle? Joe Meade? I know my mother said they first met briefly in London, and I wondered whether they ever came down here before she was sent to France."

"No, I never did, dear. Grace wrote to me once, just around V-E day it was, to say that she'd married an American officer, but that he'd been killed in France." A frown creased her soft forehead, but it was gone almost as soon as it appeared, replaced by a smile, and she reached across the table and squeezed my hand. "She wrote that she had a little baby girl over there. That would have been you, I suppose. She said she was hoping to come down for a visit, but that things were terribly difficult. It was a hard time for everyone then, but it must have been especially so for poor Grace, widowed so young."

I nodded. "My father had been a pilot with the OSS," I explained, "the Office of Strategic Services. I never knew him, unfortunately. He and my mother first met in London, as I say. I'm not sure just how it happened, but since they were both working with their respective special forces, I suppose there must have been some sort of liaison arrangement that might have brought them together."

"We often met the American boys at Red Cross dances," Miss Entwistle suggested. "Perhaps that's where Grace met your father. They were such a lark, the Yanks. Always coming up with chockies and ciggies and stockings for us girls. It didn't half make our own boys jealous, I can tell you."

"A devilishly charming bunch, those Yanks, were they?"

"Oh, ever so! 'Overpaid, oversexed and over 'ere,' we used to say about 'em," Miss Entwistle said, then covered her mouth with her hand, shocked at her own cheekiness.

I laughed. "So I heard. In any case, my mother has never really said how they met in London, just that it was later, when they found themselves together in France, that they fell in love. I've been trying to piece together how it all unfolded. I think they must have met not long before she was sent into France, because my father only arrived here around the spring of 1943, and my mother would have been sent to France not long after that, I think. He ended up flying supply missions over that fall, and he got caught behind the German lines. When his plane was shot down, my mother was among those who arranged for him to be hidden until the Resistance could spirit him back to England. That's when they really fell in love, she told me, during those weeks of hiding. They were secretly married by a priest who was working with the Resistance."

"Oh, my! It's all very romantic, isn't it?" Miss Entwistle said, eyes wide behind her spectacles.

"Very. Unfortunately, when they were finally ready to try to get back to England, they had to separate. My mother said that, even though she knew she was pregnant by then, she insisted my father go out ahead of her because he was at greater risk. He didn't speak French, you see, so it wasn't as easy for him to pass unnoticed in the streets. He never made it out of Paris. The Germans had stepped up their pressure on the Resistance, and had unleashed all their forces to try to shut the entire opposition network down. Hundreds of Parisians were being rounded up, and my father got caught up in that net. When the Gestapo realized he was neither French nor a regular enemy soldier, they shot him as a spy."

"Oh, dear, how awful! I'm so sorry."

"In the end, Mother didn't get back here to England until after the liberation of France."

Miss Entwistle removed her spectacles to wipe them with a tissue pulled from her dress pocket, then gave her damp eyes a pat. I leaned over and squeezed her hand, but it seemed extraordinary to be explaining about my parents. I was used to everyone telling *me* about them, especially about my father, who was, after all, a local hero in Havenwood. I suppose I'd just assumed that when I landed in my mother's hometown, her own life story would be just as well known. That's the kind of supreme self-importance that growing up in small towns can sometimes foster, but I thought I'd lost it after years of living away from Havenwood.

"I'm sorry, Miss Entwistle. I didn't mean to upset you. I thought you must have known all of this."

"No, I'd no idea, dear. Poor, poor Grace! How ever did she manage, losing a young husband, giving birth alone in a terrible place like that. And after she'd already lost her father and poor John..." She caught herself and pulled up short, glancing nervously at me.

I decided to help her out. "That would have been the naval officer she was engaged to when the war broke out? I understand he died early in the war."

"John Emory, yes," Miss Entwistle said, looking relieved she hadn't let any cats out of the bag. "Such sad times those were. But we mustn't dwell on them, must we? You say Grace is a journalist now? Fancy! I'm not surprised, of course, her knowing as much about the business as she did, working with her dad as she had."

"I wouldn't want to give the impression the *Havenwood Herald* is the *New York Times* or anything of that caliber," I said. "It's a very small town. Only a couple of thousand permanent residents, though that rises in summer when the cottage people are in town. It's a resort town, you see."

"Lovely. Here, dear, help yourself to some cheese and bickies, won't you?"

"Mother says she was born with ink in her veins, though," I added as I took a wedge of Stilton and a few crackers.

"Oh, that's true. Adored her dad, she did, loved to work in the print shop with him. She was with him right up to the day he died."

"That was in 1941?"

"Was it?" She paused, the teapot poised over my cup for a refill. "Yes, I suppose it must have been. I'll never forget that night. It was fall, I remember. We'd had rain, but the skies were clear. I was having tea with your Mum and her dad when the sirens went off, as a matter of fact. Their flat was over the print shop. Grace and I had been planning to go to a dance later that night over at the Grand. We'd half been expecting another raid, though. You never knew when the Germans were going to come—whether they preferred a clear night so they could see their targets or cloud cover for protection from the anti-aircraft guns. Never knew, either, whether they'd drop their bombs here or just fly over on their way to London. They'd been doing terrible damage to the East End, you see. The Queen Mum, God bless her, had been doing walkabouts, trying to keep spirits up. She said she was glad when they bombed Buckingham Palace, because she finally felt she could look the East Enders in the eye. Here in Dover, though, we hadn't been hit in a bit, so we guessed we were overdue."

"And that was the night my grandfather died?"

Miss Entwistle nodded. "Oh, a terrible thing it was. When the sirens went off, Mr. Wickham sent Grace and me out to the Anderson shelter."

"That was a homemade bomb shelter, wasn't it?"

"That's right. You granddad had built one in the back garden. You'd dig a big pit, you see, and cover it up with corrugated iron, then pile the earth back over. They were surprisingly sturdy, actually. Could hold half a dozen people, if you squeezed in there. Mr. Wickham had built his big enough to hold him and Grace and all the fellows who worked in his shop, if need be, although that night, there was just Grace and me in it."

"Her father didn't go down with you?"

"Oh, no. He was an ARP warden, so he'd to be on fire watch that night. Air Raid Precautions, you know. It was the incendiaries they really worried about. They did much more damage than the bombs themselves. Round balls of fire the Germans would drop onto the rooftops. Next thing you know, an entire neighborhood would be caught up in a firestorm. The government issued shovels and buckets of sand to the wardens, and they'd position themselves up on the rooftops and try to scoop the incendiaries and drop them into the buckets before they could do too much damage."

"In the middle of the bombing raids? That sounds awfully dangerous."

"Oh, yes, it was. They were ever so brave, were our wardens. So that night, Grace and I were alone in the shelter while her dad was up on the roof. We knew it was going to be a bad one. We could hear the antiaircraft guns and the engines of the planes roaring overhead, then dull thumps as the bombs started falling." Miss Entwistle illustrated by knocking her clenched little fist on the table, making the teacups rattle. "Suddenly, there was a dreadful, awful roar, and the next we knew, there was dirt flying all 'round us. One had landed very close, no doubt about it. Grace and I held on to each other, shaking like leaves. It seemed to go on forever, but the shelter held, and finally, the All Clear sounded. Grace ran out straight away. I was right behind her, but as I came up into the garden, I nearly knocked her down. She'd stopped cold and was staring at their house. They'd their flat on top, as I said, and the presses were down below on the ground floor."

I nodded.

"Well, half the building was gone. Just sliced away, vertical, like," Miss Entwistle said. "The parlor upstairs, where we'd been having our tea just a few minutes before? It looked like a set on a theater stage. The dishes were still on the table, exactly as we'd left them. Her father's chair had been knocked on its side, that was all. Otherwise, the room was completely intact. The other half of the building was just a pile of burning rubble. The shop downstairs was burning like mad—because of all the paper in there, you see."

"And my grandfather?"

"We couldn't find him. Not at first. We called and called, but there was no answer. We ran everywhere, looking—in the rubble, in the road. It was Grace who found him. He must have been blown off the roof. There was a chemist's shop across the road, and Mr. Wickham was sitting on the sidewalk in front of it, his back propped against the wall of the chemist's, as if he'd just sat down for a minute to catch his breath. He looked almost untouched, but his eyes were open and staring, and you could tell straight away that he was dead."

"Oh, my God, how awful," I breathed. My mother had never told me this part, just that he'd been killed when a bomb hit his print shop.

"Oh, it was worse than that, dear. His hair was on fire, you see. There he was, sitting on the sidewalk, looking at us, like, his hair burning away. Grace stood there, frozen in place. And then, she started to scream. Screamed and screamed, until finally one of the other ARP wardens from down the lane came running. They had to go 'round after the All Clear and bring out the dead, you see. Anyway, he took one look at poor Mr. Wickham, then went and smothered the flames with his jacket. When the flames were out, he left it over the poor man."

Nellie stared glumly into her tea, which had long since gone cold. "Poor Grace! He was all she had, what with poor John Emory already lost at sea. They'd to bury her dad in a cardboard coffin, you know. There was a shortage of wooden ones, with so many people dying, night after night."

We sat in silence while the awful image seared itself into my brain: my grandfather propped dead against a building with staring eyes and hair aflame. And now, I wonder if perhaps that was the moment—the bend in the road when my mother's virtue first took the awful turn it did.

CHAPTER 14

Havenwood, Minnesota
Friday, January 12, 1979

Being an outsider was nothing new for Cruz. He knew he wasn't the only stranger in the roadside café that morning, but he was the only one who looked so out of his element. He'd considered dispensing with the tie today, but there didn't seem to be much point. While his gray topcoat and black leather shoes might be inconspicuous in a city of bureaucrats, in this world of plaid flannel, steel-toes and sweat-stained ball caps, they marked him as clearly as if he'd had the words "desk jockey" tattooed on his forehead. Back in the motel room, cleaning crystalline deposits off his brogues—the Army spit-polish routine deeply ingrained by now—he'd debated dropping into a general store he'd spotted last night to see if they carried rubbers to protect his shoes from the salted slush, but after taking a look at the morning breakfast crowd, he decided against it. Better ruined shoes than wrecked pride.

The day had dawned sunny, with the promise of some small measure of warmth. It had taken him till nearly 4:00 a.m. to fall asleep. Each time he started to drop off, the whine and swish of tires passing on the highway would pull him up short, his body tensed, ears pricked, listening for movement as he stared out into the blackness around him. Finally, he had dropped off, the biting smell of pine trees and gasoline fumes sparking bizarre dreams of wandering lost in burning forests. A razor-sharp slice of light had awakened him around seven-fifteen, shining in through an uncurtained bathroom window, and he'd stepped outside to a big, open sky so blue it hurt the eyes.

Walking over to the café from his room, Cruz noticed for the first time that there was a two-story, clapboard-sided house sitting on a small hill directly behind the gas station-motel-café complex. Both lots had been planted with the same variety of juniper trees, leading him to the conclusion that Norbert Jorgenson and his wife obviously lived where they worked, keeping a close eye on their business.

Two sixteen-wheelers with out-of-state plates were parked in the lay-by of the truck stop. One was a moving van, and he spotted its thickset driver through the café's big picture window, sitting on a red, vinyl-covered stool at the semicircular counter, leaning over his plate, "Allied Van Lines" embossed on the back of his jacket. The other long-haul rig was out of New York State. As he was walking past the gas pumps, Cruz saw the driver jump down from the sleeper box behind the cab, then pause on the tarmac to tuck in his shirt, zip his fly, and fasten the belt on his pants. He strutted over to the café, Cruz close behind him.

Inside, while Cruz took a corner spot, his back to the wall, the rig driver settled into a booth near the front window overlooking the gas pumps outside and the highway beyond. There were half a dozen or so others having breakfast—a couple of linemen from Ma Bell, some truckers and a few old-timers with faces weathered and lined like the Martian plains—local farmers, Cruz guessed, by the International Harvester and Monsanto logos on their billed caps.

Two waitresses were working that morning—the older woman

whom Jorgenson, the owner, had said was his wife, and a teenage
girl with a dark ponytail who might have been a granddaughter.
The girl had no sooner taken a coffee cup, cutlery and menu over
to the big rig driver than he looked up—all the men in the place
looked up—to see a pretty but wan young girl in frayed jeans,
tight T-shirt and fringed suede jacket emerge from the pay
shower down the hall near the rest rooms. She hesitated for a moment until she spotted the driver, then walked over and set her
grimy green canvas backpack next to his booth. She slid into the
bench across from him, smiling uncertainly. The glance the
driver gave her conveyed a world of reactions—smug familiarity, cockiness, contempt, and only the barest measure of guilt.

Cruz watched as the young waitress grabbed another coffee
cup, a set of utensils, and a menu from behind the counter and
took them over. The girl nodded at the cup but shook her head
at the proffered menu, her long, muddy-colored hair sticking
wetly to the shoulders of her brown suede jacket. Mrs. Jorgenson was working the counter, but keeping an eye on that table,
Cruz noted. As soon as the girl shook her damp head, the woman
grabbed a pot from the coffee-making unit behind her and came
out from behind the counter.

"You should eat," she said bluntly, filling the girl's cup almost to the brim.

The young girl looked up at her. Despite the black mascara
ringing her tired eyes, she looked childish and frightened.

The older woman turned to the driver and took his cup to fill
it. "A person needs a good breakfast," she said, smacking it
down in front of him.

The guy was forty if he was a day, wiry and lean as old rope,
with a receding black hairline and a gold wedding band on his
left hand. He scowled at the sloshed coffee, but Mrs. Jorgenson
was obviously brooking no grief this morning. Ignoring her, he
muttered to the girl to go ahead and order, he'd pay. She took
the menu gratefully. The older woman nodded to the young

waitress to carry on, then headed over to Cruz's table, grabbing another cup and a menu from the counter as she passed by.

"Morning! Coffee?"

"Yes, ma'am," he said, then lowered his voice. "Nice work over there."

She glanced back at the other table, where the ponytailed waitress was taking down the girl's breakfast order. "Not the first time I've seen that kind of nonsense. Young girls out on the road, hitchhiking all alone, getting picked up by old farts like that— pardon my French. Enough to make you sick. Those girls think they've got it rough at home, figure they'll head out to the big city or California or somewheres to find the good life, but they find out pretty quick they're on a fast trip to nowhere."

"She looks young."

"They always do," she said grimly. "You up for breakfast this morning?"

"You bet," Cruz said, giving the menu a quick once-over. "Let's see...I'm pretty hungry. I think I'll go with the number two special."

She took back the menu. "You got it. You're the fellow my husband checked into number eight last night, aren't you? How'd you sleep, then?"

"Just fine," Cruz lied. "It's a nice room, thanks."

"I hear you're with the FBI? And that you're here about the fire over at Grace Meade's?"

He nodded. "Your husband tells me Jillian Meade and your daughter were friends. You knew the family well, did you?"

"Oh, well enough, I guess. Haven't seen much of Jillian since she and Nancy graduated. I called Nance last night to let her know what happened, though. She and her husband and their two kids live out in Seattle."

Cruz nodded. "I think your husband mentioned that. Was your daughter still in touch with Jillian?"

"No, not a whole lot. They exchanged Christmas cards once a year with news about what they were up to, but that was about it. And as a matter of fact, Nance told me when I called last night that she never heard from Jillian this year. It was the first time Jill had ever missed sending a Christmas note, although Nance said she didn't actually realize it until she was taking her cards down off the mantel after Christmas. She'd been thinking about giving her a call, just to make sure everything was okay, but she's pretty busy with her kids, you know, and with one thing and another, she hadn't gotten around to it yet. She felt real bad after she heard what happened here."

"What about Mrs. Meade? Your husband mentioned he's the deputy mayor, and I understand Mrs. Meade was very active in local affairs, so you must have seen a lot of her. What was she like?"

"Oh, well, Norbert ran into Grace more than I did. I'm pretty much tied up with this place most of the time," she said, waving her hand at the café around them. "I do some work for our church, too, but we're Lutheran and Grace belonged to the Episcopalians, so her and my paths only crossed now and again. You know—Fourth of July, weddings, that sort of thing."

"But this is a small town," Cruz said, pulling out the line he'd been hearing ever since he arrived. "Everyone knows everyone. You must have had some opinion of her."

Mrs. Jorgenson leaned one hand on the table, frowning, as she seemed to debate how to answer. "I guess you're going to hear different opinions on Grace Meade, depending on who you talk to. She was real active in social events around here, as you say, but she could rub some people the wrong way. On the other hand, there's no denying she was a darn hard worker. Grace got things done, which is more than I can say for some of the grumblers who complained about how she was always taking over or second-guessing everybody else's work. Bottom line was, if Grace took something on, she got results. Now that she's gone, no matter how much other people might have thought they wanted to run the show, stuff is going to fall between the cracks,

I guarantee you. Things won't be done as well as Grace would have done them, and a lot of stuff won't get done at all."

"But she had a difficult personality, Mrs. Jorgenson?"

She grimaced. "Oh, please! My name's Olga—Ollie, everybody calls me. Mrs. Jorgenson was my mother-in-law, and a real battle-ax she was, too. Gives me the willies every time somebody calls me that."

Cruz grinned and held out his hand. "Alex Cruz. Good to meet you. So, Ollie, was Grace Meade a battle-ax, too?"

"Well, now, that's a little strong, though it depends who you talk to, I suppose."

"How so?"

Ollie Jorgenson glanced around the café, but things looked to be under control. The younger waitress was just delivering food to the rig driver and his hitchhiker, and no one else had come in behind Cruz. "Pam?" Ollie called over, "when you're done there, you wanna bring a number two special over here?"

"No problem."

"How do you want your eggs?" she asked, turning again to Cruz. "And what kind of toast?"

"Over easy and wheat."

"Right. Over easy on those eggs, Pam, and wheat toast," she called back to the girl, who nodded and headed to the kitchen. Ollie set the coffeepot down on the table and settled into the bench across from him. "You ever had a terrier?"

"No, I can't say that I have."

"Well, Grace could be a little bit of a terrier, Norbert liked to say. Tough and yappy, the way terriers and small women can be. That's what Norbert always says, anyway. Says that's why he prefers big gals like me."

Cruz nodded and smiled, liking her more and more. She reminded him of his aunt Luisa.

"Mind you, Grace could also be charming," she went on. "And she was very attractive. Beautiful when she was young, as a matter of fact. A real knockout when she first came to town, which made her real popular with the men and real unpopular with the women, at least until they figured out she had no interest in their husbands."

"She never considered remarrying?"

"Not as far as I know. She said she could never find another man like Joe Meade, and she wasn't going to settle for less, so she was content just to keep herself busy with other things. And to be honest, to look at her, you really couldn't picture her with anyone from around here. As I say, she was a knockout. Even as she aged, she kept herself real trim and stylish. Always wore her hair in this kind of elegant bun that would have made anyone else look like an old maid librarian, but made Grace looked like...well, like Grace Kelly, actually. Cosmopolitan, I guess you'd call her. And it's true she could be a bit bossy, but that woman could also charm the socks off of anyone if she put her mind to it. Most people around here were in awe of her, to be honest, and they approached her with... Hmm...what's the word I'm looking for, now...?"

"Deference?"

"Deference. That's it. Like the Queen of England, you know. Grace really played on that. Played people, I guess you'd say, like a queen plays her subjects. She didn't have many equals in town. I wouldn't want to say she was better than other people, but she was certainly different. Most folks were intimidated by her and happy to let her be in charge of anything she wanted. A few of them practically worshipped her. She had a little clique of loyal followers who trailed after her everywhere she went."

"What about you, Ollie? I don't get the sense you'd be easily intimidated by Grace Meade or anyone else."

"Me? Oh, no, I wasn't, not at all. But don't get me wrong, Grace and I got along just fine, for as much as we ever saw of one another. We certainly weren't good friends or anything, but she'd never given me any grief personally. I've got my own busy life, what with this place, and four grown kids and seven grandkids. Frankly, I couldn't have cared less whether Grace Meade approved of me or not. She probably knew it, too, but she also knew I was no threat to her ambitions, so like I say, we got along just fine."

"Did she have any close friends?"

"She had plenty of friends, and a lot of people were probably happy to think of themselves as her close personal friends, although whether they were really all that close is hard to say, since Grace didn't strike me as the type to open up to anyone. Might just have been that English standoffishness, you know. I guarantee you, though, there's going to be a mob of mourners at her funeral."

"Who would you recommend I talk to who might have known her best—her and her daughter?" Cruz added. Jillian Meade was the real reason he was here, but somehow, he was getting the sense the key to the daughter lay in understanding the mother.

Ollie paused to consider, and while she was thinking about it, Pam, the young waitress approached with Cruz's breakfast and set it down in front of him—a big plate of eggs, sausages, hash browns and pancakes, with a side of toast. A real working man's meal.

"Ollie?" Pam said quietly to the older woman. "You know that girl over there? You think we should try to get her to stay? That guy she's with gives me the creeps."

Ollie glanced back to the front table where the two were eating their breakfasts in total silence, neither one looking at the other. "I can offer," she said, "but I can't force her to if she doesn't want to."

"Maybe she just needs to know she's got another choice?"

Ollie studied the girl for a second, then nodded and pushed herself back from the table, leaning on it to heft herself out from behind the bench. "'Scuse me for a minute, Agent Cruz?"

He watched as she walked over to the table at the front of the café. "Everything okay here?" she asked.

"Fine. We were just finishing up." the driver said. "I need to hit the road. You could bring the check."

"You want to stick around for a bit, hon?" Ollie asked the girl.

"Why would she want to do that?" The trucker turned to the girl. "Come on, I'm running behind schedule."

"Well, then, you should probably get on your way," Ollie said affably, "but personally, I think this nice young lady can do better than take the ride you're offering."

"Lady, why don't you just mind your own business? We only came in for breakfast, but I gotta tell you, the food's not all that great here, and the service definitely sucks. I think I'm gonna get on the old CB radio when I get back on the road and tell the other boys out there they should just barrel on down the interstate and give this place a miss. What do you say about that?"

"That's your privilege. You go right ahead and do that," Ollie told him, then turned back to the young girl. "But like I was saying, hon, if you want to stay, we can find you another ride to wherever you're going, or some work, if you could use a job. Could help you with a phone call, too, if there's somebody back home who might be worrying about you."

The girl's gaze shifted uncertainly "I don't—"

"This is bullshit," the driver said angrily, pushing his way out of the booth. "She's comin' with me. Come on, you, get up and let's get the hell out of here!"

Cruz was already on his feet, but by the time he reached the table, the trucker had clamped a grip on the young girl's arm. "Let her go," Cruz warned him quietly.

The driver paused to glance at him, then sneered. "You stay outta this. Come on!" he repeated, dragging the girl half out of the booth.

"I said, let her go," Cruz repeated, bringing a fist up under the other man's wrist to break his hold.

As the girl fell back into the corner, the trucker wheeled to face him head-on. "Who the hell are you?" They were eye-to-eye, but the other man leaned into his face. "This has got nothin' to do with you, asshole, so just butt out or I'll butt you out!" he snarled, his forefinger jabbing Cruz right in the middle of his inappropriate tie.

Cruz grabbed the finger and twisted it painfully with one hand while his free hand held up his leather ID folder. "FBI Special Agent Cruz," he said, "and I'll overlook this once, sir, but if you touch me again with that dirty finger, I'll have you facedown in what's left of that plate of eggs and handcuffed faster than you can say 'assaulting a federal officer.'"

"Oh, shit!" the driver said, blanching and wincing simultaneously. "Ow! That hurts!"

"Let me see your driver's license," Cruz said, releasing his finger and shoving him back. The other patrons in the place had fallen silent and were sitting stock-still.

"Okay, okay!" The trucker dug in his back pocket and pulled out his wallet, withdrawing the license. "I didn't do anything, all right? She was hitchhiking and I gave her a ride. It was cold out. You think I shoulda left her there to freeze by the side of the road?"

Cruz took the license but ignored it and the driver, looking instead at the girl. "Are you all right, Miss?" She nodded, wide-eyed. "Did he hurt you?"

The trucker took a step forward. "Look, I'm sorry. I didn't mean—"

Cruz held up a warning finger. "Back off. I'm not talking to you right now. You will not say another word until I tell you to, got it?" When the driver nodded, Cruz turned again to the girl. "You've been hitchhiking?"

She nodded guiltily, looking ready to burst into tears. "I thought I'd go see some friends in Oregon."

"Do you have some ID on you?"

She looked panicked, then nodded again, the tears starting to flow now as she got to her feet and reached under the table for the grubby green backpack. She pulled out a pink plastic wallet from which she withdrew a Wisconsin driver's license. Her name was Kelly Parkening, Cruz noted, and she was barely sixteen years old.

"Where did this man pick you up, Miss Parkening?"

"Around Eau Claire?"

"Eau Claire, Wisconsin. So, we're talking about crossing state lines then," Cruz said, shaking his head as he turned back to the driver, who was trembling now. "Interstate transport of a minor for immoral purposes. Definitely a federal offense, Mr....um..." He read the trucker's license. "Mr. John Dinelli, of Trenton, New Jersey. And you've got New York plates on your rig out there."

"Oh, Jesus, please! She's a minor? I thought she was older, at least twenty-one. I mean, look at her!"

"Mr. Dinelli? Shut up. I won't tell you again. Miss Parkening," Cruz said, turning back to the girl, "don't cry. You're not going to be charged with anything, I promise."

She nodded, sniffling. Ollie Jorgenson reached into her apron pocket and pulled out a clean tissue. She handed it to the girl, then put an arm around her shoulders. "Do your parents know where you are, hon?"

The girl shook her head. "I told them I was going to spend the night at a friend's. By now, they'll know I didn't, though. I had this boyfriend, see, who moved out to Oregon to live on a farm with a bunch of other people, like a commune? And we really missed each other, and I thought..." She started to cry again. "It was such a dumb idea!"

"Miss Parkening? Kelly? Listen to me," Cruz said, ducking down so he could look at her eye-to-eye. "It was definitely a dumb idea, but it can be fixed—for you, anyway. But no matter how dumb a thing you may have done, Mr. Dinelli here is an adult and should know better. He can face federal criminal charges if you're prepared to testify against him."

"Oh, sweet Jesus!" Dinelli cried. "I've got a wife and three kids!"

"Well, maybe you should spend a little more time thinking about them."

"Agent Cruz, can I talk to you for a second?" Ollie asked.

He nodded. "Miss Parkening, have a seat over at the counter there, will you? And you," he ordered Dinelli, "sit down and be quiet."

Dinelli dropped back into the booth while Pam, the other waitress, took the young girl over to the counter and settled her there, standing protectively by while Cruz and the older woman withdrew a couple of feet off to the side.

"She's a stupid kid who made a bad choice," Ollie whispered. "And don't get me wrong, I think that creep deserves to be hung up by his you-know-whats. But if you charge him and force her to testify, it turns a dumb choice into a horror that'll go on for months or years."

"I know that."

"Then let me take her in hand. If I can get her to go back to her family, would you let that creep off with a warning? Look at him. He's shaking so hard he looks ready to wet himself."

Cruz gave the trucker a glance, then looked over at the tearful girl. "She's got to go home, and she's got to agree to stay there at least until she graduates from high school. And, Ollie?" he said, lowering his voice even further. "She should be looked at by a doctor as soon as possible."

She nodded. "I'll take care of it, I promise."

"Okay, then." They walked back over to the group. "Miss Parkening, if I gave you the choice," Cruz said, "what would you like to see happen now?"

"I want to go home," she told him tearfully.

"And you'd stay there? And you'd go back to school and work hard?" She nodded. "You're absolutely sure of that?"

"I promise," she sobbed. "I just want my mom!"

"Okay, we'll see what we can do. But remember, I'm going to hold you to your promise." He pulled out his notebook from his back hip pocket and jotted down her name and address. "I'm going to be calling you from time to time, and you'd better still be there, or I will be very upset. And you don't want to get me upset, because I am a nasty FBI agent and we have a very long reach. Do you understand?" he asked, handing her back her ID.

She took it, nodding solemnly.

"And as for you," Cruz said, turning toward the trucker as he noted his license details, then peered outside to take down the plate information from his rig, "I am going to run your name through the system."

"There's nothin' there, I swear! I've never been in trouble, ever. This was just real bad judgment on my part, too."

"Mr. Dinelli, the only bad judgment in your case was your mother's when she decided not to strangle you at birth." Ollie Jorgenson snorted. Cruz slapped the man's license down on the table. "My advice to you is to go back to New Jersey and find yourself a job that keeps you closer to home and that poor, benighted family of yours, God help them. One thing you don't ever want to do, however, is get picked up for something like this again, because your name is going to stay in the system. And if you ever do this again, I will find out about it and I will be on your case like a dog on a bone. It will not be pretty, I guarantee you."

"No, sir, never. I swear."

"Hit the road."

"Yes, sir. I'm outta here!"

The man grabbed his license and sprang to his feet, but as he made to scramble out of the booth, Cruz had another thought. "Hold it!" He stuck out his arm, clotheslining the guy clean in the Adam's apple. Dinelli let out a choked scream and grabbed his throat. "Did Mr. Dinelli here pay for these two breakfasts?" Cruz asked the young waitress.

She nodded at the cash the driver had thrown down.

"Does it look like there's a good tip in there?" Cruz asked.

She grimaced and shook her head. Cruz raised one brow. Dinelli still had one hand at his throat, which would be bruised and sore for days. He looked ready to protest, but thought better of it and pulled a ten-dollar bill out of his pocket, throwing it on the table. Cruz dropped his arm, and the trucker was out the door a split second later.

There was a round of soft snickers from the room, and a smattering of applause, as Ollie Jorgenson turned to the two younger women.

"Pam, why don't you take Kelly here up to the house to relax for a bit while I finish out the breakfast shift?" She picked up the green backpack and handed it to the girl. "You go and put your feet up, hon. I'll be over shortly, and then we'll give your mom a call to let her know you're okay."

The girl nodded tearfully. "Thank you. Thank you both," she added, looking shyly at Cruz.

"It's no problem," he said. "But don't forget, Kelly, I'm going to be calling, and I'm going to want to hear that you're pulling good grades."

She nodded again, and the two girls headed for the back door. Meanwhile, from the parking lot in front of the café came the rarely heard sound of a sixteen-wheeler laying rubber as it peeled out onto the highway.

Ollie Jorgenson turned to Cruz. "Well, Agent Cruz—"

"Alex."

"Alex." She smiled. "Your breakfast has gone cold over there. You go settle in and I'll bring you a hot one and some fresh coffee, on the house. And then, maybe I can point you in the direction of some people you might want to talk to on that other business of yours."

CHAPTER 15

There was so much I never knew about my mother, so many missing pieces to the puzzle of Grace Meade, left blank by her reluctance to talk about the past.

"Too many sad memories, dear," she told me when I pressed for details of the tantalizing stories hinted at but never fully told.

Other times, she cloaked her silence in the black robe of the Official Secrets Act. "There are affairs of state that can never be discussed, darling, no matter how much time has passed. The consequences, even now, could be dire. I signed an oath, and these are constraints to which I have resigned myself to being bound for life."

But there was no quieting my hunger to know—about her, about my father. I needed to understand the forces that had brought them together briefly, a bright light in the midst of those dark days, then blown them apart before we could ever be a family. Trying to fill the blanks that my mother couldn't or wouldn't, I latched on to every book, every story, every reference to wartime Europe that I could lay my hands on, searching for the roots of my own existence. Who knows what I might have become, if not for the need to fill that void inside me? As it was, I became a historian as a result of the sheer amount of time I spent living in the past.

But meeting Nellie Entwistle provided a couple of missing pieces to the puzzle that was my mother. I'd already guessed why a young woman like my mother would have consented to bury herself in clandestine work, where the life expectancy of an agent dropped behind enemy lines averaged a few weeks, at best. But Miss Entwistle confirmed my suspicions. She said that after the night she and my mother found my grandfather dead in the road with his hair on fire, my mother changed. Until then, she had been carefree and flirtatious, more interested in young men and pretty clothes than in the tedious work of war. Then, already saddened by the loss of the young sailor she'd loved, she'd lost her beloved father, as well, to a German bomb. She could have spent the rest of the war pining, but instead, being the strong person she was, she became determined to defeat the evil responsible for their deaths.

Miss Entwistle was also able to provide a clue as to how my mother even found her way into those top secret circles. Her recruitment, it seems, had actually been initiated over a year before she actually went up to London, back in the early days of the war.

When France fell to the Nazis in 1940, the Germans sat poised across the Channel, getting ready to invade Britain, the last bastion of resistance to Hitler's ambition to rule all of Europe. While the Nazis planned their invasion, the British prepared their own secret plans to undermine Hitler's war machine from within. But how had my mother figured into those clandestine plans? I wanted to know. It was Nellie Entwistle who filled in that blank.

"Why, it was that mysterious gentleman who showed up down at the docks, I should think. Very posh, that one, hardly said a word to most folk. But our Grace, well, she surely caught his eye, she did. He kept her busy all the time he was here. He'd have been the one put the notion of going up to London into her head. At first, she wouldn't go with him, but after her poor dad died, well, I think she decided she hadn't anything to lose."

"Are you saying my mother got involved with this mysterious man?"

Miss Entwistle looked at me, startled, then blushed to the roots of her silver-white hair. She took a hurried sip of tea. "Oh, no, nothing like that, dear," she said, when she'd recovered her poise. "In the first place, she was still seeing John Emory at the time. And in any case, that other gent, he was much, much older than we were."

"What was his name, do you remember?"

"I'm not sure I do. He had an officer's rank, it turned out, although he didn't wear a uniform—not here, at any rate. But his name...? What was it now? Gordon? Gibbons..."

I felt my heart begin to race. "Was it Gubbins? Colonel Colin Gubbins?"

"Yes! That's it. Colonel Gubbins! How ever did you know, dear? Did your mum mention him, then?"

"No, she never did, but I've come across his name in my research. I work for the Smithsonian Institution in Washington," I explained to her. "My specialty is World War II history, especially clandestine operations and the various resistance movements who fought against the Nazis. That's why I'm here, actually, to look at some newly declassified files and borrow some materials for a new exhibit we're mounting."

"Fancy! And Colonel Gubbins? He's famous, is he?"

"Well, in certain circles, he is. He was head of training and operations for the Special Operations Executive, or SOE. He would have been responsible for teaching the tricks of the trade to the saboteurs they dropped behind enemy lines—things like how to send messages in code, derail trains, and kill with their bare hands. Stuff like that."

"Oh, my! That nice man did terrible things like that?"

"Well, maybe he didn't personally, but the people he recruited and trained certainly did. It was wartime, after all, and Britain was fighting for its life."

Miss Entwistle nodded, but I could see the notion of my mother being mixed up with people who strangled with their bare hands was more than a little disconcerting to her. It was one thing to watch the brave British RAF pilots engaging in air battles over the English Channel, but quite another altogether to imagine the gruesome realities of guerrilla warfare. For my part, I was amazed to think this sweet, round spinster in front of me had actually come face-to-face with the famous Colonel Gubbins of British Special Operations.

"So what was Colonel Gubbins doing here?" I asked her.

"He'd come down with the other government people to help organize the Dunkirk business, I should think. It was a huge operation. They ran it out of the castle. Did you know there were secret tunnels under Dover Castle, dear?"

I did, actually. I knew they had been dug during the Middle Ages and had been used as a defense post in every war since. During WWII, the British military had operated a major military command post and field hospital out of the tunnels under the castle, and it had been the headquarters for the operation to evacuate the beaches of Dunkirk in France.

By June of 1940, the RAF had lost half of its bombers trying to hold back the enemy advance. When the Germans overran France that month, thousands of British troops found themselves trapped at Dunkirk with their backs to the English Channel, as the Nazis prepared for the final assault on Britain. But miraculously, the Germans paused to regroup before moving on across the Channel. It was one of Hitler's first and worst strategic errors. In that brief respite, an armada of more than eight hundred British vessels, from naval destroyers to small pleasure boats, crossed and recrossed the Channel from Dover and other southern ports, ferrying out more than three hundred thousand troops. Although it was a tactical retreat, the Dunkirk evacuation turned out to be one of the greatest morale-boosting episodes of the war, allowing the stalwart British troops to regroup and go on to fight another day.

And the Dunkirk evacuation, I discovered that day at tea with Miss Entwistle, also marked the beginning of my mother's career as a spy.

"We were all down at that docks greeting the boats as they came in with the troops. Trying to help out in any way we could," Miss Entwistle said. "Some of the boats were damaged. Many were destroyed by German mines in the Channel. But the rest just kept on, going back and forth, bringing load after load of troops. And, oh, what a sorry-looking lot they were, poor dears! You can't imagine! Dirty and tired, many of them wounded. Some still had their weapons, but most of them had lost everything over there, right down to their boots. Their spirits were good, though. After all, they'd managed to slip out of the grasp of the filthy Hun, hadn't they? If it hadn't been for all those boats and the bravery of those captains who went back and forth like that, though, those boys would have ended up in prisoner of war camps—or worse."

"It certainly was an incredible episode," I agreed. "You said you were trying to help out? In what way?"

"Oh, any way we could. The Red Cross had set up down there to tend to the poor boys. Grace and I volunteered to help roll bandages, bring the boys ciggies and tea and what not."

"And that was when Colonel Gubbins showed up?" It made sense, of course, that the British government would have sent in its top intelligence people. They would have been anxious for whatever information could be gleaned from the evacuees—what armaments the Germans were using. What the morale of the French was. Would they fight the Nazi occupier? Was there any sign of organized resistance?

"Yes, the colonel showed up early on. Some of the defeated French soldiers came over in the evacuation, too, you see. And a right cheeky bunch they were, blowing kisses at all the girls." Miss Entwistle blushed, but despite her feigned indignation, I suspected

she'd adored all that male attention. War or no war, she, my
mother, and those soldiers had all been young, caught in the heat
of raging hormones that could only have been rendered more intense by the dangers they faced.

"So the colonel came down to Dover to interview the French
troops who'd escaped in the evacuation?" I asked, coaxing Miss
Entwistle's memory along.

She nodded. "They'd all to be interviewed, to make sure they were
on the up and up, I suppose. That was where your mum was really
able to help, speaking lovely French the way she did. I remember the
day the colonel came into the Red Cross canteen. Some French boys
had been chatting us up, your mum and I. Of course, I couldn't make
out a word of what they were saying, but Grace? Why, she had those
boys eating out of her hand. I noticed the colonel watching her. After
a while, he came over and asked Grace if she'd come along to the
hospital with him to do a spot of translating. He was debriefing some
of the wounded French fellows, Grace told me later. After that day,
he kept her right busy, and when the evacuation wound up, he asked
Grace if she'd like to go back up to London to work with him there."

"And that's how she was recruited into the SOE?"

"No, she didn't go, actually, not right then, in any case. She was
still waiting for John Emory to return, you see. His ship was out on
convoy duty in the North Atlantic. He was overdue, but she expected
him back any day. It was not long after that she got word his ship
had gone down, all hands lost." Miss Entwistle shook her head and
exhaled heavily. In her long sigh, I thought I heard an entire nation's mourning for all the lost young men of her generation.

"But before the colonel had left," she went on, "he'd given Grace
a card, in case she changed her mind, see. At the time, it seemed
quite a lark. Grace showed it to me. There was no name on it or
anything, just a number she was to ring if she ever decided she'd
like to come up and work for him."

"But even after John Emory's ship was lost, she didn't go right
then, did she?"

"No, not right then. A year or so later, it would have been, after her dad was killed. Grace had stayed on to help him at the print shop. She had to, him being so shorthanded and all, what with so many men off fighting. When poor Mr. Wickham died and his press was destroyed, Grace seemed lost for a time, but then she remembered that card the colonel had given her, and she rang the number on it. Very mysterious it all was, too, she told me. Said she was told to call round at a flat in London. Baker Street, it was. I remember because that was the street made famous by Arthur Conan Doyle, wasn't it? I remember telling Grace that perhaps she'd be working for Mr. Sherlock Holmes himself."

I smiled, but I already knew from my research what a large and deadly clandestine network had been launched out of two modest Baker Street houses the British Government had requisitioned for wartime use. And now, I finally had an inkling of how it was that the beautiful printer's daughter from Dover had found herself at the dangerous heart of those secret operations.

Until I met Nellie Entwistle, I'd never been entirely certain which part of the British secret establishment my mother worked for during the war, since she, in the best tradition of spooks everywhere, had steadfastly refused to confirm or deny anything. But once Miss Entwistle told me about Colonel Gubbins's arrival in Dover to interview the French soldiers evacuated from Dunkirk, his chance meeting with my mother, and—the final clue—that he'd mentioned a Baker Street address in London, I knew my suspicions had been correct, and that the SOE was, indeed, the branch that had recruited her and sent her behind enemy lines.

So after I left Miss Entwistle's thatched cottage that afternoon, I set out to retrace my mother's steps, and boarded the northbound train back to London, just as she had done after her father's death in the spring of 1941.

Knowing what I now know and given everything that's happened since, it seems incredible to think how happy I was that day, rid-

ing back to London, despite the gray skies, the bitter cold, and the
sheetlike rain pouring down the windows of the train, obscuring
the view of the passing English countryside. In fact, I was almost
giddy with delight at the thought that I was at last on the trail of
rediscovering my mother's past. When my research was done, I
thought, I would know her in a way I never had before. And given
the lengths to which I'd gone, I hoped she would appreciate my efforts, and know that I had undertaken this journey out of love for
her. Bottom line: I hoped it would bring us closer in a way we'd
never been before.

Our relationship had been strained for several years and for a
variety of reasons, some typical, some unique to us. But as I'd
grown older, I'd come around in my thinking and started to see
her as a lonely figure. She never suffered for lack of admirers in
Havenwood, of course, but I think it's fair to say that she had no
one she could feel really close to. No one there really knew her. How
could they, without understanding where she'd come from or what
she'd been through?

My mother was an outsider, of course, but she became a civic
leader because she was a chameleon, extremely skilled at adapting
to her surroundings. It was this ability that probably allowed her
to survive the dangerous undercover life she'd led during the war.
When I was growing up, I thought it was just because of her gra-
cious nature that she conformed her behavior and tailored her conversation to match the simple interests of her neighbors.

Unlike most of her friends, my mother read widely and followed
current events avidly. One event stands out in my mind. When Israeli agents kidnapped Adolf Eichmann in Argentina in 1960 and
put him on trial in Jerusalem for his war crimes, then later executed him, she was glued to the news reports. It was one of the
very rare occasions I ever heard her evoke the past, when she told
my grandparents and me that she'd lost several Resistance colleagues to the Nazi death camps—patriots who were shipped to Germany and never seen again.

And yet, as passionately as she obviously felt about this and other issues in the news, I never heard her discuss anything like this outside our house. I never heard her remind anyone in that small town, however subtly, that she'd once lived in London and Paris, much less that she'd fought on the front lines of this century's epic battle between good and evil.

Of course, most people in town knew, however vaguely, that she'd had an eventful past. But if my mother's accent was different, her ability to adapt was such that, in the end, people forgot she hadn't spent her entire life there. When you came right down to it, Grace Wickham Meade was accepted in Havenwood because she was Joe Meade's widow and Helen and Arthur Meade's daughter-in-law, and the Meades had been part of the town's fabric for as long as it had existed.

I, however, was on a self-appointed mission to give her back her full identity.

It's pathetic, really. Because the real payoff, at least as I imagined it in my pitifully insecure mind, was that my mother might look at me with newfound respect and admiration after all the effort I'd made on her behalf. That she might at last consider me a worthy heir. That she might, finally, love me in a way I never felt she had before.

As I was doing my official work in England and France, simultaneously delving into my mother's record of service, it almost felt as if it were my own steps I was retracing. I had spent so many years focusing on this period in my work and in my imagination that even if I had no first-hand memory of wartime Europe, I was on familiar turf, having read everything I could get my hands on concerning this period in my obsessive need to understand the forces from which my life had sprung.

I knew that in the dark days following the fall of France and the Dunkirk evacuation, England found itself facing a solid wall of nations under Nazi domination along its North Sea and Channel coasts: Norway, Denmark, Germany, Holland, Belgium and France, all overrun by the enemy. No sooner had France capitulated than the first German bombers began to fly over England in the Battle of Britain. With America showing no interest in joining the struggle against Hitler and the evil he represented, the British dug in and prepared to fight alone.

The RAF was doing its best to hold the Germans back, but British air, sea and land forces were vastly outnumbered and outgunned. Winston Churchill understood that the only way to slow the Nazi onslaught was to stir up rebellion and resistance within the occupied territories and thus, divert the German high command away from its single-minded focus on the conquest of the British Isles. And so, Churchill ordered the creation of a volunteer civilian force with orders to "set Europe ablaze" through subversion and sabotage—the Special Operations Executive. This was the hastily created community that Colonel Colin Gubbins, SOE head of training and operations, later its chief, had invited my mother to join.

I knew, too, that the SOE had ceased to exist in 1946. Viewed with intense suspicion and distrust by the professional spies of MI6 and Britain's military intelligence establishment, who considered it a gang of undisciplined amateurs, the organization had been disbanded soon after the war's end. But I was hoping to gain access to old SOE files through my contacts in the Imperial War Museum and the Foreign and Commonwealth Office, who'd agreed to make other materials available for the Smithsonian's WWII exhibition. Now that more than thirty years had passed, I naively expected the strictures of the Official Secrets Act would no longer apply to the files of this extinct organization and that I would find in them the details of my mother's recruitment, training and service.

No such luck.

Many SOE files, I soon learned, had been caught in a blaze of rather vague origins and either destroyed outright or left so water- and fire-damaged as to be virtually useless. Others were scattered among various government ministries, which either couldn't or wouldn't release them, especially to a civilian Yank with no official reason for access. In the vast, strategic world of intelligence operations, I discovered, thirty years is a short enough time span that some players apparently still had their hand in the game. I was told that if such files existed, they continued to be highly classified. I could only conclude from this that they contained information on sources or tradecraft that was still current and could, if revealed, prove damaging to British interests.

But a chance conversation with a military historian at the War Museum, himself a veteran of the SOE (although he had worked in the Greek section and therefore had no memory of my mother) led me to a live source of information who proved more than willing to tell me what the files probably wouldn't have been able to even if I could have gotten my hands on them.

Miss Vivian Atwater had been principal assistant to the late Colonel Maurice Buckmaster, who'd overseen the training and assignment of saboteurs dropped into France. Buckmaster's name was another one I recognized from my research. Adolf Hitler himself was reported to have raged, "When I get to London, I'm not sure who I'll hang first, Winston Churchill or that man, Buckmaster!" When I met the very astute and efficient Miss Atwater, Buckmaster's right-hand aide, I knew she was a large part of the reason the Führer never got the chance to make that deadly decision.

Miss Atwater is seventy-one years old now and officially listed as retired, although she still has a small office in an obscure corner of an even more obscure building in Whitehall, the area of central London that is home to the British Ministry of Defense, the Prime Minister's residence at 10 Downing Street and assorted other government offices. Having gotten her number from my ex-SOE contact at the War Museum, I called her from my hotel. When she heard I was Grace Wickham's daughter, Miss Atwater said she would see me the next afternoon.

I trudged on foot to her office through misty rain, thrilled that

I was about to meet a woman who was herself a wartime legend. The address she'd given me was a low brick building at the end of a cul-de-sac just off Whitehall. A brass plaque on the door had the lion-and-unicorn crest of the British Crown and noted the building's address: 24-B Camden Court, but there was no indication of exactly which Crown ministry might be housed inside the premises. Neither was there a bell on the black-painted front door and so, after hesitating for a moment, I depressed the latch on the big brass handle and walked in.

I found myself in a small, walnut-lined lobby whose only occupant was a wizened little man sitting on a tall stool behind a high, Bob Cratchet style desk. Although he wore a dark suit pinstriped in gray, I wouldn't have been surprised to see him in an eye shade and arm garters, so much did he resemble some lowly clerk out of a Dickensian novel. Behind him stretched a long hall with closed doors on either side. It seemed to stretch to infinity, black and white tiles on the floor marching in ever-diminishing formation to a distant vanishing point.

I approached the old man, who was sitting hunched over what turned out to be one of the seamier British tabloids. I coughed softly to indicate my presence and the sound echoed down the cavernous hallway. The old man looked up, startled, and quickly slipped the tabloid under the desk, then folded his hands in front of him. "Can I help you, Miss?"

"I'm here to see Miss Vivian Atwater."

"I see. Is she expecting you, then?"

"Yes, I telephoned her yesterday. I have an appointment at three. My name is Jillian Meade."

He pulled a leather ledger out from under the desk and opened it, running a tobacco-stained finger down a handwritten list. Reading upside down, I spotted my name before he did, the last on the list and the only one with that day's date on it. The name listed above mine belonged to someone who'd apparently been by a couple of weeks earlier. Whatever else went on this building, it was clearly not a high-traffic area for visitors.

"Do you have some identification you can show me, Miss?"

I handed him my passport, which he perused page by page, pausing to check my face carefully against the photo inside. Then, after handing the passport back, he consulted his pocket watch and noted the time next to my name in the ledger, then turned it around for me to sign in.

"You'll find Miss Atwater in room 323. Third floor, end of the hall on your left, Miss. The lift's just there," he added, directing me to an ancient, screened-in elevator set into one side of the lobby, the kind with inner and outer accordion-style doors just waiting to pinch unwary fingers.

I took it up to the third floor. My War Museum contact had told me Miss Atwater's office and some small measure of administrative support had been granted to her in perpetuity (or for as long as she wished to take advantage of them) in recognition of her long and sterling service to the Crown, which even the SOE's detractors did not deny.

When I knocked at the heavy oak door of room 323, a woman's voice from within called, "Come!"

I opened the door to a wood-paneled room with a floor-to-ceiling bookcase covering one entire wall, all of it made warm and cheery by the glow of several Tiffany-style lamps, a small gas fire and the rich tapestry of a red Persian carpet that extended over most of the floor.

A rather prim-looking elderly woman sat behind a cherry-wood desk angled across the far corner of the room. Her hair was steel colored and rolled at the sides in a style that probably hadn't changed since the forties. Her long, lean face was lined with age but it was alert and intelligent-looking. Its only embellishment was a slash of bright red lipstick. She wore a gray woolen twin set and, I noted as she unfolded herself and rose from her chair, a matching tweed skirt. Her rather large feet were clad in laced brown leather Oxfords that squeaked as she made her way around the desk to greet me. If I had run into this woman on the street, I would have taken her for a librarian or the headmistress of a private school for girls. Certainly not a trainer of spies—which only goes to show, I suppose, how little we ordinary folk understand the real world of espionage, where anonymity is probably the greatest of all virtues.

Miss Atwater was tall, close to six feet, I guessed as she came over and extended a hand gnarled with arthritis. In spite of the infirmity, her grip was vicelike. "So you're Grace Wickham's daughter! How do you do, dear?" Her voice was raspy and rather loud, which led me to suspect she might be a little hard of hearing.

"It's very good of you to see me at such short notice, Miss Atwater."

"Not at all. Delighted, delighted. Let's have a seat over by the fire, why don't we? Damnably cold out there today."

Her manner was forthright and blunt compared to most of the British officials I'd encountered, but the smile she gave me was nearly as warm and welcoming as Nellie Entwistle's, with the same look of frank curiosity in her intelligent brown eyes.

"Remember Grace?" she bellowed in response to the question I posed as we settled into deep armchairs upholstered in worn and cracked green leather. They were arranged on either side of a low table in front of a small gas fire. "Course I remember her. Four hundred we sent over from F and I remember them all, every last one of them."

"F", I already knew, stood for the SOE's French section.

"Handled them all from A to Zed, you see. Interviewed them myself, recommended each one for duty."

"How did you recruit your agents, Miss Atwater?"

"Oh, they came to us mostly by way of in-house recommendations. We had talent-spotters out there, you see, looking for just the right kind of person. Most of the ones we took on in F Section were like your mum, half English, half French. General de Gaulle's doing. He insisted we leave the pure French nationals to him for his Free French army. Fair enough. His people were doing their bit to undermine the Nazis, of course, but his aim was to roll back into Paris, take the Elysée Palace, wasn't it? But we had strategic and defensive objectives he didn't necessarily share. Needed people we could control on our own."

"I was told it was Colonel Gubbins himself who spotted my mother," I said. "In Dover, it would have been, during the evacuation of Dunkirk."

"Did he? Well, that's possible. She showed up here in the fall of '41, as I recall. Had a flood of willing bodies after the damage done during the Blitz."

"How did you know which ones could do the job?"

She pursed her lips. "Instinct, more than anything. Had to have MI5 vet them before we could take them in, of course. Double agents could compromise operations, make a right mess of things, so we'd to be very cautious. Some of it was the skills they could offer. Had to have what we needed or it wasn't worth the candle, was it? Eliminated a lot of them on the first round of interviews. Did those myself at the old Northumberland Hotel. We'd requisitioned it for the duration of the war, you see. Brought 'em into a room, just me, two chairs, a table and lightbulb. Put 'em through their paces. Had to speak French like a native, obviously, or they'd never survive undercover. Had to understand the risks, too. Told 'em right off that they had a one-in-two chance of being captured and shot. Average life expectancy of our wireless operators was only six weeks. That was enough to frighten off a good lot of them, I can tell you."

"But not all, obviously. You still convinced four hundred to take up the challenge."

She nodded soberly. "A fine bunch they were, too. Absolutely dedicated. Several, like your mum, had already lost loved ones to the Germans. Highly motivated. Wanted to make Hitler's boys pay."

"So what happened after the initial interviews?"

"Sent them away."

"You sent them away? Where?"

She waved a hand airily. "Wherever. Didn't matter. Sent them off to think, because there was no turning back once they'd gone over, was there? They'd to think about what we were asking, decide whether they were prepared to make that kind of sacrifice. Course, it gave us time for MI5 to finish up the background security checks, as well."

"And after that?"

"After that, if we took them on, there were several weeks of training. Varied, of course, depending on what we wanted them to do. Most of them did four weeks at Wandsborough Manor outside the city, taking physical fitness, small arms training, map reading and the like. After that, it was up to Scotland for commando training. Or to Thames Park in Oxfordshire for wireless and cipher work. Depended on their skills and talents, you see."

"And then you sent them off?"

"Not quite. Once they were operationally ready, we still had to brief 'em on how to get on in occupied France. Even if they'd been before, you see, they had to be brought up to date on the curfews and regulations and such that the Nazis had imposed when they took over the place. Needed *cartes d'identité* and other bits of ID that could pass inspection. Continental clothing, accurate down to the smallest label. Couldn't have somebody caught wearing a shirt with a Dorset laundry mark on it, now could we? Filled their pockets with genuine ticket stubs and receipts—theater chits, worn ration books, authentic letters and keepsakes. Whatever it took to help them pass as locals."

Her high forehead corrugated in a frown. "I helped them draw up their wills, too, before they left." She fell silent for a moment and her gaze drifted down to the multicolored carpet. "I stood on the runway as each one of their planes took off for France, you know," she said quietly. "Wrote to their loved ones while they were out of touch to let them know they were safe and still alive."

"You obviously cared deeply about your agents, Miss Atwater."

She looked up once more and leaned her tall, angular body back into the chair. "Oh, yes. My ducks, they were. Fretted over them all. Monitored all the wireless traffic. Kept track of where they were, how they were getting on, whether they were getting enough to eat. Found myself counting heads every morning, worrying whether we still knew where each one was."

As I listened, I suddenly understood why, at seventy-one, Miss Atwater was still coming in to her small office every day, working so hard to keep the memory of the SOE alive. Why, as my museum contact said, she gave interviews and spoke to veterans' organizations. Why she was writing her memoirs. She'd never married, never had children of her own. This was her family she was talking about. Those agents had been her children, and like every mother who's ever lost a child, Miss Atwater was still haunted by the faces of the ones she'd watched take off in those airplanes bound for occupied France—and especially, I imagine, by the faces of those who never returned.

"Miss Atwater, I've been told that, when the war was over, you took it upon yourself personally to track down the ones who didn't make it back."

She nodded, sighing. "Oh, yes. Felt we owed it to them after all they'd done."

"Did you lose many?"

"One hundred and eighteen out of the four hundred we sent into France," she said without hesitation, the number clearly seared into her memory. "All but one of them caught by the Nazis and either shot outright or shipped off to concentration camps where they were subsequently murdered."

"All but one? What about that last one?"

Her broad, thin shoulders lifted in a dismissive shrug. "Disappeared in Monte Carlo. Compulsive gambler, it turned out. Bit of a bungle, I must say, taking that fellow on." She waved one gnarled hand dismissively. "But, there you have it, confusion of wartime and all. Bound to have one bad egg in the bunch, hey? Can't say he did any real damage to his cell, thank God. Wasn't in action long enough. Still, he had three million francs of secret service money when he vanished, the bugger. I'd like to get my hands on him, I would. The rest of them, though—absolutely solid. Heroes every one."

I leaned forward in my chair. "I read in a book about the Nuremberg war tribunal that your evidence helped to convict some of the Nazi leaders who were prosecuted there. That you personally went over to the continent to follow the trail of the agents you'd lost and interview their former captors."

"Oh, well, yes, had to do it myself, didn't I? Only person who could, you see. Hitler had issued a directive that all captured Resistance fighters were to vanish without a trace. 'Disappear in night and fog'—*Nacht und Nebel*—that was the operative phrase. Objective, of course, to instill fear in the general population. People simply vanished. Picked up and shipped back to Germany in total secrecy. Those left behind never knew if they were dead or alive. Even after the Nazis were defeated and the Allies got access to their records, we couldn't be certain about the fate of our own SOE agents, since they'd all been operating under fictitious names, documentation forged to conceal their true identities. But I knew every detail about my ducks—real names, code names, every hair on their heads. Could spot their tracks, couldn't I, no matter what?" Her lower lip jutted in grim satisfaction. "Tracked down the fate of every last one that we lost. Made sure their killers, if they were still alive, were brought to trial. Tea, dear?"

I'd been listening so intently that I was taken aback by her abrupt switch in direction, but I nodded and watched as she stretched out a long arm and pressed a button I hadn't noticed on the side of the low wooden table. Not that I really needed yet another cup of milky English tea, but I was eager to enjoy Miss Atwater's voluble hospitality for as long as she was willing to extend it. From somewhere outside her door and down the long, arched hallway, I heard a buzzer sound. Miss Atwater leaned back in her chair, lacing her arthritic fingers together in her tweedy lap. While we waited for something—I wasn't sure what—to happen, I returned to the charge.

"I was told it was you who got the confession out of Rudolf Höss, the commandant at the Auschwitz concentration camp. The confession that helped ensure his conviction at the Nuremberg war tribunal. What was that like?"

She placed a hand against her cheek, brown eyes flashing, and shook her head. "Bloody awful, to tell the truth. Terrible man! Accused him of having murdered a million and a half people at Auschwitz, and do you know what he answered, the vile bugger?"

I shook my head, although I imagined that Höss had probably resorted to the standard excuse of those who'd run the death camps—that he'd simply been following orders.

"He was offended!" Miss Atwater exclaimed. "Offended! Imagine! As if I'd insulted his professionalism. Told me, indignant as can be, 'Oh, no, Frau Atwater, if you please, not one and a half million. We exterminated two million, three hundred and forty-five thousand at Auschwitz.' Just like that. Can you imagine? Bloody Kraut, not the slightest sense of guilt, and still proud of his damnable efficiency!"

I agreed that it was an abomination. Miss Atwater sat in silence for a moment.

"I think of them every day, you know," she said at last. "The ones who went over. The ones who didn't come back. I remember how young they were, how much they had to live for. Thirty-nine women we sent in. Twelve of them died. One who was murdered at Auschwitz was the mother of three little girls. And yet, when she was asked to serve, she went willingly. They all died incredibly bravely. And it wasn't in vain, you know. I know that. But it was a terrible, horrible waste."

There was a short knock just then on the heavy wooden door of her office. Then a second, louder one when she appeared not to hear the first.

"Come!" Miss Atwater bellowed over her shoulder.

A young batman in military uniform entered carrying a tray, which he set on the table in front of us. It held a teapot, strainer, sugar bowl, two cups, and a plate of the inevitable Peak Frean biscuits. The milk, I noticed, had already been poured into the cups.

"Splendid! Thank you, Prescott," Miss Atwater told him. "We shall manage nicely from here."

The batman nodded and scarcely gave me a look as he turned and disappeared silently out the door, closing it firmly behind him once more. When I looked back at Miss Atwater, I saw a troubled expression furrowing her brow as she poured the tea.

"You say your mother is well, dear?" she asked.

"Quite well, yes. She still lives in the small town my father grew up in. It's in a rural area of Minnesota. She's made a comfortable life for herself there. She never remarried, but she has friends and she keeps busy. She seems content."

"I'm very glad to hear it. I must say, she's one I've fretted over. Thought about her often since the war ended, wondered how things went for her. For a couple of months after we retook France, you know, we thought we'd lost her."

I looked up, startled. "Really? I never knew that. Although to be honest, there's a lot I don't know about her wartime service. She almost never talks about the past."

"Hmmm..." The older woman's frown deepened. She handed me a cup and extended the sugar, which I declined, although I did accept a digestive biscuit.

"What do you remember about her, Miss Atwater?"

She took her own cup, dropped in two sugar cubes and stirred, her gaze fixed on the milky brown swirl. Putting down the spoon, she took a tentative sip, then said, "Well, she was beautiful, of course. To be honest, my first impression when she came to the Northumberland Hotel was that she wouldn't be any good at all for undercover work. You look for people who'll pass unnoticed in a crowd, you see. No chance of that with Grace. She had skills we could use, of course, but my initial recommendation was that she not be sent over. And, in fact, we didn't, not until...oh, the late spring of '43, I think it would have been."

"But she was recruited when?"

"Late summer or early fall of 1941, as I recall. The worst of the

Blitz was pretty much over by then, though I know Grace had lost her father during a German bombing run just a few months earlier."

I nodded. "I just got back from Dover. While I was there, I spoke to an old friend of my mother's who was with her the night my grandfather died. She said it was in June of '41. She said my mother had been carrying around Colonel Gubbins's card since the Dunkirk evacuation a year earlier, but that she never did anything about following up on it until after her father died."

"Yes, that's right. Now that you mention it, I remember her telling me that. And that her father's printing shop had been destroyed. Course, when I learned she'd worked with her dad and knew the trade, it was manna from heaven. Knew we could make good use of her, even without sending her into the field. We had a false documents section we were running out of an old roadhouse up in North London, you see. As I said, our agents needed all sorts of papers—identity cards, travel passes, work permits that would allow them to be where we needed them to be—that sort of thing."

She took another sip of her tea, then set the cup down on the edge of the table. "And your mum was brilliant, I must say. Spoke flawless French, and even a little schoolgirl German, which didn't hurt. But it was her abilities as a forger we found invaluable."

"A forger!" It was the first time I'd heard what my mother might actually have done in the war. But, of course, it made perfect sense when I thought about it. Forgers are simply, after all, skilled printers who ply their craft for nefarious ends.

"Yes, and a bloody brilliant one, as I said. Given a little time and the right materials, there wasn't anything Grace couldn't copy, we soon discovered. Could tell at a touch exactly what kind of paper a document was printed on. Knew at a glance the printing method that had been used—ink, typeface, the whole ball of wax. Bloody marvelous! She could produce a facsimile of any document so letter-perfect that even the originator would be hard-pressed to tell her copy from the real thing."

I felt a swell of pride as I listened to Miss Atwater speak of my mother's wartime role. I was already thinking how pleased my mother would be to know she was still remembered with such awe and admiration by someone like Miss Atwater, who'd been such a formidable force in her own right. But then, another frown moved in on Miss Atwater's features, like the arrival of a sudden storm front.

"I've often regretted that we moved her out of that section. She wanted to go over, of course. Had been pressing from the outset to move up to the front lines. She was young, of course. Restless as only young people can be, eager to be at the center of the action. But my instincts said it wasn't a good idea."

"Because of the way she looked?"

"Partly, yes. She drew too much attention to herself, even when she didn't mean to. Half the men who met her fell in love with her. And a right nuisance it was, I must say! Try to get a decent day's work out of a man who's mooning like a love-struck oaf. Ridiculous! Never had this sort of bother with the French, you know. They simply copulate and that's that. Very sensible. The bloody English, though, will insist on falling in love."

I laughed and was rewarded with a broad smile that lit up Miss Atwater's austere features. "I see your point," I said. "That was one more complication I'm sure you didn't need."

"How true," she agreed ruefully. "Bloody pain in the arse, to tell the truth."

"So, what happened? Why did you end up sending her into France?"

"Because in the end, there was so much more she could be doing over there. We had a cell outside Paris that had been asking us for months to send in a small printing press and someone to help organize an anti-occupation journal. The Germans were beginning to suffer major reversals on the front lines, and it was more important than ever to beef up the harassment of their forces behind the lines. There were millions of potential French recruits for the Resistance, good people who resented the German Occupation. Hated the Nazis' arrogance and brutality, and the appropriation of scarce food and valuable properties that rightfully belonged to

them. But at the same time, people were frightened. They needed
to know the Resistance was alive and strong, and had a real chance
of defeating the Nazis and throwing them out of the country. There
was so much someone with Grace's skills could do to help, and not
just by printing an underground journal, either. The Resistance
needed to plant disinformation to confound the Occupiers. We
wanted to flood the market with phony ration books and information on the black market—anything to undermine occupation
controls and rationing. Deny the Germans the resources they
needed to hold the country, you see. And Grace, with her skills as
a forger, could help with all of that."

Her broad shoulders lifted in a shrug. "The bottom line was they
needed her desperately and Grace herself wanted to go. There was
no question she could pass. Spoke perfect French with a slight Norman accent. Knew the country like the back of her hand. Compe-
tent and self-confident—although maybe too much, in my view."

"Too self-confident?"

"Oh, yes. She was very competitive, was our Grace. Tough-
minded, determined to win at all costs."

"Not surprising, after what the Germans had taken from her,
was it? And surely those are good qualities in a wartime scenario?"

"In principle, yes, but not if they lead an agent to take unnecessary risks."

"And you thought she would?"

"I fretted about it, yes. Right from the start. Even more so when
I talked to her about drawing up her last will and testament. It
was standard procedure, you see, in case they didn't make it back."

"And my mother?"

"She had no family anymore."

"There were a couple of uncles and some cousins in France."

"Yes, but she wasn't fond of them, it seemed. Actually disliked
them, in fact. Ended up naming the Red Cross as her only beneficiary. Totally cut the family off."

I smiled ruefully. "She did tell me that her cousins had been awful to her when they were growing up. I get the sense there was no love lost between them."

Miss Atwater nodded. "There you have it, then."

"But why should that make a difference to her operational potential?"

"Because, dear, when agents have loved ones they're hoping to come back to, they think carefully before they act. Avoid unnecessary risks. But Grace, you see, was leaving no one behind. Had nothing to lose. And that, I've found, can lead to fatal mistakes."

"But it didn't in her case, did it? After all, she was one of the ones who did come back."

"Yes, but she wasn't the same. Not the same at all."

"Is that so surprising?"

"Perhaps not." Miss Atwater reached for the teapot and raised one eyebrow in my direction to ask whether I wanted a refill.

I shook my head and sat, lost in thought for a moment while she topped up her own cup. "You said you lost track of her about the time France was retaken by the Allies," I reminded her. "That you thought she might have been captured and killed by the Nazis."

"Yes. We'd lost contact with her in June of 1944. Paris was liberated at the end of August, but when we sent people in to try to find out what had happened to her and to some of our other missing agents, they came up empty-handed."

"I was born on July 14, 1944," I said.

Miss Atwater studied me with a frown. "Yes, I know. Bastille Day. We only learned that later, of course, when Grace showed up again over here with you in tow. As it was, we'd no idea she'd had a child over there. It was partly our fault, of course, for leaving her in situ so long, but all reports said she was doing marvelous work." Miss Atwater's gray head shook sadly. "Utter madness for her to have stayed on, once she knew she was pregnant! She'd managed to avoid detection by the Gestapo longer than we'd ever have expected, but we'd never have left her in country if we'd known she was pregnant. As it was, she soldiered on, kept it a secret. Never the slightest hint in her wireless messages that anything was amiss."

"But then you lost her signal."

"Yes. The Paris Resistance circuit was like Swiss cheese, full of holes. When Grace stopped transmitting, we were certain she'd been betrayed. And so she had, it turned out. Was caught by the Gestapo, taken to their headquarters on Avenue Foch. Tortured, I expect, though she refused to talk about it. Severely traumatized, I would imagine. Ended up in the Drancy transport camp."

"My God!" I breathed. The name of that Parisian suburb was listed in my official documents. I had seen it a thousand times, and yet the penny had never dropped. I never realized until that moment that I'd been born not just in Drancy but in the transit camp that the Nazis had run there. "They shipped people to Auschwitz from Drancy!"

Miss Atwater nodded. "And so Grace would have been, too, except she gave birth to you and somehow missed the last train for Auschwitz. She was still at the transit camp when it was liberated by the Americans. When Grace told them the father of her child had been an American pilot who'd been shot down, rescued and sheltered by her Resistance cell, the Yanks took her in—took in the both of you, and gave you shelter until things settled down enough that she could make her way back here to England."

"And in all that time," I said, "neither she nor the Americans got in touch with you to let you know she was alive and well?"

"No. Turns out Grace didn't let on she was one of ours. Just said she was half English, half French, and had been living in France throughout the war, working with the Resistance. The Yanks treated her as just another war bride. Eventually arranged for her to sail to America with a shipload of war brides."

"But why didn't she get in touch with you?"

"That's what I asked her when I finally got wind of the fact that she wasn't dead or captured. Far from it, she was back here in England, living in a bed-sit up in the north end of London, waiting for passage to America. I went to see her, but she was in a terrible state. Didn't want to talk to me."

"Why?"

Miss Atwater exhaled a heavy sigh. "Because she was furious with us. Your father had been betrayed as the Resistance was trying to smuggle him out of France, you see."

"Yes, she did tell me that."

"We knew Grace's cell had been sheltering a downed American pilot, of course. Didn't know he and your mother had fallen in love, of course, much less that she'd had his child. When he was captured, though, she became convinced the leak had come from our end. We think it was a double agent working for the Gestapo inside the Paris circuit who told them where they could find him, but nothing I said could convince your mother, and, of course, I couldn't prove it. It was a very confusing period when your father was killed. There'd been a theft of gold not long before, you see, a rather large cache that the Nazis had appropriated from Jewish families they'd deported to the concentration camps. They were getting ready to send it back to Berlin when it vanished, stolen by the Resistance. Hitler was enraged, they say, and ordered the Gestapo in Paris to pull out all the stops to roll up the Resistance and find the gold. The pressure on everyone on the ground there would have been dreadful. I tried to point out to your mother that any number of people could have betrayed him."

"But my mother didn't believe it?"

"No. Or, at the very least, she thought that even if the leak hadn't come from our side, we'd known in advance that the Germans had got wind of your father's presence and were setting a trap to capture him. She thought we knew about it but kept silent because to do otherwise would have revealed our source of information."

"She thought you sacrificed my father in order to protect your own operations?"

"In essence, yes, that's what Grace believed."

"And so he was betrayed, captured and then shot by the Gestapo," I finished quietly. I drew a deep breath and considered carefully before asking the next question. "And did you, Miss Atwater? Did you stand by and do nothing while the Germans set a trap for my father?"

She shook her head sadly. "No, dear. I can't prove a negative, of course, but I swear to you on my honor—on the memory and soul of every one of my murdered agents—that we played no role, by act or omission, in your father's death. I only wish you could convince your mother of that. And convince her, too, how dreadfully sorry I was—and still am—for her terrible loss."

CHAPTER 16

Havenwood, Minnesota
Friday, January 12, 1979

One of the fringe benefits of a career so closely associated with sudden death, Cruz often thought—although "benefit" might be putting too positive a spin on it—was that it provided a constant reminder of the virtue of a simple life. It's difficult to keep up appearances when you're dead. Other people are left to settle your affairs, and so they end up sniffing through your personal belongings and picking apart your unfinished business. God help you if you've been putting up a false front or hiding skeletons, because when you die, the truth will almost invariably come out. Some might say it only matters if the dead can be held to account for themselves. The corrupt among us gamble on the odds of an afterlife—if there's none, they're home free. But if more people felt a little anticipatory shame about how they'd be judged once they were no longer able to cover their tracks, Cruz thought, they might lead their lives in ways that put them in less danger of postmortem humiliation.

Grace Meade had solved part of the problem by managing to die in an inferno that had consumed all her material possessions. She'd also arranged for sympathetic mourners. Chief among these were Tom and Sybil Newkirk. After he met them, Cruz knew they would do their utmost to polish Grace's legacy to a golden luster. If she was watching from her afterlife, all she had to worry about were any old secrets she might have been hiding—because old secrets, Cruz knew, had a nasty habit of coming out of dark hiding places after death like snakes slithering out after a rain to bask in the glare of the sun.

Ollie Jorgenson had told him that Grace's Lakeshore Road neighbors were her closest friends in Havenwood. Given Jillian's current unfortunate state, the task of organizing the funeral and memorials had fallen on the Newkirks. In addition, Ollie said, word was already out that Tom Newkirk, the town's mayor and only practicing lawyer, had sole power of attorney over Grace's affairs and had long ago been named executor of her estate. The Grace Meade groupies in town apparently saw this latest bit of news as further evidence of Jillian's shameful neglect of her mother. Obviously poor Grace had felt she had good reason to mistrust her daughter. Why else, they asked, eyebrows raised, would she have felt it necessary to appoint an outside executor to keep her daughter's fingers out of her affairs? Those with a more conspiratorial turn of mind were even going so far as to wonder if Grace had had a premonition Jillian intended to do her harm.

"Do you believe that, Ollie?" Cruz asked as he finished his breakfast. "That Jillian Meade hated her mother? I spoke to her boss at the Smithsonian, and he said she'd been very concerned about her mother's cancer scare last year. That doesn't sound to me like a daughter who means her mother harm."

Ollie Jorgenson let out a snort of contempt. "Course she didn't. Jillian's always been a good kid."

"So why is this town so divided in their opinion of her?"

"Oh, I don't know. People like to talk, and whatever they don't know for sure, they'll just go ahead and make up. And what did that P. T. Barnum fellow say about public relations?"

"You mean, 'all publicity is good publicity'?"

"That's it. For better or worse, Grace was a one-woman PR machine for herself. The grumblers' biggest complaint was that she took on more than her fair share of the top jobs and so, of course, got all the glory and credit that went with them. Jillian, on the other hand, was invisible—out of sight and out of mind for the most part. Even when she lived here, she was so far back in her mother's shadow that not many people really knew her all that well. And have you ever noticed how most people will mistrust anyone they don't know real well? It's pretty stupid, but I guess that's just human nature."

"Jillian told her boss she was coming back here to spend Christmas with her mother, but I gather she never came. Do you have any idea why?"

"None at all," Ollie said. "I haven't spoken to either Jillian or Grace in quite a while. Until the fire, I hadn't even heard Jillian was back in town, although Norbert tells me she was here that afternoon, buying gas. News to me. I must have been up at the house when she came by, because I didn't see her. As for why she didn't come at Christmas...well, I honestly don't know what happened there. I'd talk to the Newkirks, if I were you. If anyone can tell you why she changed her mind, they might."

When Cruz posed the question to Sybil Newkirk a short while later, she paused to rip a tissue from the box at her side, then shook her head. "I have no idea why Jillian showed up out of the blue like that," she mumbled through the tissue between bouts of nose blowing. Her eyes were red-rimmed and rheumy, her skin florid, and damp gray tendrils of hair stuck to her temples. She looked as if she had a bad case of flu—or, as it soon became evident, had been crying for the better part of the last two days.

A small, round woman, she'd met Cruz at her back door wearing a lime-green jumpsuit made of some kind of stretchy material that was not kind to a person of her girth, the one-piece outfit cinched with a wide, black patent leather belt. She'd given a knowing nod when he introduced himself, word of his presence in town obviously preceding him once again.

Before he could explain why he was calling on her, he was interrupted by the ringing of the telephone. Mrs. Newkirk gave a weary sigh and waved at him to follow as she tottered unsteadily on flapping, low-heeled mules up the three or four steps from the back vestibule into the kitchen. The smell of juniper seemed to permeate the house, no doubt from the large stand of evergreens that lined the road and driveways. Cruz stood by while she took the call, puffing from the exertion, her belt buckle straining mightily to hold the line.

The call was from a florist, it seemed, regarding funeral wreaths for the church and cemetery. After she had dispatched the call, reiterating several times that Grace would have wanted white flowers—and white flowers only—she hung up, rolled her puffed eyes in exasperation, and invited Cruz to sit down at the kitchen table.

It was nestled into an alcove where a multi-paned window offered a panoramic view of the frozen lake and the burned-out rubble of the Meade home next door. Mrs. Newkirk had obviously been working at the table before Cruz arrived. Spread around her now were a pad and several loose sheets of paper covered with scrawled lists, a tissue box, a glass of ice water, and the telephone, its long, coiled cord stretching to the counter behind her. She sniffed one last time, then tossed her tissue onto a soggy pile at her elbow that was beginning to spill over onto the floor around her, although she took no notice.

"Jillian was supposed to come for Christmas this year," she said. "Grace told us way back around Thanksgiving that she was, and I was glad to hear it. That girl didn't come home nearly often enough, not even for the holidays. That's just not right, is it?"

It was not a rhetorical question, apparently, because she fixed Cruz with an arched eyebrow and a wide, expectant stare that allowed him to see every tiny red branch of the delta of blood vessels crisscrossing the slightly jaundiced whites of her eyes. He gave a vague, noncommittal nod, which seemed to be all the agreement Mrs. Newkirk needed.

"There you go, then. The girl was spoiled, if you ask me. Poor Grace did her best, but having to raise Jillian without a husband's help...well, kids need discipline, don't they? And Helen and Arthur...Grace's in-laws, you know...Joe's folks? Bless their souls, they were good people, and nobody should say any different, but they were already old when Grace and Jillian came to live with them. They couldn't be the firm hand the girl needed. They doted on her, and she could do no wrong in their eyes. But it doesn't do to spoil a child that way, does it?"

"What did Mrs. Meade say when Jillian failed to show for Christmas?"

"Oh, the usual," she said, reaching for her glass and taking a sip. "Something about Jillian's work keeping her too busy, I don't know. What could be so important that she couldn't take a few days off to spend the holidays with her mother?"

"I have no idea," Cruz said honestly. "What about the trip Jillian took to Europe about three or four weeks ago? Did you hear anything about that?"

"Jillian was in Europe?"

"England and France, apparently."

"Really? Grace never mentioned it. But, isn't that just typical? She has time to go traipsing off to Europe, but not to visit her mother."

"So you don't know whether or not Mrs. Meade was aware her daughter had gone over there?"

"Oh, I'm sure Grace didn't know, or she would have mentioned it." She frowned. "She did get a call from Jillian, oh, about a month ago or so, I think it would have been. At that point, Jillian was still planning to come for Christmas, but I'm sure Grace never said anything about her going overseas. Of course, knowing Jillian, it's no surprise she never mentioned it. A person never really knew what was going on with that girl."

"Did she—"

Just then, the telephone rang again. "Oh, hell's bells, I'm sorry!" Mrs. Newkirk said. "I've got to get this. The funeral's tomorrow, you know, and there's just so much to do."

"It's not a problem."

She gave him a brave smile as she picked up. "Hello?...Oh, Hilda, yes, thanks for getting back. ...Oh, yeah, you can say that again. I'm just sick over it." She fumbled for another tissue. "Yes, it was me called it in. I was just heading off to bed, you know, when I noticed the smoke and a funny light coming from over in Grace's front room. Flickering orange and red, it was. Just awful. Tom was down in Minneapolis that night, so I called Nils Berglund. He got here a couple of minutes later, and the fire trucks weren't long after that, but it went up so fast, you can't imagine! ...Well, yes, thanks, hon. I'm coping best I can. Keeping busy, what with the arrangements and all. It's the only thing I can do for poor Grace now," she added, her voice breaking.

She fell silent for a moment, sniffling, while a tiny voice escaping from the phone made 'there-there' noises. Then, Mrs. Newkirk took a deep breath and soldiered on. "I know, I know, Hilda. Thanks. Anyway, there's someone here, so I can't talk right now, but I was wondering if I could put you down for that jellied salad of yours for the luncheon? You know, the one you brought to the Founder's Day dinner? ...Oh, I'm sure it doesn't matter if it's orange instead of lime. It's real nice, either way. ...Uh-huh, basement of the church. I'm just having everyone drop things off before the service. The auxiliary will finish setting up the food while we're out at the cemetery. ...Oh, good. Thanks, hon. ....Uh-huh. Eleven o'clock.... Okay then, see you tomorrow."

She spent a moment wiping her eyes and blowing her nose again, then took a deep sip from her water glass before turning back to Cruz. "I'm real sorry. It's been like this ever since the night of the fire."

"No, I'm the one's who's sorry, Mrs. Newkirk. I'll try not to hold you up too long. I'm sure this must be awfully difficult, losing your friend like this."

"Oh, it is! I still can't believe she's gone, you know? Grace and I, we were like sisters. It's been over thirty years since she came to town, and we saw each other almost every day. In fact, just a little while ago," she said, nodding at the papers before her on the table, "I was working on her obituary notice for the *Herald,* and I said to myself, 'I should pop over next door and see what Grace thinks, she always knows just the right thing to say,' and then I looked over at that—that thing over there...." Her voice trailed off and she waved her hand miserably in the general direction of the blackened rubble next door, while a few more tears traced a ragged trail along her rounded cheeks.

"You're certainly going to miss having her around."

"Oh, my gosh, yes." She sniffled into her tissue. "Twenty years now we've been next-door neighbors. There wasn't a day went by Tom or I wasn't over there, or she wasn't over here."

"Mr. Newkirk's not home right now, is he? I was hoping to speak with him."

"No. He was going to take the day off to help me with these arrangements, but really, there's nothing he can do here. He'd just be in the way, and he's got more than enough to do at the office."

"Someone told me he's the executor of Mrs. Meade's estate."

"Uh-huh, he is. I don't really know much about that, though. Tom did all Grace's legal and business work for her." She fell silent for a moment as her gaze wandered back next door. "We actually own that lot, you know. Tom bought it right after the war, same time he bought this one to build our house on. We never planned to build over there, at least not until our kids were grown. He bought it on spec. Ours was one of the first lake-front places built at this end of the town, but Tom knew this land would be in demand as the town grew. We thought one of our kids might want to be next door one day, but then, after Helen and Arthur died, Grace and Jillian were on their own out at the Meades' place. Way across on the other side of town it was, you know. Took a lot of upkeep, and Tom couldn't see how Grace was going to manage a big old place like that all on her own. He did his best to help her out, but he was already putting in real long hours at work. The kids and I hardly saw him, he was that busy, what with setting up his practice and then his various community activities. He was the one had the idea to lease Grace the lot next door. He let her have it for next to nothing, a couple of dollars a year, you know. Helped her hire a builder, plan her own brand-new house. Wrote it up so she could have that lot for the rest of her days."

"That was very generous of him."

"Oh, for sure. But then, Tom's like that, and where Grace and Jillian were concerned.... Well, he and Joe Meade had been best friends, you see, ever since they were little boys. Like brothers, really. After Joe was killed in the war, Tom felt it was his duty to keep an eye on Joe's wife and daughter. That's just the kind of fella he is. Of course, he knew I'd be real pleased to have Grace for a neighbor, too."

"Your husband sounds like a very good man, Mrs. Newkirk."

"Oh, he's a keeper, all right. Next year's our thirty-fifth anniversary, you know."

"Congratulations."

"Thank you. I'm real sorry you missed him, Agent Cruz."

"I may try to catch up with him in town," Cruz said. He nodded at the phone. "I heard you saying you were the one who called in the fire alarm?"

Mrs. Newkirk nodded. "I was just putting a glass in the dishwasher before heading off to bed when I looked over and saw it."

"Had you noticed anything unusual over there earlier in the evening?"

Mrs. Newkirk looked down at her hands, wringing her tissue. Suddenly, she reached for the glass at her side, but her hand missed and knocked it a sideways so that some of the contents splashed on the table. Using the side of her hand as a blade, she wiped the spilled drops onto the floor, and then lifted the glass to her lips. When she set the glass down again, her movements were slow and painfully deliberate. "I told Nils Berglund," she said, "so I guess I can tell you, too."

"Told him...?"

She exhaled heavily and slumped forward, arms crossed on the table. "That they'd been arguing."

"Who?"

"Jillian and Grace. I heard them. Jillian seemed halfway to hysterical."

"Do you know what she was upset about?"

"No idea. You know, I haven't actually talked to her since she got in. Grace had called that afternoon to tell me Jillian had come on a surprise visit, and she invited me over. But Grace was heading out to the hairdresser shortly, and I didn't feel comfortable going over there and getting stuck with just Jillian, you know, so I decided I'd wait and pop over after dinner. I was barely out my back door, though, when I heard the yelling."

"Who was doing the yelling?"

"Oh, Jillian mostly. I could hear Grace answering, and she sounded upset, but she was nowhere near as loud as Jillian. Of course, Grace wouldn't be. Mostly, though, it was Jillian I heard."

"What was she saying?"

She shrugged. "I honestly couldn't tell you. The windows were all shut up tight, of course, in this weather, so I couldn't really make it out, even when I stood right up close to the door." She caught herself and looked up at him. "Not that I was trying to eavesdrop or anything. Of course, I wouldn't, but a person can't help hearing, can they? All I knew was that they were having a big argument and it probably wasn't a good time to visit, so I turned around without knocking and tiptoed on back home."

"So, you have no idea what the argument was about?"

"Nope. I couldn't hear a thing clearly, except once or twice, when Jillian yelled, 'Tell me!' What all that was about, though, I couldn't say."

"Had you ever heard them argue like that before?"

"Never. Never, never, never," she said firmly, shaking her head vigorously. "I still can't believe Jillian would speak to her mother in that tone. It sounds awful to say, but she's always been kind of a wimpy sort. And, as for Grace, it certainly wasn't like her to get into a big row like that. She was a very sophisticated person, you know. Here, look," Mrs. Newkirk added, sitting upright and rummaging around among the papers until she found a couple of photographs under the pile. "I was looking for a good picture to run with her obituary. I knew I had plenty of snaps of her, but most of them had other people in them. I did come across a couple of her alone, though, and I was just trying to decide which one to use. This one's the better shot, I think, but it was taken years and years ago."

She pushed a saw-tooth edged black-and-white photo across the table to Cruz. It was an outdoor shot of a very pretty woman from the waist up, sitting at what looked like a wooden picnic table, a line of pine trees behind her in the distance. Her pale gaze was direct, amused, her blond hair smoothed back and caught somehow behind her head. The collar of her dress was the sort of off-the-shoulder, rolled style that Cruz remembered his aunt wearing when he was a kid, although he never remembered Aunt Luisa having as voluptuous a bosom or as tiny a waist as this woman had. The string of pearls around Grace's neck barely grazed the top of her collarbone, and her skin of her neck and shoulders looked like fine porcelain. The smile she gave the camera was as cryptic as the Mona Lisa's.

"Everyone has told me she was a beautiful woman," he said. "I can see why."

Mrs. Newkirk nodded. "Tom took this shot of her out in our backyard here one Fourth of July. It must have been...oh, 1955, 1956, maybe? And then, there's this other one," she added, pushing a second photo, also black and white, across to him. "It's really not as good—she's farther away, and it's not as clear as the other one. This one was taken just last year, when Grace was emceeing the Christmas concert the Sunday School choir from our church put on for the seniors' center."

In this shot, Mrs. Meade stood at a podium, smiling warmly out at the camera, which must have been situated front and center in the audience, because its sight line was uninterrupted. One of her delicate hands gripped the top of the podium, while the other extended gracefully out to her side, as if soliciting applause for the unseen choir. She wore a dark-colored, two-piece sweater set with what looked to be the identical set of pearls at her throat. Her classic hairstyle was much the same as it had been in the photo taken more than twenty years earlier, Cruz noted. The only difference between the way she looked then and now was that her hair was lighter, possibly silver rather than blond, and her body and her face were slightly rounder. Her skin, however, was still remarkably clear and smooth. Altogether, Cruz thought, a very handsome woman.

"This is a good shot, as well," he said.

"Tom took that one, too. He always did take a good picture. Of course, Grace was a good subject. But which one do you think I should send in to the paper?"

"It's a tough choice. Which do you think she would have liked to see used?"

"Oh, Lord," Mrs. Newkirk said, holding her hands up, "neither! Grace just hated seeing her picture in the paper. She used to hold up her hand in front of her face if someone tried to take her picture and tell them to go shoot someone or something else.

And if they got one of her, anyway, when she wasn't looking and she caught the editor of the paper getting ready to put it in? She always made him take it out."

"A modest lady."

"Well, there you go. That just proves it, doesn't it?"

"Proves what?"

"What a good person she was. You know, Agent, you're going to hear talk as you go around, but you mustn't listen to it."

"Talk about...?"

She waved an impatient hand. "Oh, that Grace hogged the spotlight. But that's just jealous people talking. It's not true at all. Grace worked real hard, and if she'd really been trying to hog the spotlight, there wouldn't have been a single issue of the *Herald* that didn't have her in there for one thing or another she was doing. I can tell you, no one in this town planned anything without checking with Grace first, because you never wanted to have a conflict with anything Grace was organizing. That was one way to make very sure no one showed up at your do. Grace managed everything beautifully, but she didn't do it for personal glory or so she could get her picture in the paper every week. She just didn't want that kind of attention. But I can tell you," Sybil Newkirk said, her lower lip trembling and her eyes brimming once more, "she's going to get her picture in there now if I have anything to say about it". She picked up the two snapshots, looking from one to the other and back again. "If I could only decide which one! What do you think?"

"Well...to be honest?" Cruz said. "Speaking strictly as an outsider, I think you should go with the more recent one. As you say, Mrs. Meade was always front and center organizing things here in Havenwood. I guess I'd have to say this one really speaks to her civic involvement." He tapped the shot of Grace Meade at the podium.

Mrs. Newkirk gave him a look of teary gratitude, and for a moment, Cruz was afraid she was going to leap up and hug him.

"Oh! You're so right! That's real good thinking! It's just the kind of thing Grace would have said." Mrs. Newkirk began searching through the papers on the table once more.

"Anyway," Cruz said, watching as she paper-clipped the photo to a handwritten sheet that must have been the obituary she'd been preparing when he arrived, "you were saying that it seemed to be Jillian doing most of the shouting that night when you heard them arguing."

"Uh-huh. What I started out to say was that you can see from these pictures what a lady Grace was, can't you? I don't think I ever heard her raise her voice in all the years I've known her. She didn't have to. If Grace wasn't happy about something, you knew it, but to raise her voice the way Jillian did the other night? Never. That's why I tiptoed away when I heard them arguing. I knew Grace would be have been mortified. She raised Jillian better than that, I can tell you. I think she would have been embarrassed to think I'd overheard. And, anyway," she sniffed, "I knew Grace would tell me all about whatever this latest problem of Jillian's was after she'd gone back to Washington. As I say, we were just...like...sisters...."

At that, her voice completely broke and the tears started again. Cruz patted her hand awkwardly, racking his brain for an exit line. He doubted there was much else to be gotten out of this distraught woman, but he sensed Sybil Newkirk would sit here offering tributes to her friend for as long as he was prepared to be her audience. He stole a glance at his watch. After eleven already, and he still wanted to get over to Montrose to see if Jillian Meade was better and try to convince the shrink to let him have a couple of minutes with her. Otherwise, he had no chance of getting out of town today, and his weekend would be shot—not that he had any plans, anyway.

He was just about to take his leave when Mrs. Newkirk looked up, startled at the sound of tires pulling into the drive outside. A moment later, a car door slammed. She grabbed another tissue and was drying her tears as the latch on the back door clicked and a tread announced itself on the vestibule step. Cruz turned in his chair to see a silver-haired man entering the kitchen.

"Oh, Tom, you're home!" Sybil Newkirk said, jumping to her feet. One of her mules seemed to have slipped off her foot, and she stumbled. Cruz grabbed her elbow for support while she righted herself and slipped the shoe back on, then set about tidying her papers. "This is that fellow from the FBI, Tom," she added, smiling over her shoulder. "His name is...is...?"

"Special Agent Alex Cruz," he said, getting to his feet and slipping around her in the tight space to face the other man.

Mrs. Newkirk nodded quickly. "Yes, that's it. I'm sorry, I'm just so bad with names. This is my husband, Tom," she added. "Tom, the agent here just dropped by to see you, but I told him he'd probably find you at the office."

Newkirk studied her and the clutter on the table. There was a moment of silence, and a tension Cruz couldn't quite put his finger on seemed to fill the room, but it vanished so quickly he wasn't sure he hadn't imagined it, because Newkirk smiled broadly and leaned over to give his wife a peck on the cheek. Then, he turned and offered his hand. "Agent Cruz, welcome to Havenwood. I only wish you'd found things in a little happier state than they are right now."

"I'm sorry for your trouble," Cruz said. "It's a nice town you've got here, Your Honor."

"Oh, please, none of that 'your honor' stuff here. It's Tom, just Tom. And thanks for the good words. It's just a small town, but I guess we're all pretty attached to the place."

Like every politician he'd had ever met, Newkirk retained a rock solid grip on Cruz's hand longer than was absolutely necessary. He couldn't seem to resist slapping his shoulder while his blue-gray eyes fixed Cruz's with that approximation of an honest man's regard that must be taught in political hack school.

Newkirk was as tall and lean as his wife was short and

round—Jack Sprat and his spouse. Somewhere in his sixties, he had a high forehead and swept-back fins of silver hair that curled stylishly over an open-necked, striped shirt. He wore a black wool sweater over the shirt, and a two-tone bomber jacket with a crest on the left breast that featured two stylized *H*'s. Havenwood High? Cruz wondered. Mature, seasoned, but with a measure of casual cool was the look Newkirk seemed to be going for. No doubt it appealed to the ladies and the younger voters.

"So, what are you up to here, honey?" he asked his wife, his smile never wavering.

"I was just working on the arrangements for the lunch after Grace's funeral and her obituary and the flowers and all."

"And how's it going? Everything coming together?"

"Oh, yes, really well. I've had a very busy morning, but I think it's all in place now. Can I get you something? Some lunch maybe, or a cup of coffee? I offered one to Agent Cruz here, but he said no."

"No, I don't need anything, either, thanks. I'm having lunch over at the Elks in a little while with Charlie Peterson and some of the boys. I just dropped by to make sure you were all right."

"Oh, I'm fine, really!" she said brightly, her eyes sparkling.

"Do you think maybe you should go and lie down for a while, now that you've got this in hand?"

She glanced from him to Cruz and back. "Well, maybe that wouldn't be a bad idea. I haven't slept a wink the last two nights since...well, since everything. I think I will at that. You remember that we have to go over and see Reverend Allsop at four about the order of service?"

"I remember," her husband said. "I'll be back here in plenty of time. Why don't you go and stretch out, and I'll switch off the phone ringer so you won't be bothered. I'll be sure to wake you in time to get ready."

She nodded and reached for her glass, but Newkirk held out his hand for it. She gripped it to her ample bosom. "Tom, I want this."

"Sweetheart—"

"I really need it today," she argued, her eyes pleading. "Please!"

In her voice Cruz heard the desperate whine of the addict, and he suddenly knew it wasn't water in the glass. The odd juniper smell that had been bothering him since he'd walked in came from gin and not the trees, and Mrs. Newkirk's flushed features and jaundiced eyes were the result of more than just grief over the loss of her friend. Newkirk shot an uncomfortable glance in his direction, then nodded at his wife. She gave them both a nervous smile.

"Well, I think I will go and lie down for a little while. It's been a really stressful morning. It was nice to meet you, Agent... um...Agent. And thanks for your help with the picture."

"My pleasure, ma'am. And once again, I'm very sorry for your loss."

She nodded and smiled through teary eyes, then tottered over to her husband and reached up for a kiss. He dodged her lips and gave her another peck on the cheek, his smile strained as she turned and shuffled out of the room, the heels of her mules clacking on the tile floor. He and Cruz stood in silence for a moment, listening, as a slight clatter sounded from a nearby room, the unmistakable sound of ice cubes being dropped into a glass, followed by a liquid gurgle. Then, her heels tapped on the hall floor once more, a distant door latch clicked, and the house fell silent.

Newkirk turned to him, and to the man's credit, Cruz thought, he neither explained nor apologized. The problem he lived with was all too clear, but Tom Newkirk had obviously chosen to stick it out and carry on.

"What did my wife mean about you helping her with a picture?" he asked.

Cruz nodded at the papers on the table. The sheet with Grace Meade's picture paper-clipped to it sat on top of the pile. "Your wife was trying to decide what picture to give to the paper for

Mrs. Meade's obituary, that one or an older one taken at a Fourth of July picnic."

Newkirk frowned and stepped over to the table, shuffling through the papers until he turned up the older photo. He stared at it for a long moment, then laid it down on the pile.

"She was a beautiful woman," Cruz said.

Newkirk nodded. "Yes, she was. But I think it's silly to run old pictures like that in death notices, don't you? Who are we trying to kid? We all know what the person really looked like."

"I think you're right, although in this case, she had nothing to fear from just about any picture anyone chose to run of her, I would think."

"That's true." Newkirk turned to face him. "Sybil said you had some questions for me?"

"Just a couple. I gather you're the executor of Mrs. Meade's estate?"

"That's right."

"Can you tell me who the beneficiary is?"

"Well, Jillian, of course, gets a good chunk of it, although most of what she's getting is the reversion of her trust from Helen and Arthur Meade, her grandparents."

"How's that?"

"They left the bulk of their estate to her, although she was just a child when they died, so it was put into a trust. Grace had borrowed from the trust to build her house next door, so much of it was tied up in that property."

"Was that legal, if the trust was Jillian's?"

"Oh, completely. The terms of the trust allowed Grace to draw on it for Jillian's care and upkeep. Grace had very little income of her own, just a small widow's pension from her husband. She also got the proceeds of her own father's estate in England, although that was mostly in dribs and drabs because of the currency controls that were put in place after the war to keep capital from fleeing the country."

"What about the grandparents' house? Mrs. Newkirk said Grace and Jillian were living in it after they died, but that it was too much to keep up. Wasn't the sale of the old house enough to finance the building of the new?"

"Well, yes, it was, but the house was part of Jillian's inheritance, so the sale money went into the trust. As I say, though, I'd helped to set up the terms of the trust, so I knew Helen and Arthur would have no problem with Grace borrowing on it to build the new place. It was, after all, primarily to give Jillian a good home that it was built. The trust came to Jillian free and clear when she turned twenty-five, but by then, she was starting to make her own living, and she agreed to leave things as they stood. She had no interest in turning her mother out of her home."

"So that house next door—or rather, the insurance on it— that's not part of Mrs. Meade's estate?"

"No. What's in her estate is primarily the income on her investments from what she was able to set aside from her father's estate when it was finally settled and closed out in the early sixties, plus the proceeds from her life insurance policy. That's about it."

"So she wasn't a wealthy woman."

"Not at all. She lived comfortably, but not extravagantly. I think some people in town thought she was well off because her home was nicely put together and Grace was always well turned out. But she was one of those people who believed in paying a little more to get the best quality, whether in clothes or furnishings or whatever. It was cheaper in the long run, because they lasted forever. Grace was pretty shrewd, really, about things like that."

"And you own the land the house sat on, your wife said."

"Yes, that's right. It reverts back to me, now that Grace is gone."

"Mr. Newkirk, who do you think killed her?"

He passed a liver-spotted hand over his lined, handsome face. "I don't know. Chief Lunders thinks it was some drifter looking to score drug money."

"Nils Berglund's not quite so wedded to that theory, it seems, though."

"No."

"But he doesn't think it was Jillian, either."

"Neither do I. Jillian would never kill her mother." Newkirk glanced down the hall, then back at Cruz. "No matter what anyone might tell you."

"Your wife did mention an argument the two of them had that night."

"Agent Cruz," Newkirk said, his voice dropping, "this is a little awkward. My wife...well, her nerves are bad. She was very fond of Grace, and this has really upset her, naturally. But I think you have to take what she says with a little grain of salt. She's been under the weather for some time, and she sometimes misinterprets things."

"So you don't think there was an argument?"

"I have no idea whether there was or not. I only know that it would be out of character for Jillian to behave the way Sybil says she did, and I'm also virtually certain that she wasn't the one who killed Grace."

"So you ascribe to the Berglund theory that there's still an unknown perp wandering around out there somewhere?"

"I'm certain there must be, and if Nils is, as well, it's because of what I told him I'd seen that day."

"I thought you were away on a business trip the day Grace Meade died."

"I was. I'd left for the Twin Cities early that morning. I had a meeting with the governor, who was then catching a noon flight out to Washington. I went along to the airport with a number of other people to see him off, and I ran into Jillian there. She came in on the same plane the governor was going back out on."

"So, you saw her at the airport when she arrived?"

"Yes, I did."

"And did you speak to her?"

"Very briefly. I was pretty surprised to see her, as you can imagine, but real glad, too. She's a very nice girl. I guess you could say I've always had a soft spot for Jillian. Felt sorry for her, you know, growing up without a dad."

"I understand you and her father were close friends."

Newkirk nodded. "Best friends, Joe and I, right from kinder-garten—pretty much inseparable. We were in the service to-gether right up until his plane went down in France."

"So you felt you should be a substitute father to Jillian?"

"Well, I don't know if I could ever do that, but I did feel a re-sponsibility to watch out over her, for sure."

"Did she say why she never showed up at Christmas?"

Newkirk frowned, then glanced at his watch. "Do you mind if I walk you out while we talk, Agent Cruz? I don't want to dis-turb Sybil, and I've got a couple of errands I need to run before that lunch date."

"No, it's not a problem at all. I really need to get going, too." Cruz picked up his coat off the kitchen chair, took one last look at the two photos of Grace Meade with her lovely, cryptic smile, and followed the older man toward the vestibule and out the back door. "So, Jillian? Christmas, Mr. Newkirk?" he coaxed.

Newkirk held out his hand to lead Cruz forward, as they walked over to the two cars parked side by side in the wide driveway, Cruz's rented Buick and a blue Oldsmobile. The smell of burnt wood once again insinuated itself into Cruz's nostrils, but at least it cleaned out what he now realized was the cloying scent of gin.

"Jillian just said she'd been in Europe to collect materials for an exhibit," Newkirk told him. "It was for some kind of show they were doing at the museum where she works in Washing-ton. She said the follow-up work had to be done by the new year and there was more of it than she'd expected, so she'd had to stay back and finish up."

"And now? Why did she say she was here?"

"We really didn't have a chance to get into it. As I say, I was with the party seeing off the governor, so I only exchanged a few words with her."

"You didn't come home after the governor left, though? Mrs. Newkirk said you were out of town Tuesday night."

"Yes, I was. I was attending a regional development meeting in the city to talk about a new irrigation project for the western part of the state, and there was a working dinner planned for that night, so I stayed on and drove back the next morning." He frowned and looked over at the burn site. "I can't help wondering if it would've made any difference if I'd have skipped the dinner and come on home, instead."

"No way to know, I guess," Cruz said. "Did Jillian seem upset in any way when you talked to her at the airport?"

"No, I wouldn't say so."

"And you're convinced she had nothing to do with what happened over there that night?"

"Not Jillian, no. And Nils said it looked like she might have been hit on the head, so...." He spread his arms and lifted his shoulders in a gesture that said that the truth, if not self-evident, at least lay down a different path.

"And that's what you told Deputy Berglund? That you'd run into Jillian when she arrived at the airport?"

"No. What I told Nils is that she wasn't alone when I saw her."

"Who was she with?"

"Some fellow. She was talking with him as they walked off the plane. To be honest, I thought at first it was just somebody she might have sat next to who'd struck up a conversation with her, but then, when Jill spotted me and stopped to talk, he stopped, too."

"Did she introduce him?"

"You know, she did, but I didn't really catch the name. The place was noisy, and I was with other people, and it was all kind of rushed."

"A new boyfriend she was bringing home, maybe?"

Newkirk shook his head. "Somehow, I don't really think so. In the first place, Grace had never mentioned anything about Jillian having a fella, which might not be that surprising. But this fellow and Jillian, you know, they didn't look all that chummy. As I say, I was still thinking, even then, that this was just some guy who maybe met her on the plane, was trying to pick her up."

"What did he look like?"

"Your height, I'd say. About your age, maybe a little younger. Black, curly hair—kind of an Afro, I guess you'd say. Mustache."

"Eyes?"

"I couldn't say. Brown, maybe? He was kind of on the swarthy side. Looked Spanish or Italian or something."

"Did he speak with an accent?"

"Not that I noticed, but then, I don't think he said much more than 'how do you do,' if that, so it's not like I really got a chance to notice."

"Do you remember anything else about him? What he was wearing?"

"He had on a leather jacket, I think, black or dark brown. That's all I remember."

"And when Miss Meade and you separated—?"

"She headed toward the baggage claim and he walked off with her."

"And you gave Deputy Berglund all this information?"

"Yes, I did. Anyway, Agent Cruz, that's about as much as I can tell you. I'm running a little late, to tell you the truth, so I'm afraid I'm going to have to let you go now."

"No problem," Cruz said, wondering why it was that people always said they 'had to let you go' when what they really meant was, 'Hit the road, Jack.' Newkirk was obviously not going to leave until he did, so Cruz headed for the driver's side of his rental and opened the door, casting one last glance up the drive of Grace Meade's destroyed house. And then he stopped and looked over the roof of the car. "Mr. Newkirk...?"

"It's Tom, please," the other man said, his politician's smile a little strained by now.

Cruz let it pass. "How did Jillian get here from the airport? Did she rent a car, or is there a shuttle that passes out this way, or what?"

"Hmm...you know, now that you mention it, I have no idea. I did ask if her mother was meeting her when I ran into her at the airport, but she said, no, she was going to make her own way and surprise Grace. I never thought to ask if she was renting a car."

"You got back to town the morning after the fire?"

"Around eleven, yes."

"And you didn't see a car in the drive next door?"

"No, but maybe it had already been towed, especially if they had to get it out of the way of the fire trucks. Nils would probably know."

Cruz nodded. "I guess he would at that. I'll have to remember to ask him." And, Cruz thought, ask Berglund why he'd failed to mention that Jillian Meade was seen arriving at the airport with someone else.

CHAPTER 17

War brings out the best and the worst in the human spirit. In wartime come extreme examples of both heroism and treachery, personal sacrifice and venal cowardice. Spending that afternoon with Miss Vivian Atwater, I got a rare glimpse of an extraordinary group of men and women who valued freedom more than their own lives. The volunteers of the SOE committed themselves to the front lines of the battle against a great evil, which they faced unprotected by even that paper-thin veneer of civility that governs the rules of war. They were not uniformed soldiers. If they were caught by the enemy, no Geneva Convention would protect them. Yet, despite grave warnings, each one of Miss Atwater's agents was prepared to pay the price of his or her life if it meant freeing future generations from Hitler's oppressive, mad and racist vision of empire. One hundred and eighteen of them did, indeed, end up making the ultimate sacrifice.

And what about my mother? Well, to be fair (I am still her daughter, after all, and so I suppose I feel the need even now to defend her), it's worth remembering that she was very young, only twenty-two, when she pledged her life to the cause. How many of us can say for certain that our own courage wouldn't falter when put to the test? It's impossible to know until the moment arrives.

I'd read enough about the history of the Resistance movement to know, intellectually at least, what singular courage and resourcefulness was shown by those who populated the anti-Nazi underground— people who were, for the most part, a fairly ordinary bunch. They came from the full gamut of backgrounds—professionals and tradespeople, aristocrats and salt of the earth types. Some were young, like my mother; some were weathered veterans of the last great war and other skirmishes that had come between. Their only common denominator was a stubborn refusal to knuckle under to fascism. Sitting in Miss Atwater's office that rainy afternoon, listening to her memories of her "ducks" and all that they'd accomplished, I felt more in awe of them all—and closer to my mother—than I ever had before.

While my mother remained in England, Miss Atwater said, she was put to work in the False Documents Section. One of this section's strengths lay in the lists it maintained, updated regularly on the basis of communications from the Resistance about all the towns in France where records offices had been destroyed by bombing. Where there were no records offices, there were no originals of documents against which the Gestapo could compare false papers. The False Documents Section also kept updated lists of French citizens known to have died or left the country before the war. Once again, barring acts of betrayal, the Gestapo was hard-pressed to spot these false but credible identities.

"The Germans were efficiency mad," Miss Atwater told me, "real fiends for paperwork, so we set out to defeat them at their own game. We had an absolutely marvelous collection of identification cards, passes, permits and certificates, plus rubber stamps from nearly every police prefecture and municipal office in France. There was no piece of documentation Grace couldn't reproduce. All that was left for the holders of her faked papers was to memorize every detail in them, know them better than they knew their own names so they'd be able to recite them back faithfully, no matter what. And they did, too. Even under torture, it was the rare agent who cracked or missed a beat."

"And when she went over to France?" I asked. "How did she operate there?"

"We set her up as the niece of the owner of a print shop in the north of Paris. During the day, they printed religious pictures and texts. By night, they were a veritable factory for the mass production of false papers, anti-occupation tracts and fake ration books."

"They were never caught?"

"Not for their printing efforts, no. Many of the members of that cell, including your mother, were picked up for questioning on several occasions, but the Germans never did find their underground workshop. And it was, literally, underground. They'd a couple of masons and municipal sewer workers in their cell, you see, fellows who helped construct a series of caverns and passages under the print shop and some surrounding buildings occupied by partisans and sympathizers. The whole subterranean spiderweb was so well bricked up with false fronts that the Gestapo never did uncover it. The facility itself remained intact right up to the Liberation, even if it was no longer operational."

"When did it cease to be operational?"

"It only worked in fits and starts once the roundups started in earnest. There just weren't the bodies to get the job done anymore, although the Germans were on their last legs in France by then, in any case."

There was so much Miss Atwater was able to tell me about my mother's assignments, both before and after she was sent over to France, right up to the D-Day landings in June of 1944, which marked the beginning of the end of the Nazi Occupation of France. But there were still some major holes. The biggest of these, from my perspective, at least, involved my parents' time together in France, and the reason my mother had never communicated to her SOE handlers that she was pregnant—although, on that score, Miss Atwater had developed a theory.

"Quite simple, really. I think Grace knew we'd pull her out *tout de suite* if we knew she was going to have a baby, and she was just too stubborn to walk away from the fight. She'd great spirit, as I said, even if she was prone to more risk-taking than I cared to see. She was competitive and she liked to play on the winning side. Since the tide of the war was beginning to turn, I can only think she wanted to be there to see it through to the end."

"You said that at the time she disappeared off your radar, her cell had been working on a plan to smuggle my father out of the country," I pointed out. "Maybe she was simply afraid of what would happen if she went out first and left him behind."

"Perhaps that was part of it. I'm sure it would have been. As I say, the Gestapo was on a rampage right about then, after the theft of the gold bullion. With the war going so badly for him, Hitler was desperate for resources. Losing that cache was a disaster. They really did pull out all the stops to try to find it. The Gestapo offered a reward of one million francs to anyone with information on the 'Anglo-Saxons, Jews and Bolsheviks' who'd done the nasty. Was enough to bring some very slimy chaps out of the woodwork, I can tell you—the kind who used this sort of opportunity to settle personal scores. Hundreds were rounded up. We lost track of dozens of our agents during those terrible weeks, and we feared the worst. The 'Night and Fog' decree had set out a long list of executable offenses—the usual stuff: espionage, sabotage, aid to the enemy, possession of arms, that sort of thing. But there were a few catch-all categories, too, such as 'fraudulent movement' or 'acts likely to stir unrest.' You'd no way of knowing, once the Gestapo had you in hand, whether or not they'd trump up charges under one of those categories. Next thing you knew, it was a bullet to the back of the head or a one-way ticket to the gas chambers. Most of our agents who were rounded up eventually reestablished contact, I'm glad to say, but still, there were many partisans lost in that affair."

"Plus my father," I said glumly. "And for what? Some stolen gold. So, did the Nazis ever find it?"

"Ah, well," Miss Atwater said, heavy brown eyebrows rising high above her long, equine features, "no, as a matter of fact, they never did. It's one of the great, unsolved mysteries of the war."

"You mean no one else ever recovered it, either?"

"Not as far as I know. It was so well bunked away that the Gestapo couldn't find it, despite ripping apart any number of likely Resistance hidey holes. It was a brilliantly executed bit of work, really—every step of the operation compartmentalized to cut down on the damage if any corner of the cell sprung a leak. Seems whoever did the actual hiding of the cache must have gotten picked up and executed, either by the Gestapo or in the concentration camps. Took the secret to their graves."

"Maybe not," I suggested. "Maybe whoever did it just laid low until after the war, then recovered the booty to use for their own personal benefit."

Miss Atwater's head dipped in a thoughtful nod. "Well, yes, quite right. Entirely possible someone's taken a bunk with it. Living the good life on the Riviera even as we speak." She sighed. I could see she was beginning to tire, and I knew it was time to take my leave, but before I did, there was one more thing I was anxious to learn from her.

"Miss Atwater, my mother once told me she actually met my father first here in London, although it was only after he started flying supply missions and then was shot down and harbored by her Resistance cell in France that they fell in love. My father was with the American OSS, but it's never been clear in my mind how an OSS and an SOE agents' paths would have crossed."

"Oh, easily enough, I should think," she said. "The first six OSS operatives showed up at our Baker Street digs in early '43, as I recall. Like *jeunes filles en fleur* straight from finishing school, they were, all fresh and innocent, eager to start working in our frowzy old spook brothel."

"So it was your people who trained the OSS operatives?"

"Oh, yes. Had to take them in hand. General Eisenhower was

mad keen to help beef up the Resistance in France before he launched his Operation Overlord to retake the continent, but the Yanks were still so wet behind the ears, weren't they? Hadn't a clue, really. As late as the spring of 1944, our shop was launching ten times the number of sorties as the Yanks. Still, they were 'fresh meat,' as they say," she added mischievously. "And they had ever so many aeroplanes, which we needed desperately. We and the OSS concluded an operational pact, set up a combined Special Forces HQ. Took the Yanks through their paces, trained 'em just like our own lads—up in Scotland, Milton Hall, Wandsborough, Thames Park. Gave 'em the works, as those boys liked to say."

"Including the False Documents Section, I imagine."

"Oh, yes, quite. And since Grace was on hand there into the summer of '43 before we started preparing her to be dropped behind the lines herself, I should think it entirely likely their paths would have crossed."

So there it was—another piece of the puzzle snapped into place.

In all, I spent more than four hours with Miss Atwater that afternoon. By the time I left her Whitehall office, the busy London rush hour was over. The rain had ended, and streets and buildings, washed clean, were sparkling under the street lamps like the Crown Jewels as the dinner and theater crowds headed out for their evening's entertainment. I had no desire for crowds or conversation or distraction. My mind was racing with everything she'd told me. Lost in thought, I strolled alone, watching the lights of Big Ben and the Houses of Parliament reflected in the never-ending flow of the Thames, witness to so much history. As I walked the Embankment, a fine haze began to settle, precursor to the inevitable London fog that would roll in by midnight.

And as the brume grew thicker, I was reminded of Hitler's decree that anti-Nazi partisans in the occupied territories be snatched in total secrecy and made to vanish without a trace. I could imagine the kind of terror and confusion those disappearances would have struck in the hearts and minds of their loved ones left behind. But little did I know how aptly that term "Night and Fog" would come to apply to my own efforts, as well, as my search would dredge up a finale to this story that was so much darker and murkier than either I or the honorable Miss Atwater could possibly have imagined.

German efficiency is no myth, and as Miss Atwater said, the Nazis were fanatics for record-keeping, so I thought it would be a simple enough matter to obtain in Paris details concerning my mother's various arrests by the Gestapo. Miss Atwater was not so sure. I might or I might not find what I was looking for, she said. Some of the voluminous records the Nazis kept were destroyed as the war wound down, torched either by fleeing Germans fearing retribution, by angry mobs who overran their strongholds, or by the random bombs and incendiaries that fell as control of territory teetered back and forth between opposing forces in the waning days of the conflict.

She herself had gone over to the Continent again and again after the German defeat, obsessed with finding out what had happened to her agents who hadn't come home—and determined to bring their murderers to justice. My mother's name had been on her list at first, but when Miss Atwater learned she'd been spotted in England, then found her living in a bed-sit in the north end of London, bitter, angry, but very much alive, she'd crossed her name off the list and gone back to looking for her other missing agents. There were simply too many lost souls to worry about.

"I was dreadfully sorry for what had happened to her, of course," Miss Atwater said. "I wished I could make her understand that, as far as I knew, it was nothing we'd done that had led to the capture of her young man—your father—but Grace didn't want to hear it. I had to get back to looking for the others, and it seemed best to give her some time. The next I heard, she'd left on a transport the Yanks had set up to take British war brides and their children to the United States. In the end, I decided to let it lie and hope things went well for her."

"She's had a good life, I think," I said, anxious to ease this good woman's conscience. "She seems quite content. She has a lovely home on a lake, and she's made good friends over there."

"I'm glad to hear it. Still, I can't help thinking we let her down."

Poor Miss Atwater, still grieving over her "ducks." How could she have known all the details of what any of them went through, especially in those final days? As the war sputtered to its ugly end, Europe was in chaos. Millions of people were dead, missing or displaced. Cities were in ruin. Civilian authority was nonexistent or ineffectual, and villains and victims alike were getting lost in the shuffle.

Little wonder, then, that Miss Atwater had few details concerning my mother's final weeks in France—and no idea at all of the shocking act of betrayal that I myself was about to discover.

CHAPTER 18

Havenwood, Minnesota
Friday, January 12, 1979

Emotions in Havenwood were running high over the death of Grace Meade, but cases got compromised when investigators let personal feelings get in the way of reason. In this regard, Cruz decided, he had several advantages over the Havenwood deputy police chief—first among them the fact that he'd never been in love with the prime suspect. He was an outsider, with no personal knowledge of either the victim or her daughter, but he had instincts that had been honed on far more homicide case experience than Berglund. He also had no vested interest in this case. Finding out who killed Grace Meade was not a career-maker or -breaker for him as it might be for the deputy, heir apparent to his ailing chief. Cruz needed to know what had gone down while Jillian was in England, but otherwise, he was strictly an observer here, willing to do what he could to help out, but uninvolved. He could afford to keep a cool head.

That's what he told himself. So why was it, he wondered, that every time his mind flashed on the image of Jillian Meade lying crushed and broken-looking in her hospital bed, his gut knotted and adrenaline surged in his veins, leaving him jumpy, suspicious and irritable? Why was it that from the moment he'd opened this file, he'd been picking up the unmistakable smell of evil, a faint, underlying stench that seemed to hover in every unexplored corner of this case, growing stronger with every bend in the road?

Nobody in town seemed neutral on this complicated mother-daughter duo. There were reams of unexplored subtext in every mention of their names, and while Berglund himself was also implicated in some of this back story, he had insights Cruz could never match on the interrelationships between Jillian, her mother and the rest of the town. His cooperation would be critical in getting to the bottom of the puzzle of Jillian Meade.

So after leaving the Newkirks, Cruz stopped by police headquarters to have another talk with the deputy, try to make peace, and offer the Bureau's help following up on Tom Newkirk's report of seeing Jillian at the Minneapolis-St. Paul Airport in the company of a stranger who may or may not have been traveling with her.

When he walked into the low-slung Havenwood police building, Verna was once again working the front desk—although to call what she did "work" was a pretty elastic use of the term, since her job as receptionist and dispatcher seemed to leave her plenty of time on her hands. She'd remembered her glasses today and was happily working her way through another mystery novel.

"Well, hi there, Alex!" she said, peering over the top of her glasses as he pushed the door closed behind him. "Still kicking around our fair town, are you?" She slid a plate across the counter to him. "Have a date square."

Cruz smiled. "No thanks, Verna. I'm still carrying a load from Ollie Jorgenson's trucker-sized breakfast over at the Whispering Pines. How do these guys here get into their squad cars when you spoil them like this, though?"

She pulled off her glasses. The ear pieces were attached to a gold chain slung around her neck, and when she let the glasses dangle, they settled comfortably on the broad shelf of her bosom. "I raised four sons. Guess I got used to feeding the multitudes. I can't seem to break the habit, even though my boys are all grown and gone. Keeps me busy, anyway, the baking and helping out over here."

"As long as it keeps you out of trouble. Is Deputy Berglund in this morning?"

"He was, but he's out on a call right now. Is it urgent? I could get him on the radio."

"When do you expect him back?"

"He said he'd check in before noon. It's quarter of now," she added, glancing at the wall clock above the window to the squad room. It seemed empty.

"Maybe I'll wait for a few minutes, see if he checks in. It's not really urgent, but I wanted to have a quick word with him." He unbuttoned his coat and leaned an elbow on the counter, nodding at the novel in her hand. "Good book?"

She folded over the corner of the page she'd been reading, then closed the book and set it aside. "Not great. I think I had the killer figured out by page 50. If I get to the end and it turns out I'm right, I'm going to chuck it across the room. I go through about five of these things a week, mind you. After a while, you get so's you can spot what's coming a mile away, but what the heck, it helps pass the time."

"You said you help out here? Are you a volunteer?" That would certainly explain why she got away with kicking back like this, he thought.

She nodded. "Town budget's real tight. They needed another patrolman, but they didn't have money for that and for an officer at the front desk full-time, so they decided to make this a volunteer job. Suits me fine. I needed something to keep me busy, especially in winter when I can't be out in the garden.

There's just me at home now, like I said. The mister died when my youngest was two."

"Sorry to hear it."

"Oh, well, thanks, but it was a long time ago. My baby's thirty-two now. Anyway, I've always loved the mystery stories," she said, flicking a finger toward her disappointing book. "Not that anything this dramatic ever happens around here—at least, not before poor Grace died it didn't. I have to admit, though, I kinda get a kick out of working for the fuzz after all these stories I've read."

He looked askance at her. "Working for the 'fuzz,' Verna?" She blushed. "I'll bet they're glad to have you," Cruz said. "I've never seen a desk sergeant who bakes cookies."

"Oh, go on with you. I know it's dopey, but old habits die hard, you know? I try to cut back." She patted her ample stomach, which was camouflaged today by a candy-striped sweater that hung halfway to knees clad in fire engine red stretch pants. "It's not like I need the calories myself, but if I'm baking for a church sale or a social or something, my hands just seem to do up double and triple batches automatically. The boys here are real good about polishing off the extras."

"Yeah, it's a dirty job, but somebody's gotta do it. I guess Sybil Newkirk called you, too, about baking for the church lunch after Mrs. Meade's funeral tomorrow?"

"She didn't have to. I told Tom I'd take over some baking. It's going to be a big affair, that one, and you can never have too much food."

"Were you close to Grace, then?"

"I wouldn't say real close, but we both kept busy with the horticulture club. Grace had a real green thumb. The English, you know, dogs and gardens, that's their thing. Grace used to say, 'The reason mad dogs and Englishmen go out in the noonday sun is there's always one more weed that wants pulling and the dogs are too daft to leave their idiot masters out there alone!'"

"How about Jillian, Verna? How well do you know her?"

"Oh, not real well. Not anymore, anyhow. My next-to-youngest boy and she used to hang out with the same group when they were in high school. Him and Jill and Nils Berglund and all, they were about the same age. Used to go to dances and swimming together and what not, but I haven't seen much of Jill in, oh, years now."

"So, being a mystery-lover, do you have a theory on what happened the night Grace Meade died?"

"No clue. Chief Lunders figured it was a drifter broke in."

"What if it wasn't? Do you think Jillian might have had a reason to do her harm?"

"No, not me, although I guess there's people around town who'll tell you different. I just can't imagine her doing something like that, though. She's a quiet, educated girl, and that was her mother, for heaven's sake. Grace gave up her home to bring Jillian here to be with family. Nice girls don't go around torching their mothers' houses after they've gone and made that kind of sacrifice."

Cruz nodded, but was there anything worse, he wondered, than being the unwitting cause of someone else's noble sacrifice? How many times in her life had Jillian been reminded that her mother had paid the price of a homeland in order to bring her here? How many times had he himself heard that said since her name had first crossed his desk? Even her boss, Haddon Twomey, had mentioned it. But isn't that what it was all supposed to be about, each generation doing for the next? You don't expect slavish gratitude for doing what comes naturally. In any case, Grace hadn't done badly for herself, ending up in a pretty lakeside house in a town where she was obviously respected and admired. Yet, he had the impression Jillian had never been allowed to forget that her mother had uprooted and transplanted herself for her benefit. How sick to death would she have been by now of having that dubious sacrifice rammed down her throat?

"Did you know Jillian and Grace to disagree?" he asked Verna.

"Don't all mothers and daughters? I raised boys, so I wouldn't know about daughters, but they say mothers and daughters, fathers and sons—oil and water. Although mind you, my boys really never got the chance to butt heads with their dad. No matter how much kids and parents argue, though, they usually don't kill each other."

"I was told they were heard arguing the night of the fire."

"Who told you that? No, wait, let me guess—Sybil Newkirk?" Cruz didn't answer, but Verna took absence of denial as affirmation. She sighed, glanced around the empty lobby, then leaned forward, voice lowered. "You know, the thing with Sybil is, Alex, she's kind of a silly woman. And I hate to say it, but you can't always rely on what she says as being fact. She's got a little...um...medicinal problem." Verna cupped her hand and made a tippling motion, just in case Cruz had missed what kind of medicine she meant. "Anyway, Sybil was Grace's loyal sidekick. You never saw Grace at any event but that Sybil wasn't trailing right behind her, bright-eyed and bushy-tailed. No matter what kind of problems Grace and Jillian might have had—and, like I say, all mothers and daughters do—you can be sure Sybil would've taken Grace's side."

"It seems both the Newkirks were Grace Meade fans."

"I guess so," Verna said.

"How about you?"

"Oh, we weren't real tight or anything, but her garden was something else, and we used to share cuttings back and forth. Grace was never stingy, I'll give her that." Verna tapped her ample chest with her thumb. "Mind you, this is one Norwegian-Irish girl whose garden is not too shabby, either, if I do say so myself. Come the annual garden show, Grace and I were always neck and neck in the race for the ribbons."

"Friendly rivals, then."

Verna nodded. "I guess you could say that. I felt kind of responsible for her, too."

"How so?"

"Well, because of her being Joe's girl," Verna said, as if it were self-evident. "The mister and I, we were real good friends with Joe. The bunch of us—Tom and Sybil, too—we all went through school at the same time, and then the boys joined up and went off to fight together, too. Tom and Sybil had gotten married just before the boys left. My Ed and I'd been married three years already. Had two kids and another one on the way, so he could've easily stayed home, but once he heard Joe and Tom were going, there was nothing for it but he had to go, too. Tom was the only one of the three who came back all in one piece, mind you. Joe was killed over there, of course, and my Ed got shot up real bad. Lost a leg from the knee down just six months after he left. Never really did get his health back. Had a heart attack in 1949. He was only thirty-one when he died, and really, I think it was on account of the injuries he got fighting over there." Verna waved a hand as if to shoo off her own long-windedness. "All this to say, I guess I felt like Grace and I were both war widows, in a way. Something else we had in common."

"Tom Newkirk really seems to have watched over Grace."

Verna hesitated. "What do you mean?"

"Well, Mrs. Newkirk told me he gave her the land next door to them that she built her house on, and helped Grace manage her finances and things."

"Oh, that. Well, yeah, Tom's real good that way. He's helped me out, too." She grimaced. "Course, he is a politician, you know, likes to be seen as helpful. Still, he made sure I got my widow's pension and my boys got college money. Like I said, those fellas were real tight, and Tom's a good one for watching out after his buddies' families."

"Did they all serve in the same unit over there?"

"Tom and Joe did. My Ed ended up in an infantry unit, and like I say, he came home minus half a leg. Tom and Joe were there to the end, though. Tom actually met Grace over there, too, you now, same time as Joe, so when Helen and Arthur Meade heard from her after the war, Tom was able to tell them a little bit about her. After that, they decided to invite her to bring the baby out here to live with them."

"Tom Newkirk met Grace over there?" A new picture was beginning to form up in Cruz's suspicious mind, still fuzzy in its details, but the broad outlines beginning to come into focus. A beautiful widow. The dead husband's solicitous best friend, who arranges for her to come to town, and eventually, to live next door. His wife, too silly and gin-besotted, maybe, to see something developing between her husband and her best friend.

"Anybody tell you about Grace's war service?" Verna asked.

Cruz nodded. "I gather she did some kind of secret work behind the lines over there?"

"Uh-huh. The boys met her in England, except she was then sent behind the lines. Tom didn't see her again till after the war. It was just by chance that Joe happened to run into her in France and the two of them got together. Poor guy never made it back, of course. But Tom and my Ed? They sure did come back with the old war stories. Let those two get a couple drinks under their belts and they'd bend your ear half the night if you let 'em."

"And Grace, too? She was right in the thick of it, from the sound of things."

"No, not Grace. She never liked to talk about the war. It must be a guy thing."

"Well, that was her home turf getting blown to bits. I guess it would take some of the shine off the adventure."

"There you go, then. Anyway, she was never one to sit around rehashing it all."

Cruz nodded. For his part, he shared Grace's aversion to old war stories. They say memory is selective—that it forgets the bad times and remembers only the good—but he'd never found it to be the case. He only wished his own memory would be so cooperative.

The radio set behind Verna squawked, and Berglund's deep voice suddenly crackled from the speaker, calling in.

"Hey there, Nils," Verna said, picking up the mike, "you got a visitor here. Your FBI fella's back. Over."

"I'm just on my way over to Montrose. He need anything in particular?"

Verna turned to Cruz and raised an eyebrow. "Do you mind?" he asked, indicating the microphone.

"Be my guest," she said. "Just push the button here when you want to talk."

Cruz stretched across the counter and took the mike from her hand. "This is Alex Cruz, Deputy. I came in to see if you were able to follow up on a report that Jillian Meade was seen arriving with someone at the airport on Tuesday morning. Over."

There was silence for a moment, and then, "You been talking to Tom Newkirk?"

"Affirmative," Cruz replied. "If you like, I can ask the FBI field office in St. Paul to follow up, get a passenger manifest from the airline so we can figure out who this guy might have been."

The response was again delayed. Berglund was either busy driving or unhappy with Cruz for sticking his nose in once again— first the arson investigators, now this. In the end, though, he seemed to decide not to look a gift horse in the mouth. "Go ahead and do that. You can use our phones to make the call, if you need to. But Cruz? I want to know the minute you hear back. Understand?"

"You have my word. Are you going up to see Jillian?"

"Later. I'm on my way to the coroner's first to pick up the final autopsy report on her mother."

"How about if I meet you at the hospital?"

Again, a delayed response. Look, Cruz wanted to say, you don't like a fed breathing down your neck. Fine, but I need what I need, and I'm not about to ship out until I get it. We can do this the easy way, or we can do it the hard way.

"Whatever," Berglund replied finally. "Over and out."

Cruz handed back the microphone. "I don't think your deputy chief likes me much."

"Oh, I wouldn't worry about it," Verna said. "Nils is all right. He doesn't mean to be unfriendly. This case is just real tough on him, especially with Chief Lunders laid up right now. It's real tough on everyone around here."

"Fair enough. So, do you think I could use a phone?"

"Sure. He said you could. Why don't you go on through to the squad room? There's nobody in there to bother you right now. And here," Verna added, handing him the tray of date squares, "take these and put them inside, would you, before I start in on them myself?" She picked up her book once more, opened it to the page she'd marked and slipped her glasses back on her nose. "I'll get back to my story, but you just holler if you need anything else."

CHAPTER 19

France was the next stop on the tour of my mother's past. This is where the trail grew murky, dank and overgrown with lies and half-truths. This is where I first began to uncover the contradictions between what I believed and what could be proven by fact—the unbridgeable chasm between what I had thought was true and what I now know to be true. This is where I began to wish I'd never started down this road, but by the time I realized I'd gone too far, I had stumbled blindly over the edge of a precipice. I am in free-fall now, propelled by forces I can no longer control.

They say history is written by the victors. Stories of the dead, the betrayed and the vanquished only surface years later, if at all. Most times, if the details conflict with popular mythology, they are simply buried. But to those who take the trouble, eyewitness accounts of small events and the paper trail of obscure documents are like the signs read by the old Indian trackers in those Westerns we used to love to watch as kids, who found evidence of their prey in broken twigs, bits of dung and flattened blades of grass. My prey was the truth about my mother's past—and my own—and I went after it armed with more than a decade's worth of experience at following the indistinct historical markers that most other people walk right on by.

Our side won the war and the Nazis lost. Inevitably, therefore, the tales we tell ourselves of that period are limited almost entirely to heroic accounts of the battles fought and won against the German war machine, both the overt battles and the covert ones. Nowhere is this more true than in France, which fell early in the war, when the Germans simply walked around their supposedly impregnable Maginot Line of defense fortifications. In June of 1940, Paris surrendered unconditionally and without a fight. It was not the nation's proudest moment.

There was, of course, a patriotic and incredibly brave anti-Nazi underground movement, both in the occupied north and the collaborationist, Vichy-controlled south, a Resistance born the day the first German tanks rolled onto French soil and active throughout the entire four years they were there. There are those who would have us believe the vast majority of French citizens were members or supporters of this opposition, but the records of the German Occupation demonstrate otherwise. The Resistance movement was strong and ably assisted by a largely sympathetic population at the very beginning of the Occupation, when the Nazis first rolled in, and it grew stronger again toward the end, as the Nazi stranglehold on Europe began to weaken. But for much of the period between the fall of Paris in 1940 and its liberation in August of 1944, the movement and its partisans were betrayed, over and over, by a population in which the majority of people seem to have decided, for a variety of reasons, to go with the Nazi flow.

Of course, it's easy enough to sit in judgment from the safe distance of another era, but when the Germans forced an armistice on France in 1940, many citizens were relieved to think the country could sit this war out and be spared a repeat of the horrifying devastation it suffered in the First World War. The use of fear was also a potent weapon in the Nazi arsenal, and Hitler's henchmen were experts in its use, employing all the tools of the police state—secret files and card indexes to keep track of people. Passes and permits to control their movement. Censorship of information in the press and on the radio, which were restricted to spouting Third Reich propaganda. Intimidation, beatings and assassination by jackbooted thugs. Mass arrests. Brutal interrogation centers and prisons. And, of course, the Night and Fog decree—the secret, silent deportations of the regime's opponents—real, potential or imagined—to slave labor and concentration camps in the east, filling the gas chambers, stoking the crematoria fires. All of these tactics played a role in inducing paralytic terror throughout occupied Europe.

Psychologists tell us that living like this induces a kind of inertia, keeping people docile even where they don't support the regime or its goals. It becomes easier to obey and pay lip service than to oppose. We resort to "inner emigration," retreating into our own mental worlds, keeping our thoughts to ourselves while outwardly conforming our behavior to what the oppressor says it should be. We self-censor and self-control until we are little more than docile sheep, going where the yapping, snarling dogs of power tell us to go, doing what they tell us to do. Knowing this, we can only be amazed that the Resistance managed to recruit as many partisans as it did.

And my mother? How did she manage to survive and carry on, given that kind of intense physical and psychological pressure?

Here was what I knew to be true, based on my research to date, including some of the old files I'd sifted through and my interview with Miss Atwater: Grace Wickham was recruited by the Special Operations Executive in September of 1941 and was trained as a document forger, a job at which she excelled. She probably first met U.S. pilot Joe Meade in England, sometime in mid-1943, when the British SOE and the American OSS concluded an operational pact to work together to support the French Resistance. In August of 1943, she was parachuted into occupied France carrying forged documents that identified her by her late mother's name, "Sylvie Fournier." She landed on a moonless night in a clearing at the edge of a wood near the town of Beauvais, about fifty miles north of Paris, along with a supply drop of several cylindrical aluminum canisters containing various kinds of paper, inks, blank rubber stamps and a small, hand-cranked press. She was met by a local cell of the French Resistance code-named "Magpie" and hidden in a series of safe houses in Beauvais for about two weeks until it was deemed safe to move her down to Paris, where her skills and her precious cargo were in great demand. When the coast seemed clear for a transfer, the "Magpie" group handed her off to another cell named "Persimmon", who handed her off to another, and then another, until finally she landed at the door of an old French printer named Viau, who lived in the Parisian suburb of Gentilly.

Viau, a widower in his seventies, had been producing religious tracts for local Catholic parishes for over fifty years, and although his workshop was investigated by Occupation forces on several occasions, his age, frail health and the evidence in his shop apparently convinced the Gestapo he was harmless. When my mother moved into his spare room, she was introduced to neighbors (with a couple of years shaved off her true age) as Viau's twenty-year-old grandniece from Normandy, left orphaned by a stray British bomb that had missed its German military target and landed instead on her parents' stationery shop in Rouen.

Miss Atwater told me that some clever SOE handler had come up with this cover story for my mother. It had a dual advantage, they decided—it was close to her true history, which meant she could convincingly describe both Normandy, where she had spent so much of her childhood, and the bombing of the shop, including graphic details like how it had turned into a paper-stoked inferno and the horror of finding her father dead in the road with his hair on fire. It also gave her a plausible pretext to feign an anti-British bias, which would stand her in good stead should she find herself being interrogated by the Gestapo.

Her cover story may have been too clever by half. As a new face in the neighborhood, conspicuous because of her beauty, she was bound to be noticed and picked up for questioning. And so she was, I discovered, although this in itself was not unusual. People were yanked off the streets every day, partisans and nonpartisans alike. It was one sure-fire method to keep the population nervous and off-balance.

In the course of being repeatedly interrogated, I think it's possible my mother may have begun to believe her own cover story. She seemed such a formidably strong woman that some people would find it difficult to accept she might have cracked under pressure. But she was young, after all, only twenty-two when she was sent into France, and this after already having lived under incredible strain and facing terrible losses since the first days of the war four years earlier. Who knows exactly what happened to her while she was in custody. What kind of pressure they exerted on her. What they did to her.

It sounds as if I'm trying to justify her behavior, I know, but can any of us really say for certain we could stand up against those odds? Because one thing seems almost certain now—once cut off from the constant support and moral reinforcement of her SOE comrades, my mother's loyalties *did* waver—and grievously.

No one could have been more shocked than I to discover this, although in retrospect, I don't know why it had never occurred to me that the truth would turn out to be more convoluted than the simple legend that had always surrounded my mother. Our heroes almost always turn out to have feet of clay, and there should have been no reason to think she was different than so many others. Except....

Except that she had managed to convince me—convince us all—that she was cut of finer cloth than most mere mortals.

But there was something I once heard my mother say, long ago, when I was still very young. It was in the middle of a Fourth of July party at someone's house. I remember a crowd of people standing around her, and although I don't recall the context of the conversation, but the memory of what she said has stuck with me all these years because there was such contempt in her voice. "You Americans are so incredibly naive." There was such contempt in her voice.

I thought about that not too long ago, and with the advantage of age and a little experience, I decided she must have been referring to the innocent, gung-ho enthusiasm of a nation that had forgotten what it was like to experience the terrible destruction of warfare on its own soil. Now, I know she meant so much more. What fools she must have thought us all!

I say she wavered in her loyalty, possibly buckling under the pressure of interrogation, but even now, I wonder if the blame lies entirely with the enemy, or whether there was a fatal flaw in her character that made it inevitable she would crack at the critical moment. There are certain people, after all, who go beyond passive acceptance of evil—individuals who embrace it. Who, at the very least, accept the philosophy of whoever is in power at the moment because they want desperately to play on the winning team. Who seek to ally themselves with the strong, even if it means changing sides—more than once, sometimes, as the fortunes of the game change.

I've spent my entire life believing I was heir to a more noble tradition than that. That my mother made her choice early on to be on the side of decency and sacrificed everything rather than waver in that commitment. As little as I felt I knew her, I always thought at least that I knew what she stood for.

Now, I know I was wrong even on that score. She duped me. Worse—far worse, in my mind—was that she duped my grandparents, who loved and sheltered us, and whom I adored. She made fools of an entire town that welcomed her, followed her and admired her. So what does that make me heir to now, except a fine family tradition of treachery, betrayal and murder?

CHAPTER 20

Montrose, Minnesota
Friday, January 12, 1979

Cruz put in the call to the FBI field office, where the Special Agent in Charge took down the details of Jillian Meade's arrival from Washington and promised to cable a copy of the passenger manifest to him within twenty-four hours. That done, Cruz headed over to Montrose to meet Berglund, take a look at the final autopsy report on Grace Meade and find out what their odds were of interviewing their suspect/victim/patient today.

He was getting mental whiplash from the contradictory views of Jillian Meade he'd been picking up around town, but the dominant image he retained was the one from the previous day, when he and Berglund had stood at the viewing port of her room. Now, Cruz found himself increasingly inclined, despite the uncertainty gnawing at his gut, to see her as another victim rather than a suspect, an inclination fed by Tom Newkirk's report of seeing a stranger with her at the airport. Was he grasping at straws, he worried, looking for an unknown suspect, letting fuzzy empathy for an admittedly attractive woman in distress overrule clear-headed analysis of the evidence?

He couldn't get the picture out of his head, the way she'd looked on suicide lock-down yesterday—a far cry from the pretty woman in the glamorous red dress pictured in Haddon Twomey's photo. Instead, he'd seen a disheveled, disoriented, pathetic-looking creature curled in a near-fetal position. Her long hair had been matted, her deep brown eyes hollow and shadowed with fear and exhaustion. Periodic tremors had shaken her body like tiny seismic storms, yet she'd seemed oblivious to discomfort, totally absorbed in the feverish scribbling that her psychiatrist had likened to an act of self-exorcism, while her free hand kneaded the covers like a thing possessed. It had been a sight to stir the hardest of hearts, and even Cruz's naturally suspicious mind had had to concede that she looked severely traumatized, and that a psychiatric ward might well be the best place for her.

It was that image, he finally realized, that had been troubling him throughout his restless night at the Whispering Pines, so that when he'd hit the road that morning, he'd been determined to make peace with Berglund. It was little bloody wonder the deputy was stressed. Seeing her in that state was enough to make even a stranger want to gather her up and shelter her from the harsh world—and this was someone Berglund had known all his life and had once loved enough to consider marrying.

But when Cruz arrived at the Montrose Regional Hospital, he was forced to revise his opinion of Jillian Meade yet again.

He found Dr. Kandinsky on the third floor, getting ready to leave the psychiatric ward after completing her morning therapy sessions. Berglund had not yet shown up, but the doctor agreed to postpone her departure in order to take Cruz for a look at how her patient was coming along. Today, Kandinsky was dressed in the same navy cardigan she'd worn yesterday, this time over matching slacks and a white blouse. The geriatric cases were once again in the day room, where there seemed to be a little excitement going on. The doctor paused briefly on her way past to look in on them, Cruz beside her. Three patients were hunched in front of a television screen, their vacant stares broken only by the occasional slow motion blink of an eye. A fourth, an elderly man with an upright shock of sparse hair, was more agitated. He leaned forward in his wheelchair, elbows on his knees, fully absorbed in the soap opera.

"That's right, that's right!" he shouted at the screen. "You tell him you've been two-timing, you cheap floozy! You just tell him!"

As he bounced up and down in his seat, another old-timer shuffled past behind him, seemingly unaware of his surroundings. When he reached the far wall, he paused, looking confused. Then, he pivoted unsteadily and started back for the other side of the room, his pajamas and slippers loose-fitting, as if he were shrinking a little inside them with every step. If he kept this up much longer, Cruz thought, the old man would completely disappear inside the wrinkled nightclothes, like some ancient tortoise withdrawing into its shell. On the far side of the room, sitting by a window with the sun streaming in, an elderly woman in a squeaking wooden rocker hummed a warbled lullaby to the rag doll cradled in her arms, watching the snowbound prairie like someone patiently waiting for spring's release.

"Are you all right, Agent Cruz?"

He looked over, startled, to find the doctor studying him curiously. "Me? I'm fine. I was just thinking how familiar this all looks."

"You've encountered dementia before? Someone in the family, maybe?"

"No, I was thinking of VA psych wards I've been in. These are just an elderly version of some of those guys. Same tics. I guess symptoms are similar no matter why the mind disconnects."

"Have you spent much time in Veterans Administration hospitals?"

He gave her a grim smile. "You asking if I've been committed myself, Doc?"

"Have you?"

"No. Been poked and prodded by your colleagues a little, but most of the time I've spent in places like this I was working homicide cases for the Army. I've interviewed a few in this condition, most of them flipped out from combat shock or recreational pharmaceuticals."

"Are you a Vietnam vet?"

"Yup. Got a problem with that?"

"Not with any veteran, no. The war itself, yes, and the government that sent our boys over there. But," she added wearily, "I guess that's all history now."

"Not hardly, Doc. Not for everyone. You only wish."

She nodded wearily. "I guess that's true. Come on, why don't we go take a look at Miss Meade."

Cruz was stunned by the dramatic change in the patient occupying the room at the end of the hall. As he and the doctor stood once more on the outside of the glass partition, observing without being observed, he found himself growing irritated, wondering yet again whether this supposedly traumatized, but otherwise intelligent, reserved (some said cold) woman wasn't one of the more devious manipulators he'd run across in all his years of dealing with the worst of the worst.

"How did you manage this?" he asked the doctor. "She barely looks like the same woman."

The hospital bed on which Jillian had lain the previous day, bedclothes rumpled and tangled around her, was neatly made now, and she was sitting in the high-backed chair off to one side of it. She looked relaxed and calm in a white terry robe buttoned up to her throat, long, shapely legs demurely crossed and peeking out from between its front flaps, her feet clad in soft, matching ballet slippers. Her hair was clean and brushed, tumbling over her shoulders like a spill of mink, gleaming in sunlight that shone down from the high, mesh-reinforced window. The thick black notebook was propped on her knee, and she was writing again, but her pace was measured now, calm and considered. She seemed to have worked her way through about two-thirds of the book. As they watched, she paused briefly, brown almond eyes looking off into the middle distance as her mind seemed to search for some elusive word or memory. Then, her gaze dropped to the page once more, and she resumed her writing. She could have been composing her grocery list or a letter to an old maiden aunt, Cruz thought, for all the emotion she displayed.

"I can't take much credit," Dr. Kandinsky said. "Part of what you're seeing here is the effect of the drugs finally working their way out of her system. She seems to have had a very averse reaction to them. Mostly, though, it's Jillian herself who brought about the transformation."

"Has she said anything?"

Kandinsky nodded. "A little before eight this morning, she spoke briefly to the nurse, and then she asked to see me."

"What did she say? Did she tell you anything about the fire or what happened to her mother?"

As Kandinsky shook her head, a tendril of frizzled gray hair fell loose. She grasped it between her fingers, twisted it into a rope and coiled it around the loose knot on top of her head before nesting her hands in her sweater pockets once more. "No, nothing like that. Our conversation was much more banal. Utilitarian, for the most part, more along the lines of how she was feeling and attending to her personal needs. I didn't want to push her too far, too fast, or make her talk for too long. It's taken her all this time to simply recover her voice, physically as well as psychologically. As you can see, she's only just come off the oxygen line. Her lungs and bronchial passages are finally starting to sound clearer after all the smoke she inhaled the other night. Mentally and emotionally, her progress is a little less self-evident, although there's obviously been a change for the better."

"Did you get a chance to look at what she's writing in that notebook?"

The psychiatrist turned to him. "You know, Agent Cruz, I don't mean to be difficult, but there are doctor-patient confidentiality issues that need to be kept in mind here. I know you're in the middle of an investigation and that you've got a job to do, and I don't dispute the seriousness of it. A woman is dead, after all. But at the same time, you have to understand that my job is to tend to my patient's needs, not to act as an information conduit from her lips to your ears."

"I know that, and I respect it. And, frankly, Doc, my hat's off to you. If anyone had told me yesterday afternoon she'd be looking this good today, I'd have thought they needed your help even more than she did. Whatever you did to draw her out of her shell, you've obviously got one hell of a bedside manner. I can think of a some VA shrinks who could take a lesson."

"Well, you're very kind, but as I say, the initiative really came from her. You know that old joke, 'How many psychiatrists does it take to change a lightbulb?'"

Cruz nodded. "'Only one, but the lightbulb has to really want to change.'"

"There you go," Kandinsky said, smiling. She turned back to the viewing port. "This lightbulb was ready for a change this morning. She was the one who asked to talk to me, as I say. She did it on her own time and according to her own agenda."

"And what exactly is her agenda, do you think?"

Kandinsky's shoulders rose and fell. "In the long run, I can't say."

"How about in the short run? Why was this morning different, aside from the fact that she's finally clean and sober? What made her break her silence now?"

"She needed something."

"What?"

"More writing material. The staff tells me she kept working right up until lights out last night, and then slept with the notebook tucked tightly under her. Whatever she's getting down there, it's obviously important to her. Apparently, she started writing again at first light, but by the time they brought her breakfast tray this morning, all the markers I'd given her yesterday had run dry."

"And that's why she asked to see you? Because she wanted more markers?"

Kandinsky grimaced and nodded. "So much for my therapeutic skills, hmm? Actually, what she really wanted was a pen. She doesn't like writing with the markers, it seems. She didn't come right out and say so, but I get the impression she finds them altogether too frivolous. In any event, the nurses weren't about to take the responsibility of handing her anything with a sharp point, given the reason she was brought in here in the first place, and they more or less told her so. That's when she kicked it upstairs and asked to see me."

"Which suggests she was fully aware of your presence yesterday and simply chose to ignore you," Cruz pointed out. A fairly calculated strategy, he thought. A stall to give herself time to come up with some explanation for her actions, or grounds for a plea of temporary insanity.

"At some level, I'm sure she was aware of me," Kandinsky agreed. "As I told you and the deputy yesterday, I knew she was listening to my words, even if she wasn't yet able to respond."

Able? Cruz wondered. Or, more to the point, willing? He let it slide. "So what did you tell her when she asked for a pen?"

"I explained that I couldn't let her have anything sharp until I was confident she wouldn't try to hurt herself again."

"And she promised not to do that, I suppose."

"No, she didn't bother—not that I would have been prepared to accept such a promise at face value, anyway. As it was, she seemed to have no desire to discuss her self-destructive urges. She simply reiterated that she needed something to write with, preferably not in colors like Tangerine Orange and Rikki-Tikki

Lime, if I could manage it. On the other hand, if that was all she could get, she'd take it. In the end, I brought her some black felt markers. She seemed content with that."

"And this?" Cruz asked, nodding toward the room. "Getting cleaned up like this? Was that her initiative, too?"

"Nope. That was my side of the bargain. I said I'd get her more writing materials if she'd take a shower first and eat some breakfast. She had absolutely no interest in either, I can tell you, but I made it clear those were my terms, take it or leave it. It was critical to get some fluids into her, at the very least. I came in here this morning prepared to have her strapped down if necessary and an IV drip put in. I told her as much when she tried to refuse. In the end, she made it easy on herself. She just nodded, got up and said, 'Fine, let's get it over with.' I get the impression our Miss Meade is very focused," Kandinsky added dryly.

"No kidding. You weren't tempted to sneak a look at the notebook while she was showering?"

"No. As I told you yesterday, I promised her I wouldn't. I'm never going to gain her confidence if she thinks she can't trust my word. In any case, she wasn't leaving anything to chance. She held on to it all the way to the shower room, and if she could have taken it into the stall with her without ruining it, she probably would have. As it was, she made the nurse who took her down promise not to touch it. Even then, the nurse told me she insisted on leaving it just outside the stall where she could keep an eye on it. She cleaned herself up, put on a fresh gown, ate a little, brushed her hair and her teeth, and then, when I brought her the felt pens, took them without a word, sat down and went right back to work. She hasn't budged from that chair since."

"How long has she been at it?"

The doctor glanced at her watch. "About two and a half hours this morning. She paused a few minutes ago when her lunch tray was taken in. Drank some tea. Didn't eat much, unfortunately. Then, she went back to her writing. I thought I'd see how things go this afternoon. I was planning to have another go with her a bit later."

"Her mother's funeral is tomorrow. Don't you think she should know about that? She might want to be there for it. She'd have to go under close supervision, of course, but if it were me, I think I'd want to know about it, at least." Innocent or guilty, Cruz thought. "She certainly appears strong enough to deal with it now."

"Appearances can be deceiving, but you could be right. I'll play it by ear. I was planning, in any event, to look for an opportunity to raise the general subject of her mother and see how she reacts to that before broaching the fact that she's dead. No matter what happened that night, Agent Cruz, there's a good chance she's struggling with guilt at having survived when her mother died."

"Unless she was the one who killed her."

"Is that where the investigation stands right now? You people think she did it?"

"It's one of the possibilities."

"How do you explain her own concussion, then, if not by the fact that whoever attacked her mother also went after her? The deputy said he pulled Jillian out of that house and that she'd said she was out cold before he got there."

"She could well have been struck by an unknown third party," Cruz conceded. "Her mother seems to have died of a gunshot wound, though, so I'd have to ask why she was shot and Jillian wasn't. On the other hand, if Jillian *was* the attacker, then maybe her mother struck back in self-defense. Or maybe Jillian slipped and fell and hit her head while trying to run out of the house. From the description of her mother's injuries, there would have been a fair amount of blood in the house, and the ambulance drivers reported that Jillian was barefoot when they picked her up. You must have seen the blood on her feet and hands when she was brought in here. The evidence, what little of it there is, points in any number of directions," Cruz said. "I'm keeping an open mind."

"An open mind? Really?"

"You have some reason to doubt that?"

"Well, don't take this the wrong way, but it would be a refreshing change from most law enforcement officials I've dealt with in the past." Her crepe soles squeaked as she pivoted to face him. "You still haven't told me why, exactly, the FBI is in on this case. You said something about Jillian having information pertinent to another case you're working. Is that a murder?"

"A double murder, actually, of two elderly women in England." He nodded at the woman in the room. "She was with both of them just before they died."

The lines deepened in Kandinsky's face as she frowned, taking that in. "What was her business with those women? I was told she was an historian and a writer. How on earth could she have anything to do with not just one murder but multiple murders? This doesn't make any sense."

"I wish I could give you some answers, Doc. I can tell you, though, that this seems to be a lot more complicated than two women in an isolated house being attacked by some drifter. That said, I'm damned if I know exactly what's going on or how Miss Meade fits into it all."

Inside the room, Jillian shifted position and recrossed her legs, then went back to writing, but after a moment she stopped, frowning, and looked at the felt pen in her hand. She shook it, put it to the paper and tried again, then repeated the action, a crease of irritation spreading across her brow. Setting the notebook carefully on the bed, she got to her feet and picked up the bell cord attached to the head of it. A moment later, a light went on over the window, and Cruz heard a ding down the hall at the main desk.

"Looks like she needs a new pen," he said.

Kandinsky nodded. "I'll go in and talk to her."

"Let me go with you."

"Oh, I don't think it's a good idea just yet."

"Dr. Kandinsky, please. Three women are dead. I'm not necessarily convinced Miss Meade is responsible, but I think she knows something that can point us in the direction of whoever is. Every hour in a murder investigation is critical. If a suspect isn't identified in the first forty-eight hours, chances are he or she never will be. It's already been more than that since the death of her mother, never mind those victims in England. If she's not responsible for what happened to them, then I've got to believe she'd want us to find out who is."

He waved a hand at the room, where Jillian was pressing again on the button, her look of annoyance growing. "Look at her, Doc. She's not the same woman who was brought in here two days ago. Even I could see what kind of state she was in yesterday, and that's why I didn't press it. You've done a good job of giving her a chance to get back on her feet. Now, give me a chance to do my job. I promise you, I'll go real easy with the questions and make every effort not to upset her. Like I told you, I've done this before with people in iffy mental states. I think she can handle a few questions."

"Excuse me?" Jillian's voice called from inside the room. The bell cord was still in her hand, and from the front desk came the repeated sound of dinging as she stared blindly at the glass, which she must have realized was a one-way window. "Is someone out there?"

Another voice, male, sounded from down the hall. "Dr. Kandinsky?" They turned to see an orderly peeking around the corner from the reception area. "Oh, hi. You are still there. So, I guess you know Miss Meade's been ringing?"

Kandinsky nodded at him. "Yes, I know, Bob. It's all right, I'll handle it." She glanced at Jillian, then turned to Cruz. "All right, look, maybe she is ready to take a few questions today— if," she added, "you keep it non-confrontational. I also want you to promise to stop when I ask you to."

Cruz nodded. "It's a deal."

"I mean it. I'm going to be in there with you, and we're going to keep it short. I'll introduce you and we'll take it slow while I gauge how she's reacting. She's made good progress today, but if she starts to backslide, I'm going to have to ask you to leave. Are we clear on that?"

"Clear."

Still, the doctor hesitated. "Why don't you take off your coat and jacket. You look like something out of *Dragnet*."

Cruz shrugged out of his overcoat and tossed it over the handrail that ran the entire length of the hall. He debated removing his sport coat, but then remembered the gun holster clipped to the back of his belt. He had no intention of leaving it out here where any passing psycho could pick it up, and it wasn't going to do a patient any good to see it, either. "The jacket stays," he said.

"Well, could you loosen your tie or something? Or at least try not to look so ferocious?" She watched for a moment as he did his best approximation of a non-threatening demeanor. "That's it, huh?" She sighed. "All right, let's go and talk to her."

He stepped back, letting her pass in front of him to open the door to the left of the viewing window. He followed her inside, but he was hidden by the door, and Jillian seemed not to notice him at first.

"Oh, Doctor, I'm glad you're still here." Her voice was low and dusky, still hoarse from the smoke, maybe, but clearly articulated, like a teacher's or a singer's.

"I heard your bell," Kandinsky said. "How are you doing?"

"These felt pens have dried up. I really need more. I'm not—"

Jillian froze as Cruz stepped around the open door. He closed it behind him and stood quietly against the wall, waiting for the doctor to take the lead.

"Fresh pens are not a problem, Jillian. Those ones I gave you came from the desk up front, and I guess there wasn't that much ink in them. I'm sorry about that. I'll go and get you some new ones out of the supply room in just a minute. But before I do, this is Mr. Cruz. He'd like to ask you a couple of questions. Would that be all right?"

Jillian looked nervously from the doctor to Cruz and back again, then snatched up the notebook and clutched it to the front of her robe. "I have work to do."

"We know you do," the doctor said reassuringly, as she made a palm-downward movement to Cruz behind her back.

He looked around for a place to sit, guessing that she wanted him to lower himself into a less threatening posture, but there was only the chair and the bed, and he would have to come around her to get to them. He didn't think the nervous patient would tolerate any shrinking of the physical space between them. Instead, he took a step to the side and settled on the edge of a small ledge beneath the mirrored viewing port, stretching out his legs and crossing them at the ankles, slipping his hands into his pant pockets. It was the best non-threatening pose he could muster, under the circumstances.

Jillian stole a look at him through lowered lashes, her fringe of bangs half covering her eyes. "Who are you?"

He glanced at the doctor for guidance and she gave him a nod, which he took to mean that honesty was the best policy. "My name is Alex Cruz, Miss Meade. I'm with the Federal Bureau of Investigation."

"The FBI?"

"That's right. I know you've been through a difficult time. I'm sorry for your trouble."

She looked uncertainly to the doctor.

"Why don't you have a seat, Jillian?" Dr. Kandinsky said.

Jillian hesitated, then perched on the very edge of the chair, still clutching the book, her gaze dropping to the floor. The doctor settled herself nearby on the bed, like a referee or a guardian angel. "Oh, Lord, it feels good to sit," she said, smiling. "I've been on my feet all morning. So, how are you feeling, Jillian? I see they brought your lunch in. You didn't eat very much, though. I wish you'd have a little more."

"I'm not hungry."

"Maybe not, but you'd feel better if you ate. How's the breathing? Still painful?"

Jillian lifted her thin shoulders, but her eyes stayed down. "A little. It doesn't matter."

"Well, we'll want to keep a close eye on that. I don't want infection setting in there." Jillian said nothing. "You've been keeping busy, I see," Kandinsky added. "At this rate, I'm going to have to get you a new notebook soon, too."

Jillian glanced up, then looked at the notebook in her hands. She shook her head. "I don't think I'll need another one. I'm nearly done. This one should be enough."

"Enough for what, Miss Meade?" Cruz asked. She flinched, as if she'd forgotten he was there, but didn't answer. "Can you tell us what it is you've been working on?"

Her thumbs began stroking the nubbled surface of the black notebook, and she rocked ever so slightly on the edge of the chair. She was stalling, Cruz thought, irritation at this helpless act growing, although he was careful not to let it show.

When she finally did answer, it was only with evasion. "You were here before," she said.

"Excuse me?"

"You were here. I heard your voice outside with the doctor and Nils Berglund. I suppose that mirror is a one-way window?" she added, glancing over at the doctor.

"Yes, you're right, Jillian, it is," Dr. Kandinsky said. "I'm sorry, I guess I should have mentioned it to you, but frankly, I'm so used to it being there, I forgot all about it. It's just a safety precaution, so we can look in on patients without disturbing them. I'm sure you understand."

Jillian nodded slightly, then turned back to study the floor in front of Cruz's feet, as if she were reading code in the speckled linoleum. "You were here, weren't you? I'm sure that was you I heard...yesterday, I suppose it would have been?"

"Yes, ma'am, I suppose it was."

"Why are you here?"

"I had some questions I wanted to ask you."

"Questions?"

"Yes. But before I do," Cruz said, glancing at the doctor, then taking the plunge, "can you tell us whether you know why you're here, Miss Meade?"

"Because...something happened," she said. "I was hurt. This is a hospital."

"Do you remember what it was that happened?"

Her rocking increased a little. She kept her eyes on the floor, but as Cruz watched and waited, one tear rolled down the soft incline of her cheek. Damn, but she was good, the cynic in him said.

She looked over at the doctor. "I have work to finish," she pleaded softly.

"I know, Jillian, and we can't stay long. But can you answer Agent Cruz's question? Do you remember what happened before you came here?"

She nodded slowly, looking back at the floor. "There was a fire," she whispered.

"That's right, there was," the doctor said. "Anything else?"

"My mother died," she said, then pressed her lips together as more tears started rolling silently down her cheeks.

"Miss Meade, I'm very sorry for your loss," Cruz told her.

She stole a quick glance at him, then nodded.

"Can you tell us what happened that night?"

Her lips were pale and bloodless, pressed tightly together. She shook her head.

"You can't say? Or you don't want to talk about it?"

"Not now. I need to finish. Please," she said, appealing directly to him now. "I need to finish." Her eyes were large and pleading, and her pale skin was tracked with tears. The sight of her left him feeling like scum for even thinking about how much he wanted to grill her until she cracked and told the truth. Damn, but this was hard. He'd spent a decade interrogating enlisted guys who knifed each other in drunken bar fights, dopers who flipped out on their whores, and grunts who got shit-scared in rice paddies and fragged their COs rather than take another step toward the enemy. But what had ever made him think he could do this?

"It's all right," he said. "No one wants to stop you from finishing your work. Just...don't cry, please."

"I'm sorry."

"Maybe there's something else we could talk about?" the doctor suggested, arching one eyebrow at him in an obvious effort to steer him in another direction.

"Yes, there is," Cruz agreed. "Actually, the real reason I'm here, Miss Meade, is because I wanted to ask you about a trip you made last month. To England?"

She raised her head, her eyes still damp, but curious now, too. "Yes. I was in England and France."

"I was wondering if you could tell me what you were doing over there."

"I was...I was collecting some artifacts and information for an exhibit at the museum where I work."

Cruz nodded encouragement as she paused to wipe her cheeks with the back of her hand. The doctor grabbed a box of tissue from the table next to the bed and reached across to hand her one. "We'd been offered material from various archives over there," Jillian went on after wiping her eyes. "We're mounting an exhibit on covert American support to the French Resistance during the Second World War. It's...it's sort of a specialty of mine, so I was appointed to curate."

"And that's all you did while you were there? Gather material for this exhibit?"

She looked away uncertainly.

"Miss Meade?"

"I was doing...personal research, too."

"What kind of research?"

Her thin shoulders lifted in a shrug. "Family history."

"I've heard a little about your parents," Cruz said. "Your father was an OSS pilot. They say he flew supply missions to the Resistance."

She nodded. "And my mother was behind the lines."

"And they met over there?"

"Yes."

"And so, on this trip last month, you were...?"

She exhaled heavily, although there was as much shudder as sigh in it. "I was trying to retrace their steps. See where they'd been, talk to people who might have known them there."

"Does the name Vivian Atwater mean anything to you?"

She frowned. "Yes. She recruited my mother."

"Who did your mother work for?"

"The British SOE—Special Operations Executive. Miss Atwater was one of her handlers while she was behind the lines in occupied France."

It was Cruz's turn for a puzzled frown. The query from Scotland Yard had said only that Vivian Atwater was a retired civil servant. He should have known. It was typical intelligence smoke, the need-to-know restriction ensuring that anyone who really *did* need to know would probably end up being kept in the dark. "And were you able to meet this Miss Atwater while you were in London?"

"Yes. One afternoon, I called on her at her office."

"Do you remember the date?"

"I...I'm not sure. A Thursday...I think. The middle of last month. I'm not sure of the exact date. It would be in my agenda. You could check. It's in my..." She froze and looked up. "It was in my purse, in the house... But it must be..."

"It doesn't matter right now," Cruz said. "We can try to find out later. So you went to see her at her office? How many times?"

"Just the once."

"And did you see her again after that? At her home, maybe?"

"No, just that once. I spent about four hours with her in all. We had tea in her office and we talked about the war."

"And that's it. You didn't see her again that evening? Maybe she invited you back to her apartment in Bloomsbury?"

Jillian frowned. "No. I only spoke with her at her office. I signed in and out at the front desk there, and we had tea and talked. Why? What's this about?"

"How about another woman, Miss Meade, a lady named Margaret Ellen Entwistle?"

"Nellie Entwistle?"

"Is that what she was called? Was she with the SOE, as well?"

"No. She was a childhood friend of my mother. They grew up together in Dover and..." She looked up suddenly. "What do you mean, 'was'?"

"Did you see her while you were over there, too?"

"Yes, I did. Why? What's happened?"

"When did you see Miss Entwistle?"

"A couple of days before I met with Miss Atwater. What's this all about?"

"So if you saw Miss Atwater on a Thursday, that would have been...what? Monday or Tuesday?"

"The Tuesday afternoon, I suppose. I had tea with her, too, at her house in Dover."

"Tell me about that."

"What do you want me to tell you? She was a sweet little old lady who lived in a cottage covered with vines, and she told me about growing up in Dover with my mother. She was with my mother the night my grandfather died, so she was able to tell me about that, too. He was killed in a German bombing raid during the Battle of Britain."

"And that was all?"

"Well, no, there were a lot of other details she was able to give me, as well, about the early days of the war and Dunkirk and—"

"I guess what I meant was, did you leave her in good health?"

"I only saw her the once, and she seemed fine." Jillian looked from Cruz to the doctor and back again, her growing distress evident. "Why? What's happened to her?"

"Who went with you when you visited these women?"

"No one."

"Are you sure?"

"Well, yes. I think I would have noticed, don't you?"

Cruz ignored the sarcasm. "Did you discuss your meetings with anyone over there? Have business with anyone who might have taken an interest in them?"

"No. I told you, this was strictly a personal project."

"Was Miss Atwater alive and well when you left her?"

"Yes, of course she—" Jillian leapt to her feet. "Tell me! What's happened?"

"You don't know?"

"How could I know? Know what? What's happened to them? Why are you here?"

"Agent Cruz," the doctor interrupted, "this is not—"

"They're dead, Miss Meade. They were murdered, both of them."

"But—how?"

"I think we should get into this at another time," Dr. Kandinsky said. "Agent Cruz, I think Jillian's given the answers you need for the time being, and—"

Jillian raised a hand to her, then turned back to Cruz. "Tell me what happened. How could they have been murdered? This can't be."

"Miss Atwater was found bound, beaten and shot in her Bloomsbury apartment. Miss Entwistle was also killed in a similar manner. Both their homes were torched afterward. Sound familiar?"

"Agent Cruz!" the doctor said sharply. "This was not what we agreed!"

"What happened, Jillian?" Cruz pressed. "Why were they killed?"

"I have no idea! Oh, God, no. Why would anyone kill them? It makes no sense. They were just a couple of sweet old ladies. They knew nothing!"

"Knew nothing about what?"

"Agent Cruz, that's enough of that!"

But he was already on his feet. He crossed the room in two long strides and took the woman's thin shoulders between his hands, not roughly, but firmly enough that Jillian had no choice but to look at him. "What didn't they know, Jillian? It's really important that you tell me or their killers are going to get away with this."

"Oh, please, no..."

"That's enough!" Dr. Kandinsky ordered. She, too, was on her feet but before she could reach them, a bang sounded from behind them and Cruz felt the back of his jacket gripped in a vise. He was lifted off his feet, hurled aside like a rag doll.

"Get out!"

Cruz landed at the open door and grabbed the frame for support. Recovering his footing, he turned to see Berglund standing between him and Jillian, the deputy's broad features distorted by as murderous a look as he'd ever seen.

"I said get the hell out!" Berglund ordered.

When Cruz didn't move fast enough, the man charged forward and bulldozed him out through the open door, then slammed it shut behind him. Cruz steadied himself on the handrail opposite the door. Berglund was inside the room, and Cruz looked through the viewing window just in time to see Jillian's knees buckle. The deputy caught her, lifting her in an easy swoop and carrying her to the bed. Dr. Kandinsky was right beside him as he laid her down, one of her hands reaching above the head of the bed to slam an intercom button on the wall. From down the hall to his right, Cruz heard the sound of her muffled orders and then feet running. Berglund was leaning over Jillian's still form, and as Cruz shifted position, he saw the deputy stroking her forehead, his lips moving. A nurse approached with a covered tray, which Cruz suspected held a sedative, and entered the room. Dr. Kandinsky held up a hand and she stood off to the side, waiting, while the doctor spoke to Berglund. Looking reluctant, the deputy nodded and turned away from the bed where Jillian lay, deathly pale, her eyes closed. She may or may not have fainted, but her hands, Cruz noticed, were still gripping that damn notebook. As Berglund made his way toward the door, the nurse and the doctor closed ranks around the bed.

Cruz braced himself as Berglund barreled out into the hall and was on top of him with a speed that was incredible for a man of that size. His fists wrapped in Cruz's lapels and he rammed him against the wall. "What the hell were you thinking?"

"I asked her a couple of questions, that's all! The doctor gave her permission. And get your damn mitts off me right now, Deputy," Cruz warned, shoving him back. It was like trying to push off a solid brick wall, but Berglund gave a grunt of disgust and dropped him of his own accord.

"I don't care what the doctor said. I told you to leave her alone."

"She was fine."

"The hell she was! Look at her."

Cruz glanced back at the room, where Dr. Kandinsky was pulling a blanket up over the still form on the bed. He turned back to the deputy.

"You didn't see her ten minutes ago. Dammit, Berglund, she's conning you! She's the biggest damn con artist I've ever seen! You would not have believed the change in her. I wouldn't have, if I hadn't seen it for myself. She was sitting in there, cool as a cucumber when I got here. Look, I know you've known her a long time and that the two of you have some history, but you need to consider the possibility that she's been gone a long time and may no longer be the same girl you once knew. The doctor said herself, Jillian's focused and she knows how to get what she wants. She got up today, demanded more writing materials, and then, when the doc made it conditional on her getting cleaned up first, that's what Jillian did, no problem. She only puts on that fragile act when she thinks it'll help her dodge the tough questions."

"We agreed your questions could wait."

"No, you agreed. I was willing to take it one step at a time. As it happened, the timing was right when I got here. The doctor agreed she was strong enough to take a few questions. You weren't here, I was. Simple as that. And if it's any help to you, we did ask her first what she remembered about the other night."

"What did she say? Does she realize Grace is dead?"

"Yes. She's clear on that and clear on the fire, but she didn't to want to go there right now. Fine. I was trying not to upset her. The doctor agreed it might be all right to ask her about her trip overseas last month, so that's what I did. Jillian only flipped out when I told her about those two women being murdered. But she knows something," Cruz added. "She's not the total innocent you think she is, Berglund, I swear to God."

"She's not capable of murder. I know her, dammit! She could not have done this."

"Maybe you're right. Maybe she didn't fire the gun or light the match herself, here or in those other cases. Look, I admit, I'm not sure about that myself. All right? But sure as we're standing here, she knows something about why those women were murdered, and we are never going to get anywhere until we stop being conned by this helpless act she puts on."

Berglund shook his head. "You're way off base."

He turned abruptly and walked to the window at the end of the hall, staring out—a man obviously struggling to get his over-wrought emotions under control.

"Come on, let's get out of here. You can follow me back." He was already in motion, heading for the exit.

"Where are we going?" Cruz asked, catching up to him.

"Back to my office. You need to call your special agent in charge over there in St. Paul. I got a radio message from Verna. She said he phoned twenty minutes after you left, fit to be tied."

"What did he say?"

"Just for you to call him back pronto. Verna said the guy sounded like he was spitting nails. Call me crazy, but I'm guessing he got a hit on that suspect Tom Newkirk saw at the airport the other day."

"This fast?"

Berglund paused at the door to the lobby. "Well, what do you know, Agent Cruz? You think it's possible that maybe we've got a for-real bad guy on our hands? Somebody you can go sic your big, tough dogs on so you can call 'em the hell off that poor girl back there?"

"Maybe so," Cruz said. "God knows, there's nothing straight-forward about this case. But just remember—Tom Newkirk said this guy, whoever he might be, got off the plane with that same poor girl down the hall. She knew the guy, Berglund. She introduced him to Newkirk."

"Yeah? And so?"

"And so, if this guy, whoever the hell he is, does have something to do with Grace Meade's death, what do you suppose are the odds that Jillian's an innocent bystander? Me, I'd say they're pretty slim."

CHAPTER 21

I'm running out of time. An FBI man showed up out of the blue with questions for me, but they made no sense. About Miss Atwater and—oh, God! Nellie Entwistle! My mind's a fog, but I'm sure he said they're dead. How can that be? It makes no sense! It has to be a lie. Obviously he wanted me to confess to...what? My mother's murder, no doubt. But then, why bring those other two women into it?

I should have remained calm. Why couldn't I just stay calm and either ignore him or hear him out? Ask questions. Insist he stop lying and tell me what he really wanted. Whatever. Just let him say what he came to say and then leave, so I could get back to work. Instead, I allowed him bait me, and I reacted. Stupid, stupid Jillian!

And then? What happened then? I think Nils burst in, and—then what? They gave me another sedative. It was after Nils was gone, both he and that horrible FBI man. Poor Nils. He looked terrible.

I asked the doctor not to give me any more drugs. I told her I can't handle them and needed to finish this, but either I wasn't making any sense or she simply chose to ignore me. Now, I have no idea what time it is. I slept again—I don't know for how long, but I've lost the thread of what I was writing. Now, I don't know if I'm going to have time to finish.

Damn! Why couldn't they just leave me alone and let me finish? What did I ever do to deserve this?

Oh, Jillian—you know very well. There's no escaping this. The blood price has to be paid.

So much blood.

I keep drifting off to sleep and each time I do, I find myself back in my mother's kitchen. Her body lies on the floor in a pool that shines brilliant red on the black and white tiles. Her porcelain blue eyes are open, staring and accusatory. I feel my throat aching to cry, and my face is soaked with tears. But despite the dense smoke filling the house, I can't move. I am transfixed by my mother's furious eyes.

Snakes of flame creep across the floor, pausing briefly at the pool of blood around her, temporarily stymied. But as the blood begins to sizzle and boil away, the snake-flames move forward again, licking at her body. I stand there, helpless and horrified, as her soft, pink skin begins to burn. Shrinking and curling, it peels back on itself like brittle parchment, exposing red, fleshy muscle, tendons and organs beneath. These blacken and fall away in flaming strips, slowly revealing a bare, bleached skeleton. The bones are small, birdlike, incredibly fragile, and as I watch in horrified fascination, a spiderweb of hairline cracks forms and spreads across them. Then suddenly, they crumble into fine, gray powder that the gusting inferno blows high and wide.

Ashes to ashes, dust to dust.

And with each layer of my mother's body that is revealed, then consumed in that crematorium of my nightmare, our terrible secrets, too, are exposed for all the world to see. Except in reality my mother's secrets—and mine—are still shrouded in that veil of lies she wove. Now that she's gone, no one will ever know the truth unless I tell it. All of it.

The truth...

For weeks now, ever since I caught its first glimmer through the murk of half-truths and deception that defined our lives, I've been struggling over what it would serve to talk about it now, after all these years. Who it might help. Who it would surely hurt. My mother, of course, would have done anything to prevent the truth from coming out—for many reasons, but at this point, I think, mostly out of pride.

The damage to her reputation will be unavoidable now, but at least she won't be here to see it. For that one small mercy, she might have been grateful. I have to admit that I, too, am relieved she'll be spared the indignity. Even now, after everything I've learned, I suppose the child in me still clings to the memory of the mummy I adored. I would not have wished to see her suffer public humiliation.

I slept again, and my mind is a little clearer now. I have to do this. I have to finish. Where was I?

I remembered....

It was the math that started me wondering—dates and events that refused to line up in the proper order. For people in my field, this kind of thing happens often enough, of course. History gets written, then rewritten, then rewritten yet again as new evidence comes to light. When facts don't jibe, we question their accuracy, we develop new interpretations, and ultimately (far too often, I'm embarrassed to admit) we massage the details until they fit into our preconceived notion of the truth. But numbers don't lie, and it was on the numbers that I really started to run into trouble.

As I followed my mother's and father's separate trails into France and their reacquaintance there in 1943, I started wondering exactly how and when it was that their paths had crossed to ensure my own emergence the following year.

The average human gestation period is forty weeks from conception to birth, give or take a couple of weeks either way. I've never had a child myself, but I gather the common wisdom is that first-born children often arrive late, so I tried to factor that possibility into my calculations, even though my mother had never dropped any hint that I might have been tardy arriving on the scene—or, for that matter, early. I was born, she said, on July 14, 1944—Bastille Day—which was exactly six weeks before Paris was liberated from the Nazis. I was a normal, healthy baby, she said. She didn't know my exact birth weight because there was no scale on hand when I was born. I might have been a little on the small side, she said, but frankly, all newborns seem small, don't they? Without a scale, how can you be sure if they're underweight or not?

I don't know if there was a doctor or midwife present when I was born. I don't know if my mother's labor was long or short, difficult or easy. I don't know if she was disappointed that I was a girl instead of a boy. There are so many vague and missing details in my mind concerning my earliest days, but I've never been able to fill them in because I always knew that this period was the blackest part of that black hole of her past, one she was particularly loathe to revisit. And so I learned early on not to ask too many childish questions of the "Where did I come from, Mummy?" variety. The only thing I've ever felt quite certain of was that my arrival did very little to assuage her grief over the death of my father several weeks earlier.

(This is not a bid for pity, merely an explanation of why I may have been just a little obsessed with filling in some of these blanks.)

In any case, since I was born on Bastille Day, I calculated that I had to have been conceived at the end of September or very beginning of October, 1943. And therein lies the problem with the math. Because after meeting with Miss Atwater and her remarkably encyclopedic memory, I now know that my mother was parachuted into occupied France in early August, 1943. And Joe Meade, I learned from the declassified OSS files sitting back in my office, didn't make his first covert supply drop until October 16th, 1943—a gap of over two months when they could not possibly have been together. Yet this was the very time when they were supposed to have been busy making me.

And not only that. I also know now that it was only on his eighth sortie, in early February, that Joe's plane went down, forcing him hide out with the Resistance—this, of course, being the period, according to the lore I'd been fed all my life, in which the two of them fell in love and were secretly married. Which either means that I was born just five months after his plane crashed and he was taken in and sheltered by my mother's Resistance cell, or, an alternative explanation, that they "did the deed," as it were, long before the enforced confinement that followed the crash of his plane. And why not? They were young, full of raging hormones, and engaged in high-risk activities from which any chance intimate encounter would have offered a welcome respite. Well, so what? I thought. Obviously, I was conceived out of wedlock.

Fair enough, but the problem of the math remains. I couldn't have been conceived before my mother left for France, obviously, or I would have been born no later than May, instead of in July. So, let's presume they met again at Joe's very first landing behind the lines in occupied France (that was October 16th, remember). Let's presume that for some reason, Joe didn't simply off-load his cargo and take off again as fast as possible, which was normal procedure for these pilots, who were anxious to avoid detection by the Germans or the French milice. That, instead, he delayed his departure to spend a little time alone with "his girl" (about whom he had already written to his parents, although in the vaguest of terms because of the top secret nature of their work). And that in that brief space of time, they managed to conceive me.

That would have accounted for my birth on July 14th, a scant thirty-eight weeks later, in the Drancy transit camp, where, according to Miss Atwater, my mother reportedly spent the last two months of the Occupation. It would mean that I was born a little premature, and yet I managed, despite harsh conditions, poor hygiene and the deplorably meager prison rations given to the inmates, to survive until the camp was liberated at the end of August.

Fair enough. It's all possible—*if* my mother and Joe Meade were together the night of that first-ever supply flight he made behind the lines.

But they weren't.

What I learned when I went to Paris was that there was almost certainly no way my mother could have been in the woods a hundred miles north of Paris on that night of October 16th—not when the archives of the German Occupation list her as having been in custody at Gestapo headquarters on the Avenue Foch in Paris from October 12-26, 1943, detained for questioning in one of the periodic Gestapo sweeps of neighborhoods in the Nazis' tireless effort to uproot and destroy the Resistance. She was one of over twenty people rounded up in Gentilly on that occasion and held for two weeks, her arrest ordered by a newly arrived Gestapo Obermeister reputed to be ruthless in his determination to infiltrate and destroy the Paris Resistance network.

The more I dug into the records of the Occupation, the more I found myself regretting the task I'd taken on, dreading the truth I'd been so determined up to then to find. Suddenly, I was sick at heart with anticipation of what my mother might have been put through when she was at the mercy of the Gestapo. Terrified to think what she might have been driven to do.

But it was too late. Pandora's box had cracked open, and now I had to know. Because if my mother wasn't with Joe Meade when I was conceived, then who was my real father? And when—and why—had she decided to lie about it to my grandparents, to me and to the world?

CHAPTER 22

Havenwood, Minnesota
Friday, January 12, 1979

Cruz and Berglund convoyed back from the Montrose hospital to Havenwood, the police cruiser leading the way along what were probably the same corrugated secondary roads they'd taken the night before when Cruz, as passenger, had suffered the uneasy sense of hurtling through a black void toward the edge of the world. But in today's brilliant sunlight, he saw there were no sudden drops, no stomach-plummeting surprises in this flat, snow-drifted prairie. It rolled away to infinity, recalling bygone days of massive buffalo herds and hunters riding bareback under an immense blue sky—the kind of sky that made everything beneath it seem small, fleeting, and inconsequential.

It was all Cruz could do to keep up with the black-and-white as Berglund sped along with the ease and familiarity of someone who'd been traveling these frost-rutted back roads all his life. When they arrived at the offices of the Havenwood police, they found Verna at the front desk deep in conversation with a younger, petite woman in a powder-blue ski jacket, jeans and brown leather hiking boots. Her sandy hair was caught up in a ponytail fastened by a punctured bit of leather, held in place by what looked like a long, pointed wooden chopstick. Both women turned at the sound of the opening door, and the younger one's expression warmed at the sight of the deputy.

"There's the absentminded professor now," she said cheerfully.

She wasn't classically beautiful, Cruz thought, but she had the kind of clean, honest looks that made a man breath a sigh of relief. Her buffed, rosy skin looked soft and inviting to the touch. Her blue eyes were as wide and guileless as the prairie sky, and the tiny lines at the edges of her eyes and mouth suggested the warm smile she wore now was pretty much habitual.

Berglund seemed a little thrown off his stride to find her there, but he bent to receive the kiss she stretched on tiptoes to plant on him. "What's up?" he asked. This must be the wife, Cruz realized, studying them with interest.

She nodded to a thermos flask and a brown paper bag sitting behind her on the counter. "You forgot your lunch. I was heading out to pick up some groceries and thought I'd drop it off."

"Guess I was rushing this morning." Berglund glanced around the lobby. "Where's the baby?"

"At home with my mother. She's putting her down for a nap while I do the shopping. I didn't want to drag her around with this bug she's got."

"She okay?"

"Grumpy as all get-out. I got her in to see the doctor at the clinic this morning, though. He says she's got another ear infection. I picked up the ear drops and the pink stuff at the drugstore on the way home. I dosed her up and gave her an early lunch, then called Mom to watch her."

Berglund nodded, then looked over her head to Verna. "Any calls?"

"Just that one from the FBI fellow in St. Paul."

"You want to get him back on the horn? The agent here can take it in the chief's office."

"So," his wife said, smiling past him to Cruz, "this is the mysterious FBI agent."

Berglund made a grudging introduction. "Agent Cruz—my wife, Sharon."

Cruz nodded. "Ma'am."

"Nice to meet you. Alex, right? I hear you play a mean game of shuffleboard."

That's right, Cruz thought, one of the women from the pub last night had been her sister. Sharon Berglund was smaller than her sister and the younger of the two, he was guessing, but otherwise the resemblance was strong now that he'd made the connection. Same light brown hair, same eyes, same friendly manner. The sisters were as outgoing as Berglund was reticent, the kind of women who radiated loyalty and warmth, and invited a lifetime of trust.

"I had a little beginner's luck," he said, watching as she leaned comfortably into Berglund, who absentmindedly slipped an arm around her shoulder while his free hand flipped through the pile of mail on the counter. Cruz felt a pang of loneliness in the face of such easy familiarity. They'd obviously been together for some time with—what? Three kids, was it? Three kids and this easy intimacy he'd never managed to pull off with any woman. Was it him, Cruz wondered, or was it just that he'd never found the right one?

He ignored the ache kicked up by the thought of his solitude. "I gather I was just filling in for you last night," he said. "Your sister and her friends were shorthanded."

Sharon's smile widened. "From the sound of things, I think they were just as happy it worked out that way. You made quite an impression. I hear Carla wants to make you a home-cooked meal."

Cruz felt his face go warm, and he looked to Berglund to get him off the hook here, but the deputy's habitual frown only deepened as he went on perusing the mail.

"I was supposed to go last night," Sharon added, "but then, our little girl was under the weather and Nils here was tied up." She smiled at Berglund, pausing to pick an invisible something off his green nylon jacket and flick it aside. Lint? A stubborn bit of ash still clinging from the fire? Or perhaps a long brown hair?

Cruz recalled her sister's touchiness about the fact that Sharon here was Jillian's successor in Berglund's life. Did Sharon have any idea of her husband's raw sensitivity where that woman over in Montrose was concerned? Was that the real reason she'd come to his office today, the forgotten lunch a convenient pretext to check up on the state of her marriage in light of the return of this blast from his past? To check up on him? If so, Berglund seemed oblivious.

Cruz felt a sudden urge to kick the guy, just to wake him up. Berglund was as taciturn and hard to read as ever, nothing in his manner hinting that only an hour ago he'd lost it, undermining his professionalism and risking his career by manhandling a federal agent, ready to tear Cruz to pieces for upsetting Jillian. There was no sign now of that rage. No one who hadn't seen the effect that woman's distress had had on him would suspect the tenderness with which the stone-faced deputy had scooped her into his arms and settled her onto the bed, all the while whispering soothing phrases. But had she truly been distressed, Cruz wondered, or had she simply played a card she knew would work on an ex-lover who was obviously still vulnerable to her wiles?

He could only pity the poor wife. The two women were as different from one another as it was possible to be. How could Berglund let himself get so emotionally tangled up over Jillian Meade when he had a sweet thing like this at home to share his life, help raise his children and warm his bed? How the hell could one guy be so lucky and so stupid at the same time?

"I'll put that call through whenever you're ready, Alex," Verna said.

"I'm ready now, Verna, thanks. Good to meet you, Mrs.

Berglund," he added, nodding to her before heading into the squad room, looking for a place to redirect his frustration. If the FBI field office was getting back to him this quickly, it meant they had something on Jillian Meade or her reported travel companion or both. The sooner he found out what it was, the sooner he could get to the bottom of what was going on with that bloody woman. And the sooner he did that, the sooner Jillian Meade could get the hell out of these people's lives and leave them in peace.

The Special Agent in Charge of the FBI field office in Minneapolis-St. Paul was named Sheen, and when he found out it was Cruz phoning back, he pulled himself out of a meeting to take the call. "Glad you got back to me, Agent Cruz."

"Yes, sir. I called as soon as I got the message."

"We've got a hit on that fellow who came in from Washington on Tuesday morning."

"That was fast."

"One of my men was already over at the airport working another case," the SAC said. "When I got your call, I asked him to run down the passenger manifests from Tuesday's flights. You mentioned the governor took the plane in question back to Washington, so it was a simple enough matter to find out from his office that it was United's morning flight to Dulles, and then request the manifest for the inbound trip. A Simon Edelmann was listed as occupying seat 14-B on that flight, while your Miss Meade was in 14-A. Ergo, I'm thinking he's your man."

"Simon Edelmann." Cruz rummaged in his pockets for his pad and pen, then settled into the chair behind the chief's desk while he made a note of the name. "You're sure this is the right guy?"

"Physical description checked out. My man at the airport talked with a United ground attendant who saw him and a woman stop to talk to someone in the governor's entourage. This Edelmann?" Sheen added. "He's an Israeli. Turns out he entered the country six days ago on a flight from Paris to New York/La

Guardia. Came in on a visa issued out of our embassy there. Problem is, he should never have gotten the visa, or been allowed to slip past the INS watchers at La Guardia, but somehow he managed to fly in under the radar. A series of errors, maybe, or somebody deliberately looking the other way."

"Why is he barred?"

"He was put on the FBI watch list not long ago, which means Immigration and Naturalization is supposed to clear it with us first before issuing a visa. Normally, in a case like that, the request is forwarded to the Bureau liaison in the embassy, then back to headquarters for review. It didn't happen here. They just went ahead and issued the visa without checking back."

"Any idea how they fouled up like that?"

"I just got a call from the New York port of entry and it turns out the visa was signed by someone working under embassy consular cover over there."

"Somebody in the CIA station?"

"You got it. As far as the Company's concerned, I gather, the visa was a simple spook-to-spook courtesy. Had they bothered to check the watch list, they'd have seen this guy was a no-go, but either they didn't bother to check, or they knew it and just didn't give a damn."

"Spook-to-spook courtesy? Are you saying this Simon Edelmann is with Israeli intelligence?"

"Looks like it. It's all a little murky. Don't know exactly what the deal is there. I called it in to our own counterintelligence guys for clarification. They confirmed the guy checks out as Mossad, but other than that, they wouldn't get into details on the phone."

"But both the Bureau and the CIA liaise with Mossad on a regular basis," Cruz said, frowning. "I had dealings with them myself when I was in the Army and stationed over in Germany. We work the same side of the street more often than not, so why would this guy be on the watch list? What's he supposed to have done?"

"You got me. I gather it's Justice that requested he go on the watch list, but it's their file and closely held. Bottom line, though, is that the front office wants to know where he is and what he's up to. Have you got him under surveillance?"

"I wish," Cruz said. "Like I told you this morning, all I have is an eyewitness report the guy was seen arriving at the airport Tuesday in the company of this woman I'm here to interview. She started out looking like a material witness on those U.K. homicides I'm working, but I'm wondering about that now."

"What does she say about the guy she flew in with?"

"She doesn't say anything, although to be frank, it's a question I haven't been able to put to her yet. Her mother was murdered not eight hours after she hit town."

"Jesus! What is she, the frigging Angel of Death? Did she do it?"

"Not clear, and she's not talking. For my money, she looks to be playing the not-guilty-by-reason-of-insanity card. Tried to off herself the other night—allegedly. Flubbed it, very conveniently—twice, as a matter of fact. Still, she's managed to be convincing enough that the locals have got her on psychiatric lock-down."

"And Edelmann? Is he anywhere around?"

"Not that I know of." From the corner of his eye, Cruz picked up movement in the squad room outside. Berglund was striding across the floor toward the corner office, his wife obviously dispatched, the brown bag and thermos container she'd brought in gripped in one massive hand. "I'll let you know if we do sight him," Cruz told the SAC. "Meantime, is there anything else you can give me?"

"Not yet. I've moved up the feeding chain at headquarters to see if I can get anything else out of them on this Edelmann. I'm waiting for the call now. They're supposed to be sending us a photo of the guy. We're under instructions to locate and detain ASAP."

"Is somebody going to ream out the CIA over this visa snafu?"

"Maybe. I doubt it," Sheen said. "It's not like they're gonna give a good goddam. Those fellas have their own agenda, and in my experience, they do what they want to do, regardless of how many interdepartmental feathers they ruffle. How much longer do you figure on being out there?"

"I'm not sure. I'd hoped to get a statement on those British cases and get back on the road later today, but that's not too likely now. I'm in for another twenty-four hours at least by the look of it."

"Well, check back by end of business today and I'll see if anything else has come in. I'll make sure the weekend officer on watch is up to speed, too, and calls me if anything new comes down the pipeline. If this Edelmann does show up, you're asked to request local authorities take him into custody, then get in touch with us and the INS. HQ says there's a nationwide alert going out. I've been told to put some manpower on it myself. We'll attempt to pick up his trail from point of arrival in state— check out the car rental agencies here in the Twin Cities, hotels, that kind of thing. If we find he headed your way, you could be getting some backup in short order."

"Fair enough, but frankly, we're just playing catch-up at this point. It's been over seventy-two hours since the last confirmed sighting, and of all the spooks you ever want to deal with, there's none as adept at fading into the woodwork as the Mossad-trained guys. I'm guessing Edelmann's long gone by now, having a drink back in Tel Aviv even as we speak."

"Yeah, that's my bet, too, but we'll go through the motions. Meantime, if you don't hear from me before then, check back in by seventeen hundred hours."

"Yes, sir. Will do."

As Berglund entered the office, Cruz realized he should get up and give him the chair. It was cracked, fake leather, and it squeaked and wasn't very comfortable, but it occupied the place of honor behind in the chief's desk, the seat of whatever law enforcement authority existed around here. For the time being and as long as the chief was laid up, it rightfully belonged to the deputy—except Cruz was in no mood to relinquish whatever meager advantage he held at the moment. What he'd thought would be a routine inquiry, an in-and-out interview, was getting thoroughly bogged down in this bloody freezing, middle-of-nowhere town, looking less and less clear-cut with each passing hour. There was precisely zero chance he'd be catching a plane today, and for all he knew, he was going to be stuck here all weekend and into next week. He was out of clean shirts and he was out of patience. Jillian Meade was playing a stalling game, and Berglund, who should have been his main ally in cutting through the crap she was slinging, was so wrapped around her little finger that his value as a fellow investigator was rapidly dwindling to nil.

So he'd hold on to the chair for now, Cruz decided as Berglund dropped the lunch bag and thermos on the desk. "Have a seat," Cruz said, nodding to the straight-backed gray metal chair on the other side of the desk.

Berglund hesitated, then scowled and settled. "Gee, thanks. Make yourself at home. You hungry?"

"Beg your pardon?"

"Hungry," Berglund repeated, nodding at the brown bag. "You know...lunch?"

"I wouldn't dream of taking the lunch your wife made for you."

"Well, there's more than enough, I guess. Turns out she brought over a couple of sandwiches for you, too."

"She brought lunch for me?"

"Yeah. Go figure, huh?"

"She seems like a real nice lady."

"She is."

"Well, tell her thanks from me. I'll pass for now, but maybe in a while. I had a big breakfast."

"So I hear," Berglund muttered.

"What does that mean?"

"I heard Ollie Jorgenson bent your ear for an hour or so over breakfast this morning. So what is it with you and the ladies, Cruz? First those women last night, then Ollie and Sybil

Newkirk this morning? Not to mention Verna out front there, who's already on a first name basis. Hell, you've even got my own wife cooking for you."

Cruz shrugged. "It's a friendly town. But what's the deal? Have you been keeping a tail on me since I arrived?"

"I just hear things, is all—although maybe I *should* be keeping a closer eye on you. Either that or lock up all the women. You even sweet-talked that shrink into letting you in to see Jillian after she'd already told me no way. Guess that makes you some kind of real lady-killer, huh? So what's the secret? Is it the FBI badge, you figure, or that Latin lover thing you've got going for yourself there?"

"You're kidding, right?"

Berglund leaned back and laced his fingers over his stomach as he tipped the chair on its rear legs. "Not at all. I'm taking notes. Me, I'm just a small-town cop. I figure a big-time fed like you can give me some tips on how to handle your average female witness."

"Oh, for chrissake, Berglund, give it a rest, will you? You've got yourself a great wife there, a family, and a town that obviously looks up to you and has a lot of respect for you. You don't need pointers from anybody, least of all me."

Berglund said nothing for a moment, just rocked on the chair legs, his gravel-eyed gaze taking Cruz's measure. "You married yourself?" he asked finally.

Cruz shook his head. "Not anymore."

"But you were once?"

"Briefly. It didn't take. The lady figured out pretty fast the grass was greener elsewhere."

"She left you for another guy?"

"Yup. One of my buddies. Former buddies. It was a year or so after I re-upped in the Army. She was a therapist at Walter Reed Hospital. He was going through physio there after getting shot up in 'Nam. I was on the road too much. I came home early

from a field assignment one day and found the two of them playing doctor in our bed."

"So she left you and married the guy?"

"Last I heard, that was the plan. Don't know if they're still together or not. We didn't really socialize much after that, as you
can imagine. I got a transfer out and lost track of them."

"Sorry to hear it."

Cruz shrugged. "It was a two-way street. I get too caught up
in the job, and I'm probably not real easy to live with. You, on
the other hand, look like you've got a good thing going here. Your
wife's a pretty lady, and she seems real devoted to you and your
kids." He leaned back in the creaky chair and laced his own hands
together. "That's why I'm having trouble understanding—"

Berglund held up a hand. "Look, I know what you're going
to say. I know I lost it back there at the hospital, okay? It was
stupid and unprofessional. Sorry."

"No big deal. Maybe I did push a little too hard, but Jillian
seemed like she could handle it. Only now," he added, grimacing as he pushed the phone back into the corner of the desk,
"we've got another monkey wrench in the works."

"Verna got you through to your field office okay?"

"She did."

"And? They say what the big panic was all about?"

Instead of answering, Cruz posed a question of his own.
"What do you know about Grace Meade's politics?"

"Her politics?"

"Yeah. Was she active in any party? Drum up support for any
particular causes that you know of?"

Berglund shook his head. "Not that I know of. I saw her wearing a campaign button when Tom Newkirk was running for re-
election last year, but that was more out of friendship than
anything, since she couldn't even vote for him herself."

"Why not?"

"She wasn't an American citizen. Didn't have the right to vote."

"How's that? I thought she'd been here since after the war."

"That's right. More than thirty years."

"But she never took out citizenship?"

"Apparently not."

"Why not?"

"No idea. Just never got around to it, I guess. There's no law says a person has to. She paid her taxes, did her bit for the community, but she was never on the voters list. Plenty of people thought it was too bad, because they wanted her to run for town council. She'd probably have been a shoo-in, but she said she had no interest in politics. Come to think of it, that's about the only activity I can think of that Grace sat out."

"How about international politics?"

"How do you mean?"

"I don't know...the Middle East, say? Arabs and Israelis, Palestinian refugees, the occupied territories, stuff like that? She ever express any opinion on them?"

From Berglund's expression, he might have been asking if Grace Meade believed in little green men from Mars. "Not that I knew," the deputy said. "Not much interest in that kind of stuff around here. We've got enough on our plates, what with low crop prices and the high cost of gas. Why?"

"How about Jillian?"

"What about her?"

"She was a U.S. citizen," Cruz said. "A dual national, actually, according to her file, although, as far as we know, she generally traveled on an American passport. What do you know about her politics?"

Berglund's broad shoulders lifted in another shrug. "Not a thing."

"She ever travel in the Middle East?"

"Beats me. What's this all about, anyway?"

"You never heard her talk about the situation over there? Like, maybe she was a supporter of Palestinian rights, or the return of the Arab territory the Israelis occupied after the '67 war?"

"Not that I know of, but she's been gone seventeen years, and I've only seen her off and on in all that time—never long enough to talk about anything more than the weather and where some of our old friends have gotten to. But even when I knew her better, I never knew her to be interested in anything political, aside from World War II, but that was only because it was how her parents met. What's this all about, anyway?"

Cruz nodded at the telephone. "That call from the local field office? Turns out they got an ID on the guy Tom Newkirk says he saw arrive with Jillian at the Minneapolis-St. Paul airport. Turns out he's a known agent of Mossad."

"Mossad?"

"Mossad LeAliya Bet, otherwise known as the Institute for Intelligence and Special Services, otherwise known as 'The Institute,' otherwise known simply as Mossad. Probably the most efficient intelligence agency in the world—the Israelis' CIA. Deals mostly with security threats to Israel and counterterrorist ops."

"You saying she's hooked up with terrorists?"

"I don't know, but I can't think why else Mossad would be on her tail. You remember that incident a couple of years back when some terrorists hijacked a plane-load of Israeli tourists and forced it to land at the Entebbe airport in Uganda, then held them hostage, demanding the release of a bunch of Palestinian prisoners in Israel?"

"Yeah, vaguely. It fell apart, didn't it? I seem to recall seeing on the news that there was a commando raid on the plane. All the hijackers got killed, right?"

"That's right. And those commandos who raided the plane? That was Mossad. And you remember the '72 Munich Olympics, when Black September murdered eleven Israeli athletes? They got away, but not for long. Mossad hunted them down. Picked 'em off wherever they found 'em, one after another, using Uzis, car bombs, whatever. Got all but one, I think, but that doesn't mean they won't eventually get him, too. That's the kind of organization we're talking about. They're patient and methodical, and they've got long memories and a long reach. Not the kind of people you want to piss off."

"I get your point, but what's this got to do with Jillian?"

"That's what I'd like to know." Cruz nodded at the phone. "My Bureau contact said the guy Tom Newkirk saw at the Minneapolis airport with Jillian the other morning is with Mossad. His name's Simon Edelmann, and he flew into New York from Paris six days ago. That in itself wouldn't be so unusual. We and the Israelis are often targeted by the same terrorist groups, so our intelligence guys maintain pretty close ties. But this Edelmann character was on a Bureau watch list, for some reason. He shouldn't have gotten a visa, but he did. Obviously Edelmann doesn't know he's on our watch list, or he wouldn't be traveling under his real name. Now, my people want to know what he's up to, and so do I. And what's Jillian Meade doing hanging out with him?"

"This doesn't make any sense. Jillian wouldn't be involved in that kind of business."

"So how come she knew this guy? And she did know him. She introduced him to Newkirk, remember."

"Tom told me he thought they might have met on the plane. Maybe this guy—what's his name, again?"

"Edelmann. Simon Edelmann."

"This Edelmann must have targeted her for some reason."

"Possibly. But why?"

Berglund's chair dropped back to all four legs and he leaned forward, elbows on his knees, tapping his fingertips together as he studied the floor, deep lines of concentration striping his brow. "I don't know, but now that you mention it, maybe that explains who was there the night of the fire."

It was Cruz's turn to lean forward. "He was there? How do you know?"

Berglund shot him a grimace. "I know you think I've been sitting on my thumbs here, but I do know a little about conducting a criminal investigation, believe it or not. Sybil Newkirk said she thought she saw a stranger in the woods Tuesday night. I didn't give it a lot of notice at the time, partly because the place was crawling with firefighters and I thought she might have been confused on the time. Besides which, every time Tom's out of town and Sybil's had a few drinks, she starts seeing strangers lurking in the woods. I've lost track of how many times I've had to go over there and convince her there was no mad rapist out there waiting to get into her pants. That's what I thought it was all about the other night when I got her call, only instead, I found Grace's house on fire."

"And the guy in the woods?"

"I think there might have actually been someone. I went back the next day to look around. The place had been pretty thoroughly tramped over by the firemen, of course, and it had snowed some that night, too, but I found a couple of tracks down near Grace's dock."

"Footprints?"

"Snowmobile tracks. Between the woods and the shoreline, mostly. They carve a pretty deep rut, so you could still see them, in spite of the snow that fell that night. It looked like someone had come in off the lake and then gone back the same way. Footprints were harder to spot, because the machine had pulled up into the wood and the brush is pretty tangled in there, masks any prints. But on the other side of the tree line, between the woods and the house, I did manage to find a couple of clear prints in a spot that was sheltered from the wind by a small incline in the terrain. One full boot print and another partial."

"Did you take a mold?"

"No, but I took a picture of them and called the State Bureau of Investigation. They've got a file on most common shoe and boot impressions, so I sent the prints off to St. Paul. I just got a call back on it this morning."

"And?"

"They didn't have it on file. The guy I talked to said they had sole prints for every boot, shoe or sneaker sold in North America, but this one wasn't there. Said it was a hiking boot, men's size nine, but that was about as much as he could tell me. Whoever wore it didn't buy it in this country. He was going to pass it on to your guys for a look. Apparently the FBI keeps files on a lot of European and Asian makes, too, but God only knows how long it'll take to get anything back from them. Meantime, I've also been trying to run down those snowmobile tracks."

"That can't be easy. It looks like there's almost as many snowmobiles as people around here, especially now, with this ice-fishing derby on."

Berglund nodded. "That's a fact, but the derby traffic really only heated up yesterday. Those tracks I found down by Grace's dock had to have been made sometime between Sunday night and Wednesday morning, when I found them."

"How do you know it wasn't before Sunday?"

"Because we had a heavy snowfall on the weekend. Everybody had to dig out their cars to get to church Sunday morning. It would have buried the tracks if they'd been made earlier, but there was just a light dusting on them, which makes me think they were made between Sunday and those flurries we had Tuesday night. I showed the tracks to Arne Olsen. He's a guy who sells and repairs snowmobiles here. I figured he might be able to identify the make of the machine that made 'em."

"And did he?"

"Sort of. He figured it was a newer Bombardier Ski-Doo. Apparently they've got some kind of new tread design. Course, there's probably fifty Bombardiers in town, between the locals and the cottage folk. My guys are doing the rounds now, trying to find out if anyone who owns one might have been out at Grace's recently."

"What about the hotels and restaurants? They have any strangers show up who might match Edelmann's description?"

"Like I told you, there's just the Lakeside and the Whispering Pines open this time of year, and nobody checked into either of them Tuesday night. Restaurants is a tougher call. They get a lot of traffic off the interstate, especially Ollie Jorgenson's place. She says she doesn't recall seeing anyone. I've got a guy hitting surrounding towns, trying to find out if anyone there might have spotted anyone matching the description of the guy Tom saw with Jillian. If your Israeli was the same guy who drove the Ski-Doo in off the lake and onto Grace's land, he would have had to have bought or rented the machine in the last few days, so somebody would remember that, I'm thinking."

Cruz leaned back and gave an appreciative nod. "I think you're right, and I can see you've been busy. 'Course, it might have helped if you'd told me a little of this before now."

"I didn't have anything much to report until I got that call back on the boot print. I was planning to tell you about it when we met at the hospital, only things got a little out of hand."

"Point taken."

"No," Berglund said, "the point is that you and everybody else in this town who's in such a big hurry to nail Grace's murder on Jillian are barking up the wrong tree."

Cruz wasn't so sure. "Look, I know the two of you have some history—"

"You don't know what you're talking about, so don't even go there," the deputy said gloomily.

"Jesus, Berglund, is she really worth it? You've got a nice wife and kids—"

"That's not what this is about. I love my wife and kids. This has got nothing to do with them."

"Then what the hell are you doing, letting yourself get so worked up over this woman?"

"Because I owe her, all right?" Berglund stared at the floor, his big boots tapping out an irritable rhythm on the spotted linoleum tiles. Finally, he exhaled heavily. "I let her down once.

I'm not going to do it again. You don't know her, Cruz. She's a
good person, but she got a raw deal from the get-go, starting with
that mother of hers. No matter what anyone tells you, Grace
Meade was no saint. There was a real mean streak to that woman.
She kept it well hidden, but oh, man! It was there. And as a parent?" He snorted. "She was just plain unnatural, is what she was.
She used to make a big show in public of being the perfect, loving mother, but to tell you the truth, I don't think she much cared
for the job. People say Jill abandoned Grace because that's the
pitiful tune Grace always played to anyone who'd listen, but the
truth is, it was the other way around. Grace wanted Jill out of
the house just as soon as she turned eighteen, and she made very
sure Jill understood she'd have nothing to stick around for."

"Why?"

"Because that's the way she was. Grace wanted to be top ba-
nana, she wanted her nice home, and she wanted it all to herself."

"Tell me something," Cruz said, the chair under him protest-
ing as he leaned back, "were she and Tom Newkirk lovers?"

Berglund's eyebrow arched. "Now there's the worst-kept secret in town. You figured that out on your own, did you?"

"You mean everybody knows?"

"Probably. It's such old news nobody even talks about it anymore. Tom's a real popular guy, and Grace was very careful
about her own image. They were real discreet. You never saw
them alone together, and as long as it wasn't rubbed in anyone's
nose, people eventually decided to ignore it."

"What about Sybil? Is that why she drinks?"

Berglund shrugged. "That's a chicken and egg story, I would
think. Her drinking, the rocky marriage—which caused which?
You met her. She's not the brightest bulb in the chandelier for
sure, but I'll give her this—she figured out fast that if she couldn't
beat Grace, she'd join her. Grace let Sybil be her sidekick, and
Sybil loved that, because it meant she got to be in the middle of
everything Grace was into. If she didn't rock the boat, she got to

be the mayor's wife and Society Grace's chief lieutenant. It was probably a better deal than she could have hoped for otherwise."

"So all these years they've had a little ménage à trois. What about Jillian? She must have known about it."

"She wouldn't talk about it. You have to realize, for a kid, a teenage girl especially, it was just too embarrassing." Berglund shook his head grimly. "She got it in spades. The whole town was so mesmerized by Grace that most of them never even noticed that sweet girl standing in her shadow. And me? I was the worst of all, because I did see and I didn't help her. If I'd had any brains or decency at all, I'd have packed her up and taken her away from here as soon as I got the chance."

"Maybe you should go a little easier on yourself. You were just a kid."

"That's no excuse. We could've gotten married before I went into the Navy. She was underage, and everybody said we should wait until after the draft board was done with me, but Grace would've signed off in it. She wouldn't have been cared. In fact, it would have suited her just fine. Jill could have come with me to San Diego, and gone to school or gotten a job...something. I should have known nothing good could ever come of her staying behind, but the problem is, I'm a small-town guy. I couldn't imagine living anywhere else, so I asked her to wait here for me to come back. Grace went to work on her, making sure she'd leave, and by the time I realized what an idiot I'd been not to get Jill away, it was too late."

"In the end, she left without you," Cruz pointed out. "And she seems to have made out okay."

"Until now," Berglund replied. "And at what price? I always hoped she'd find somebody else who could make her happy, but who was she going to trust after that? She didn't deserve any of it. Anyway, like I said, I let her down, bad, but I'm not going to do it again."

C H A P T E R   2 3

After I left Miss Atwater, I went over my notes, preparing to do the research legwork in Paris, considerably more nervous than I'd been when I'd started out in London. My verbal skill in French is nowhere near as proficient as my mother's (in this, as in everything else, she outshone me), but I can stumble along in conversation, and I read the language well enough, if I could just find someone who might be willing to help me wade through the morass of old files and fading memories I hoped to find there.

It was only when I reviewed the notes I had made from my interview with Miss Atwater and from days of digging through files to which I'd been given access at the Imperial War Museum, the Ministry of Defense and other British and American sources that I began to be troubled by the fact that dates and events were not quite lining up as I'd expected. The more I learned, the less well things fit together. By the time I got to Paris, I felt more trepidation than pleasure at what I was finding out. No longer was I strolling down memory lane, gathering rosebuds of nostalgia to present as a Christmas gift to my mother. Now, I began to suspect that it was vindication I needed to find—for her actions and for my own existence.

The more I learned, the more unanswered questions I had, some of them troubling. What had happened to her after she was arrested by the Gestapo? If Joe Meade wasn't my father, what did that mean? Had there been another lover no one knew about? Or had she'd been raped while in custody? It happens to countless women in wartime, so why should my mother have been any different? Was that the reason I'd always sensed in her an inability to love me as unconditionally as other mothers seemed to love their children? I'd inherited nothing of her beauty, but was that the only reason for the disappointment she was never quite able to hide? Or did she see a torturer's face every time she looked at mine? My poor mother, I thought. I could forgive her so much if it turned out that was the source of the problem that had plagued our relationship all these years.

I also wanted to know the circumstances under which she and Joe Meade had met up again and married. Had he known she was carrying a child that couldn't possibly be his, as I'm now convinced was the case? I wanted to believe he'd known about me. And he had to have, I thought. She couldn't possibly have hidden her pregnancy by the time they married, but what I hoped was that he had loved my mother enough to accept me as his own child. I needed to believe that he wanted us to be a family.

Most of all, I needed desperately to know that my mother had not perpetrated a terrible fraud on my grandparents—that Joe Meade had blessed my entry into his family and had been smiling down on us all when my mother finally brought me to America. Because whatever real warmth and joy I remember from my childhood is associated with time spent with that wonderful old couple. I can't imagine what my life would have been without my Nana and Grandpa. I didn't want to believe that their love for me had been a mistake.

My relationship with my mother was not so much quarrelsome as cool. When I was growing up, I knew girls whose mothers were overprotective and smothering, wanting their daughters to remain babies forever. Mine didn't really care for babies.

"All that leakage, and from every possible orifice!" I once heard her exclaim in mock horror to the twittering St. John's Episcopal Ladies' Auxiliary. I couldn't grow up fast enough for my mother, and she expected decorum from me even as a gap-toothed first-grader.

I also had girlfriends whose mothers wanted to be their best friends, sharing their deepest secrets—first schoolgirl crushes, first kisses, first broken hearts. Heather Pilsky's mother even confided to her about the first time she'd had sex (in her father's hayloft, apparently with a young tank gunner on leave from General Patton's 7th Army, a fellow who'd later died in Sicily). But my mother was not a great one for confidences—or warmth.

It was my grandmother who tried to make up for what my mother lacked in nurturing maternal instinct, and who tried to explain it to me in a way that might quell my sense that it was my fault.

"You have to understand, Jilly, she's British," Nana said when she found me in my room once, crying on my bed—quietly, of course, because Mother didn't approve of overwrought scenes. "It's just the way she was raised. They don't show their feelings like we do. She loves you very much."

"No she doesn't. She hates me."

"She doesn't hate you."

"She does. She called me a millstone. She said she gave up her life for me."

I saw the shock in Nana's face, although she did her best to hide it by taking me into her arms. "Oh, sweetie, she didn't mean that. She was just upset. You know, I think she must get real homesick sometimes. Imagine how hard it is, being suddenly uprooted the way she's been, a widow with a tiny baby coming thousands of miles to live with in-laws she's never even met in a place where she didn't know a soul."

"Why did she bother if she was going to be so miserable?"

"Your life would have been awfully hard if she hadn't, angel,"

Nana said gently. "And there isn't a single day that I don't thank God that she did bring you here," she added, pulling me closer.

I settled into her soft, pillowy body, closing my eyes and inhaling her familiar smell—Ivory Snow soap, the "Evening in Paris" perfume that Grandpa bought her every single Christmas, and over that, the delicious aroma of the cinnamon buns she'd just finished rolling and set out to rise on the kitchen counter under a cotton tea towel.

She kissed the top of my head, and I heard the catch in her voice when she added, "You're all that remains of my little boy, Jilly—my precious baby Joe."

The best place to start in Paris, I decided, would be with a lawyer by the name of Bernard Cohn-Levy, reputed to be the single greatest repository of information on the German Occupation. Anybody who takes the slightest interest in World War II and regularly reads a newspaper will have come across the name of this famous French Nazi hunter. Cohn-Levy has been working for over thirty years to locate, expose and prosecute war criminals, particularly those responsible for the persecution of the nearly seventy-five thousand Jewish citizens and refugees who were deported from France to the Nazi death camps in the East.

I hoped he might also be a good source of information on the Resistance per se. Much of what we can learn about the Resistance is based on the memories and oral testimony of partisans from a variety of backgrounds and professions, but these were people better skilled at subversion than scholarly documentation for the most part, and after all this time, their memories can be sketchy on details. But the Final Solution, Hitler's sick obsession with ridding Europe of its Jewish population, left a malodorous paper trail in France, as elsewhere. As soon as the Nazis overran a country, anti-Semitic laws were promulgated, the imprisonment and deportation of Jewish citizens and foreign residents methodically planned, carried out and written up in duplicate and triplicate, the policy's "successes" dutifully reported back to Berlin. Some of

the noblest acts of the Resistance—as well as some of the most sor-
did and cowardly acts of Nazi collaborators—had revolved around
efforts to conceal people slated for deportation, so I thought it was
possible that Cohn-Levy's files might shed light on a few dark corners of that Resistance history I was researching.

I met him in his Sixth Arrondissment offices early one evening
a few days later. He's a very busy man, of course, but luckily, my
Smithsonian credentials seemed to help when I called for an appointment. When I got there, Cohn-Levy had just returned from
arguing a case in court and still wore the flowing black robes that
seem to be the norm for most European legal practitioners. In his
sixties, he was a big man, over six feet tall, with a barrel chest that
his legal robes did little to conceal, a shock of thick, white hair and
wild, dramatically black eyebrows over what were possibly the most
beautiful brown eyes I have ever seen on a man. His office was also
the most paper-cluttered, jam-packed, chaotic workspace I've ever
seen, and yet as our meetings progressed, that evening and the next
day, I was astonished again and again by his ability to put his
hands on exactly the piece of paper he was looking for amidst all
that housekeeping anarchy.

When the Germans overran France in 1940, Cohn-Levy had
been in his twenties, a strapping, handsome young barrister just
beginning a career in his father's well-regarded legal practice, married, with a two-year-old son. The war's end found him in the
Auschwitz concentration camp, one of the few left behind as the
Nazis fled the advancing Russian army, leading most of the re-
maining inmates on a forced death march. Cohn-Levy had been
among those deemed unfit for evacuation.

"The SS guards left behind were given orders to shoot us," he
said, "but they were so terrified of the Russians that they ran away
as soon as the camp commandant departed. It's the only reason
we few survived."

His six-foot frame weighed a scant seventy-eight pounds by
then, he told me, and he was so wasted and weak that when the

Russian soldiers who liberated Auschwitz went to separate the living inmates from the dead, they assumed he was among the latter, only to be startled by his moans as they trundled his body onto a cemetery-bound cart. Nursed back to health by the Allies, he eventually made his way to Paris, but not before learning from eyewitness accounts that his entire family, including his parents, wife and young son, as well as a sister and various aunts, uncles and cousins, had been murdered in the camps. Of the more than seventy-five thousand French Jews deported during the Occupation, only 2,500 survived. Cohn-Levy was among them, and his life ever since has been dedicated to documenting the atrocities of the Holocaust and to bringing those responsible to justice—ex-Nazis and collaborators alike.

His English was as good as my French was bad, so that was the language in which our interview took place. Faced with such a daunting figure, I was more than a little nervous about explaining what I was up to and had decided to limit my questions to finding out what, if anything, he could tell me about the activities of Resistance cells in the Gentilly suburb of Paris. I knew Cohn-Levy had a voluminous collection old German files, so I also hoped he'd have records from Gestapo headquarters on the Avenue Foch that might confirm the dates my mother had been arrested and detained. I was fairly certain, as well, that his files held whatever documentation remained from the transit camp at Drancy, northeast of Paris, the last stop in France for most of those who were deported from that country—all the "Jews, Bolsheviks, and agents of Anglo-Saxon capitalism" whom the Nazis had targeted for annihilation. I was curious to see if my birth had been recorded in the transit camp's files.

I certainly had no intention of revealing my greatest fear to him—that I may have been fathered by some jackbooted thug. Under gentle cross-examination from this wily old barrister, however, I suddenly found myself tearfully blurting the whole story of where my research had led me thus far.

I was astonished at Cohn-Levy's reaction. He rose from the big, red leather chair behind his desk, came around and settled beside me, enclosing my hands in both of his. "You have absolutely nothing to be ashamed of, Miss Meade. Children do not choose the circumstances of their birth." I started to speak, but he shushed me with a gentle squeeze of my hands. "Every soul on this earth begins life as an innocent, no matter their lineage. We are judged by our own actions, not the acts of those who came before us."

"That may be," I said dubiously, "but can you see how this changes everything? What about my grandparents—Joe Meade's parents? They went to their graves thinking I was their grandchild."

"Yes, and what of it? Tragically, they lost a son, but then, a beautiful little girl came to bring them joy in their final years. Think how sad and empty their lives would have been if not for you."

"But if I wasn't really their flesh and blood—"

"To them, you were. When they took your little hand in theirs, do you think they gave any thought to your DNA? I don't. I think they were looking only at you, loving only you, taking great pride in every little step you took."

"I'm not so sure. My grandmother was always saying how things I did reminded her of my father—of Joe. Of course, I know now it was pure imagination on her part."

"Does it really matter? Nothing was going to bring back her child, but you helped her recall happy memories of him."

Cohn-Levy was so persistent, his warm brown eyes so forgiving that I had to smile just a little. "You're very kind," I told him, "and very wise. I think you should have been a rabbi instead of a lawyer."

He returned my smile with a mischievous one of his own as he shook his white mane. "I am far too fond of the comforts and battles of this bad old world to be a man of God, I'm afraid." Then, his expression sobered. "But on this, dear girl, I know whereof I speak. I, too, lost a son, you know, as well as my wife and others from my family."

"I did know that," I said. "I'm so very sorry."

"So am I. But after the war, in the displaced persons camp, I met a lady who had lost her husband and two children in the Holocaust. There was a little girl there, as well, an orphan, just ten years old. Hers was an incredible story. Her family had lived in hiding until mid-1944, when they were found and put on a train bound for Auschwitz. Only along the way, Miriam's mother had pushed her off the train, and she was able to survive by hiding out on a farm in Belgium until the end of the war."

"Her mother pushed her off the train?" I repeated, stunned at the mental picture of that.

"Well, not off so much 'off' as 'out'—through a loose floorboard, you see, at a moment when the train slowed. A couple of other prisoners, the smallest of them, managed to get out as well, although most of the others were recaptured. It was a miracle Miriam survived, because children were always among the first to be gassed when they arrived at the camps. But by sheer luck, Miriam did, and that was how we came to meet her in the refugee camp."

"And you and the lady adopted her and made a new family for yourselves, didn't you?"

"Exactly. And now, that incredible little girl is a lawyer and mother herself, and I am a grandpa to two fine young boys. So this is how I know what your grandparents would have felt, you see. Neither Miriam nor my adopted grandsons can take the place of my poor lost boy, but I love them very much, indeed, and they make my life rich."

I could only hope he was right and that my grandparents would have forgiven me for not being the person they thought I was.

By this point in the interview, of course, I was an emotional wreck. The hour had grown late, in any case, and M. Cohn-Levy had an evening commitment, so I took my leave of him. But before I left, he invited me to come back the next afternoon, when he would see if he had any of the information I was seeking.

I hated to waste his valuable time and told him I was adept at digging through documents, if he'd be willing to let me at his files, but he waved a gnarled hand over his office, which looked as if a bomb had landed on it, and gave me a rueful smile.

"You would be at it until judgment day, I'm afraid. I no longer remember how many secretaries and assistants have quit in frustration after failing in their attempts to organize me. There is a system here of sorts, believe it or not, and I can usually find what I'm looking for, but for anyone else, it is an impossible task. Come back tomorrow at twelve-thirty. I will take you to lunch, and then we shall see what nuggets of gold we can dig out for your research."

CHAPTER 24

Havenwood, Minnesota
Friday, January 12, 1979

While Cruz and Berglund were sitting in the chief's office, comparing notes and eating the sandwiches Berglund's wife had brought them, Verna called through on the intercom. "Nils, you there?"

Berglund leaned across from the wrong side of the desk, turned the telephone to face him, then hit the speaker button. "What's up?"

"Kenny just radioed in to say there's some kind of a fight brewing down on the town dock," Verna's voice crackled. "Said there's a couple of out-of-towners who've had a snootful and are giving the derby organizers what-for about where their fishing shacks are gonna go. Apparently Pete Seddon tried to tell 'em they gotta be spaced out no closer than fifty yards apart—on account of distributing the weight on the ice there and making sure people's lines don't get all tangled together, you know?"

Berglund glanced over at Cruz and rolled his eyes. "Uh-huh. So what's the problem?"

"Well, Kenny says these boys figure all the best spots have been hogged by the locals, like the fix is already in. He says they're looking to push over a couple of shacks if Pete and the rest of the organizing committee doesn't give 'em what they want. Kenny thinks they could use a figure of authority like yourself out there right about now."

"Oh, for the love of..." Berglund sighed. "Okay, Verna, tell him I'm on my way, would you?"

"Will do."

"I'm gonna have to go take care of this," the deputy told Cruz, rising wearily. His face was drawn, with dark hollows under his bloodshot eyes, and he had the fatalistic expression of a fighter on the ropes dreading the knockout punch.

"Go ahead," Cruz said. "Okay with you if I run over to the fire scene and take a look at those tracks you were talking about?"

"Suit yourself," Berglund said, shrugging into his green khaki police parka once more. "Don't know if there's much left by now, but see what you think. The snowmobile tracks run to the south side of Grace's dock. If you follow them back in a straight line through the wood, they'll lead you to that boot print on the other side, toward where the house stood. Although," he added, "it's probably drifted over by now."

"There's something else I've been meaning to ask. Do you have any idea how Jillian got to town from the airport on Tuesday?"

"I assumed at first that she got a ride out with Tom, but then I realized she couldn't have because he stayed over in the city that night. Then I thought Grace had driven in and picked her up."

"Newkirk says not. And it seems to me that Carla from the hair salon and somebody else...now, who was it...?" Cruz flipped through his notes, then snapped his fingers. "That's right, an old guy I overheard talking to Ollie Jorgenson's husband at their garage. Both of them said Grace had no idea Jillian was coming."

"Yeah, I heard that, too. Turns out she'd rented a car, though. It was in the drive the night of the fire, and I guess I saw it there, but I didn't look at it that closely. I thought it was Grace's. We had it towed out of the way of the fire trucks. It was only afterward when we found Grace's burned-out car in the garage that I took a closer look at the one that had been towed and realized it was a rental."

"Where is it now?"

"Parked out back of here. We called Hertz at the airport. Jillian had rented it from them. They're arranging to have it driven back there over the weekend."

"I'd hold off on that if I were you."

"Why's that?"

"I think it should be dusted for prints."

"Why—oh, right. I see where you're coming from. To see if this Edelmann was in it."

Cruz nodded. "Kind of important to know. I'll see if we can get a copy of his prints."

"I'll get somebody on to dusting the car. Nobody's mentioned anything about Jillian arriving in town with this guy, though."

"I know," Cruz agreed. "In fact, Sybil Newkirk told me Grace had phoned her to say Jillian was in, but if she had brought a guy with her, it seems like the kind of thing a mother would have mentioned. Maybe we should double-check that with Mrs. Newkirk?"

"I can do it," Berglund said.

"Okay by me," Cruz said, just as happy to dodge another encounter with the woman. "The Bureau guys in the city are checking out car rentals, too, so we'll know soon enough if Edelmann rented one, as well—unless, of course, he has an accomplice or is using multiple names."

Cruz got to his feet, grabbed his own coat and gloves, and followed Berglund out of the building. While the deputy headed for the town dock, Cruz headed back toward Lakeshore Road, beginning to get a feel for the layout of the place by now. The town money looked to have cornered the properties on the near side of Lost Arrow Lake, a long stretch of sprawling, custom-built homes. Among the photos in Sybil Newkirk's collection, Cruz had seen a shot of the Meade place before it was destroyed, taken from the Newkirks' yard, a mock-Tudor, two-story affair with a steeply pitched, black shingled roof, many-paned windows, its rough stucco siding bisected by the kind of half-timber cross beams probably inspired by the cottages of Stratford-upon-Avon—a little piece of England in the American heartland. How nice, Cruz thought dryly, that Tom Newkirk had arranged for Grace to be so comfortably settled close by with the help of her daughter's trust fund.

When he arrived at the Lakeshore Road property, a young mother towing a couple of toddlers on a toboggan was standing at the bottom of the driveway, staring at the burned-out shell. At the sound of his motor, she turned, startled, then smiled shyly and gave him an embarrassed little wave. When she moved on, a black and white border collie bounded out of the trees at the sound of her whistle. Cruz watched the dog leaping joyfully over snowbanks and pausing to sniff at every other bush as they made their way down the road.

He pulled into the yard and parked at the end nearest the rubble-strewn foundation. The destroyed house was still circumnavigated by a line of rope hung with Police signs. Next door, the Newkirks' driveway was empty, and their house seemed quiet. Either Sybil was still napping and Tom at his lunch, or, Cruz thought, glancing at his watch, they'd left early for their meeting with the minister to go over the funeral service. In fact, the entire neighborhood was silent, he realized, struck by the absence of the kind of noises urban dwellers took for granted—car horns, sirens and the constant hum of traffic like waves rolling on a distant shore. Only the occasional bark of a dog or warble of a yellow grosbeak or grackle broke the afternoon stillness. Positively eerie.

He climbed out the car, instinctively breathing through his mouth to avoid inhaling the stink of charred destruction that lay over the site like a blanket of death. He knew vets who hated rainy days because they brought back memories of slogging through jungle downpours, expecting to hear at any second the sibilant whiz of the enemy bullet that would end their lives. For his own part, Cruz doubted he would ever again be able to sit by a campfire or in front of a warm, crackling hearth without his memory dredging up the image of Darryl Houghton's face melting like a wax effigy left out too long in the sun.

It was Pfc. Billy Kennedy who'd turned the flame-thrower on the lieutenant's body as it lay slumped against the base of a palm tree. Kennedy had been just a kid, a couple of months off a Pennsylvania farm. Cruz had been second-in-command of the infantry unit led by Houghton, an arrogant Yalie whose rich daddy would have been better served wangling him a stint in the National Guard. That morning, Cruz had gone ahead down the trail to try to scope out the Viet Cong sniper who'd been taking pot shots at them for the past couple of hours. They'd already lost one guy and the other four in the squad—all kids like Kennedy, with acne and best girls they hadn't even gotten around to laying yet—were terrified to move. But the lieutenant, reckless, stupid and hot for promotion, kept pushing them on without bothering to reconnoiter the way ahead, leaving them exposed on all flanks in his hot dog determination to be first through the enemy lines—even if it meant climbing to glory on the cold, dead backs of his men.

Cruz had finally convinced Houghton to hold their position while he tried to get behind the sniper. He'd been gone nearly an hour and had managed to slip around the VC, who turned out to be all of fifteen, maybe. The muzzle of Cruz's .45 was biting into the kid's temple before he even realized he'd been made. Cruz was leading his captive, hands bound and feet hobbled, back to the unit when the distinct sound of M-16 fire froze his blood—three retorts in rapid succession, and then, about twenty or thirty seconds later, a fourth. He knew. Even without being there, Cruz had known the last shot was a coup de grace.

He'd started running, pushing the stumbling kid ahead of him down the trail, berating himself for having left the others. The guys had been coiled so tight that he knew they were bound to snap if that idiot Houghton so much as looked at them wrong, but Cruz had hoped that by clearing the trail, he could defuse the tension a little. But by the time he reached the squad, the lieutenant was dead, gut-shot three times with a finishing shot to the head, and Billy the Kid had fired up the flame-thrower in a panicky attempt to destroy the evidence of the murder. Cruz and his captive had emerged from the bush just in time to see the lieutenant's face melt like a superheated marshmallow.

It was classic overkill. If the unit hadn't despised Houghton so much that they'd go this extra, gruesome step, they could've said he was killed by sniper fire and probably gotten away with it. The fragging of officers was more common than anyone was willing to admit in the confusion of a messy and unpopular war. Nobody was looking too closely at all those black vinyl body bags being shipped Stateside. In the absence of a specific accusation, nobody was doing autopsies or ballistics tests, so more than a few grudges got settled by friendly fire falsely attributed to the enemy.

All Houghton's killers would have had to do was make a clean, simple kill, tell a credible lie, and maintain the conspiracy of silence among themselves. Instead, they'd made a mess of it, then begged Cruz to put in the fix. Their final mistake. He would have died for them, and they knew it, but he couldn't bring himself to lie for them. Not about this. So the four men had gone down for the crime, and though Cruz himself had walked free, he, too, had been paying the price ever since.

He walked around the blackened ruins of Grace Meade's house to the far side of the yard, where a sloping lawn led down and around a strip of trees to a small wooden dock. Grace's back lawn, dead and mostly snow-covered now, flowed into the

Newkirks', making for a large common yard surrounded on two sides by a wooded area of mixed evergreens and white birches and by the lake on the third, with both houses set well back from Lakeshore Road.

As he approached the dock and looked to the south of it, Cruz saw the signs Berglund had mentioned—a yard-wide track coming in off the lake, up the snowy bank and into the strip of bush that jutted into the corner of the lot. Cruz knew nothing about snowmobiles, so he would accept Berglund's expert opinion on the make of the machine that had left this track. But if it was Grace Meade's killer who'd left it, he'd chosen the route least likely to draw attention, hidden as it was from view of both the Meade and the Newkirk houses by the short, jutting peninsula of trees. The dense wood around the two lots would also have hidden any intruder from the property to the south, where the house was set well back from the lake, impossible to see from this vantage point.

Cruz followed the track from the shoreline back into the trees, where it seemed to come to a stop. The underbrush there was trampled, but so dense that it was impossible to make out individual footprints. On the clearing at other side, however, back toward the house, he found a circle of beaten snow, probably where Berglund had moved around the boot print to photograph it. It was so drifted over now that none of the prints, including the deputy's, could be distinguished clearly anymore. Useless for evidence.

A sudden, whining buzz rose off the lake, cutting through the silence like a rusty chain saw. Startled, Cruz turned on his heel just as three snowmobiles raced by a couple of hundred yards out on the ice. A cold wind blew up and bit into his neck. He flipped up the collar of his overcoat, crossing his arms in front of his chest and clapping his leather-gloved hands against his sleeves in a fruitless effort to warm himself as he watched the heavily bundled drivers pull a wide U-turn, then zigzag back and forth toward town, skis bouncing at every irregularity in the surface of the ice. Cruz had enough memory of his motorcycle dirt-riding days to wince with every bone-slamming bump. Across the frozen lake, the midwinter sun was already beginning to sink, silhouetting the trees and scattered cottages, creating a woodcut image of an idyllic winter playground. Had the killer been watching the Meade house from one of those cottages on Tuesday night, waiting for the right time to strike? The ice on the lake was scarred with so many striations that any single trail was impossible to discern.

The bigger question still loomed: Why exactly had Grace Meade been killed? And what about the two women in England? What was the link? And now the confusing bits of information passed on by the local field office. None of it seemed to fit with anything else.

Jillian Meade and her mother had had a strained relationship, by all accounts. Some people made Jillian out to be an uncaring, ungrateful daughter, but Berglund had called Grace an unnatural mother. For his money, Cruz thought, the two women had probably deserved each other, but even so, how was it that Jillian had suddenly arrived unannounced from Washington in the company of a known agent of Mossad? The number one target of the Israeli intelligence service were those forces dedicated to the destruction of the State of Israel. But neither Jillian nor her mother were known to have had any particular interest in the Middle East or in politics generally. Grace Meade hadn't even bothered to take out citizenship so she could vote, while Jillian, from the sound of it, lived primarily in the past, all her attention focused on her historical research into World War II. Nothing in what Cruz had been able to learn suggested either woman was the type to get mixed up in the tangle of modern Middle East politics.

And then, a light flashed on his brain. He very nearly slapped himself upside the head for not having seen it right off the bat. Sheen had said Simon Edelmann was on the FBI watch list because of information contained in a closely held DOJ file. Mossad. The Department of Justice. World War II. That was the connection!

The Justice Department had a war crimes unit dedicated to rooting out those suspected of committing atrocities during the Second World War, in particular known members of the Nazi Party and others who had aided and abetted in the Holocaust. Thirty years after the war, information was still surfacing on war criminals who'd evaded retribution by concealing their past and getting lost in the flood of post-war emigrants to countries like the U.S.A., Canada, South America and Australia. The DOJ war crimes unit had been known to exchange intelligence with Mossad, who also worked with dedicated private Nazi hunters around the world like Wiesenthal, Cohn-Levy and Klarsfeld. It was Mossad who'd kidnapped Adolph Eichmann from Argentina and taken him back to Israel, where he was tried, convicted and condemned to death for his role as chief architect of the "Final Solution" to rid Europe of its Jewish population. Mossad who'd been hunting Dr. Joseph Mengele for over thirty years now in an effort to bring him to justice for the pseudo-scientific medical experiments he'd conducted on concentration camp inmates, including children. Mossad who continued to flush former high-ranking Nazi officials and collaborators out of their post-war hiding places.

Did Edelmann belong to one of those select, highly trained, highly secretive Mossad units—one of the Nazi-hunters? But if so, and he was persona non grata in the eyes of Justice, Cruz reasoned, it could only mean that he was suspected of carrying out operations with "extreme prejudice." By law, the DOJ was required to do things by the book. If they had cut links with Edelmann, it could only mean he'd been known to bypass legal niceties like extradition, indictment and courtroom prosecution of suspected war criminals, proceeding directly to the judgment and execution phase.

And Grace Meade? How would she have shown up on the radar of an operator like that? Reportedly, she'd been on the front lines of the battle *against* the Nazis, working underground for the British in occupied France—one of the good guys. But was she really? Or had she been a double agent and a collaborator? Was that why she'd been so averse to seeing her picture in the paper, so publicity-shy that she would rip her photo off the proof sheets of even as innocuous and narrowly distributed a publication as the *Havenwood Herald*? And was that what Sybil Newkirk had overheard Grace and Jillian arguing about the night of the fire? Had Grace's past finally caught up with her, her St. Peter at the Gates taking the form of a daughter-turned-historian-turned-executioner, aided and abetted by one of Mossad's avengers?

How was he going to find out?

Jillian Meade was off-limits for the moment, but it occurred to him that there was someone he could contact who might be able to tell him more about this Edelmann character. And, he realized, shaking snow off his sodden shoes, there was one other person right here in Havenwood who might be able to shed a little more light on Grace Meade's wartime record.

He turned away from the lake and headed back toward his car.

Tom Newkirk's blue Oldsmobile was parked outside a redbrick church whose lawn sign proclaimed it to be St. John's Episcopal Church, presided over by a Reverend Stewart Allsop. Newkirk was listed as a Deacon of the church and, as Cruz could have predicted by now, Grace Meade's name was there, as well, next to the title of Chairwoman of the St. John's Ladies' Auxiliary.

Cruz moved his car into one of the diagonal parking spots across the street, in front of the Good Buy dry goods store, adjusting the rearview mirror so that he could keep an eye on the church and on Newkirk's car. Hunched down in the front seat, he killed the ignition and tried not to think about the cold as the benefits of the car heater dissipated and his breath began to come out in small, white clouds. The light was fading fast, rendering him nearly invisible inside the darkened car, which was just as well, since there was a steady stream of townspeople in the street, running last minute errands before the start of the weekend.

In the window of the dry goods store, a sign announced the Eleventh Annual Havenwood Ice-Fishing Derby. According to the notice, it was scheduled to kick off that evening with a 6:00 p.m. ceremony featuring a performance by the Havenwood High Marching Band, a welcome from Mayor Tom Newkirk, the official lighting of the warm-up bonfire by this year's Miss Havenwood (one Ainsley Gustavsen), and a street dance.

Cruz glanced at his watch: just after four. By the time the Newkirks finished with the minister and Newkirk got his wife back home again, it would nearly be time for the opening ceremonies. (Somehow, he couldn't picture Sybil Newkirk, with her gin-soaked grief and flapping, teetering shoes, taking part in the outdoor festivities.) This meant he had zero chance of taking Newkirk aside for a quiet and more detailed interview until after the mayor had dispensed with his derby duties.

A truck passed on the street behind him, rocking the car in its back draft and sending a shiver through Cruz's body. If he was to do any more outdoor surveillance, he decided, he was going to have to come up with some warmer clothes. He climbed out of the car and headed into the store, where he resisted the temptation to replace his conspicuous city overcoat with one of the snowmobile jackets hung to catch the eye of would-be derby contestants. He settled instead for a down-filled vest, which he could wear under the coat, and for some heavy-duty wool socks and a pair of tundra-worthy hiking boots that would have cost him half again as much had he bought them at some trendy urban outfitter's back in D.C. Ignoring the curious stares he was getting from other customers and the clerk at the cash register, he decided to head back to the motel, thaw out a little, change into his sweater and the cold-weather gear, make a couple of phone calls, and then catch Newkirk after the opening ceremonies.

He was back in car and just about to turn the ignition when a rap at the window startled him. He turned to see the beaming face of Carla from the pub last night. "Uh, Carla, hi," he said, rolling down the window.

"Hi, Alex! I heard you were still kicking around and here you are! I was in the shop when I spotted you coming out of the Good Buy," she said, nodding at the low white building a couple of doors down from the dry goods store, which Cruz only now realized was the Set 'n Style hair salon. Carla had sprinted out to catch him without stopping to put on a coat. She had on a floral-print cotton smock which was open at the front to reveal a pink angora sweater with a low-cut neckline. When she bent down and crossed her arms on the open car window, Cruz had an ample view of some positively monumental cleavage. Somehow, he didn't think it was accidental.

"Needed a couple of things," he said.

"So you're sticking around for the weekend? That's great! There's a street dance tonight, and then another big bash at the town hall tomorrow. Part of the derby festivities, you know? There's gonna be a live band tomorrow, and—"

But Cruz shook his head. "I'll probably be gone by then."

Her face fell. "You will? Darn! Why don't you stay on an extra day or so?"

"I don't think I can do that."

"Well, how about that dinner? I got some nice fat steaks back at my place, and a big bottle of wine—"

"Oh, no, Carla, thanks, but I really can't," he said, reaching for the ignition.

"You have to eat sometime."

"Yes, I do, but it'll have to be takeout. I've got a ton of paperwork, and some phone calls to make. I'm going to be at it all evening."

"Always on duty, huh?"

"That's what they pay me for."

"I heard you talked to Sybil Newkirk." Carla grinned and cupped her hand, pantomiming taking a drink. When Cruz didn't respond, she nodded. "No, of course, you'd never say you found her three sheets to the wind, would you? Have to keep everything confidential. I guess Tom and Sybil are pretty stressed out about it all, though. Saw them going into St. John's a while ago. I hear they're making the funeral arrangements."

"So it seems."

"Has Tom been to see Jillian over there in the loony bin in Montrose?"

"Should he have?"

Carla shrugged. "I guess I just figured he would've, seeing as he was sort of her substitute dad all the years she was growing up—though if Jillian really did do Grace in, I guess Tom wouldn't be so keen to help her now."

"You know, you really should get back inside, Carla, before you catch your death of cold out here."

"Oh, I don't feel the cold at all. Prairie born and bred, you know. Winter doesn't get to us the way it does you hot-blooded types." She grinned and punched him playfully—painfully—in the shoulder.

Cruz winced and rubbed the spot. "Got a good right cross there."

"Comes from growing up with brothers. It's not the only thing I'm good at, if you get my drift." The thin line of her eyebrows danced up and down. "Come on, what do you say I do up that steak for you later, after you get your work done?"

"I appreciate the offer, Carla, but there's an ironclad Bureau rule says we're not allowed to mix business and pleasure. Seeing as how I'm on the job here, I'm going to have to take a rain check on that offer, tempting as it is."

"I'd never report you." When he didn't reply, she sighed. "Oh, okay, you big party-pooper. You'll never know what you missed, though."

"I've got a pretty good idea. But maybe you'll find a taker for those steaks among the derby contestants. Looks to me like there's a mess of hungry guys in town this weekend."

"That's a fact. No other handsome G-men, but I guess a girl could do worse than look them over, hey?"

"There you go." Cruz turned the key in the ignition. "Happy hunting, Carla."

"Yeah, you, too, Alex." She straightened and slapped the roof of his car. "Catch lots of bad guys."

Back in his motel room, he put on the warmer clothes he'd bought, then settled on the edge of the bed and pulled the phone onto his lap. There was a directory in the drawer of the bedside table, and after flipping through dozens of pages of useless information, he finally found how to reach an information operator for Washington and managed to get the number for the Israeli Embassy. He glanced at his watch. Nearly 6:00 p.m. in D.C. It was still a reasonable time to find people at work in most offices back there—except, he realized suddenly, it was Friday evening, and if the sun was going down in Minnesota, it had already gone down in Washington, which meant the Jewish Sabbath had begun. He happened to know that Z'ev Mindel was neither Orthodox nor even particularly observant, but who knew if there would even be anyone in the embassy at this hour who could put him through to him.

Fortunately, a telephone operator at the other end had apparently received dispensation to break the Sabbath rules. Although Mr. Mindel was out of the office, she told Cruz, she'd see he got the message. When he said it was an emergency, she promised to try to reach him as soon as possible. He settled back against the headboard to catch the TV news. The newscast was only a couple of stories into the lineup when the telephone rang.

"Alex! Is that you, you old son of a gun?"

"Hey! It's me, all right. How you doing, Z'ev?"

"Like that watch, I take a licking but keep on ticking. Where are you, anyway? I don't recognize this area code."

"Minnesota."

"Minnesota! What, are you crazy? Don't you know people go to Florida for winter vacations? What's wrong with you, fool?"

"I'm on the job. Believe me, I can't think of any other reason to be here right now. Do you know that even as we speak, there are people out on a lake near here trying to catch fish through holes in the ice?"

"This only confirms what I've always suspected—you have no sense at all. And what's with this 'on the job'? Last I heard, you were resigning your Army commission and heading out to California to fix up that motorcycle you promised to sell me for a very reasonable price."

"Whoa, slow down. We never talked price. I said I'd consider selling it if I managed to find that Triumph I've been looking for. As it turns out, I've been too busy to hunt down the new bike. The Harley, meanwhile, is still sitting back in my old man's garage."

"You couldn't get it running?"

"It's slow work when I have to stop to argue with him over every seal and clutch cable. He thinks I wasted my money buying the thing in the first place, but now, as long as I've got it, I should keep it together with chewing gum and a little string."

Mindel chuckled. "You two still haven't patched things up?"

"Let's say we've agreed to disagree."

"Well, that's progress. If I'm going to buy this machine and use it, though, maybe you want to work a little faster? I'm not getting any younger, you know. And what's this I hear about you joining the fibbies?"

"Guilty as charged."

"I'm away for a few days and you change careers without consulting your wise old advisor?"

"You were laid up for a year, Z'ev, and the job offer came up out of the blue. How are you feeling, anyway?"

"I've been worse. Your father's right about that chewing gum, though. You'd be amazed what they can do with that stuff these days. It's the only thing that's holding me together."

Cruz smiled. Mindel was fifty-eight. He'd been an Israeli Army officer for over twenty years before moving over to work as a technical advisor with Israeli intelligence. Cruz had met him while posted in Germany, when they'd both gotten caught up in the investigation into the murder of the eleven Israeli athletes at the Munich Olympics. They'd kept in touch off and on ever since. The previous year, Mindel had had a stroke that had threatened to end his career, not to mention his life. Only a few days earlier, Cruz had been surprised to learn that Mindel had been named intelligence liaison officer at the Israeli Embassy in Washington—although, by now, nothing the guy did really surprised him. Mindel had an eighteen-year-old spirit and razor-sharp mind trapped in a tough, wiry little body that was beginning to betray him after years of hard campaigning.

"So what's the deal on this fancy embassy job?" Cruz asked.

"Feh! Fancy, schmancy. I shuffle papers, I go to meetings, I smile at cocktail parties until my teeth dry out. Where's the fun? Where's my Uzi? Where's that motorcycle you promised me, godammit? I thought we were going to be Sleazy Riders."

"All right, all right. I'll see what I can do. Maybe I can get it shipped out to D.C. Then you can nag me about seals and clutch cables."

"Now you're talking. So tell me, what's this job they have you doing in the FBI?"

"Not unlike yours. International liaison, only with me, it's cops from other countries I'm talking to instead of the spooks."

"Aha! But last I heard, bubbelah, Minnesota was still part of America, no? You couldn't find some cops in the Bahamas who needed talking to? I'm thinking maybe you're not the smart fellow I took you for."

"Can't argue with you on that. The thing is, Z'ev, I need some information on a case I'm working out here. Official channels are doing what they can, but that means I'll probably get it sometime next year when it's too late to do me any damn good. I was hoping you might be able to help me out."

"I can try. What do you need?"

"Ever hear of a guy named Edelmann? Simon Edelmann?"

"Should I have?"

"From what I hear, he's one of yours."

"This is news to me, my friend, but I can look into it. Personally, I don't recall the man, but that doesn't mean much. Business like ours, there's lots of people you never hear about. Also, stuff seems to slide off the old brain these days, so who knows? Maybe I did meet him and just forgot. What else do you know about this Edelmann?"

"Zip, except that he's here in the United States—or at least he was as recently as Tuesday. That's about it. I need to know why."

"You think he's up to no good?"

"I don't know. I know he was spotted with someone who's a material witness in a couple of cases—"

"Got to be murder cases, right, Alex, for you to be looking at them?"

"Yeah, they are. So what do you think? Can you run the guy, let me know what you find out?"

"I can try. It's the Sabbath, you know, so some people, they don't answer their phones, but I'll see what I can do. Can I call you back at this number? You're going to be there another day?"

"Unfortunately. This is just a motel, mind you, and I haven't got anything like a secure line, much less a security-cleared secretary, so if I'm not here, just leave a message with a number and a time I can call you back, okay?"

"I'm on it as soon as we hang up. But Alex?"

"What?"

"Think chewing gum. And think Mojave in April. They say

it's a very nice time to see the desert, and that a motorcycle is the only way to go."

"I'll give it some serious thought."

CHAPTER 25

The next afternoon, unseasonably sunny and warm for mid-December in Paris, I met Bernard Cohn-Levy again at the café Aux Deux Magots, that literary crossroad made famous by Ernest Hemingway and countless other novelists, musicians and poets. We sat in the lee of a windbreak on the terrace, lingering and enjoying the last good weather of the year while we talked over crusty baguettes and Niçoise salads, drinking good French Chablis that we chased with strong espresso coffee while across the street, devout old parishioners filed out of the noontime mass at the church at St.-Germain-des-Près.

It was such an idyllic setting that I found it hard to imagine leather-coated Gestapo officers sitting in this very same café but I had seen an old wartime photograph of the place in which white-aproned waiters stood nervously by Germans in their polished black boots and pressed gray uniforms, the Nazis sneering at the passing crowd, cruel masters of all they surveyed. Paris had been the jewel in the crown of Hitler's vast empire, which extended for a terrible, painful time from the Atlantic Ocean all the way to the Volga River, and pride of possession had been evident in the face of every Nazi occupier I'd ever seen in those old pictures.

I could only imagine what dark memories resided in M. Cohn-Levy's mind. When the Nazis arrived, his family, Parisian born and bred for generations, would have suddenly found itself subject to more than a hundred anti-Jewish statutes and decrees which stripped them of their legal rights, their worldly possessions, their liberty, and eventually, in most cases, their lives. From the fall of France until 1942, when the deportation of Jewish citizens got underway in earnest, they were subjected to special censuses, had their material goods and bank accounts inventoried and appropriated, were excluded from all economic and political life and ordered to wear an identifying Star of David. Finally, they were rounded up and interned, first in work camps, then in concentration camps where the "Final Solution" was being carried out with brutal efficiency. Thousands of French *gendarmes,* local authorities and ordinary people had aided and abetted in these outrages, so it was hard for me to imagine how someone like Cohn-Levy, who had lost so much, could have come back here and picked up his life, knowing how many of his fellow citizens and national institutions had turned their backs on decency during that terrible time.

But, of course, there were also individuals who had acted with great courage and heroism. It was the sight of a couple of nuns hurrying across the Boulevard St.-Michel, their black and white habits billowing around them like wind-puffed sails, that reminded M. Cohn-Levy of something he'd been meaning to tell me. "Last night, lying in bed, I thought about what you asked," he said.

"About...?"

"About Resistance activities at Gentilly."

I nodded. "There was an old man, a printer named Viau, who lived there and was my mother's host when the SOE dropped her here. She'd learned the printing business from her father, so it was a natural fit. Did you know this man?"

"No, not personally, but I do seem to remember that the name came up in connection with an incident at a convent school in the neighborhood of Gentilly."

"This Viau was a Catholic, I gather, a printer of religious tracts."

Cohn-Levy nodded his white-maned head. "Exactly. They say he used to deliver prayer cards and such to the nuns for use in the school. Sometime in 1944-mid-'44, I think it was, but we can check the dates when we get back to my office—the convent school was discovered to be sheltering four Jewish girls and their teacher. The mother superior was taken into custody by the Gestapo and never seen again—no doubt shipped back to Germany as per the Night and Fog decree. The convent and school were closed, the other nuns detained for the duration of the war."

"And the four little girls?" I asked, already fearing the answer. In the terrible logic of the Final Solution, there could only be one answer.

"They were held for a time at the Vélodrome d'Hiver, the bicycle track here in Paris. From there, they were sent to the Drancy transit camp. It was an especially tragic case, as I recall, because they were shipped out of Drancy on July 31, 1944, on the very last train to leave for Auschwitz. And, of course, because they were children..." Cohn-Levy's voice trailed off and he turned away, head shaking.

My throat had tightened up, but if he could talk about this without crying, I was determined I would, too. Still, I pushed my plate aside, my appetite gone. A fork fell to the ground and M. Cohn-Levy bent to pick it up. When he rose again and saw my face, he patted my hand, seeming to read my mind.

"I, too, have cried, Jillian," he said quietly, "but it does no good. The dead have no use for our tears. They ask only that we remember them and bear witness to what was done to them. That we take action against those responsible and work to ensure that it never happens again."

I nodded glumly. "What about Viau, the printer? Was he the one who betrayed those children and their teacher to the Gestapo?"

Even as I asked, a darker question was forming in my mind. Had it been the old man, or perhaps a young French-English partisan who worked with him? My mother might well have learned the convent school's secret in the course of living and working with Viau, and I knew she'd been rounded up by the Gestapo on more than one occasion and subjected to God only knew what kind of intimidation. Had she broken under torture? Or volunteered the information in an effort to save her own skin?

"I don't think anyone knows for sure," Cohn-Levy said. "It's entirely possible they weren't betrayed, at all, but merely discovered by accident in the course of a Gestapo hunt for something else. There'd been a major Resistance coup not long before, you see, a theft—"

"Of gold?" I asked, grasping for any explanation that might exonerate my mother.

"You've heard of that incident?"

"Only in the vaguest of terms. I understand entire cells of the Resistance were wiped out after a hoard of Nazi gold was stolen, but I don't know all the details."

"I'm not sure anyone does. What we have learned, on the basis of eyewitness accounts and documents we obtained from the Prefecture of Police, is that the gold came from those deported to the concentration camps—seventy-five thousand Jews alone, plus thousand of others detained for various reasons. All their valuables were confiscated at the transit camps like Drancy. Most of these people were not wealthy, but even so, it's a lot of people, and most of them would have had a wedding ring, or earrings or a necklace or some other bauble."

I nodded. "It would add up to a lot. Even if they confiscated just one ounce of gold from each person, that would make—"

"Thousand and thousands of ounces. I once heard an estimate that the stolen shipment was worth over two million in 1944 U.S. dollars."

"Which would be worth a lot more now with the price of gold skyrocketing the way it is these days."

"Ten times that, I should think," Cohn-Levy agreed. "But even in 1944, that much gold carried a enormous amount of purchasing power. There were other valuables taken, as well, jewelry and watches and the like. All the confiscated goods were inventoried, then put into storage in a safe deposit box at the Banque de Paris— a strong room, actually, because there was no box or vault large enough to hold it all. The official line is that it was being held for eventual restitution when those from whom it had been stolen would no longer be deemed a threat to the regime. But since the Nazis believed this so-called threat to their plan to 'Aryanize' Europe would only be gone once we were all dead, it is a bit of a mystery how exactly these valuables were supposed to be returned."

Cohn-Levy gave a short, bitter laugh, then took a long draught of his wine. "In any case, when the war ended and the vaults at the Banque de Paris were opened, the jewels and fountain pens and watches and what have you were still there, minus a little that had been pilfered at various stages of the chain of control. But every last gram of gold was missing."

"I'd heard that Hitler himself ordered that the gold be shipped to Berlin."

"Exactly. He needed more money for arms. Coins were to be left intact, since they were easily negotiable, but all the jewelry had to be melted down before it could be traded."

"Was that done here or in Germany?"

"Here. We've been able to learn that it was melted down into bars at a foundry northwest of Paris by a small contingent of French workers operating under close Gestapo supervision. The bars, something like a thousand of them, plus crates of coins of various denominations, were then loaded onto a heavily guarded freight car and moved to a railroad siding at Gentilly to await a train that was scheduled to depart for Berlin a day or so later."

"And that's when it disappeared?"

"Possibly. Nobody really knows for sure. You see, the car was padlocked at the foundry, and it was only when it arrived in Berlin and the padlocks were removed that the theft was discovered. The gold had vanished somewhere between the foundry and the Berlin rail yard, replaced with ordinary bricks spray-painted gold, in case anyone checked through the peephole." Cohn-Levy's broad shoulders lifted in a typically Gallic shrug. "Maybe they did check, maybe they didn't. Who knows? All we know is that nobody actually opened the sliding door until Berlin, and when they did, bricks was all they found."

"What a coup," I breathed.

"Indeed. Unfortunately, the aftermath was horrific. It was normal practice to take massive punitive reprisals against the civilian population whenever the Resistance made a blow against the Reich. All the foundry workers involved in the meltdown were immediately arrested, interrogated, tortured and shot. Then, the Gestapo started moving down the rail line, rounding up anyone and everyone suspected of having Resistance connections. They did a house-by-house, building-by-building search, trying to learn where the gold had been stashed."

"But it was never found?"

"Not as far as we know. Hundreds were arrested, but an operation of this sophistication would have been tightly compartmentalized. Probably only one or two people knew all the details of how it was carried out, and they either carried the secret of the hiding place to their graves, or," Cohn-Levy said, his shoulders lifting in another of those resigned shrugs, "some enterprising soul found the gold, hid it until after the war, and went on to live—how do you Americans say...?"

"The life of Riley?"

"Exactly. Went on to live the life of Riley."

I frowned into the dregs at the bottom on my demitasse of espresso. "So, during the Gestapo's search for the gold, is that when the convent and school were searched?"

"Yes. The children were all moved into the chapel when the Gestapo arrived. The *Obermeister* at that time was a particularly nasty fellow by the name of Kurt Braun. They say he was a cousin of Hitler's mistress, Eva Braun. Like Adolf Hitler, this Colonel Braun had been raised a Catholic himself, so once the little girls were together, he went down the line one by one, asking them questions on the catechism. When he got to the four Jewish girls, of course, they could not give the correct answers, so they were all taken into custody. Their teacher stepped forward when she saw what was happening and insisted on going with them. And that," Cohn-Levy added grimly, "was the end of that melody."

We finished our coffee and he called for the check and wouldn't hear of my paying. We were walking down the Boulevard St.-Michel a few minutes later when a thought occurred to me. "How did he know?" I asked.

"Who?"

"The Gestapo man, Colonel Braun. How did he know to question the little girls on their catechism?"

"I don't know. He was a cruel man with a tendency to indulge in capricious drama, they say. Perhaps he thought to play the role of the wise catechism teacher, rather like Marie Antoinette playing at being a shepherdess—only in this case, he accidentally stumbled across four little black sheep in the flock."

"Or maybe he knew those children and their teacher were hiding there because he'd been told," I said unhappily.

I was right back at square one, my dark fears about my mother lurking once more. But I had yet to learn the full story of what had happened that day at the convent school, and my biggest shock was yet to come.

CHAPTER 26

Havenwood, Minnesota
Friday, January 12, 1979

When Cruz arrived back at the town dock for the opening ceremonies of the ice-fishing derby, Tom Newkirk was nowhere to be seen. The Havenwood High band was playing the theme from *The Bridge on the River Kwai,* accompanied by the off-key whistle of dozens of boot-tramping fishermen and other party-goers waving bottle-shaped brown bags and Thermos jugs of what Cruz suspected held more than just coffee. He walked around the small stage set up on the hill overlooking the town dock, trying to see if the mayor was among the crowd of derby officials back there, but instead, he found Nils Berglund.

The deputy chief nodded as he approached. "You looking for me?"

"I was actually trying to find Tom Newkirk. I know he's slated to do the kick-off ceremonies and I was hoping to get a chance to sit down with him afterward and ask him a couple of questions."

"About what?"

"About the guy he saw at the airport with Jillian. Also, to find out what he knew about Grace Meade's war record. Someone told me he and Grace's late husband served together during the war. I thought that if Newkirk had met her over there, too, he might be able to tell me a little more about her service record."

"Why would you be interested in that?"

"I was trying to put bits and pieces of this business together. I couldn't figure out where the Mossad guy fit into it until it occurred to me that it might have something to do with the war—maybe something Grace might have seen or done over there."

"Get outta here. That was over thirty years ago."

"Like I told you, those Mossad guys have long memories. I can't think of any other common denominator, so I figure it's worth looking into. So what about Newkirk? Why isn't he here?"

"He canceled."

"You're kidding."

"No. He gave his speech notes to Norbert Jorgenson." Berglund cocked his head toward the stage, where Ollie's husband, the man who'd checked Cruz into the Whispering Pines the previous day, was standing off to one side, nervously folding and unfolding a piece of paper as the high school band played on. "Jorgenson's the deputy mayor," Berglund added.

"So I heard. How come Newkirk ducked out?"

"He said he wasn't up for the party scene tonight, what with Sybil so upset about Grace, and then having the funeral arrangements and all to take care of." Berglund shuffled his big feet. "I imagine it's hit him pretty hard, too."

No doubt, Cruz thought, especially since it seemed Newkirk and Grace had been more than mere neighbors. "So I guess I'd find him at home?"

"Probably. You really think you need to do this tonight?"

"Tomorrow's not going to be any better."

"No, I guess it isn't," Berglund agreed. "By the way, one of my guys was checking out the cottages across the lake. He found one that looks like it's been broken into, and it's got a direct line of sight to the Meade place. We called the owner in Minneapolis, who told us there should have been a Ski-Doo in the shed over there, but when we went back to double-check, it was nowhere to be seen. There are tracks, though, and they look to be identical to the ones I saw over at Grace's."

"You dusting the cottage for prints?"

Berglund nodded. "You going to get me Edelmann's prints anytime soon for comparison?"

Cruz grimaced. "I called in the request, but I wouldn't look for them to arrive much before next week."

"Lotta good that does me."

The Havenwood High marching band finished playing to a chorus of cheers and stomping from the crowd. Norbert Jorgenson and a young woman, whom Cruz presumed was Miss Havenwood, stepped up onto the platform.

"Listen, I should tell you something else," Berglund added quietly. He appeared to be watching the ceremony, but from the deep ridges lining his brow, Cruz knew his mind was far from ice-fishing and crowd control. "I talked to Dr. Kandinsky a little while ago. I wanted to see how Jill was doing after that episode this morning."

"Uh-huh. And what did she say?"

"Said she settled down okay after they gave her a mild sedative. I asked if she thought Jillian should be told about the funeral tomorrow."

"And?"

"She thought she should. She knows her mom's dead, after all, and the doc thought she should be given the option to go if she seemed able to handle it."

"She thinks Jillian should attend?"

"Not necessarily. I hope not, as a matter of fact, but the doctor said she was going to try to have a quiet talk with her again tonight and feel her out on it. For some people, apparently, attending a funeral helps them get 'closure' or some damn thing. Seems like a real dumb idea to me, but what do I know?"

"So there's a chance she'll actually be here tomorrow?"

"Yeah, I guess so. Physically, Dr. Kandinsky says, there's no reason why she couldn't leave for a couple of hours, and if it would help her come to terms with all this..." Berglund's voice faded as he rammed his hands into his jacket pocket and watched Jorgenson take up the microphone and start delivering Tom Newkirk's welcoming remarks.

The cold night wind picked up the smell of gasoline fumes wafting over the shoreline. Down by the ice, a couple of locals were dousing a ten-foot high log pile with fuel in preparation for the lighting of the bonfire. Cruz felt the familiar knot in his gut twist and tighten. Time for him to hit the road.

And then, it hit him what the deputy had been trying to say.

"Oh, Jesus, Berglund, tell me you're not planning to bring her to the funeral yourself."

The deputy's face screwed itself down into a stubborn frown. "If the doc says she wants to go, I'll pick her up."

Right. And how thrilled would his wife be with that? Cruz wondered. How much more grist for the gossip mill did this town need? "Why you? Why don't you let Tom Newkirk go and get her?"

"He's got his hands full with Sybil, and God knows, we don't want that woman within arm's reach of Jillian right now."

"You're afraid Sybil will rip into her?"

"I don't know. Where Sybil's concerned, you never know what she's going to do next. A lot of people's emotions are pretty raw right now. No telling how anyone's likely to react. Like I say, I don't know that it's even such a hot idea for Jillian to come, but it *is* her mother, after all. If she thinks she needs to go to the funeral, then I guess that's what she should do." He turned to face Cruz head-on. "The thing is, if she does come, I'm going to have plenty on my hands without worrying about you setting her off again. It's going to be hard enough keeping Grace's old cronies in line. The last thing I need is you sniping at her, too."

"Sniping? All I did was ask her some straightforward questions."

"Same difference."

"Hardly. In any case, give me some credit. I'm not going to give her the third degree at a funeral."

"I should hope not. But after what happened over at the hospital today, I don't even think she should see your face there. And nothing personal, Cruz, but you also seem to have attracted a certain amount of attention around here. This is going to be a three-ring circus as it is without having a bunch of women climbing over each other to get at you. Like I said, nothing personal. I'm not saying it's your fault. Things can get pretty dull around here, I suppose, so when a little fresh meat shows up, well...you know."

"You're saying you want me to stay away altogether?"

"I think it'd be for the best. With all the curiosity your being here has stirred up, if both you and Jillian show up at that funeral, things will deteriorate in short order."

"All right, I won't show my face," Cruz said reluctantly. "But just for the record, I also think it's a real poor idea for you to bring Jillian."

"Yeah, well, it's her call and the doctor's."

"Like it or not, you know," Cruz said, "she's still a suspect as long as the investigation into her mother's death is pending—not to mention those other homicides that brought me here in the first place. If she's taken off lock-down, she should be kept under close watch."

"All the more reason for me to bring her."

"Maybe, but your hands are going to be full just trying to run herd on all the looky-loos and people with an ax to grind one way or the other. Tell me you're going to have additional men covering that funeral."

"I am, but I can only spare a couple of guys. As it is, I'm pulling them off derby duty, but the funeral's at eleven in the morning and the party animals will barely even be out of bed by then, so it should be okay. You and I are clear on this, though, right?"

"As a bell."

"I have your word you won't complicate things by showing up or trying to ask Jill any more questions until after Grace is safely buried and we see how she handles it all?"

Cruz nodded. "You've got it."

Another cheer went up from the derby crowd, and they looked over to see Jorgenson and Miss Havenwood heading over to the woodpile with a lit torch. Berglund turned up the collar of his jacket. "I better go keep an eye on things, make sure these clowns don't burn down the whole town."

"I'm going to have a talk with Newkirk."

Berglund hesitated. "You probably want to go a little easy on him right now, too, you know."

"Understood."

Berglund studied him for a moment, then nodded curtly and walked off.

Cruz looked down to the shoreline just as a deep *whumpf!* announced the lighting of the bonfire. A cheer went up from the crowd, and then music began to blare from loudspeakers mounted high on the light standards. Windows rattled to the back beat as couples formed up and began to dance. A lone young woman near the fire slipped her jacket off her shoulders and held it out to either side of her, undulating and swaying her hips in a winterized version of the Dance of the Seven Veils that drew stomps and whistles from the half-inebriated crowd.

Cruz headed for his car and away from the town center, leaving the noise behind as he made his way down silent residential streets. But as he rounded Lakeshore Road, he was blinded by the headlights of a car coming from the opposite direction, aiming directly at him. He was about to yank the steering wheel and take his chances on the ditch when the car suddenly veered, then careened past him and took off toward town. Shaken, Cruz slowed and looked over his shoulder at the receding red taillights but it was too dark to make out the model. Another party animal rushing to make a night of it.

At the Newkirks' driveway, he cut his own headlights, not wanting to draw attention to himself when he realized Tom Newkirk's powder-blue Oldsmobile was not parked in the drive. Through the wide front window, Cruz could see Sybil Newkirk curled on the couch in the living room, which was dark except for the flickering blue light of the television set, the reflection bouncing off a glass as she lifted it to her lips. She took a long draught, then set it aside and used the heel of her hand to wipe her nose.

Cruz cut the engine, opened his car door quietly and slipped out, walking over to check out the double garage, but when he looked through the window, he saw only the round outline of a Volkswagen beetle next to the empty spot where Newkirk's Oldsmobile should have been. He debated his next move. He could knock on the door and ask Mrs. Newkirk where he might find her husband, but that might turn into a long weep-fest, which he wasn't up for. Instead, he climbed into the car once more and rolled it quietly back down the drive, keeping the headlights off until he was out on the Lakeshore Road again. There were only half a dozen streets in the center of the town, and not many more in the surrounding residential neighborhood. How hard could it be to find the man?

But after two circuits of the town center, where the bonfire by the town dock was burning brightly now and the party in full swing, Cruz had still not run across the blue Olds. He was giving the downtown one last sweep before widening his search to include all the residential streets, when he spotted the Olds's bumper in a parking lot at the rear of a redbrick building that stood next to the Lakeside Inn. It looked as if Newkirk had gone into the pub. Cruz hesitated, loathe to take on all that smoke and noise and boozy bonhomie. It was no place for a quiet talk, and trailing a politician as he glad-handed a crowd was no way to conduct an interview. On the other hand, as he'd told Berglund, if he didn't catch Newkirk tonight, he'd have an even tougher time of it tomorrow.

With all the central parking spots taken by the derby crowd, he was forced to park about three blocks away from the pub. He walked back along street, his feet unconsciously picking up the pace of the music blasting from the speakers at the dock—the inescapable "Stayin' Alive." Inside the pub, the din was even more deafening than it had been the previous night. While he would have thought everyone was outside at the bonfire, this place, too, was jumping, the Wurlitzer volume cranked to the max. Newkirk, however, was nowhere to be seen. The same blond waitress who'd served him the night before gave him a smile as she passed with her tray.

"Hey, you're back!" she bellowed over the din.

"Just looking for the mayor," Cruz told her.

She cupped a hand behind her ear. "Who?"

"Tom Newkirk! Know where I can find him?"

She shook her head. "Hasn't been in tonight."

Cruz nodded, frowning, but as he looked the room over, he realized the crowd was too young to draw a man of Newkirk's age, even if he had wanted to drown his sorrows. He slipped back out the door and debated returning to the bonfire to see if Newkirk had decided to show up there, after all. But when he glanced at the redbrick building behind the inn again, he saw the dim glow of a lamp in the front window. He walked over to the low building, where he found a shingle next to the front door that said these were the law offices of Thomas Newkirk, Esq.

He tried the front door handle but there was no give. Cruz walked around to the back where the Olds was parked. A security light was on over the rear door, and when he tried the doorknob, it was unlocked. It could only happen in a small town.

He walked in and found himself in an office supply room, with the door leading to a carpeted hall that went straight through to a front lobby area. A soft, golden light shone from another open doorway off to one side the hall. Cruz moved toward it and saw an office taking up one entire side of the building. Toward the rear of it, a broad wooden desk was angled across a corner, its high-backed chair turned away to face the low credenza behind it. A pair of highly polished leather brogues were propped on the cabinet.

Cruz rapped lightly on the door frame. "Excuse me? Mr. Newkirk?"

He knew the man was there, but even so, he was startled by Newkirk's voice as it cut through the stillness. "Come in, Agent Cruz. I saw you trying the front door. You managed to track me down, I see." The shoes dropped to the floor and the chair pivoted around. "I thought I might be seeing you again."

Newkirk had thrown his overcoat and jacket over another chair in the corner of the room and was sitting in his shirt-sleeves, tie loosened and collar unbuttoned. There were pouches under his eyes, and the deep purple cast of the five-o'clock shadow on his cheeks left him looking haggard and gaunt. His chromed hair was still slicked back at the sides by some sort of industrial-strength hair cream, but a few strands had come loose, lopping messily over his forehead. Like his wife, Newkirk had a glass in his hand, nearly empty.

"I'm sorry to bother you, sir," Cruz said. "I was hoping to have a word. I stopped by your house, but when I saw your car wasn't there, I didn't want to bother your wife."

"I thought that might have been you I passed at the corner."

"I guess it was."

"Mmm... Small town, you know. Not much goes unnoticed around here."

"No, sir, I suppose not."

"Come on in, have a seat." Newkirk tipped back his glass, a brandy snifter, and drained it, then rocked the chair forward and got to his feet. "I was just about to pour myself another. Care to join me?"

"Thank you, maybe I will," Cruz said, settling into a wing-back chair on the client side of the desk.

"I'm drinking cognac myself, but I can offer you Canadian whiskey, or—"

"Cognac would be fine, thanks."

"Good choice." Newkirk slid open a door under the credenza and withdrew another snifter, then filled both from the bottle on his desk and handed the fresh one across to Cruz. "Picked up a taste for it in France during the war. Cheers."

Cruz raised his glass in reply, then took a drink and felt a sweet burn travel down his gullet. Newkirk settled into his chair once more and propped his feet up on the desk.

"Were you over there at the Liberation, sir?"

"It's Tom, please," Newkirk reminded him, ever the politician, even in this state of liquid mourning. "Yes, I was. Quite an occasion, rolling into Paris. Thousands of people out in the streets, cheering us on, throwing flowers and kisses, handing bottles of champagne and cognac up into our jeeps. They'd been hiding it from the Germans since the beginning of the Occupation, but, boy oh boy, the good stuff sure came out after we chased the Jerrys off. I collected close to a dozen bottles myself."

"No kidding."

Newkirk picked up the bottle by the neck. "I drank most of it over there, but this is the last of my stock. Courvoisier 1939."

Cruz's eyes went wide and he stared at the bottle, then at his glass. "Forty years old? Incredible."

"I've been saving it all these years. For what, I'm not sure. Something momentous, I guess. Decided this was the night to crack it."

"To toast Grace Meade?"

Newkirk paused, then nodded. As he lifted his glass, Cruz noticed a shake in the man's pale, mottled hand. "To Grace," Newkirk said. His Adam's apple bobbed visibly between the wattles of his neck as he drained his glass once more.

Cruz raised his own glass and took another small sip, then let a respectful silence float between them. "Tell me about her," he said finally.

"What would you like to hear?"

"Well, I know she was beautiful."

"Yes, that's right, you saw pictures of her, didn't you? Not that they really did her justice. I don't think I've ever seen a more beautiful woman. She had skin like silk and blue eyes a man could swim in. And her voice—it was low, you know. Surprisingly low for a woman. Made you ache to hear it. Like a cat's purr or something. I don't know. Just electric, really. I've seen men blather at her, do anything, just to get her to talk to them."

"You loved her."

Newkirk didn't even try to deny it. "It was impossible not to."

"That must have been awkward, you being married and all."

Nor did he shy away from that. "It was," he agreed. "You might judge me harshly for saying this, but I didn't give a damn. Grace was worth it. I fell in love with her the very first time I ever laid eyes on her, and my feelings never changed. Even as she aged, she was still worth ten of any other woman."

"When did you meet her?"

"May 11, 1943, not long after I arrived in England. It was at a training facility just outside London."

"You were with the OSS?"

Newkirk nodded. "Joe Meade and I both flew for them. His dad had had a crop dusting service before the war and he'd taught us to fly. Were you ever in the service yourself, Agent Cruz?"

"Yes, sir, the Army. Twelve years."

"Infantry?"

"At first. Later, I moved over to criminal investigation."

"I see. So that's how you ended up in your present line of work?" When Cruz nodded, Newkirk went on. "Joe and I started out with the infantry, too, but when the OSS came looking for pilots we volunteered. Sounded like exciting business, flying supplies and people behind the lines to the Resistance. Dangerous work, but it beat slogging through muddy cow pastures with all the other grunts."

"Did you and Joe both meet Grace at the same time?"

"Yes, during training. British Special Operations had been running people behind the lines from the get-go, so they had a lot of experience to share when our guys finally got into the game. Grace was in their False Documents Section, putting together identity papers and such for the people going over."

Cruz frowned. "I thought she'd been behind the lines herself."

"She was, but not till fairly late in the game. She was young and hungry for adventure. We all were, I suppose. In any case, after helping to train so many other people to get along behind the lines, Grace wanted a shot at it herself. Her mother had been French, you know, so she spoke the language like a native, and she had skills the Resistance could use, so the Brits finally agreed to send her in. That was a couple of months after I first met her. As a matter of fact, it was me who flew the plane that took her over. Just about killed me to watch her strap on that parachute and jump out of the plane. Like I said, I'd fallen hard for her. I didn't want to see her get hurt."

"What about Joe?"

"What about him?"

"I heard you guys were best friends."

"Since we were kids, that's right."

"So you must have been rivals where Grace was concerned."

Newkirk exhaled heavily. "Not exactly. I was already married then, and Grace knew it, so I wasn't really in the running, much as I wanted to be. I'd gotten Sybil in the family way, you see, so we'd had to get married just before Joe and I shipped out."

"So it was Grace and Joe who hooked up?"

"Not right off, no. Grace had a thing for Joe the way I did for her, but he didn't feel the same way—not at the beginning, anyway. Not that Grace had much time to pine over him, with all the fellows standing in line for her."

"But not Joe?"

Newkirk shook his head. "He was never one to go after what everyone else wanted. Instead, he'd ask the quiet girls to dance, and the ones with glasses, just so they wouldn't feel overlooked."

"Sounds like a nice guy."

"He was always like that, watching out for the little guy. I'll give you an example. The summer we were ten, Joe's folks said he could have a dog, so he and I rode our bikes out to a farm where there was a litter looking for homes. Wouldn't you know Joe would pick the mangiest, scrawniest one of the bunch? Elderchuk, the farmer, tried to talk him out of it—said that runt was too sickly and he was going to drown it, which was all Joe needed to hear, of course, to convince him that pup was the only one for him. Even his parents thought he was crazy, but she turned out to be the best dog—loyal, smart, followed him everywhere. He called her Queenie," Newkirk added, grinning. "Said it would build her confidence. To this day, you drive around this town, half the dogs you see are Queenie's descendants because everybody loved that dog and wanted one just like her. And you want to hear the strangest thing?"

"What's that?"

"Apparently she died on the same day Joe was killed over in France. His folks said she just took sick one morning, lay down and never got up. It was only after the war that they learned Joe had been shot by the Germans on the exact same day the dog died."

"That is weird," Cruz agreed. "And he and Grace? How did they get together?"

"They met again behind the lines."

"Were you surprised to learn they'd been married, after him not showing any interest before?"

Newkirk took a long sip from his glass. "You have no idea how surprised I was."

"How's that?"

"Well, for one thing, Joe had met another girl by then. It happened after Grace went over, but from the way he talked, it sounded pretty serious. I never met the girl myself, mind you. I'd ended up in hospital with a bout of jaundice, but Joe came in to see me a couple of times, so I knew he was seeing this French girl. One of General deGaulle's Free French, she was, getting ready to be shipped over. Her name was Isobel, but that's all I know about her. After she was dropped behind the lines, they lost contact with her."

Newkirk sat quietly for a moment, his finger circling the rim of his glass as his mind seemed to wander through the distant past. "To tell you the absolute truth," he said finally, "when Joe's plane went down, I half suspected he'd ditched it so he could go looking for her, but I'm guessing she'd already been caught by the Germans. One of the thousands of partisans who vanished. Hazards of war and all."

"Do you really think Joe ditched his plane?"

"I wouldn't put it past him to do a foolhardy thing like that, but, of course, there's no way of knowing for sure."

"So instead of this Isobel, he hooked up with Grace? No wonder you were surprised."

Newkirk nodded. "Grace said Joe showed up with one of her Resistance contacts one day. They were passing him off to the Resistance cell in Paris that Grace belonged to. I guess Joe ended up hiding out in the house where she was staying, and one thing led to another. Grace said they were married by a local parish priest, but Joe got caught up in a Gestapo sweep not long after. It wouldn't have taken the Jerries long to figure out he was no Frenchman, of course. As a downed pilot, he should have been sent to a POW camp, but he wasn't with his plane and he wasn't in uniform or even part of the regular armed forces, so instead, the Germans did what they always did with spies."

Cruz studied the other man, trying to read between the lines of this tale he was telling. "Why does it sound like you don't entirely believe this?" he asked.

Newkirk exhaled heavily. "I have no doubt that Grace and Joe met up in Paris. She told me Joe had mentioned to her that a buddy of ours had lost a leg and had just been shipped home to the States. That was Ed Rasmussen—Verna's husband, you know? I imagine you've met her over at the police station."

Cruz nodded.

"Well, Ed was finally shipped home not long before Joe's plane went down, so Grace could only have heard about it from Joe."

"But there was still something fishy about Grace's story, right?"

"Yes. The marriage part. Not many people knew about Joe and his French girl, but to me, it seemed odd that he'd marry Grace so soon after losing her. Mind you, Grace had gone through some tough times herself by then, and Joe being Joe, that would be just the kind of thing to bring out those protective instincts of his."

"Could Grace have been pregnant with Jillian by then?"

Newkirk swirled the brown liquid in his glass, staring down into the fragrant eddies. "Well, yes, she would have to have been. I suppose it's possible Joe could have married her for that reason."

"Because she was carrying his child?"

"His child?" Newkirk took another long drink from his glass, then shook his head. "Not a chance. As I said, Agent Cruz, Joe was a hell of a good guy, and he might have married Grace because he knew she couldn't possibly marry the real father of that child."

Cruz almost heard a chunking sound, a mental "aha!" as another piece of the puzzle fell into place. "So Joe Meade wasn't Jillian's father. Are you sure? Did Grace actually tell you?"

Newkirk shrugged his shoulders, which seemed suddenly thinner than they had been. Once again, Cruz had the sense of a man shrinking right before his eyes. "She didn't have to. I have fingers and I can count. I knew Joe couldn't be the father because he wasn't anywhere near Grace at the time she would have gotten pregnant."

Another thought occurred to Cruz. "Is that it? Are you Jillian's real father?"

Newkirk arched an eyebrow. "Funny you should ask. Jillian called me from Washington last week, and that's what she wanted to know, too."

"She phoned you? Last week, even before she came out here?"

"Yes. It seems she'd gotten her hands on our old OSS service records. She was checking dates and had figured out that Joe and Grace weren't together at the, shall we say, auspicious moment? She saw that I'd been flying missions into France at about that time, though, and apparently it got her wondering."

"What did you tell her?"

"I told her what I'll tell you, Agent Cruz. I would be proud and delighted to be her father. Jillian's a lovely, intelligent young woman, and I loved her mother with all my heart. Even though I already had a wife and child back here, I would have gotten a divorce in a New York minute if Grace had asked me to be father to her child. Unfortunately, she didn't." His eyes narrowed. "I'm sure you must have heard gossip by now that she and I were...close friends. I won't deny it. I don't see the point, especially now that she's gone. It would be an injustice not to admit how I felt about her. Our affair started after the war was already over, however. And, in case you're wondering, Sybil did know about it. But I fulfilled all my marital obligations, and she seemed satisfied with the arrangement Grace and I had—which was, I hasten to add, both mature and discreet. At this point, frankly, I don't give a damn what anyone else thinks about it."

"And Grace was content with the arrangement, too?"

"It would seem so. I'm happy and grateful to say that after she moved to Havenwood, she never to my knowledge even looked at another man. But neither would she hear of my divorcing Sybil for her. Didn't want the scandal or the guilt, she said. So, we just went along as we did, managing as best we could. If that was the only way I could have her, then so be it. But, Agent Cruz, to answer your question—yours and Jillian's—no, she is not my daughter."

"But neither is she Joe Meade's?"

"No, although it seemed best to let everyone believe that, including Helen and Art, Joe's parents. He was their only child, you know. After he was killed, they were crushed, but when they thought there might a grandchild in the picture.... Well, as you can imagine, it gave them a reason to go on. Art Meade wrote to me over in England after the war, when I was waiting to be shipped home. He told me they'd had a letter from Grace, and he said Helen wanted to bring the girl and the baby over to the States. He asked me to go and check things out, see if that was a good idea."

"Do you think he suspected the baby wasn't Joe's?"

"No, not necessarily. Joe had written to them about meeting a girl, so the marriage wasn't a total surprise. Because of the military censors, Helen and Art didn't know anything about Joe's girl, except that she was a foreigner. Art was worried she might not be happy here, and he didn't want to get Helen's hopes up if it wasn't going to work out. That's why he asked me to go and see Grace before they made the offer."

"So you were basically the vetting committee?"

"I suppose you could say that, yes." Newkirk reached for the bottle and refilled Cruz's glass, then his own. "And yes, I know what you're thinking, Agent Cruz."

"Do you?"

"That I had a selfish interest in making sure Grace was able to come here. Which I did, of course. And I imagine you're also thinking to yourself about now that I must have blackmailed Grace—told her I'd vouch for her with the Meades in exchange for sexual favors."

"And did you?"

His shoulders gave another irritating lift. "She didn't really need me to vouch for her. She had a marriage certificate from a church parish in Paris to prove they'd been married. The U.S. government was content with that."

"A marriage certificate, right," Cruz said wryly. "Did the American authorities know she'd worked in false documents? As a forger, I imagine?"

A small smile turned the corner of Newkirk's thin lips. "I'm not sure they did, as a matter of fact. Things were very confused around that time, you know. With a war to be mopped up and countries to be rebuilt, not to mention millions of people dead, displaced and missing, there were much bigger things to worry about than one young widow and her baby."

"But you were onto her game, weren't you? You didn't really believe Joe had married her, and yet you vouched for her with his parents, anyway."

Newkirk sighed. "That's basically what Jillian accused me of having done when I told her I wasn't her father. I can understand that she was upset, of course. Who wouldn't be, under the circumstances?"

"Were you able to tell her who her father really was?"

His lower lip jutted out as Newkirk shook his head. "Not entirely. And not willing to, even if I were able. I told her it was something she would have to discuss with her mother."

Cruz frowned. What had Sybil Newkirk said she'd overheard the night of the fire? The two women arguing, Jillian's voice especially loud? What was it she'd been saying? "Tell me!" Was that what she'd been so anxious to know?

"You say you wouldn't tell Jillian. Does that mean you've got a pretty good idea who her real father was?"

"I only know what Grace told me when I tracked her down after the war. She'd been picked up by our Army units after the Liberation—she and the baby. When she showed them the certificate to support her claim to be Joe's widow, they arranged transport back over the Channel for her, then helped her get a letter to his folks. When I caught up to her, she eventually admitted that Jillian wasn't Joe's, but she said he'd known about the baby. I wanted to believe her and frankly, it sounded like something Joe would have done, making sure Grace would be taken care of after what she'd been through. Make sure that poor little baby girl would have a name, too."

"And what was it Grace said she'd been through?"

"Use your imagination, Agent Cruz. She'd been arrested by the Gestapo. You must know what they were like with female prisoners. A blond, blue-eyed beauty like Grace? And those bloody Nazis with their obsession about the Aryan race? What do you think happened? They'd have seen a girl like that as a prime breeder in their quest to build the master race."

"So you're saying she was raped and Jillian was fathered by some Nazi?"

Newkirk nodded. "So you can understand why Grace wanted to bury the past and just live a quiet life here in Havenwood."

Right, Cruz thought, not to mention why their mother-child bond had been tainted. But then, he thought about Simon Edelmann. Did Edelmann know something that Grace apparently hadn't revealed when Joe Meade's best friend had paved the way for her to escape to America after the war?

"You're convinced it was rape? Or is it possible she took a German lover and then had to hide the fact after the Liberation? You know what happened to women like that after the war if they were caught by the mob, don't you? Their heads were shaved and they were paraded through the streets to be spat on and have people throw garbage at them. Besides which, who knows who she might have betrayed in the process? As an agent of the British government, she'd have been doubly guilty if she were found to have collaborated. She could have been put on trial for treason."

Newkirk drained his glass and set it down on the desk. "I honestly don't know, Agent Cruz. But it's ancient history now, isn't it? Grace is gone. All I can tell you is that she said she'd been raped and I saw no reason not to believe her. I knew it was possible the marriage document could be a forgery, but Grace needed my help and she was grateful when I gave it to her. That was enough for me."

CHAPTER 27

Where was I?

I was writing about Bernard Cohn-Levy, and how he had offered to help me go through his files. And how, as we sat in dappled sunlight under the chestnut trees outside Aux Deux Magots, I remembered wartime photographs I'd seen of that same spot, where aproned garçons stood in nervous attendance on a host of strapping Gestapo men looking smugly down their Teutonic noses at all the conquered Parisians.

The image of those leather-coated Nazis must have stuck in my mind, because in the midst of the jumbled nightmares that followed my sedation yesterday, one lucid memory seems to have jarred itself loose from the dark recesses of my mind, a bizarre-but-true recollection of my mother and a leather coat that seems suddenly, in light of what I know now, to have taken on new significance.

By way of background, I should note she was never the kind of mother who appreciated the commotion of children, so when I was a child, friends were rarely allowed to play at the house unless she was out and my grandparents were alone with me. As we grew older—and therefore more interesting to my mother—she became a little more tolerant, however. But by then, I think I began to resent how she always seemed to end up the center of attention when my friends were around.

I don't think my mother ever resigned herself to the idea of growing old. Beauty, charm and indomitable will, those were her trademarks. As my friends and I turned into young adults, she seemed to feel the need to dazzle the boys and to compete with the girls as if to prove—to us? to herself?—she was still more beautiful, more alluring than anyone else. Still the infamous femme fatale who had used her charm and talents to such devastating effect during the war. Not even her daughter was exempt from that competition.

Nils was my first boyfriend, the only one I ever had in Havenwood, although at the time, he was all I could have wanted. We'd known each other forever, but only really noticed one another swimming down by the town dock the summer I was sixteen and Nils was seventeen. For the next two years, we were inseparable. I think my mother hated every minute of it. When she wasn't finding fault with his family, his looks, or his prospects (all of which seemed just fine to me), she was busy reporting that he'd been sighted in the company of someone prettier or cleverer than I and commiserating over the inevitable dumping I was bound to suffer at his hands.

"I know it isn't fair, darling. No one can say you don't do the best you can with what you have to work with, but you know how fickle men are. So easily distracted by a pretty face, aren't they? You mustn't take it personally."

The afternoon she came home early from a shopping trip to Minneapolis and caught us in my bed, asleep in each other's arms, she was icily terse as she ordered Nils out of the house. After he'd left, she directed her cold, blue glare at me. "Well! I suppose you think you're the cat's pyjamas, don't you? What a stupid, pathetic little girl you are," she spat, before turning on her heel and walking away.

For weeks afterward, I was frozen out of all but the most unavoidable communication. I thought she absolutely despised Nils and despised the idea of any daughter of hers associating with him, but I couldn't imagine giving him up. Eventually, in any case, she got bored with the effort of maintaining all that indignation, and so the situation finally thawed enough for him to feel safe entering the house once more.

One day, he was over working with me on some school project. I had hung his leather football jacket on a hook in the back vestibule, and at some point, I headed there to look for something in my own coat pocket. As I rounded the corner, I came upon my mother clutching his jacket against her breast, one sleeve held up to her face. She didn't hear my step. Her eyes were closed, her nose pressed into the buttery leather, and the look she wore as she inhaled its scent was positively erotic.

I was seventeen at the time, and seventeen-year-olds do not think of their mothers as sexual creatures, no matter how beautiful they may be, so naturally, I was mortified to have caught her in such a pose—and with my boyfriend's football jacket, no less. My face burning with shame, I slunk away without her seeing me and shut that image away in the locked mental closet where life's most humiliating moments are hidden. Only now, after all these years, has it shaken loose, leaving me to wonder about its real significance.

They say smell is the most evocative of all the senses, the most able to carry us back to other places and other times. What was it about that leather jacket? I wonder. Was it Nils she lusted after or did the smell of it conjure up more distant memories? Was she recalling what it felt like to be held in the arms of a handsome young American pilot wearing his flight leathers? Or, I suddenly thought this morning, was it that other leather-coated man in my mother's life whose memory summoned up such an erotic response?

CHAPTER 28

Havenwood, Minnesota
Saturday, January 13, 1979

Cruz had promised Berglund not to show his face at Grace Meade's funeral, but that didn't mean he wouldn't station himself nearby to do some surveillance. After all, the deputy chief had said he was shorthanded, and in a pinch, Cruz reasoned, one cop was as good as another. The service was scheduled for eleven in the morning. His plan was to head into town early to snag a parking space that would give him good vantage point to observe St. John's Episcopal church and see who came out to mourn Grace Meade.

In particular, if Jillian attended the service, he wanted to see her and see how she reacted when surrounded by the people she'd grown up with, who would all be watching her for clues as to what had happened last Tuesday night. Cruz's own inability to cut through the riddle of that night and that woman was becoming a major irritation. And what about Simon Edelmann? If it was, in fact, he who'd broken into the cottage across the lake from Grace Meade's house and stolen a snowmobile so he could slip

over there Tuesday night, what was the motive for the attack? And
who was the actual target, Grace or Jillian—or both? Not Jillian,
Cruz decided. If she'd been targeted by an agency like Mossad,
which was known for its lethal efficiency, she'd have been dead
by now—and she wouldn't have had to do the job herself.

At about nine-thirty, he wandered over from his motel room
at the Whispering Pines to the café to grab some breakfast. The
coffee shop was empty except for Ollie Jorgenson, who was busy
at the horseshoe-shaped counter wrapping pies in cellophane.

"Hey, there, Alex!" she said cheerfully. "I was wondering
when you were going to show yourself. I thought you'd given
my breakfast menu the thumbs-down."

"No chance of that," he assured her. "I was up late, that's all,
and then I had some phone calls to make before heading out
this morning."

The first of those had been to the home phone number Z'ev
Mindel had given him the night before, but the housekeeper there
had said Mindel was out. Nor did he seem to be in his office at
the Israeli Embassy, so Cruz resigned himself to waiting for
Mindel to get back to him on the mysterious Simon Edelmann.

Cruz's next call was to Gordon Kessler, the inspector in charge
of the international affairs and liaison section at FBI headquarters—Cruz's boss. Kessler had left a message the night before
telling him in no uncertain terms to call in first thing in the morning, Saturday or no.

"You mind telling me what you're still doing out there?"
Kessler asked when Cruz reached him at his Bureau office.
"This was supposed to be an in-and-out deal—you were going
to locate the woman, interview her and be back at your desk yesterday. All of a sudden I've got the SAC from the St. Paul field
office calling to say you guys are tracking some Mossad agent?"

"It got complicated," Cruz told him and went on to outline
where the investigation had led him since he'd first picked up
the file on Wednesday.

"All right, look," Kessler said, "this has obviously gone way beyond a simple courtesy response to a foreign police query. I'm pulling you back in. We'll leave it to the field office to interview the woman as soon as they can get access."

"It's a pretty complex case, sir, not the kind that's real easy to hand off."

"None of us is indispensable, Cruz, much as we might like to think we are. I'll follow up with the INS on that visa snafu, and I'll also have a talk with the intelligence rep at the Israeli Embassy, see if we can't get to the bottom of what the hell this guy of theirs is up to. But I need you here on other business, so you'll just have to leave this one where it lies for the time being."

"Uh, actually, sir, I already did that."

"Did what?"

"Talk to Mindel, the Mossad liaison man. I'm just waiting to hear back from him."

"You mind telling me who the hell gave you permission to contact a foreign embassy?" Cruz heard the all-too-familiar sound of an exasperated sigh hissing through the phone line. "Look, Cruz, you're still on the learning curve, as far as Bureau procedures are concerned, and you come with a good investigative reputation, so I'll cut you some slack this time. But for future reference, you don't do that, understand? There's a chain of command around here. Any formal contact with a foreign embassy liaison office gets cleared through me first."

"Noted and understood, sir. But this was an informal contact. Z'ev Mindel's an old friend."

"Excuse me?"

"I've known him since the '72 Munich Olympics, back when I was with Army CID. We both worked the Black September investigation."

"How the hell did you end up assigned to a case like that?"

"I was based in Germany at the time, working another investigation into a neo-Nazi cabal that had sprung up in one of our

Army units over there. When the Israeli athletes were murdered, we got word that it was some Americans who'd let their killers into the Olympic Village. Some of our units were on security duty, and we thought there might be a link, but it turned out it was members of the U.S. Olympic team sneaking in after curfew who'd done it. Bunch of them had been out touring the Munich beer halls and the idiots were too drunk to notice that the strangers sneaking in with them were carrying automatic assault weapons."

"And Mindel was working the case for Mossad?"

"Yes, sir. We've been in touch off and on ever since."

"You might have mentioned this before, you know."

"I wasn't aware that contact with Mossad carried the same kind of reporting requirements as with an agent from behind the Iron Curtain."

"Don't be a wise guy," Kessler snapped. "You know it doesn't. Just the same, like I said, there are chain of command issues now that he's their intelligence liaison."

"Yes, sir. I'll keep that in mind."

"Fine. As far as this interview with the Meade woman, you'll pass the file over to the local field office for follow-up and come on in. We've got an Iranian situation heating up at the moment and I need a full complement back here. I want to see you at your desk first thing Monday morning, understood?"

"Yes, sir."

But, Cruz reflected after hanging up the phone, there were still two days and a dozen Minneapolis-to-Washington flights he could catch between then and Monday morning, and so he could think of no reason not to go ahead and do what he'd planned to do that morning—starting with breakfast.

At Ollie Jorgenson's café, he settled onto a stool at the counter. The place smelled incredibly good—bacon, apple, cinnamon and pastry scents setting his stomach to grumbling and his mouth to watering—but he was the only one in the place to appreciate the treat.

"Where is everybody?" he asked. "It looked like most of your rooms were booked last night."

"Ha!" Ollie ripped off another sheet of plastic wrap and draped it across the top of a golden-brown, lattice-topped pie that looked like blueberry.

Could he have pie for breakfast? Cruz wondered, watching with regret as she set it aside.

"You're a real diplomat, you are," Ollie said. "Sounded like they were all booked, is what you mean to say. Those darn ya-hoos kept me up half the night, too. Supposed to be here for the derby, but I guess nobody told them the early bird catches the worm—not to mention the fish. The serious fishermen will be pulling in their lines in a coupla hours, but most of the party animals who checked in here yesterday haven't even shown their faces yet."

He grinned. "So no big winners there, huh?"

"You got that right. Sorry if they bothered you."

"Didn't make a whole lot of difference. I'm a night prowler myself. I'd have been up with or without them."

"You ready for some breakfast, then?"

"Oh, you betcha," Cruz said, unable to resist imitating the distinct Minnesota accent that after a couple of days was already worming its way into his brain. Ollie seemed not to notice. She paused in her wrapping long enough to set a coffee mug and spoon down on the counter in front of him, then lifted a glass carafe from the Bunn warmer and filled the cup to the brim.

"I forget, now. Do you take cream?"

"No, ma'am, black and strong is perfect."

"You got it. You get started on that and I'll get your breakfast going in just a sec, as soon as I finish this."

"Are you on your own here this morning?" he said, studying her freshly done hair and the nice skirt and blouse under her bib apron.

"For now," Ollie said.

"What happened to your granddaughter?"

"My granddaughter?" She looked puzzled. "Oh, you mean Pam, the girl who was here yesterday?" When Cruz nodded, she said, "She's not my granddaughter. She just works here. She's coming in a little while to cover the lunch crowd while I go to the funeral."

Cruz nodded at the pies. "Are those for the church luncheon afterward? Sybil Newkirk put you to work, too?"

"Uh-huh. Are you going to the funeral?"

"No, Deputy Berglund asked me not to."

"Why's that?"

"He thinks it might upset Jillian to see me there."

"Really? Does that mean you got a chance to talk to her, then? I've been wanting to run over to see her, but Nils told me to hold off for another day or so. But you've seen her?"

Cruz nodded. "I saw her on Thursday afternoon, and then I spoke with her briefly yesterday."

"How was she?"

"She looked pretty good yesterday, a lot better than she had the day before. At least, she was doing better until I got there."

"That didn't go well?"

"Let's just say I've done better interviews in my time."

"Oops. So, Nils figures you should lie low, huh? I guess that makes sense. There's a time and a place, and this is her mother's funeral, after all." Ollie set aside the pies and fired up the grill behind her. "By the way, what would you like for breakfast this morning?"

"Same as yesterday? The lumberjack special?"

Ollie grinned. "Oh, I do like a man with a good appetite." She pulled down a pan and eggs and started cooking, talking to him over her shoulder as she worked. "So you were saying Jillian's coming to the funeral?"

"Depends how she's feeling and whether her doctor gives the green light. Physically, as I say, she seems to be doing much better, so if the doc figures she can handle the strain of it, there's no reason why she shouldn't go." As Cruz watched her crack eggs over the griddle, a sudden thought occurred to him. "Say, Ollie, whatever happened with our young hitchhiker from yesterday?"

She was dropping bread into the toaster, but she paused and slapped her forehead. "Oh, darn! That's right. I meant to leave you a message to let you know how it all ended up." She depressed the lever on the toaster and went back to tending the eggs. "Her folks showed up about suppertime last night. Seemed like real nice people. I told them how you'd stepped in to encourage Kelly to go home and go back to school. They were real grateful. I said you might be calling one of these days to see how she's doing. Did you mean it, by the way?"

"Absolutely. I thought I'd let her get settled back in, then maybe give her a call from D.C. next week."

"That's real good of you, Alex. I think she learned her lesson. I hope she did, anyway. I called over to your room before they left last night. Kelly wanted to say goodbye, but you weren't in. I told her I'd say goodbye for her. She said to be sure to tell you thanks again."

"It was my pleasure."

"I think she was real glad to be going home," Ollie said, turning his eggs. "Just so you know when you call though, we agreed not to go into too much detail with her folks about that business with the trucker. We did get her over to see the doc, like you said, and then Pam spent the afternoon with her."

"Pam made a good call when she spotted the two of them yesterday."

The older woman grimaced. "Yeah, well, she would. Been there, done that, poor thing."

"Are you saying she was a runaway, too?"

Ollie slipped his eggs onto a platter and lifted the cover off a warming pan to scoop out a large helping of home fries and bacon, grabbed some utensils, and then, with precision worthy of a circus acrobat, snagged the toast at precisely the moment it flew up out of the machine.

"Two years ago," she said, turning around and laying his breakfast down in front of him, then sliding condiments and the napkin holder to within reach. "The only difference between Pam and Kelly was that Pam didn't have folks back home worrying about her, ready to jump in a car and drive two hundred miles to come get her. Far from it, matter of fact. She was better off out of there."

"What was the problem? Was she being abused?"

Ollie paused, then gave a reluctant nod. "Her stepfather. When he wasn't smacking her around, it seems, it was the other. Mind you, she only broke down and told me the whole sad story a few months back. We saw his name in the paper one day. He'd gotten himself arrested for raping a woman over in Fargo. That's when Pam broke down and told me the whole messy business."

"I guess she's pretty grateful to you for taking her under your wing," Cruz said, nodding appreciatively as he dug into his food.

"Well, we all just do what we can, hey?" she said, reaching for a box and loading her pies into it.

"We try. Thanks for this," Cruz said.

"Uh-huh. So, anyway, what's the deal with Jillian? You said she was doing better physically. What about her mental state? Trying to hurt herself like that, poor thing. I can hardly believe it."

Neither could he, Cruz thought grimly.

"Is she doing better now, do you think?" Ollie asked.

Cruz frowned and glanced around, but they were alone. Through the open door leading to the motel and garage office where he'd first checked in, he could see Ollie's husband, Norbert, dressed in white shirt with a loosely knotted tie around his neck, probably in anticipation of the funeral he and his wife would be heading out to shortly. But he was talking with a customer and seemed to take no notice of what was going on in the coffee shop.

Ollie seemed to read his mind. "I don't mean to snoop, Alex. I only ask because I'm real fond of her. Like I say, she and my

Nancy practically grew up together, and Norbert and I were close to her dad and his folks, too. I can't tell you how many times Jillian slept over here, especially after Helen and Art died. I hate to see her in a bad way. It just seems like there's been too much sadness in that family, you know?"

"Yeah, I guess that's true, but to be honest, even taking all that into consideration, I really can't figure her out."

"You're not still thinking she had anything to do with Grace's death, are you?"

"Well, aside from their strained relations, the gas can Jillian filled that day, and the nasty argument they apparently had that night, no, of course not. It was the ideal mother-daughter relationship."

Ollie paused, taken aback, then grimaced. "Now you're making fun of me."

"No, ma'am, I would never do that. She sure seems like one troubled lady, though. Tell me something, was she always so self-contained?"

"How do you mean?"

"So focused? Emotionally closed down?"

"Well," Ollie said, leaning a hip against the counter, "she's always been quiet. Always agreeable, mind you, and ready to do whatever you asked her, but so much so that you never knew what she honestly felt about anything. Whatever she was thinking, she kept it all inside." She shook her head sadly. "Maybe she's got good reason to be that way. There's more than one kind of abuse, you know."

"You think she was an abused child?"

"Well, now, that might be too strong a word for it, but Jillian always seemed to be.... I don't know...kind of a sad little thing, you know?" She straightened and wiped her hands on a tea towel. "But what do I know? It just seems that once Helen and Art died, there was nobody really there for her. Not that Grace was negligent or anything like that, mind you, but she was always so busy with her own activities that—I don't know.... Jillian just seemed to be on her own more often than not. Norbert and I tried to do what we could. She spent a lot of time over here, like I said, but we had four kids of our own, and a new business to get off the ground, and...well, you know how it is. Just the same, I feel a little guilty about Jillian, like maybe there was something more we could have done for her."

"It sounds like you did a lot. I don't think you've got any reason to feel bad." Cruz pushed the eggs around his plate, thinking. "I shouldn't be doing this."

"Didn't I make them the way you like them? I thought you had over easy yesterday, and so I—"

"What? Oh, no, not the food. It's great."

"What then?"

"What I was going to say was, I shouldn't be putting you on the spot or involving you in this, but I can't figure it out."

"What's that?"

Cruz sat back on the stool. "Berglund and her. What's the deal there? Why did they split up?"

"Did you ask Nils about it?"

"Sort of."

"And what did he say?"

"He says he let her down. Says he should have gotten her out of Havenwood and away from her mother when he left to join the Navy. Only he didn't because he wanted to live back here when he was done his service, so he asked her to wait for him, instead."

"And that's it?"

"Pretty much. So I just don't get it. The guy is obviously carrying a whopping load of guilt about her, but everybody's got an old flame in their past. You don't go around whipping yourself for the rest of your days just because it didn't work out."

"Do you think it's affecting Nils's judgment, or the way he's doing his job?"

"To be honest, I don't know. He's as conscientious a cop as I've ever seen, but I'm not sure he's capable of impartiality where she's concerned."

Ollie started polishing the already spotless counter, a classic avoidance ploy if ever Cruz had seen one. He knew it was unprofessional and unethical to be discussing Havenwood's deputy chief of police with a civilian, but having seen her in action, he trusted Ollie's judgment. As sounding boards went, she was the best he had at the moment.

"Your daughter must have known something about what went on between the two of them back then," he pressed. "Is there any reason you can think of that he should be especially touchy on the subject?"

She braced her arms on the counter and shook her head. "I don't know, Alex. I know you mean well, but it's all so long ago that I can't imagine it's got much to do with what's happened now. Even at the time, there were things I found hard to believe. Some stories you just can't credit, you know? I don't see what's to be served by repeating them now."

A cuckoo clock on the wall over the cash register began to bong, ten rings. The little door over the clock face opened and a mechanical girl with blond pigtails and a green dirndl skirt circled out on a tiny turntable, spinning to a tinkled chorus of "Lilli Marlene." Ollie looked up at it and smiled. "My younger brother brought it back from Germany. He was stationed over there in the fifties."

"Army?"

She nodded.

"Me, too," Cruz said. "I was there in '72–'73."

The tune ended, the mechanical girl returned to her little house, and Ollie went back to wiping the counter until Cruz stopped her by laying a hand over hers. "I think Jillian is in real trouble. And I think Nils is on the verge of going over a cliff himself, too. Maybe doing something stupid he'll regret forever."

"Bad trouble? You really think so?"

"Yeah, I do. I'm still trying to put the pieces together, but I think Jillian's gotten herself mixed up in some very dangerous business. I can't figure it out, though, much less help her, if I don't know where she's coming from. I'm really stumbling blind here, and I could use a little insight right about now."

Ollie's shoulders slumped, and she nodded reluctantly. "Like I said, I haven't seen much of her for a long time now, Alex, so I really don't know what's been going on in her life lately. But all I can tell you is this—if Nils Berglund feels guilty.... Well, if what my Nancy heard is true, he bloody well should."

CHAPTER 29

My head is finally clear, and I want to finish this record of events, but Dr. Kandinsky says Nils is coming shortly to take me to the funeral, if I think I'm up to it. I could sense her feeling me out, trying to decide if I'm sane enough to be let out of this place, even temporarily and even in the company of a burly police officer. I suppose I must have passed muster because in the end, she left it up to me to decide.

How can I refuse to go? I'm the only living relative. I should be there to see my mother laid to rest, shouldn't I? I can just imagine how insulted she'd be to think that I'd stay away. On the other hand, wouldn't she be equally scandalized by the notion of her funeral as freak show? Frankly, I'm absolutely terrified to face all the people who are bound to be there. I can only guess what they must think of me by now. Little do they know that the truth is even worse than they imagine.

I should just bite the bullet and go, but I need to finish this journal. I'm so angry about the time I've lost. Half of yesterday vanished in a grief-filled, drug-induced fog after that awful FBI man left. I can't even let myself think about what he said about Nellie Entwistle and Miss Atwater, or it will drive me even madder than I obviously am already. Now we have their blood, too, on our hands, my mother and I.

If I'm fully honest, though—and that is my intent here—then I have to admit that it was I, and I alone, who led death to their doors. If I hadn't begun this quest, those two women might still be alive. It might have been better if I'd never started down this road, but if I let myself be stopped now, their deaths will be rendered even more tragic by the fact that it was for nothing. So all I can do is go forward.

I've said that my mother was caught up in repeated Gestapo arrest and detention sweeps. Every time the Paris Resistance mounted an operation, whether it was successful or not, mass arrests and punishing reprisals were the inevitable consequence. But trying to stomp out the Resistance was like stepping on an ant hill. Partisans would scatter in all directions, scurrying to find new hiding places where they could reestablish their bases, then pick up from where they'd left off, harassing the Occupation forces.

Cohn-Levy's files provided me with the information on her arrest and detention at Gestapo headquarters. It was in their meticulous lists that we found the name "Sylvie Fournier," my grandmother's maiden name and the nom de guerre my mother had adopted when she went behind the lines. It showed up for the first time among a list of those detained in an October 12, 1943 sweep of the north Paris suburb of Gentilly. Twenty-two people were rounded up that day, according to the records. A new Gestapo *Obermeister* had recently arrived in Paris, a secondary but still powerful functionary by the name of Colonel Kurt Braun. Braun's assignment, it seems, was to root out Resistance partisans and sympathizers in the northern quarters of the city, deemed especially sensitive because they were the gateway into the capital should the Allies invade from across the Channel.

For his part, Braun was anxious to demonstrate a ruthless get-tough attitude to impress his Berlin masters, the Resistance and the general population—as if the country hadn't felt the Nazi boot firmly enough over the past three years. I've seen a photo of this Col. Braun. He looks tall and lean in his crisp Gestapo uniform, dark hair swept back under his stiff-peaked cap, the eyes also dark, hard-looking.

Objectively speaking, I suppose one would have to say he was handsome, but with a cruel twist to his mouth. He'd been an accountant in Bavaria before the Nazis rose to power in Germany in the 1930s, Cohn-Levy told me, but his fortunes began to rise when he elected to follow the siren call of a fascist house painter with a vision of a thousand-year Reich—a fanatic who had taken Braun's cousin as his lover and, briefly at the end, as his wife. Kurt Braun himself was said to have had a wife back in Bavaria, but his reputation in Paris was that of a notorious womanizer, with a taste for good food, fine wine and beautiful lovers—all of which the Occupiers were in a position to appropriate freely.

Not that compulsion was always required. In fact, it wasn't all that hard for men in his position to secure whatever they wanted, including the freely given attentions of beautiful women. As I've researched this period, I've been struck again and again by how much effort was expended by ordinary people on the simple matter of finding food. Wartime rationing is always difficult, but in Nazi-controlled Europe, conquered populations suffered more than just minor deprivations or the absence of a few luxuries. They faced serious malnutrition unless they could get their hands on a few black market rations over and above the miserly weekly allowances set by the Occupation forces. An extra few ounces of bread. A little tea or ersatz coffee. Sugar. Milk. The occasional egg, for God's sake.

Unlike the rest of the population, however, beautiful young women were never limited by ration coupons—not if they were sufficiently accommodating. They had the currency of their bodies and their smiles to trade for access to the nearly unlimited storehouses of the Occupier: meat, wine, chocolate. Dinner at fine restaurants.

Champagne and warm feather beds. The wherewithal to shop for dresses, stockings or a new coat. Hunger saps the will. Constant deprivation, especially in the face of easily gotten plenty, is a great thief of morals.

After the war, if the mob got its hands on them, these women paid a terrible, humiliating price for fraternizing with the enemy. They were stripped, their heads shaved, paraded through the streets by angry, spitting mobs. But during the Occupation, being young, hungry and faced with limited options, casting their lot with the victor may well have seemed like the smart decision.

And my mother? She was twenty-two and beautiful. Once she was arrested, what were the chances she wouldn't catch the eye of a womanizer like Braun? Non-existent, it turned out. It was exactly the sort of problem Miss Atwater had feared when she'd first recruited the stunning blond, blue-eyed printer's daughter—that Grace Wickham was too conspicuous for her own or anyone else's good.

I have no doubt my mother genuinely meant to fight the good fight when she volunteered to go behind the lines, but she'd been accustomed all her life to being admired, feted and doted upon. She wasn't constitutionally equipped to suffer indefinitely the humiliation of conquest. What were the odds she'd resist the temptation to live at the top of the food chain when offered the chance? Also nonexistent, it turns out. She simply wasn't wired for long-term sacrifice.

That first time she was arrested, she was detained for two weeks on the express orders, the files said, of the *Obermeister.* There's no way of knowing exactly what happened to her in that time, but it doesn't take a lot of imagination to guess. For the Gestapo, as for all despots, the method of choice to break the spirit of prisoners is the lavish use of humiliation, pain and bribery—not to mention seduction.

Whatever Braun did to her, it apparently worked. The arrest files from the Avenue Foch list only detention and release dates, but in a copy of a minor security file, Cohn-Levy and I stumbled across the name "Sylvie Fournier" in a far more damning context. On the evening of October 18, 1943, a driver recorded in his trip log that he had driven Col. Braun and a guest to Maxim's for dinner, and from there to the Hotel George V. In an addendum from the next day, the driver notes that he was sent back to the George V to retrieve a handbag accidentally left behind by the colonel's guest—a handbag belonging to one "Mlle. Fournier."

My heart sank when I found that small, inconspicuous notation, but at least it pointed us in the right direction. As we searched through the trip logs for the days that followed, we found no fewer than eleven references to excursions to the Galeries Lafayette and shops along the Boulevard Faubourg-St. Honoré, to the Lido, the Moulin Rouge, Maxim's (again), and various other Paris nightspots—all ending at the same hotel, all listing one "Mlle. Sylvie Fournier" as being among the colonel's guests. While her comrades in the Resistance were being harassed, hunted, tortured and shot, my mother, it turns out, was eating truffles, watching cancan dancers, drinking champagne, and being bedded under the crystal chandeliers and Louis XIV tapestries of the Hotel George V.

On October 26th, the records show, she was finally released from custody and sent back to the northern suburbs to rejoin her cell. It is true, as Miss Atwater noted, that Sylvie Fournier is listed in the files of Gestapo headquarters as having been detained for short periods several times after that, but Miss Atwater didn't look far enough. Once she found out that Mother was alive and well and back in London, she simply stopped hunting for references to "Sylvie Fournier." If she hadn't, she might have stumbled across the truth, as I had, and my mother might have been arrested and charged with treason. No bloody wonder she was upset and uncooperative when Miss Atwater discovered her in that north London bed-sit.

Poor, conscientious Miss Atwater, searching for her missing "ducks." She'd had no time to unravel that web of lies, but almost nothing she believed about my mother's final months in occupied France is borne out by the more obscure administrative records I found buried in Bernard Cohn-Levy's rabbit warren office—records that show my mother again and again stepping out with Colonel Braun on occasions when she was supposed to have been languishing in a subterranean jail cell.

Did her Resistance colleagues not suspect what was going on? Possibly not. She was frequenting restricted nightspots far from Gentilly, so her chances of being spotted by the printers, masons and shopkeepers of that neighborhood were practically nil. And the Resistance was so compartmentalized for security reasons that any member in central Paris who spotted her with Braun could have been unaware that she was ostensibly on their side.

Or were they? I wondered. Had she possibly convinced her comrades that she could serve as a double agent? Was she that confident of her hold over Colonel Braun by then that it was feasible? Perhaps, but it would be hard to prove, Cohn-Levy and I soon realized. Ominously, few members of her Resistance cell had survived the war.

In any case, as awful as it may sound, whether or not she had betrayed the Resistance was almost a secondary consideration for me by this point. Even when faced with the hard historical evidence, I still didn't want to believe it, but the fact was, I seemed to have stumbled across the truth about who my father really was.

From that point on, everything I did was part of a desperate, futile attempt to prove myself wrong.

CHAPTER 30

With ten minutes to go before the funeral got underway, Nils Berglund and Jillian still hadn't shown up. As predicted, it looked like a packed house. It seemed to Cruz as if all of Havenwood had come out in the brilliantly cold winter sunshine to see Grace Meade laid to rest. Watching people crowd the wide front steps of St. John's Episcopal Church in an effort to get through the arched double doors and wangle a seat for the event, he couldn't help wondering how many were really there to see if the suicidal, scandal-tainted, mad, murderous daughter would dare show her face.

From his vantage point across the street, hunkered behind the wheel of his car, he tried to beat down the unnamed dread rising in his gut as he watched the milling crowd part down the middle at the Newkirks' arrival. Since the previous night when Cruz had watched him polish off the better part of his forty-year-old Liberation cognac, the mayor seemed to have completed the process of shedding his robust political veneer. He'd aged overnight, looking brittle now as he shuffled through the crowd and up the steps, lending a supportive arm to his teetering wife. Sybil was dressed entirely in black, mincing along beside him on impossibly high heels, the long mourning veil draped over her pillbox hat intended, perhaps, to evoke memories of Jackie Kennedy after Dallas.

Ollie and Norbert Jorgenson, who must have left the Whispering Pines Motel not long after Cruz, followed the Newkirks up the steps accompanied by Verna from the police station, all of them dressed in simple Sunday best. The lovely Lydia, she of the Singapore Slings and shy smile, was also in attendance, Cruz noted, along with her bruiser of a boyfriend, who, Ollie had said, was the orderly who'd yanked the air-filled syringe out of Jillian's arm in the ER the other night. The hero had a self-important look about him as he swaggered up to the church, nodding left and right to the crowd like some red carpet celebrity—although maybe that was envy talking, Cruz thought, as he watched Lydia walk up the steps on the big oaf's arm and pass through the Gothic arch entryway.

Cruz unbuttoned his overcoat, made bulky by the down vest and sweater he wore beneath it, adjusted the waist holster digging into his spine, then settled himself in for the duration.

Sharon Berglund and her sister, Shelli, arrived a couple of minutes later, and when he saw them together, Cruz was struck again by the similarity in their warm smiles and easy manner. The sisters were greeted on the front sidewalk by Carla the Amazon, who had on black patent boots with two-inch platform soles this morning and a long, tomato red coat that fluttered open to reveal a black leather miniskirt and low-cut, white ruffled blouse. She looped a hand through each of their arms as they made their way up the church steps, but at the top landing, Sharon Berglund held back, murmuring something to the other women, then stood aside while Shelli and Carla went into the church.

By ten fifty-five, it seemed as if everyone in Havenwood and the surrounding area must have turned up for Grace Meade's funeral except the deputy police chief and the daughter of the deceased. From the way Sharon Berglund bit her lower lip as she searched up and down the street from her high vantage point, Cruz suspected Berglund had informed his wife of his plan to bring Jillian if she felt she was up to it. But where the hell were they?

Another five minutes passed and the street grew quiet except for the low drone of an organ dirge spilling out the open doors and, from the lake a block and a half away, the faint, high-pitched whine of snowmobiles out on the ice. Finally, the organ fell silent. Sharon Berglund cast one last worried look up and down the street, then went inside, and the doors closed behind her. Grace Meade's funeral was getting underway without her sole surviving heir in attendance.

Cruz sat a few minutes longer, the windshield fogging as he waited to see if Berglund's black and white might still pull up. Finally, he admitted it wasn't going to happen, turned the key in the ignition and cleared the glass, then headed for the interstate, turning south toward Montrose to find out what had delayed them.

When he arrived at the hospital twenty minutes later, he found the place in a commotion. Half a dozen state and Montrose Police vehicles were parked at odd angles around one corner of the building, cherry lights spinning, and the air was filled with the static crackle of radio dispatch units sputtering terse messages. A flat area of asphalt behind the main building had been cordoned off—a patio, it seemed, surrounded by bushes that hid it from the parking lot. Several uniforms stood along the perimeter, holding back curious onlookers. As Cruz approached, a state policeman held up a hand, but waved him through when he spotted Cruz's Bureau badge.

Cruz paused at his side. "What happened?"

The cop cocked a thumb over his shoulder. "One of the patients took a gainer out of the window up there."

Cruz's gaze looked to an open window overhead, counted three floors, and realized it had to be one of the ones on the psych ward. "Oh, shit."

"S'cuse me?"

"Who's in charge here?"

"That'd be the detective over around the back," the young officer said.

Cruz nodded and loped over to the cordoned-off section, searching for Berglund among the other cops on site, but the deputy was nowhere to be seen. A crime scene investigator was taking measurements on the patio, while another walked around the bushes, snapping photographs. As he got close, Cruz saw a spattering of wet stains on the asphalt, and he felt his gorge rise. Around the building by a service entrance, a man in a coroner's jacket was tightening the gurney restraints on a sheet-wrapped body. The form under the blood-spotted drape seemed waif-thin, like the troubled woman Cruz had been studying through that one-way mirror for the past couple of days. Watching the body's dull rock as the straps were tightened, he felt a knot of guilt in his gut. Had he done this? Pushed her over the edge by trying to grill her the way he had?

He was about to ask to take a look at the body before she was carted off to the county morgue—a man should face his mistakes—but then he spotted Dr. Kandinsky at the side entrance. Our Lady of the Perpetual Cardigan, Cruz thought, watching her navy sweater-clad arms wrap around herself as she found shelter in the alcove, out of the cold wind. The psychiatrist's presence confirmed his worst fears. She was talking to a man in a rumpled suit with the universally weary look of detectives everywhere. Cruz flashed his badge once again at another patrolman who hurried forward to try to steer him away, and the cop stood aside to let him approach the shrink and the gumshoe.

"Dr. Kandinsky?"

She shaded her eyes with one hand to make him out in the brilliant sunlight. "Oh, Agent Cruz."

"How did it happen?"

She shook her grizzled head sadly, ignoring the loose tendrils whipping around her eyes. "One of the common room windows was open. Usually they're latched so that they'll open no wider than two or three inches, but somehow...I don't know...either the screws worked their way loose or they were deliberately tampered with. And with the screens off for the winter...." Her voice drifted off as she waved a hand dismally over the scene.

"Excuse me," the detective said, "who the hell are you?"

"Special Agent Alex Cruz, FBI."

The detective squinted at his ID. "What are you doing here?"

"The victim was a material witness in a case I'm investigating."

"What?" Dr. Kandinsky interjected. "Oh, no, Agent Cruz, it wasn't Jillian who jumped. I'm sorry, I thought you knew."

"Who was it, then?"

"The boy we were treating. The one with the drug problem."

Cruz's mind flashed back on the lanky, long-haired sixteen-year-old with the DTs whom he and Berglund had seen on lockdown next to Jillian's room the first day Kandinsky had taken them through the ward.

"Oh, hell, sorry about that," he said. "That's a rough one. When I saw you talking to the detective here, I just naturally assumed it must be Miss Meade, given her history."

"No, it was Stephen," she said sadly. "Such a waste. He'd been clean nearly a week now. It was the first time he'd been out of his room since he got here. I told him the worst was over. If only he could have held on a little longer, it would have gotten better." Her gaze drifted over to where the coroner's investigators were loading the gurney into a van, and she shook her head. "His parents are going to be devastated."

"The coroner found a teaspoon in his pocket," the detective said. "The point of it was chipped, like he'd used it on those screws. Looks like the kid was pretty determined, Doc."

"All the more reason for us to have kept him under closer surveillance."

"I'm really sorry this happened on your watch," Cruz told her. He'd seen a few junkies self-destruct like this, decent guys, once, who'd developed a taste for the high and couldn't live without it, until finally they reached the point where the self-loathing of knowing they'd sell their own mothers for a fix got to be too much to bear. "With some of them, you know, the need's too strong. Makes them blind and deaf."

Her expression said she wasn't about to let herself off the hook for this one. "I thought we'd made progress."

Cruz nodded sympathetically. "So, Miss Meade is still upstairs, then? You decided not to let her out for the funeral?"

"Oh, no, she went. The deputy came by to pick her up earlier. I'd thought I might go along with them, but I couldn't, as it turned out. It's been a terrible morning. One of our elderly patients had a very bad night, and I was having to deal with him. I might have sent a nurse along, but we were shorthanded here. Two of my staff called in sick. In any case, neither Jillian nor the deputy would hear of it." She sighed heavily. "There was so much confusion on the ward this morning—and then this...."

"But you thought she was all right to go?" Cruz asked.

"Yes," Kandinsky said distractedly. "She was doing much better by this morning. She's not a prisoner here, you know. I'd found her some clothes to wear, and she wanted to give it a go. I wouldn't have released her if she'd had to do it on her own, but Deputy Chief Berglund is an old friend, I gather, and he seems to have a calming effect on her."

"So I've noticed," Cruz said, his irritation welling once more. What was it about these Meade women and their power to make married men do stupid things? "They never made it to the church, though. I was outside, keeping an eye out for them over there, and I didn't see them go in."

The doctor frowned. "That's odd. They left here in plenty of time. Maybe they went in by a back door to wait until the service was ready to get underway? Jillian might not have been up to greeting other mourners."

"Possibly," Cruz agreed, kicking himself for not having gone into the church to double-check, "or maybe she got cold feet."

The doctor obviously mistook his aggravation for concern. "I'm sure she'll be fine. Perhaps Deputy Berglund took her for a drive to help her relax and get her mind off things. In any case, he promised to have her back here by two, so we'll be seeing her before long."

"Uh, if you two don't mind," the detective interrupted, "I got some business to take care of here? We do have a dead kid on our hands, after all."

"Yes, of course. I'm sorry, Detective," the doctor said, chastened.

"Right. I'll let you get to it." Cruz nodded to the psychiatrist and started to walk away, but she called after him.

"Agent Cruz? You are going to leave Jillian in peace today, aren't you?"

"Absolutely," he said. As soon as he knew where she was and what kind of game she was playing now.

Cruz returned to Havenwood via Berglund's preferred back road route on the unlikely chance they might have had car trouble. But even if they had, he reasoned, traversing the empty miles between the two towns, it would have been a simple enough matter for Berglund to get on the radio and call for help. If Dr. Kandinsky was right about the time they'd left, there was still no reason why the two hadn't made it in plenty of time for the funeral.

Back in town, the streets were still jam-packed with cars, but they seemed to have rearranged themselves on the street, leaving little doubt that the funeral service had ended and that those following the casket to the cemetery had left—including the Newkirks, Cruz realized, since the powder-blue Oldsmobile was nowhere to be seen. He watched a couple of cars pull up in front of the church again and disgorge a few people, who entered the building by a side door, and he decided to follow them in and take a look.

In the church basement, the post-funeral luncheon seemed close to getting underway. The hall was beginning to fill with loud conversation and the smell of home-cooked food, but neither Berglund nor Jillian were there. Ollie Jorgenson was over near the kitchen servery window, helping to lay out food, but none of the other faces in the place were familiar to Cruz. Turning to leave, however, he ran smack into Verna from the police station as she came out of the ladies' room.

"Alex, hi," she said, "I didn't see you at the funeral."

Cruz glanced around, then took her by the elbow and steered her around under the staircase for a quiet chat. "I didn't want to butt in, so I waited outside. I'm looking for the deputy chief, Verna. Have you seen him? He was supposed to bring Jillian to the service."

She glanced around, then lowered her voice and nodded. "That's what I heard, too, but they weren't in church, and they didn't make it to the cemetery, either. I just this minute got back from there."

"The deputy's wife hasn't heard from him?"

"No. In fact, she was asking me if I knew whether Nils had checked in. She said she'd called the baby-sitter to see if he'd been by the house, but he hadn't. At this point, poor Sharon's as stymied as anyone."

"Who's on duty today?"

"All the guys. Between traffic control here and keeping an eye on the derby crowd, nobody got the weekend off. I said I'd go in myself and man the front desk as soon as this wraps up."

"Did any of the other officers hear from him, as far as you know?"

"Well, Kenny—that's Kenny Wahlberg, you know? I guess you could say he's Nils's number two guy, what with the chief on sick leave. Anyway, Kenny led the procession to the ceme-

tery and I talked to him out there. He said Nils called in around
a quarter of ten to say he was just on his way over to Montrose
to pick up Jillian, but Kenny hasn't heard from him again since.
We tried to raise him on the radio from the cemetery, but there
was no answer. Kenny'll probably be down at the dock now, if
you wanted to check with him, see if Nils finally got in touch.
He'll be the guy in uniform with the white hair. Looks like an
albino. You can't miss him."

Cruz nodded. "I think I will do that, thanks."

"I'm sure there's nothing to worry about," Verna said, sounding as if she were trying to convince herself.

"I'm sure you're right."

They glanced back into the crowded hall where a long line
was starting to form in front of a groaning buffet table that covered most of one wall. "Just the same," she added, "I'm not all
that hungry and this din is giving me a real headache. I think I
might just head on over to the office now and have a listen to
the radio for a while, you know?"

Cruz smiled. "You're one of the good ones, Verna."

"Oh, well... Oh, hell's bells! I just remembered, I haven't got
wheels. Can you give me a lift over to the police station?"

"Sure, not a problem."

"I better go tell Ollie and Norbert I'm leaving. I came with
them, so they'll be looking for me to go home later if I leave
without saying anything."

"Grab your coat and I'll wait for you here."

"You want to fill a plate for yourself before you go?"

"I'd better pass."

"Ha! Don't dare show your face in there in case Carla gets it
into her head to bonk you on the head and drag you hog-tied
back to her cave, huh? Oh, go on with your blushing, Alex
Cruz," Verna added, grinning. "I heard how you've been breaking hearts around here. I think even Ollie Jorgenson's got half
a mind to trade Norbert in since you rolled into town."

"Yeah, well, she's another one of the good ones, but the reports of my exploits are highly exaggerated. I'm innocent, I swear."

"Oh, hon, I know that." She laughed. "You're just a babe in the woods compared to us tough old prairie chickens. So you hang on right here, and I'll be back in a jiff."

"How about I meet you outside?"

"Ha! Made you nervous, did I? Go on with you, then." She walked away, chuckling, as Cruz headed up the stairs, determined to avoid any more close encounters, especially with the dreaded Carla.

On the way over to the police station, he debated how to pose a delicate question, but finally decided this sensible woman could take it straight up. "Have you got any idea where Nils and Jillian might have gotten to, Verna? Like say, if they wanted to go somewhere and have a quiet talk without having to worry about prying eyes?"

"Hmm...that's a good question. I'm not real sure there's anywhere in town they wouldn't be spotted by somebody. And you're right, you know."

"How do you mean?"

"That they'd worry about that, especially Nils. He knows tongues have been wagging around here ever since he pulled Jillian out of that fire—like he should've left her to roast alive in there, for Pete's sake," she added, her voice dripping with disgust. "Still, people just love to have something to gossip about, don't they? You have to understand, though, Alex, Nils is a family man. Doesn't matter what he and Jillian used to be to one another, he wouldn't do anything to hurt Sharon or the kids."

"I believe you," Cruz said. "On the other hand, I think Jillian may feel she has no one else she can talk to right now, and Nils's job means he does need to get to the bottom of what happened at her mother's last Tuesday night."

"I guess that's true."

"The thing is, if she has finally decided she's ready to talk, I'd sure like to know about it."

"I guess you would at that. But it's hard to imagine anywhere around here today where they'd be able to have a quiet, uninterrupted talk. Are you sure they actually left the hospital?"

Cruz nodded. "I took a run over there, and Jillian's doctor saw them leave. I suppose it's possible they stayed somewhere in Montrose, where they wouldn't be so well known, but when they left, the doctor said, they fully intended to make it to the funeral. You can't think of any place around here they might have gone if Jillian got cold feet at the last minute? Someplace they wouldn't necessarily have been spotted? They dated as teenagers. There must be someplace where kids go when they want to be away from prying eyes to do what it is teenagers do."

"I don't know. The only place I can think of like that is Lovers' Leap."

"Lovers' Leap?" Cruz tried to imagine any place nearby that could possibly be high enough for a suicidal plunge.

"Well, that's just what the kids have always called it," Verna admitted. "It's by an old dam up the river, just out of town. All the young couples go up there to make out. It's up on a ridge and it's got a nice view of the surrounding countryside, but it's not like it's a huge cliff or anything. I really don't think Nils and Jill would go there at this time of year, though."

"Why not?"

"Well, for one thing, it's a nice enough spot in summer, but it's too darn cold today for sitting in a car very long. Besides which, families go there in winter for tobogganing, so it wouldn't exactly be very private, either. Also," she added, "if they'd been sitting out there in the squad car, Kenny would've been able to raise Nils on the radio, wouldn't he? But he couldn't. Nils isn't the kind to ignore a call."

"Fair enough," Cruz said, as he pulled his own car up in front of the police station and killed the motor. "There's nowhere else you can think of?"

"I haven't got a clue. Unless...."

"What?"

Verna turned to him. "The farm! Sharon's dad's old place out at the Neck."

"Where's that?"

"You go across the bridge at the narrow end of the lake, there, where all the summer cottages are? Only instead of taking a right after the bridge to go down Lost Arrow Road to the cottages, you take a left. Sharon's dad had a farm out on the headlands, just at the very end of the lake where it hooks up to the Mississippi. Her mom died when she was a kid, and her dad had to move into one of the seniors' apartments in town about five years ago when he had a stroke and couldn't manage on his own anymore, but the farmhouse is still out there. Nils and Sharon and the kids stay there sometimes when Nils is harvesting. And the thing is, you also can get to it from the interstate without having to come into town, so they could have gone there straight from Montrose without anyone knowing."

"Verna, you're a genius."

"Yeah, I know it. And did I mention I'm a widow, too?" She laughed at his awkward silence. "Go on with you now. And if you do find them, tell Nils to call in, for God's sake, before things start getting really out of hand around here."

"You bet. So—left after the bridge, you said?"

"Uh-huh. Then on for about three miles. You'll pass a campground on your right called Camp Arendal. The farmhouse is the next driveway after it, about a quarter mile farther along. The road hooks up to the interstate just about a mile beyond that."

"Okay. I'll check with Kenny first," Cruz said, "and if nobody's heard from them, that'll be my next stop."

"Keep me posted?"

"You got it."

* * *

Kenny Wahlberg was down at the town dock, just where Verna had said he'd be, his snow-white hair shining like a beacon as he watched the ice fishermen bringing in their day's catch to be weighed in a booth near the end of the dock.

"Officer Wahlberg?" Cruz said, coming up behind him. "I'm—"

"I know who you are," the young cop said, his white-lashed eyes giving Cruz a suspicious once-over.

"I was just talking to Verna. She said I'd probably find you down here."

"Uh-huh." He had skin as pale as death, and colorless eyes that could freeze a soul at twenty paces.

"We were getting a little concerned about Berglund. Has he checked in?"

Wahlberg pulled a pair of reflective sunglasses out of his breast pocket and slipped them on. "You don't need to worry about the boss. He can take care of himself pretty good."

Cruz looked across the lake and forced himself to count to ten. "Look, Wahlberg, I'm doing a job here, same as you, so just answer the goddam question, would you? Has Berglund called in or not?"

"Not."

"And you haven't been able to reach him on the radio? Verna said you tried from the cemetery."

"That's right."

"And," Cruz added, making a forward rolling motion with his hand, "have you tried again since?"

"About five minutes ago. No response."

"And nobody's seen him or his car?"

"Negative."

"You might want to keep trying."

"Ya think?" Wahlberg said, raising one bleached eyebrow.

Cruz ignored the sarcasm. "He said you guys had found a cottage broken into across the way and a Ski-Doo missing. Has the machine shown up yet?"

Wahlberg turned back to watching the fishing tally. "Not that I know of."

"Is anybody actually out checking these machines to see if one of them might be the stolen one?"

He shrugged. "These look legit."

"You can tell that from way up here, can you? Well, you're just a law enforcement whiz, you are," Cruz said. Asshole, he thought. "Thanks a lot, Officer. You've been a big help."

"Uh-huh."

Head shaking, Cruz headed back up the wooden dock toward the shore and got in his car. He followed Verna's directions out of town, pausing before a one-lane bridge over the narrows to let a pickup truck coming from the opposite direction reach him before inching forward himself. It would make for an interesting daily game of Chicken, he thought, to live on one side of the bridge and have to cross it into town on a regular basis. Must add real spice to the summer tourist season, as well. He took a left after the bridge, leaving asphalt for the iced-over gravel road that led toward Berglund's father-in-law's farm.

One side of the road was wooded, and as he sped past, Cruz noticed a couple of white-tailed deer grazing at the edge of a stand of birch trees. A couple of sparrows playing tag swooped and dived over a stubble-topped field on his left, but otherwise, total quiet reigned. The only sign of life was the occasional car passing on the interstate far ahead, which transected the landscape at a forty-five degree angle from the road he was traveling. Despite the cold and the strangeness of dealing with small-town foibles, he was beginning to feel the seductive draw of so much open space and tranquillity. He could almost begin to understand what it was that tied Berglund to a place like this, where roots ran deep and strong.

A wooden signboard which looked as if it had been hand-painted by the same artist who'd done the leaping fish sign on the highway, announced Camp Arundel just up ahead, with cabin rentals, tent grounds, a beach and a boat launch. A smaller sign swinging on a hook beneath the billboard, however, said the campground was closed for the season. Cruz drove past the tree-lined entry to the camp and started watching for the next drive on the right, which turned out to be closer than Verna had said it would be. There were plow-ridged fields on the left side of the road, but the lot on the right was as treed and pretty as the camp-grounds he'd just passed. A shelterbelt ran the full length of the property along the roadway, but as soon as Cruz passed it and turned into the drive, he spotted the black-and-white cruiser.

Something was very wrong here.

He slammed on the brakes and the car skidded to a stop at the edge of the drive near the road, about twenty yards from the cruiser. Reaching under his coat, he slipped his gun out of the waist holster at his back, then opened the door and climbed out cautiously, moving around the back of his rental to keep it be-tween him, the squad car and the weathered two-story farm-house beyond.

A screened-in veranda covered the entire front side of the house, its door swinging in the breeze. Likewise, the front passenger door of Berglund's cruiser also stood wide in the freezing wind rising off the lake. The cruiser was parked fac-ing into the veranda, but from a rear vantage point, it looked to be empty. Berglund and Jillian had obviously gotten out fast, and as Cruz tried to imagine why, the obvious explanation came to mind—the one-time lovebirds had restoked the fires, which had gotten so hot they couldn't take the time to close the car door in their rush to get into the house and into each other's pants.

"Berglund, you idiot," Cruz muttered.

At the rear bumper of the squad car, he dropped low, and then rose slowly to look through the window. Empty. A police cap sat on the ledge on the other side of the glass, and he could see that the radio mike was off its hook, lying on the center hump between the two front seats. Cruz inched his way up the passenger side of the car. A red silk scarf lay on the seat, as if it had fallen off in the wearer's hurry to get out. Otherwise, nothing. He took a deep breath and was just about to move toward the house when the radio squawked, the sudden noise an electric current slicing through every nerve in his body.

"Uh, two-niner, this is Wahlberg. You there, boss? Over."

Cruz hesitated, trying to decide whether to respond. What if the deputy and Jillian really were inside, going at it like rabbits? Dumb as it might be for Berglund to have put himself in that kind of position, did he really want to announce it to that pompous idiot at the dock? Cruz asked himself. On the other hand, did it not make sense to call for backup, just in case things were as hinky as they looked?

He backtracked a couple of steps toward the cruiser, keeping his eye and his gun trained on the house as the radio squawked again and the message from the white-haired deputy repeated itself. Reaching in with his left hand, Cruz picked up the microphone off the floor. He had his thumb on the talk button, but at the last second, he put it back down. First check, he decided. Then, if necessary, call the idiot for backup.

He started toward the house once more, gaze sweeping the lot, which was heavily treed around its entire perimeter except for the open area leading down to the lake. There was no movement around him, no sound, except for the slight, creaking sway of frozen branches. The veranda was deep in shadow, a sharp contrast to the brilliant sunlight bouncing off the snow in the yard, so that details were difficult to discern. But as he got closer and squinted to see through the shadow, it seemed to Cruz that the front door of the house also stood open. No way. He didn't care how hot the passion, nobody leaves the front door open when the temperature's ten below zero.

And then, out of the corner of his eye he saw the indentations made by footprints in a yard that had obviously seen no plow or visitors since the last snowfall. There were two sets proceeding away from the squad car, one heavy and large, Berglund-sized, the other smaller, like those a woman's dress boot might have made. But, Cruz realized with a start, there was also a third set, emerging from around the corner of the house as if someone had come in off the lake. On a snowmobile?

He took a two-handed grip on his semi-automatic, dropped low and moved forward, keeping as close as possible to the trees lining the drive. Instinct told him there was nothing good going on here. The air was bitter cold, but heavy with the kind of forced silence that always, in his experience, preceded the hiss of a sniper's bullet. Suddenly, he felt more vulnerable than he had ever been since that day on the jungle trail, playing cat-and-mouse with the VC who'd been picking off the men in his unit.

At the bottom step leading to the veranda, he paused and listened, but there was no sound. He took the steps two at a time, wincing at each creak, then slipped through the screen door and across the porch in a couple of strides. With his back to the wall of the house, he stood next to the front door with his gun held low, gripped once more in both hands. The inside wooden door was indeed open, and there was a light burning from a ceiling fixture just overhead. Cruz peered cautiously around the door and found himself looking down a long, narrow hall with a couple of doors running off either side. He slipped around the frame and stood quietly in the hall, listening once more. There was a staircase running up one side of the hall, and he peered up it, but there was no sign of lights or action up there.

And then he heard it—a low, crackling wheeze, coming from down the hall. It stopped, then a second or two later, it came again—wet, soggy and unforgettable. Cruz felt his stomach plunge.

"Oh, Jesus," he breathed.

Keeping close to the wall, he hurried toward a sound he

knew all too well. When he reached the frame of the first door leading into a small living room, he spotted a pair of huge, familiar boots sticking out from behind a sofa. Berglund. The deputy was lying on his back on the red linoleum floor, his green khaki jacket splayed open, blood bubbling through the center of his shredded shirt. Cruz did a rapid search of the room, but aside from the two of them, it was empty. He dropped to his knees beside the deputy and set his gun on the floor. Berglund's eyes were closed, but he was breathing, each breath producing the distinctive, bubbling crackle that only a sucking chest wound can make. He'd obviously taken a bullet in the lung.

"Berglund, can you hear me? It's Alex Cruz."

He searched frantically for something to plug the wound, but the room was stripped bare of everything but a seat-sprung sofa, a couple of slip-covered chairs, and a stained oak coffee table. He rummaged in his pockets, but all he could come up with was his battered vinyl-covered notepad. Good enough in a pinch, he decided.

Gingerly, he opened the front of Berglund's shirt, grimacing at the shredded flesh pulsating with every intake of the deputy's labored breathing. There was blood everywhere. Cruz centered the vinyl notebook over the wound and applied pressure. Immediately the awful sucking sound ceased. He looked around for something to hold it in place while he ran to call for help, but the second he released the pressure, air began to leak around the notebook and the bleeding started fresh.

"Berglund, can you hear me?"

"Uh-huh," the deputy grunted. His eyes were open now and watching Cruz's every move.

"You've got a punctured lung here. I need to call for help, but we've got to keep the pressure on it to keep it closed and help you breathe. Can you hold this in place for a minute while I make a phone call to your office?"

"No phone...off for winter," Berglund wheezed.

"Shit! Okay, I'll use your car radio. Can you hold this in place? Tight?"

"Uh-huh." Berglund lifted a hand weakly. Cruz grabbed it and slapped it over the notebook, but as soon as he took his own hand away, the big, limp hand slid off. "Sorry..."

"No, never mind. It's okay. I'll do something else."

Cruz whipped off his overcoat and folded it into the best approximation of a battle dressing he could muster, then placed it firmly over the vinyl notepad. Keeping his left hand on the dressing, he reached over to the heavy oak coffee table and grabbed it by the leg, dragging it toward them.

"Okay, buddy, I apologize for this. It isn't elegant, but if you try to keep real still, it might do the trick." He lifted the leg of the table and planted it on Berglund chest in the middle of the folded overcoat. "Lie as still as you can, okay?"

"Uh-huh."

Cruz watched him for a couple of breaths, but as long as Berglund didn't try to roll over, that heavy table was going nowhere, and the makeshift dressing would hold. He scrambled to his feet. "Okay, now sit tight."

"Not much choice with a damn table on my chest."

"Shut up. Don't talk. I'll be right back."

He flew back down the hall, out the door, and down the front steps of the veranda. At he squad car, he reached in and grabbed the mike. "Verna! Are you there! It's Alex Cruz, over!"

Nothing. "Verna! Wahlberg! Somebody! Come in, dammit! Over!"

The radio crackled. "Hey, Alex, it's Verna. What's up? You find them? Over?"

"Yes, right where you said, kiddo, but we need an ambulance out here, stat! Berglund's been shot. Over!"

"Holy mother of—shot? What about Jillian? Over!"

"I haven't seen her, but we've got an officer down, here. I need backup and I need that ambulance, fast! Got it! Over."

"Got it. Hang tight, Alex, they're on the way. Over."

"Attagirl. I'll be in the house with Berglund when they get here. Over and out."

He raced back in and found Berglund still breathing, but with obvious difficulty. Cruz lifted the heavy table off his chest and put his hand over his bloody overcoat. "There's an ambulance on the way, Nils. Hold on."

Berglund nodded weakly as Cruz peered under the coat. The bleeding appeared to be slowing a little, but the deputy had already lost enough blood to stop a small horse. Cruz pressed on the dressing once more, holding it firmly, trying to keep an eye on the deputy's vital signs and level of alertness. "I can't believe she'd do this to you," he muttered.

The big hand clamped his wrist with a strength that was surprising for a man in Berglund's state. "She saved me," he hissed. "He would have finished me off. She stopped him."

Cruz frowned. "Was it Edelmann?"

"Think so." Berglund released Cruz's wrist and his arm dropped again like a deadweight. "Came for her."

From off in the distance, Cruz heard the whine of sirens. Nice thing about a small town—short distances and not too many competing demands on the system. "What did Edelmann want from her?" he asked, turning back to Berglund.

"Don't know. When Jill saw him getting ready to burn the place down, she said she knew where the gold was."

"Gold? What gold?"

Berglund frowned. "I was hoping you knew. She said she'd take him to it if he left me alone."

"He shot you, anyway," Cruz pointed out.

"My own fault. I tried to take him down. You were right. Real tough SOBs, those Mossad guys." Berglund laughed grimly, but it turned into a strangled cough that sent blood spraying out the edges of the makeshift dressing.

"Okay, okay! Enough talking," Cruz said urgently, increasing the pressure. The sirens were close now.

"You find her, Cruz. He'll kill her next."

"Fine. Now be quiet. Help is almost here."

"I mean it."

"Yeah, yeah." Cruz lifted his head as the sirens—at least two of them, he realized—slowed their advance. They'd reached the turnoff from the road into the farmyard. "The ambulance is here," he said, turning back.

But the deputy's eyes were closed, his face unlined and still. Cruz leaned into his chest to listen, but his breath sounds seemed faint, if they were there at all. Even the awful gurgle was impossible to hear over the scream of the sirens.

"Berglund? Hang on, dammit! They're here."

He heard the crunch of tires on gravel and the sound of doors slamming and voices shouting outside. Then, in a whir of noise and movement, the house was full of uniforms. Somebody was ripping his makeshift battle dressing off Berglund's chest, taping plaster over the wound and starting CPR. Cruz stumbled out of the way, watching as they worked on him. The white-haired deputy was there, too, looking even paler than he had at the town dock as he watched the paramedics lift Berglund onto a stretcher while one of them—the lovely Lydia's heroic boyfriend—continued to breathe into the deputy's nose and mouth.

As they got ready to wheel the stretcher out of the house, Cruz searched around for his gun. He couldn't see it anywhere at first, but when he ducked low to look under the slip-covered chairs, he spotted it, kicked off into a corner by one or another of the tramping feet that had just passed through. His gun was there, and something else, too.

Cruz glanced around, but Wahlberg and another cop were preoccupied with helping the paramedics maneuver the gurney out the narrow door. Cruz swept up his gun and slipped it into his waist holster. Then, after one last check to make sure he was unobserved, he snatched up the black nubbled notebook that he'd found lying under the chair. He glanced at it just long enough to confirm that it was, indeed, the notebook Jillian Meade had been furiously composing at the hospital. Slipping it into the waistband at the back of his pants, he pulled his vest and sweater down over it, picked up his bloody overcoat, and followed the others out the door.

CHAPTER 31

I've been moving in a surreal state ever since Paris. My sense of time and space has become warped and twisted, the way it gets in hallucinations and dreams. After I left Bernard Cohn-Levy, I wanted to run—from his damnable files, from the truth, from my life—but some force carried me forward, dragging me against my will. No matter how hard I try, there is no pulling myself out of this viscous slime that has me bogged down. I am caught like a fly in amber. This is my nightmare, courtesy of my mother.

When we found the evidence of her affair with the Gestapo *Obermeister*, Colonel Kurt Braun, I was devastated and sick at heart. But Cohn-Levy offered me an alternative interpretation—although even he admitted it was small consolation. Still, it provided a way to view my mother's actions in a slightly less damning light.

"Perhaps, as you say, she could not help catching Braun's eye," Cohn-Levy said. "And given his reputation as a womanizer, he was probably bound to try to seduce such a beautiful woman. But this may not be as grim as it seems, Jillian."

"How could it possibly be any less grim? The man was obviously my father."

"So it would seem," he conceded, "but you had no control over that." When I started to protest that I may not have, but my mother certainly did, he shushed me. "Listen. If there was no way for her to escape Braun's attention, perhaps she decided to satisfy him in order to achieve her own ends."

"Is that supposed to make me feel better?"

"Had she refused him, Braun would have taken it as a slap in the face, a blow to his overweening pride. With a man like that, you must realize, there could have been only one possible result. He would have had her shot, as he did with so many others. But look at it from the point of view of the Resistance. His interest in your mother was a heaven-sent opportunity to further the anti-Nazi cause."

"You mean by co-opting Braun to work for their side?"

"Possibly. The direction of the war had shifted by then, and it was no longer at all certain that Hitler's forces were going to prevail. Others in the Reich hierarchy were busy making private arrangements to sue for peace, negotiating secret deals in the hope of better treatment from the Allies after Germany's defeat."

I thought about that for a moment, feeling a brief surge of irrational hope. "Do you really think it's possible my mother tried to entice Braun to become a double agent?"

Cohn-Levy nodded. "It's possible, although who can say whether a man like that, so wedded to the Fascist cause, would have been amenable? At the very least, though, she would have had an extraordinary opportunity to spy on the Germans. Think of it—if she gained his trust, she might have been privy to conversations and documents that could provide her comrades with intelligence on German plans and operations, and warn them when arrests were planned."

"And all she had to do was prostitute herself," I noted grimly.

Cohn-Levy placed a sympathetic hand on my shoulder. "I know this isn't easy for you, Jillian, but a beautiful woman can be a powerful weapon in intelligence warfare. This kind of thing is done all the time, you know."

"I suppose so," I said.

Even if it were true, it did nothing to diminish my shock at learning my true heritage—not to mention my anger over the fact that Joe Meade's parents had been duped into believing I was their grandchild. But such an explanation would at least put my mother's actions in a slightly less odious light. And who knew? Maybe Joe had agreed to be my surrogate father after he found Grace again.

Another thought occurred to me. "If I was born in the Drancy transit camp, then it had to mean that my mother was a prisoner of the Germans at the time of the Liberation. Whatever happened between her and Braun, their affair must have been long over by then. He must have lost interest in her, at the very least. Or perhaps he discovered what she had been up to."

Cohn-Levy nodded. "So it would seem. And perhaps he was not so interested in being a father, since he already had a wife and children back in Bavaria. You were born on Bastille Day, did you not say?"

"That's right."

He did a quick count on his fingers. "That would have been...oh, let me see...six weeks or so before the Allies liberated Paris, no? So obviously, even if she had managed to earn his confidence for a while, your mother could no longer have been under the protection of Colonel Braun at the end of the Occupation—not if she ended up at Drancy."

"Was Braun still in Paris at the Liberation?"

"Yes. The Allies landed in Normandy in June, although it took them another two and a half months to reach Paris. Colonel Braun was among the last to leave Gestapo headquarters just before the Allies rolled in, but apparently he didn't get far. He was planning to make his way back to Germany through Alsace, but he never made it out of the city. His staff car was attacked by a mob at the Porte de la Villette, a neighborhood that had been hit hard by his campaign to stamp out the Resistance. A few weeks before, Braun had ordered a lycée burned to the ground when he suspected some of its students of being involved in setting a fire at a nearby German military barracks. Four teenage boys hiding out in the school basement burned to death, and five others who tried to escape the flames were shot as they ran out of the building. They say when the mob caught Braun, they dragged him and his driver out of the car and stoned them."

"To death?"

Cohn-Levy nodded, watching me closely. Did he expect me to cry? To mourn this monster who had apparently spawned me? I had grown up fatherless in Havenwood, but at least I'd always felt sure of who I was. In the previous few days, I'd learned that I wasn't Joe Meade's daughter, after all. Now, in the space of a few hours, I had also found and lost my real father. All things considered, however, I was not about to grieve over his assassination.

"As you say," Cohn-Levy went on, "for you to have been born in the Drancy prison camp, your mother had to have fallen out of Braun's favor. The prisoners at Drancy were destined for the concentration camps—not the fate of a collaborator with as powerful a protector as Colonel Braun, which would seem to confirm the theory that your mother was, in fact, still working for the Resistance."

"Is there any way to confirm it?"

Cohn-Levy nodded as he started rummaging through his dusty bookshelves. "I have copies here somewhere of administrative files from the Drancy transit camp. All we have to do is check the admission records for the period leading up to July 14, 1944."

But after three hours of painstaking hunting, we had found no trace of the name "Sylvie Fournier," much less any evidence of a Grace Wickham or a Grace Meade. As we searched through page after page of Cohn-Levy's voluminous documents, however, we realized that his Drancy files were even more complete than he'd realized. Not only did he have the camp intake lists, but he also had the record of births that had taken place in the camp infirmary.

And here was where it really got ugly and untenable—because of twelve births at the camp in July 1944, only one was on July 14, to a woman by the name of Isobel Kempf who, the records showed, was transported to Auschwitz-Birkenau not long after.

It was beyond credible that a mother would mistake her child's birth date, but even so, we checked and rechecked the infirmary's maternity records. My mother's name was nowhere to be found. Nor, ominously, did it appear anywhere in the camp files, despite our backtracking all the way to the previous autumn, when she'd first parachuted into France. There was only one conclusion to be drawn—that no matter what my mother had told Miss Atwater, she had never, in fact, been detained at the Drancy transit camp. The only reason she would have lied about this was to conceal the fact that she had been a collaborator and a traitor.

Cohn-Levy, kind, sweet man that he was, tried so hard to come up with someone who could provide another, less damning explanation for the discrepancy, realizing how much it meant to me. We checked through Gestapo arrest files, where we found, among others, the names of the four little girls and the Mother Superior from the convent school who were found and arrested when Col. Braun and his Gestapo thugs went searching for the stolen gold. There, too, was the name of Isobel Kempf, who was among those to give birth at the Drancy transit camp and who also turned out to be the teacher who'd been sheltered with the four Jewish children. An unidentified foreign man was also listed as having been arrested at the convent that day. We found the name Sylvie Fournier among those who were picked up from the neighborhood, but there was an asterisk next to her name.

"What does that mean, do you suppose?" I asked Cohn-Levy.

"I'm not certain, although in my experience, it generally means that a prisoner is marked for special handling, although without other documentation, it's impossible to know exactly what kind."

"It's pretty obvious, isn't it?" I said bitterly. "They arrested her along with the others in order not to arouse suspicion among her Resistance colleagues. But while the others were being interrogated, she was probably relaxing back at the George V, wearing the pretty clothes Colonel Braun had bought for her and drinking champagne, toasting her own cleverness."

Cohn-Levy had to concede by then that it didn't look good, but he wouldn't give up, calling around to his contacts to try to locate any former Resistance members who might have some memory of "Sylvie Fournier" and be able explain the discrepancies we had found. But ominously, despite his best efforts, the entire Gentilly cell seemed to have been wiped out in the Gestapo hunt for the stolen Nazi gold, and no one else had anything to offer.

Despite my sorrow and regret, I thanked M. Cohn-Levy profusely for his help. Then, still unwilling to believe the truth that was right in front of my face, I went to Gentilly myself. For two days, I pounded the pavement, knocking on doors and calling in at shops, searching for anyone who could recall what had gone on in that period.

Hopeless. People had moved or died or had simply been keeping their noses to the ground during the German Occupation, a period when knowing too much could end up being a ticket to the firing squad or concentration camp. The closest I came was at a brasserie where the owner turned out to be a nephew of one of the Resistance members arrested and subsequently shot in that final operation when the Gestapo was hunting for the missing gold. Jacques Aubert, it turned out, even remembered a beautiful young woman named Sylvie Fournier.

"But I was only twelve years old at the time, mademoiselle. I remember Sylvie because I was madly infatuated with her, as only a young boy can be. I know she was old Viau's niece, but beyond that, I am not certain what I can tell you."

I tried anyway to jog his memory about any little detail he might remember concerning goings-on in his neighborhood when my mother would have been there, but his memories were mostly limited to rehashed family stories about the arrest and execution of his late uncle—and, of course, his boyish fantasies about the beautiful Sylvie on whom he'd had such a great schoolboy crush. He hardly believed me when I told him she'd been a British SOE operative whose real name was Grace Wickham.

"Mademoiselle, I am astonished," Aubert said, examining an old photograph of my mother that I pulled out of my wallet to show him as proof that we were, in fact, discussing the same woman. "English! I would never have guessed. And she is living now in America, you say?"

"That's right."

"Well, well," he said, handing me back the photograph. "That is a mystery solved, then."

"How so?"

I was treated to one of those Gallic shrugs. "It explains why she was never seen again. She was among those arrested the same day as my uncle. Old Viau had a heart attack and died during his interrogation by the Gestapo. My uncle and the others, of course, were shot. As for Sylvie, there was never any word of her. We all presumed that she, too, had been shot by the Gestapo or died in the camps."

"No, she survived," I assured him dryly. There was no way, of course, that I would confide to this man my suspicions about how exactly she had survived. Cohn-Levy had earned my trust, but Jacques Aubert's idle, prurient curiosity didn't qualify him for the same level of confidence.

But he took another glass from a shelf behind the counter, topped up my wine, and poured one for himself, then proposed a toast.

"To Sylvie. And mademoiselle," he added, after we had drunk to her health (what else could I do?), "you must stay to dinner, please. I invite you. I would very much like to hear more about your extraordinary mother."

I'm no better with drink than I am with drugs. Is that what happened? Did I say more than I'd meant to that night? Was it the wine that loosened my tongue. Or was it Aubert's stunning revelation about the arrests at the convent school that day that so many in the neighborhood vanished? That, in addition to the Mother Superior and the four little Jewish girls and their teacher who were taken, the Gestapo also discovered a downed English-speaking pilot hiding out in the school's cellar. His name hadn't shown up in the Gestapo arrest records Cohn-Levy and I had examined, I realized, but there had been one nameless man, simply listed as "male, identity unknown, possibly British or American spy."

I suddenly had a sickening premonition that the downed pilot Aubert and his neighbors had seen marched out of the convent school that day might well have been Joe Meade.

CHAPTER 32

Cruz was back at FBI headquarters at eleven on Sunday morning, less than twenty-four hours after finding Berglund shot in his father-in-law's farmhouse. Jillian's journal was still tucked into the inside pocket of his sport coat, burning a hole in his resolve to work the case according to standard operating procedures. He'd mentioned the notebook to no one, least of all Kenny Wahlberg, the pale, prickly young cop who'd shown up at the farm with the ambulance and who was apparently heading up the Havenwood Police Department now that both the chief and deputy chief were down for the count. Nor had he told the State Police or the local FBI field office about it. Both agencies had shown up within a couple of hours of getting word that a cop shooter was at large and had taken a hostage—although a hostage who, Special Agent in Charge Sheen had noted grimly, seemed to leave more bodies in her wake than the Grim Reaper. Despite Berglund's defense of her, which Cruz had dutifully passed on, Jillian Meade had been cited in state and nationwide alerts as Simon Edelmann's hostage but also as a potential accomplice, and law enforcement agencies had been warned to approach both with extreme caution.

While the doctors had been working on Berglund in the Havenwood E.R., plugging the hole in his chest in an attempt to stabilize him enough to survive a flight to Minneapolis for surgery, Cruz had phoned Dr. Kandinsky to let her know that Jillian had gone missing. Conveniently, the psychiatrist hadn't thought to mention the journal, saving him the necessity of an outright lie.

He'd arrived back in Washington around midnight, after reading through the journal twice on the flight from Minneapolis, then a third time in the wee hours of the morning. Everything he now knew about Jillian and Grace Meade, between the journal's revelations and the digging he'd done in Havenwood, kept playing and replaying in his head, and Cruz knew he was hooked. Berglund had been as clueless as everyone else about the true nature of those two women, but there was one thing on which the deputy had been dead right—it was critical to find Jillian, and fast, before the last chapter of the grim tale played itself out. There was no way Cruz could let her slip from his grasp.

Who the hell would believe him, anyway, if he tried to hand off the case? The whole bizarre thing was based on fuzzy thirty-five-year-old memories of distant events and the disjointed ramblings of a suicidal woman who, for all her painstaking research, still hadn't figured out what it was really all about, although it seemed to Cruz that the answer—stunning, unexpected, and yet perfectly obvious—was right there in her journal. He had only to verify a couple of additional pieces of information, but time was of the essence. At this point, there was only one way to close this down, and that was to do it himself.

He was already running far behind Jillian and Edelmann, but he had a notion where they were headed. If he moved fast, he might yet catch up to them before it was too late. It had been too late to catch a Saturday night flight to Paris, but he'd booked one for Sunday evening, then called the FBI weekend watch officer first thing that morning and asked to be put in touch with the inspector in charge of international liaison. Kessler had called back five minutes later, and his response to Cruz's request to follow the fugitives to Paris had been immediate and unequivocal.

"Not a chance."

"There's a major time crunch here, sir. As far as we can tell, they haven't crossed over into Canada or approached any nearby airports, so we think they're still in the country. The state police found the snowmobile Edelmann had stolen a couple of hours after the deputy was shot, abandoned across the lake from the farm. I just checked back with them, and they say a car Edelmann had rented was just found in South Dakota, where another car was reported stolen. Obviously, he's trying to stay under the radar of U.S. border controls by taking a circuitous route out of the country. He may be heading south for Texas and from there to Mexico, but he will get out, sir, mark my words. Edelmann's got the training, and if Mossad is backing him on this—"

"Speaking of which, your friend in the Israeli Embassy hasn't called me back," Kessler said testily.

Me, neither, Cruz thought, even more ticked off than Kessler was. He and Mindel had a track record of working together and they were friends, so he'd expected better cooperation.

"The point is," he told Kessler, "Edelmann will find a way to get Jillian Meade and himself to Paris. That's where the endgame is going to play out, I'm certain of it. I have an idea where they're heading, and if I can get over there fast, I might short-circuit his plans."

"It doesn't have to be you personally. None of us is indispensable, you know."

"Yes, sir, I know that. It's just that the case is complex, and there isn't time to bring anyone else up to speed. If Edelmann does make it to Paris, they'll find more bodies in short order, I can almost guarantee it."

"All the more reason to extend the alert to all border checkpoints and have them picked up as soon as possible, before they can leave the United States. Once they're in custody, there'll be more than enough time for a full debriefing on all those complex details. Meantime, I need you back at your desk. We've got other business heating up and I need every agent I've got."

There was logic in what he was saying, Cruz knew, but it didn't change the fact that a pro like Edelmann wasn't going to let himself be caught before he reached his objective. Nor did it change the fact that he himself needed to see this through, regardless of the cost.

"You're at the office?" Kessler asked.

"Yes, sir."

"Good. Sit tight. I was just on my way in myself, and we'll talk when I get there." The line went dead.

Cruz sat at his desk, drumming his fingers. He could make a stab at going through the pile of color-coded international police alerts in his "In" basket, he thought, maybe mollify the chief that he had his brief under control so the guy would cut him a little slack. He flipped through a few action items and found some he could in good conscience pass off to other agents. Halfway down the pile, he came across another item that had come in for him in his absence. It was a copy of Grace Meade's 1945 immigration file which he'd requested from the INS.

He flipped through the documents—birth certificate for herself, document from a Catholic parish in Paris certifying her marriage to one Joseph Arthur Meade, and from the U.S. Embassy in London, documentation attesting to Joseph Meade's active military status as of June 1944 when he'd gone missing in action, presumed dead. There was also a certificate from the Embassy attesting to the birth abroad of a U.S. citizen: Jillian Elizabeth Meade, daughter of that same Joseph Arthur Meade and

Grace Wickham Meade. The child was listed as having been born on July 14, 1944 in Drancy, France. A photograph of Grace Meade was also attached to the immigration file. The grieving young widow would have seemed a beautiful and tragic figure, Cruz thought. What bureaucrat's heart wouldn't have been moved by the sight of her to expedite her case so that she could take her infant child to be with her dead husband's family in America?

He closed the file and set it aside, reaching for his telephone. Z'ev Mindel had been incommunicado since the Friday-night call from Havenwood, but when the embassy switchboard put Cruz through to his office, the old soldier picked up immediately.

"Alex! Impeccable timing, as always. I was just getting ready to call you. Are you still in Minnesota?"

"No, I'm back in D.C., at my office. I thought I was the only fool who'd be in on a Sunday morning."

"You're in town? Excellent! You said you were looking for a Triumph motorcycle, did you not?"

"What? Yeah, I suppose so, but that's not—"

"Yes, I thought it was a Triumph. I have a lead on one, but it will only be available for a limited time. Can you meet me to go and take a look at it? Preferably right now?"

"Meet now? To look at a motorcycle? Z'ev, I just got back and I'm up to my ass in alligators here. I've been trying to reach you all weekend to see if you'd been able to come up with anything—"

"On that bike," Mindel interrupted. "Yes, I know. I apologize, my friend, but it took me some time to track one down. As I say, I may have a lead, but at this price, it will not last long. It really is imperative that we jump on it as soon as possible."

Cruz glanced around the office. A couple of other agents had shown up in the past half hour, maybe to work cases, maybe just to get caught up on paperwork. He stretched up to peer over the gray fabric divider between his cubicle and the next, but, of course, there was no chance Sean Finney would come in on a

Sunday. Thank God, he thought. He settled back and cupped his hand around the telephone mouthpiece.

"Let me be clear on this, Z'ev—this is the same machine you and I discussed Friday night?"

"The same. So, can you meet me, say in half an hour?"

"Not that soon. I'm waiting to see the boss. I don't think he's too happy with me right about now."

"I don't want to pressure you, Alex, but this may be a take-it-or-leave-it deal."

As Cruz opened his mouth, a buzzer sounded and a light on the base of his phone flashed red. "That's my intercom," he said. "I think he's ready for me now. Can we make it in forty-five minutes?"

"All right, forty-five minutes, but don't delay. Meet me at the Lincoln Memorial."

"I'll be there." Cruz depressed the cradle as the buzzer rang again, then pressed the intercom button. "Cruz."

"Kessler. Could you come down, please?" It was an order, not a request.

"On my way."

IC Gordon Kessler was tall, fit and spoke with typical Bureau bluntness. "You were to follow up on a high priority Scotland Yard query, Cruz, but the fact that I gave you permission to put it at the top of the pile and head out west to do the follow-up doesn't mean it warranted this much attention. If you're going to have a future with the Bureau, you're going to have to manage your time a little more efficiently."

"Yes, sir. Things got complicated out there."

"What's the status on that deputy chief of police who was shot?"

"The bullet went through his lung, and lodged against his spine. It was touch and go for a while there, but they got him medevac'd to a hospital in Minneapolis. I called this morning. He'd made it through the night, which is good, but at the moment, he's paralyzed from the waist down and there could be other complications. He's nowhere near out of the woods."

"And the woman and this shooter?"

"Vanished." Cruz gave him a brief rundown on what he knew about Edelmann and the wartime background to the case.

"And so you think they've gone back to Paris to look for the gold? And that's what got those two women in the U.K. killed?"

"Yes, sir. The British police were stymied because the two homicides were committed by someone who was a complete stranger to both victims. There also seemed at first to be no connection between the victims themselves, other than that they were both elderly women. The woman in Dover was a retired hospital aide. The vic in London was ex-British Special Operations, it turns out, so the field of suspects was probably a little more fertile there. It turned out that Jillian Meade had been the last person to call on her at her office, though, and when they followed up in Dover, they found a neighbor who was able to tell them that an American woman had also been to see that victim. From there, it was short work to find out Jillian Meade had been in Dover, as well, and that was how Scotland Yard finally made the connection. Although," Cruz added, "it was a bit of a red herring."

"You don't think she was in on those murders?"

"No, sir, I don't. At most, I think someone—this Edelmann, by the look of it—set out to implicate her in order to force her into a position where she'd have no choice but to cooperate with him."

"On what?"

"I think he or the people he represents believe she's uncovered the whereabouts of a cache of gold that was stolen from the Nazis by the French Resistance—gold that had originally been stolen from French victims of the Holocaust. The Resistance members involved in the heist were rounded up, tortured and shot by the Gestapo, but the gold was never found. It'd be worth about ten million dollars on the 1979 market. Jillian Meade apparently told Edelmann she could lead him to it."

"So that's why he's taking her back to Paris?"

"Yes, sir." Cruz debated mentioning the other nagging suspicion he had begun to entertain about Edelmann, but until he had his facts lined up, it was probably safer not to.

"Well then," Kessler said, leaning back in his chair, "we should definitely pass this on to the French for follow-up."

"Sir—"

"I want you to put in a call to French Sûreté and give them the information you have. Then, starting first thing tomorrow, there's another job I want you on. We're getting reports that the Ayatollah Khomeini's planning some kind of operation in retaliation for our support of the former Shah. We don't know if it's supposed to go down here or in Teheran, but we're interviewing Iranians who are in the States on visitor and resident visas. Let them know we're watching, see if we can't nip this in the bud. I want you to start working that file this week."

Cruz opened his mouth to protest but just then, the phone rang. Kessler held up a hand. "Kessler.... On my way." He hung up and rose from his desk. "That was the director's office. I have to go up for a meeting. I'll see you at our Monday morning staff meeting." He was at the door of his office, but he paused and turned back. "By the way, have you put in twelve months on the job yet?"

"Eleven, actually."

Kessler nodded, frowning. "Which means you're still on probation. I've cut you some slack because you're new to our procedures and you've got a reputation as an excellent investigator. But like I said, Agent Cruz, no one's indispensable. Keep it in mind."

It had started to rain by the time Cruz arrived at the Lincoln Memorial. Flipping up his coat collar, he spotted Mindel inside the monument's covered area, leaning against the statue's granite plinth, sheltering from the drizzle. He was taken aback by his old friend's appearance. Mindel had always been a bantam rooster of a man, barely five-foot-two, but when they'd first met in Munich six years earlier, the Israeli had been wiry, energetic and tough as old shoe leather, with forearms like Popeye, a woolly mat of salt-and-pepper curls, bright blue eyes and a wickedly mischievous grin. Now, the grin was still there, lighting up his face as he caught sight of Cruz, but his hair had turned pure white. When he stepped forward out of the shadow of Lincoln's granite knees, Mindel's stiff, slightly lop-sided gait was a sharp reminder of the stroke the old guerrilla fighter had suffered the previous year.

"Alex! You old son of a gun!" The strength of his bear hug, however, was undiminished. "You look like a million bucks! Being a fibbie agrees with you, I'm thinking."

"Hey there, Z'ev. You're looking good yourself."

"Feh! You're such a bad liar. I look like hell, but so what? I'm here, no? You should have seen me a year ago, slouched in a wheelchair surrounded by drooling old-timers, passing a beach ball. Pathetic. My own fault, mind you. Too much rich food, too much booze, too little exercise. The old arteries always betray us in the end. Keep it in mind."

"I'll try."

The high, covered space around the memorial echoed with their voices and the scuffle and shrieks of a group of kids running rings around Lincoln's oversized chair. Not a great place for a quiet talk, and yet the cold drizzle outside the monument was equally uninviting.

"Are you up for lunch?" Cruz asked him.

Mindel nodded enthusiastically. "I was just thinking the same thing. There's a very nice deli not too far from here. Serves a killer pastrami on rye."

"'Killer' is right. Isn't that the kind of thing that got you in trouble in the first place?"

"Yeah, yeah," Mindel grumbled, waving him off. "Nag, nag, nag. I didn't say I was going to eat it. I'll have some borscht and a salad, and you'll let me smell your pastrami." He smacked the front of Cruz's coat. "You still got a few years of decent eating before your body betrays you, youngster. Enjoy it while you can."

At the crowded deli, they managed to snag a corner table away from prying ears. After a few minutes, which they used to study the oversized menus, a middle-aged waitress doing the rounds of the room came over and stood glaring down at them, her hands on her hips. "What'll it be, boys?"

Mindel peered at her over half-moon reading glasses. "Pastrami on rye and a nice, fat dill pickle for my friend. And some coleslaw. You want to get the roughage in, Alex. It'll give you an extra year or two. And for me," he added, handing her back the laminated menus, "some borscht, no sour cream—godammit to hell—a side salad, and a large dollop of guilt and remorse."

"Uh-huh. And that's it?"

"You're not going to write this down?" Cruz asked.

She shot him a withering look. "What for?"

"The place is busy. Might help to keep the orders straight."

"You think borscht and a pastrami on rye is rocket science?"

"No, I guess it isn't."

"Uh-huh. So, it's just me that seems thick, then, is that it?"

"Oh, no, ma'am. Not at all."

"Glad to hear it. So, you got any more advice you want to offer, sonny? Or can I go put your order in now?"

"Yes, ma'am. Sorry. Carry on."

"Thank you. What to drink, by the way?"

"Ice water now, coffee later, please?" Cruz asked. Mindel gave an echoing nod.

"Right." She sauntered off, apron strings swaying across wide hips as she bellowed, "Gimme a number sixteen, a borscht and a side, Mort, and hold the sour cream!"

Mindel removed his reading glasses and tucked them into his pocket, grinning. "Fool. You haven't figured out by now that you don't tell grannies how to suck eggs?"

"I should know better." Cruz agreed. He glanced around the room, then lowered his voice. "So, Z'ev, tell me I haven't been waiting for two days to hear back from you only to learn you've found a bike but no information on my shooter."

"Nah, I don't know from the bike. I just wasn't sure who might be listening, so I had to play it cool. Because you, my friend, really set the cat among the pigeons with that request of yours."

"You were able to get something on this Edelmann?"

"Oh, yes, and an interesting fellow he is, too. Unfortunately, it turns out you've stumbled into a very sensitive area, as far as my government is concerned. This is something people would prefer not be discussed in public forums, you understand. I'm willing to share what I can with you, but there are those who would be very unhappy if they knew I had breathed a word of this to an outsider. And make no mistake, Alex, they would not be above trumping up some complaint against you and taking it to the very top levels of your own government to try to get you off the case—and maybe out of a job. I'm talking State Department, the Attorney General, maybe even the White House. For your own sake, you need to play this one close to the chest."

"I have to bring him in, Z'ev. He shot a deputy chief of police. A real good guy out there in Minnesota is fighting for his life right now. We can't have people thinking they can go around shooting cops and get away with it. Plus, there was a sixty-year-old female victim there, too—who was no angel, admittedly, but that's neither here nor there—not to mention another couple of possible victims of his in the U.K."

The feisty waitress approached just then and set down water glasses and cutlery in front of them. "Here you go, fellas. Well, whaddya know," she added, giving Cruz the raised eyebrow, "I managed to remember ice water without screwing up. So far, so good, hey?"

Cruz nodded as she rolled her eyes and flounced off once more. He turned back to Mindel. "So what's the deal? Is Edelmann on the Mossad clock these days? And is your government going to try to protect him on this?"

Mindel shook his gleaming white head. "No, not necessarily, but it's a complicated business. Nobody wants to cover for him if he's gone rogue on us, but you've gotta understand, Alex, neither do they want to see his picture on the front page of the *New York Times*. It'd be a big, fat pimple on the relationship between our two governments."

"So what do we do?"

Mindel pushed up his shirtsleeves and leaned forward on the table, like a man about to get down to brass tacks. "Here's the deal. You tell me what this is all about, and I'll tell you what I've been able to find out about Edelmann. Then, we figure out what to do next."

Over the next twenty minutes or so, between table service from the irate waitress still miffed at having her professionalism questioned and bites of the best pastrami on rye he'd ever eaten, Cruz gave Mindel a rundown on how and why he'd been tracking Jillian Meade, and what had happened since he'd found her—including what he had learned from her notebook about her mother's dubious wartime history. It sounded jumbled even to him, but when he was done, his Israeli friend only nodded.

"Yes, of course. It makes perfect sense. Of course."

"How so?"

Their coffee arrived and Mindel paused to load his up with four cubes of sugar, then put one more between his teeth before taking a sip. While he lifted the cup, Cruz noticed again, as he had so many times before, the ugly gray numbers marching down the length of Mindel's left forearm. Mindel had been raised in Hamburg, but had escaped to Belgium, then Holland after the Nazis rolled across Europe, fighting with the Opposition underground in Amsterdam until finally the Nazis caught up with him and shipped him off to Auschwitz. Cruz had once asked him why he didn't have his camp tattoo removed.

"Because it's my badge of honor," the old street fighter replied. "Proves the bastards couldn't kill me."

Frowning thoughtfully as he crunched on his sugar cube now, Mindel leaned back in his chair. "Simon Edelmann was born after the war, in Jerusalem in 1949. His father's family were German Jews from Berlin but they'd managed to escape to Palestine in the mid-thirties, when the Nazis first rose to power. His mother was French. She was with the Resistance until she was arrested, after which she spent eight months in Auschwitz-Birkenau before it was liberated by the Russians. She had tuberculosis and God knows what else, like so many others, so she spent more than a year in clinics and hospitals after the war, but eventually she made her way to Palestine where a sister of hers had ended up. That's where she met and married Edelmann Sr., and the two of them had a son."

"Simon Edelmann."

"Exactly. But the marriage foundered. After the divorce, the mother left Simon with his father and moved back to France. Simon was just nine when she left, and they say he grew up quite bitter at having been abandoned."

"Nice mom," Cruz said.

"It's not ideal, but there were extenuating circumstances. They say she's one of those who never got past her wartime experiences. Most survivors carry a great deal of grief and guilt, you know. Things happened back then that we can never forget. Most of us put those memories away and try to carry on, one day at a time, but Mrs. Edelmann was one of those who couldn't, it seems. For one thing, she'd been married before, in France, and had had another child during the war. She was pregnant, in fact, when she and her husband were arrested by the Gestapo. The husband was shot outright, but in her case, because she was half-Jewish, I suppose they thought that was too good a fate for her. Instead, she was sent to the Drancy transit camp to await transport to Auschwitz. Drancy was where she had the baby."

"Yes!" Cruz said, balancing on the edge of his seat. "Jillian mentions Drancy in her journal. Grace had said that's where she'd given birth to her, in July of '44, it would have been—except it turns out that Grace lied. She'd never been interned at Drancy at all."

"Of course she lied. I could have told you that."

Cruz was taken aback. "How so?"

"Because, Alex, your Jillian would not be alive today if she'd been born at Drancy. Not at that time, anyway."

"How do you know?"

"It's one of many atrocities of the Occupation," Mindel said. "On the day the last transport train left Drancy for Auschwitz, all the babies under two were separated from their mothers. The German guards said the little ones would be coming behind in a special kinderwagen staffed with nurses who would care for them on the journey. They said there would be cribs in this special train car, and milk and baby food, and they told the mothers they would be reunited with their babies at the other end."

"An obvious lie."

"Of course it was. A grand fairy tale to keep the mothers calm, nothing more. In fact, eyewitnesses said that as soon as the women had been shipped out, a truck pulled up to the infirmary where the babies and toddlers had been gathered together. They were in the maternity ward, which was on the top floor of the building—a dozen newborns, plus eighteen or so other little ones. The eyewitnesses testified that the guards went into the infirmary, only to reappear a few minutes later at the top floor window, open it, and start tossing the babies out one by one into the back of the pickup truck."

Cruz pushed his coffee cup aside. "Oh, shit."

"So, you see, your Jillian could not have been there. The babies were all murdered," Mindel said grimly, "thirty more tiny little victims of the Third Reich. As for Simon Edelmann's mother, it seems she never stopped grieving for her lost baby, or for that matter, for her first husband, shot by the Gestapo. When Simon grew up, though, they say he found his mother again in France and they reconciled. She's still alive, although very frail. Apparently she never really recovered her health after Auschwitz. I was told she lives in a convalescent care home near Tours."

"And Edelmann?"

"Well, after he met up with his mother again and saw what she had become—a sad, broken woman—he joined up with those who vow to see the innocent avenged and the guilty punished, no matter how long it takes and how many laws have to be bent or broken to accomplish that end."

"And that's why he went after Grace Meade?"

"Ah, yes, Grace Meade—also known as 'Sylvie Fournier.' When I first found out about Edelmann, I wondered if he was on a mission on behalf of Ariel's Claw, but—"

"Whoa, hold it. Ariel who? What are you talking about?"

Mindel set his coffee down and cupped the mug in his hands, glancing around the crowded deli. Cruz followed his gaze, but there was far too much noise in the place for anyone to be able to monitor the quiet conversation going on at the corner table. "This is where we get into the sensitive part, Alex, the part you must be careful not too talk about too freely. To be perfectly frank with you, there are those who would have my old, withered, but still fondly regarded nuts in a vice if they knew I was telling you this."

"I would never put you at unnecessary risk, Z'ev, I hope you know that."

"I would not be here if I didn't believe that, my friend." Mindel glanced around once more, then exhaled heavily. "How to begin? Ariel's Claw.... Ariel means 'lion of God' in Hebrew, so Ariel's Claw would basically be God's weapon against his enemies. This is how they see themselves, in any case."

"'They' being...who?"

"The members of this very secret organization."

"Part of Mossad?"

"There are Mossad agents who are said to belong to Ariel's Claw, but the group is by no means restricted to us. Government ministers, army officers, and many otherwise ordinary people are rumored to be members. No one really knows for sure who belongs, or even how large the organization is. Some skeptics even doubt Ariel's Claw exists, although I am not among them. Like many secret organizations, it's composed of small cells of activists with very little overlap between them, for security reasons, so that no one member knows the identities of more than a handful of other members."

"And it's objective is...what?"

"Just as I said—they see themselves as the active hand of God's revenge on those guilty of crimes against our people. They say the organization was first hatched in 1945, in Nuremberg. Eight thousand Nazis were imprisoned in Stalag 13 at the time. The Americans were guarding them while the Allies decided who would be put on trial for war crimes. In the end, as you know, only twenty-two were indicted in the Nuremberg war tribunals, and of those, only a dozen were condemned to death. Think about that, Alex—just twelve Nazis held responsible for the deaths of six million Jews, not to mention another five million Gypsies, homosexuals, political activists, handicapped people and others systematically exterminated by the Third Reich. Not enemy soldiers, mind you. Those victims were civilian men, women and children deemed subhuman by those fanatics. A little unbalanced, as far as justice goes, wouldn't you say? Or did those twelve Nazis condemned at Nuremberg manage to kill eleven million innocent human beings all by themselves?"

"Not hardly," Cruz agreed grimly. It was a well-known fact that the West, preoccupied with economic recovery, the Communist menace and the start of the Cold War after 1945 had had little appetite for any more war crimes tribunals after Nuremberg. "So, this 'Ariel's Claw' was created to tip the balance?"

"So it would seem, starting with those eight thousand Nazis the Americans were holding at Stalag 13. Ariel's Claw hatched a secret plot to put arsenic in the inmates' bread. Apparently, they did manage to kill or seriously injure several hundred. The exact number has never been revealed, mind you, since it would have caused your government some embarrassment to admit that its prisoners were poisoned right under its nose."

"And Ariel's Claw has been on the hunt ever since? Is that why each of Edelmann's alleged victims was torched after being killed? Sort of a symbolic nod to the concentration camps' crematoria?"

"I should imagine so. But you should also know, Alex, that my government disavows all knowledge of and support for Ariel's Claw. Not that we won't track down and put on trial the Eichmanns and Mengeles if we can. But the kind of frontier justice practiced by Ariel's Claw has a tendency to backfire, especially when it ends up being used as an excuse for acts of terrorism against the State of Israel. So you must believe me when I tell you that if Edelmann has done these things you say, it is without government sanction. We will, of course, do everything we can to cooperate and rein him in."

"That's good to know."

"Well, perhaps not as good as it sounds. The thing is, Edelmann has flown the Mossad coop."

"Gone AWOL?"

"Indeed. And even though he is rumored to have been an eager partisan for Ariel's Claw, I suspect these latest incidents may not be sanctioned by even that dubious organization. I suspect he's been freelancing for personal reasons."

"Why do you say that?"

"Because Grace Meade, also known as 'Sylvie Fournier,' was the one who betrayed Edelmann's mother to the Gestapo. People vanish in wartime and its aftermath, you know, but they say Edelmann's been hunting this 'Sylvie' for lo, these many years, ever since reconciling with his mother. He'd laid little trip wires all over Europe trying to find out what had happened to her after the Liberation. When your Jillian went looking for her mother's past, it would seem she set off those alarm bells."

Cruz leaned back, running his hands through his hair. "Son of a... And after that, it was just a matter of Edelmann finding her and letting her lead him right back to Grace."

Mindel nodded. "As they say in church basements all over America, 'Bingo!'"

"You wouldn't happen to have brought me a picture of this Simon Edelmann, would you?"

"But, of course," Mindel said, smiling. He reached into the inside breast pocket of his jacket and brought out a passport-sized black-and-white photograph, which he slid across the table to Cruz. The man in it was young—he'd be thirty this year, Cruz calculated. As Tom Newkirk had described from his brief airport meeting, Edelmann had dark, curly hair cut in a short Afro style, a thick mustache, and piercing eyes that Cruz guessed were dark brown.

"A neighbor saw Jillian arrive at the Minneapolis airport with Edelmann in tow," he told Mindel. "They seemed to know each other, although Jillian makes no mention of him in the journal. On the other hand, she hadn't quite finished writing all she'd intended when Berglund, the Havenwood cop, was shot, so maybe she would have gotten around to explaining what she was doing with him."

"Do you believe she's in cahoots with Edelmann?"

"No. Maybe. Hell, Z'ev, I don't know. They went out there to Havenwood in separate cars, and Berglund said she was as surprised to see Edelmann at the farm as he himself was, so no, I guess I don't."

Mindel tapped the picture. "He's a handsome fellow, and they say he's very effective when he goes to work on female targets. It's possible your Jillian was simply taken in by a smooth operator."

Cruz had been mulling over the dregs of his coffee cup, but he looked up, irritated. "She's not 'my Jillian,' so would you stop calling her that, please?"

Ignoring his request, Mindel asked, "Tell me, what did

your boss say when you talked to him this morning? Is he going to let you carry on with this case and bring her and Edelmann in?"

"Not exactly. I'm supposed to get in touch with French Sûreté to give them a heads-up that they may be headed that way."

"And then...?"

"And then, I'm supposed to drop it."

"And? Are you going to do that?"

"You know I'm not."

"Because....?"

Cruz pulled the nubbled black notebook out of his pocket and laid it down in front of him on the table. Resting the palm of his hand on it, he sat quietly, studying it without answering for a moment. "Because I know her now," he said finally. "I didn't before."

"And...?"

He exhaled heavily. "I honestly don't know, Z'ev. I can't stop thinking about what she's been through, and I think I can help her. I'd like to try, anyway. So what does that make me? Willfully self-destructive? Obsessed?"

"Or something. Is she pretty?"

"Yeah, I guess she is. Sort of dark and sad, mind you—and bloody aloof and mysterious, too. It's really irritating. I don't know what it is about her. I just know I can't get her or this case out of my head—especially not now, after reading what she wrote here. I need to see it through to the end."

Mindel leaned back and laced his fingers happily over his round little potbelly. "Good. So! We're off to Paris, yes?"

Cruz looked up, surprised. "We?"

"Of course. What Edelmann's done is partly a mess of my side's making. It's only right that I help clean it up. And, anyway," Mindel added, "I've had enough cocktail chatter for a while. I think I could use a good chase to clear away the cobwebs."

"Oh, no, Z'ev, I'm sorry. Not this time. I appreciate the offer of help, and in fact, there is something else I'd like you to check out for me. But Jillian's time is running out and I'll move faster on my own."

The waitress had dropped off the check, and Mindel waved Cruz away from it as he reached for his spectacles once more to peer at it. "You're probably right, dammit to hell. Okay, so go already. Tell me what you need and I'll be in touch as soon as I can. But Alex?" he added, peering over the top of his glasses.

"What?"

"Once that's done, maybe we think about a quick motorcycle run through the south of France? You could bring that Jillian. They say it's a very nice time of year to see Marseilles."

Cruz smiled. "I'll give it some thought."

CHAPTER 33

After I returned to Washington from Paris, I still wasn't ready to accept the truth—that my mother was not the war heroine her personal mythology had always made her out to be. That she had, in fact, been a traitor and collaborator, and had lied about ever having been imprisoned at the Drancy transit camp. That she had betrayed four Jewish children, their teacher, and the nuns who had sheltered them, sending them to certain death at the Auschwitz concentration camp. That she may have even betrayed Joe Meade, who I believed was also caught in that convent raid and whose name she appropriated in order to pass herself off as his wife and me as his daughter.

I canceled my plans to spend Christmas in Havenwood, blaming my workload at the Smithsonian—still too cowardly to confront my mother. Hoping that if I spent some time sifting through the American OSS files Haddon Twomey had obtained, I might still find some bit of evidence to contradict or explain what I'd learned in Paris. All my additional research did, however, was confirm that

Joe Meade and my mother couldn't possibly have produced me, since his service records place them hundreds of miles apart at the time I would have been conceived.

Those OSS records did give me one last irrational surge of hope that someone other that Colonel Braun might have been my father, though. Tom Newkirk, I discovered, had flown my mother into France when she'd first been dropped behind the lines and had gone back in several times after that. Neither of them had ever mentioned it in all the years I was growing up, part of the vast conspiracy of silence the two of them managed to maintain regarding so much of their life.

I've known since I was about thirteen that my mother and Tom were lovers, although it was never something I was encouraged or inclined to discuss. But it was around that age, I think—after my grandparents had died, at any rate—that I was sent home from school one day suffering from some flu or fever. When I walked in the door, the house seemed empty, but my mother appeared a moment later looking sheepish and flushed, hurriedly tying the sash of her silk bathrobe. Her hair, which had been caught up in her usual chignon when I'd left for school that morning, spilled messily over her shoulders. She said she'd been getting ready to take a bath, but the words rang false as she tried to delay me in the kitchen. When I finally did slip past her and drag my aching body down the hall, I saw that her bedroom door was pulled to but not entirely closed. That was when I spotted Tom through the crack at the hinges, tucking his shirt into his pants, his hair disheveled and flopping over his forehead.

I was so embarrassed that I hurried past and disappeared under my bedcovers, never letting on that I'd seen him or heard their subsequent whispers at the back door. But after that, I started watching, and the signs suddenly seemed quite obvious—his frequent visits to the house, ostensibly to help my mother with her taxes or one odd job or another, and the way they often seemed to disappear for a while; his close involvement in the building of our house right next door to his own; the convenient way my mother always remembered a specialist's appointment or some shopping she wanted to do whenever Tom had business in Minneapolis, leaving poor Sybil behind to watch over me.

When I phoned Tom last week to tell him what I'd learned in Europe and to ask him point-blank how long he and my mother had been lovers, he dashed any last hopes I might have entertained that my parentage, if confused, was still closer to home than the Third Reich. He told me with gentle but brutal honesty that he had loved my mother for more than thirty-five years but only became her lover after I was already born. I suppose I should be thankful that he showed enough respect not to lie to me, and that he said he would have been honored to be my father. But it doesn't change the fact that he was probably complicit in the fraud my mother perpetrated on Joe Meade's poor parents, not to mention the American government, since he more or less admitted that he, too, doubted his best friend had married her or fathered me. Beyond that, he refused to elaborate, saying only that I would have to discuss it with my mother.

This wasn't something I could do over the phone. I would have to confront her face-to-face. But although I showed up unannounced in Havenwood last Tuesday afternoon, I suspect my mother had been forewarned that I might appear with some hard questions. I arrived at the house about one o'clock in the afternoon and found her getting ready to leave for an appointment at the hairdresser, forestalling our conversation—which, given the terror I was feeling, was just as well.

While she was out, I'm ashamed to admit that I rummaged through the cedar chest where I knew she kept her important papers, although I can't imagine what I thought I'd find there. Love letters from Kurt Braun? Photos of her and the colonel at the Moulin Rouge? A full confession of her sins, to be opened only on her death? Really. Only a historian as addicted to paper trails as I am would indulge in such delusions. I didn't even find her immigration file, which was too bad, since it would have been an historic opportunity to examine one of her reputedly excellent forgeries—her parish marriage certificate to Joe Meade. But maybe she'd destroyed the evidence once it had served its purpose.

I did find my grandparents' wills, though. I'd never actually laid eyes on these documents before, although I had learned from Tom Newkirk when I was twenty-five that all of Helen and Arthur Meade's personal assets now belonged outright to me. By then, however, I'd washed my hands of Havenwood and had no interest in living here or having anything to do with the place. I didn't object when Tom asked me to sign a document granting my mother the right to remain in the house and have access my grandparents' funds for its upkeep as long as she lived. I was on my way to being self-supporting and saw no reason to cut her off. No matter how cool our relations were by then, she was still my mother, after all.

It was only when I read the wills the other day that it struck me how pointedly my grandparents had excluded their alleged daughter-in-law from their wills. Did they have their own suspicions about her? I wonder now. Or had they found out she was having an affair with a married man, their late son's best friend, and used their wills to express disapproval? Or was it her mothering skills or lack thereof upon which they were indirectly commenting? Regardless, it was obvious that Tom had managed their affairs to ensure my mother was well taken care of, whatever the intentions of those poor, trusting souls. He really did love her, poor man.

I waited all that afternoon for my mother to return, but with committee and newspaper business requiring her attention in town, she had no problem avoiding me into the early evening hours, even remembering a prior dinner engagement that she phoned to inform me of. Fine with me. I was in no rush. I poked around the house, going from room to room, looking for something I might have missed. I even went into the garage to see if there might be a trunk or suitcase with the documentary evidence I was still hoping would prove me wrong. There was nothing, of course.

I did come across an empty jerry can sitting next to the lawnmower. Growing more distraught with every passing hour, I began to wonder how I could go back to Washington and carry on preparing the World War II exhibit as if nothing had happened. I haven't had a real vacation in years, but when I saw that jerry can, it suddenly occurred to me that maybe I could drive back to Washington instead of fly—take a week or so to unwind and think about what, if anything, I was going to do next about what I'd learned. That was when I decided to fill the jerry can and put it in the trunk of my car.

I mention this because someone—the doctor? Nils? the FBI agent?—mentioned that the fire at the house was gasoline-primed and that I'd been seen filling the can that afternoon. It no doubt puts me in a bad light, and this explanation, I'm sure, will be seen as self-serving. All I can relate here is the truth. I filled the can in anticipation of a road trip to D.C. The last time I saw it was when I put it back in the trunk of my rental car at the Jorgensons' Chevron station. For all I know, it may still be there, if the rental car wasn't burned in the fire. If not, someone may have taken it out and used it. All I know is I didn't.

My mother didn't return until well into the evening—nearly seven, as I recall. I finally got her to sit down long enough for me to spit out what it was I'd come about and demand she tell me the truth. By the time I got to the end of recounting what I'd learned, I'd worked myself up into a bit of a frenzy, I admit. And how did she react? First, she laughed. And then, she became indignant.

"You rarely ring, Jillian. You hardly visit from one year to the next. Then, out of the blue, you come all the way out here in the middle of January to confront me with this rubbish? Have you quite taken leave of your senses?"

"I have the proof, Mother! Braun's driver kept notes on the colonel's every trip—and on the passengers he took along with him. Dates, times, where they went. One name is there, over and over—Sylvie Fournier. The name you chose when you volunteered to go underground."

"It's a common enough name."

"It was your mother's name! That was why you chose it. And the dates it shows up in the chauffeur's records? They correspond with every time Gestapo headquarters on the Avenue Foch has you listed among those picked up from Gentilly for questioning. That was you partying with that awful man, Mother, while your friends in the Resistance were being interrogated, beaten and shot."

"Don't you dare presume to lecture me on the Resistance, young lady! I was there. I lived it. You have no idea what I suffered. The sacrifices I made. The price I paid."

"The German Luftwaffe killed your father. Nellie Entwistle said you found him burning in the street. How could you forget that?"

"Forget it? Are you mad? I've never forgotten it. Do you imagine that I haven't seen my poor father over and over in my nightmares, just as Nellie and I found him that night? How could you be so cruel as to bring it up?"

I was fighting tears, but I didn't dare cry now. "I'm not trying to be cruel, Mother. I'm just having so much trouble understanding why you did what you did. That's all I've ever wanted, you know. To understand you and love you."

"What utter rubbish! You have never shown any love for me, Jillian."

"That's not true."

"Oh, yes, it most certainly is. You've been jealous of me your whole life. Don't try to deny it. You were a plain, dull little girl, and you've turned out to be a perfectly ordinary, dull woman."

"You're my mother, for God's sake. Why would I be jealous of you?"

"You felt I overshadowed you. Admit it. Is it my fault that I looked the way I did? Yet you held it against me. You always did."

"Mother, the only thing I ever held against you was that you seduced the man I loved."

She'd been pacing the floor, but at that, she stopped, dropped into her wing chair and raised her hands resignedly into the air. "Ah, yes! Of course. There it is, then. That's what this is really all about, isn't it? That stupid little episode with Nils Berglund. I can't believe you've spent all these years searching for a way to get back at me for that, Jillian. How very small of you."

"I'm not trying—"

"You are a vindictive creature to have plotted all this time to punish me for that. And it's terribly unjust of you, it really is. Not to mention," she added, "terribly stupid to still be carrying a torch for a man who's been married to someone else for over a decade and has three children and a potbelly to go with his mousy little wife."

"Mother, she isn't mousy, and that's not what this is about at all and you know it."

"Oh, isn't it?"

"Hardly. I got over Nils years ago. There've been other men in my life since him, you know."

"None who've stuck around, obviously."

"Well, touché, Mother. Thanks for pointing that out. But it's beside the point. The real reason I'm here—"

"—is to punish me for being so stupid as to comfort that boy. Fine. Go ahead. It was a moment of weakness on my part, I admit, but there he was in his naval uniform, proud and terrified at the same time as he prepared to head off to war. Well, I did know a little something about what he would be facing in just a few days. I'd been in a war myself, after all. And then...." She exhaled heavily, and a small, calculated tear rolled down her cheek. "Well, seeing him in his uniform like that, I just... Well, I had loved a naval officer myself once, you know. Nils caught me at a moment of weakness. Perhaps things got a little out of hand—"

"Perhaps?"

"Really, Jillian, you're old enough now to understand—Nils needed the comfort of a woman at a time like that. You certainly weren't there for him."

I was incredulous. "Mother, in the first place, I'd been sleeping with Nils since I was seventeen—as you well know, since you banished him from the house for weeks when you found out about it. In the second, I had no idea he was going to be on home leave that weekend, but I was just over at the Jorgenson's. You could have called. And by the way, I did find out that Nils had called ahead from San Diego a couple of days earlier to say he was coming. You apparently 'forgot' to pass the message on, or I would have been there to meet him. As it was, when I finally found out he was in

Havenwood, I got home as fast as I could. You'd gotten him so drunk by then he couldn't see straight."

"I didn't get him drunk. He was the one—"

"It was your booze, Mother. He was a nineteen-year-old nervous, stupid kid. You weren't much older than I am now. And yes, you were beautiful and you proceeded to get him drunk and seduce him. When I walked in, you were on top of him on the sofa like a terrier in heat."

She fixed me with a scowl that would have done Queen Victoria proud. "You are very crude, Jillian."

I was ready to put my fist through a window, but I was angrier with myself than I was with her. I could not believe she had diverted me with this old rubbish from the real reason I'd come.

"Mother, I couldn't care less what you did with Nils Berglund seventeen years ago. What I care about is what happened during the war. I can't understand it. How could you have slept with that Colonel Braun after what the Nazis had taken from you? After what they took from so many people?"

She sat there stone-faced, refusing to answer.

"You cannot deny this," I pressed her. "It happened. You can't even say there was an operational reason for it, because if there had been, you wouldn't have had to hide it the way you did. I met Vivian Atwater. She's a very pragmatic woman. She'd be the first to suggest that there are perfectly good strategic reasons for a Resistance fighter to sleep with the enemy."

Bernard Cohn-Levy had also suggested as much, I recalled, but I knew he'd only been being kind, and that it wasn't the way things had happened.

"That was never your assignment," I said. "Miss Atwater wasn't sure you had the self-discipline to do any kind of Resistance work behind the lines. I'm quite certain she didn't think you had the emotional stability to fuck for your country, Mother."

"Jillian! I will not listen to such filth! How dare you?"

"I don't mean to be crude. And I'm not judging you," I added wearily. "At least, I'm trying not to. As you say, I wasn't there. I can't possibly understand what you went through. What they did to you. What he did to you. I am trying to understand, though. Tell me, for God's sake. Why did you do it?"

She said nothing for a moment, then a strange look of triumph crept over her features. "You think I was bullied into it, don't you? You think I was a weak little pawn in the Colonel's hands—beaten, broken down, brainwashed? Let me tell you something, dearie, nothing—nothing—could be further from the truth."

"What do you mean?"

"Kurt did not control me. I controlled him. Of course I let him believe he had seduced me. He was the kind of man who liked to exercise that kind of power and control over others, especially women, so I let him think he could do it with me. By the time he realized it was the other way around, it was too late. I controlled him, and he was helpless to resist. Powerful as he was, there was nothing he wouldn't do for me. It was quite a thrilling feeling, to tell you the truth."

"How did you justify it to yourself? Did you think you were doing it for the Resistance?"

My mother's lips turned up in an indignant sneer. "The Resistance? I should think not. What a pathetic lot they were. Bloody, spineless little Frenchmen. Laid down their arms and let the German army march right in, didn't they? Then spent the rest of the war groveling at the Germans' feet. Oh, yes, once in a while one of them would peck ineffectively around their ankles. Not enough to make any real difference, though. An utterly hopeless bunch of weaklings and traitors, they were. I should have known, of course. After all those summers with the bloody cousins, I should have remembered what they were like. But when the war came, you know, one got quite caught up in the excitement and romance of it. One quite forgot the facts of life."

"Such as?"

"Such as a Frenchman will always be spineless, petty and self-serving. Next to them, I can tell you, your average German officer—well! All I can say is that they seemed like gods, strutting down the avenue in their fine, pressed uniforms—tall, blue-eyed, ramrod straight.

Quite beautiful, on the whole. Natural conquerors. And they knew how to live well. Oh, yes, my dear, they did. It was terribly entertaining. Really! I ask you, who wouldn't choose to eat caviar and drink champagne with towering gods over dry bread and chicory brew with a bunch of cowardly little runts?" Her robin's-egg eyes sparkled and her voice seemed to quaver with erotic excitement at the memory.

As for me, my own head was fairly reeling. This was not at all what I had expected. Denial, yes. Indignation, anger, self-justification. But childish pique at her Norman cousins justifying hatred and contempt for an entire nation? Not to mention self-serving collaboration with an enemy that had enslaved that nation and most of Europe? Oh, yes. It's safe to say I had not expected this.

And then, another thought occurred through the fog of my confusion. "What about Joe Meade, Mother? What happened with him?"

"He was captured and shot. He and that bloody Frenchwoman he was so enamored with."

"What Frenchwoman?"

She waved an irritated, dismissive hand. "Isobel Kempf. Some teacher from Alsace. Jewish, or half-Jewish, or some such thing. She'd been in England when the Germans invaded and she'd joined up with the Free French. Went back to work with the Resistance, was wounded, got smuggled back to England, where she recuperated. They put her to work temporarily in my shop—not that she was any good at documentation, mind you. But she'd been behind the lines, so every time somebody wanted to know how things were over there, it was bloody Isobel they called in."

"And Joe loved her? But I thought you and he had met up again in France after his plane went down."

"Went down?" She harrumphed. "The fool crashed his plane so he could go looking for her after she went back in. She was hiding in a convent along with some Jewish children she'd been sent to rescue. He couldn't very well get at her there, could he? I made sure it was our house the Resistance put him up in. There was just myself and old Viau there, you see, so we'd plenty of room. Viau came to be quite fond of him, as a matter of fact." She smiled. "He was a lovely man, was our Joe. So handsome. Such a big, strong, good-hearted Yank. Melt your heart, he did."

"You really were in love with him, weren't you?"

"Yes," she said quietly. A tear rolled down her cheek. "I really, truly was, you know, Jilly. He was ever so wonderful."

"But—?" I prodded, dreading what was going to come next yet unable to stop myself. Having come this far, I had to know.

She shrugged her tiny, perfect shoulder. "It was that woman he wanted. I can't imagine what he saw in her. She seemed to have cast some kind of spell over him."

"Isobel."

"Yes."

"And what happened to her?"

"She was found at the convent. She and the children. Kurt found them."

"How did Colonel Braun know they were there?"

"I don't know."

"I think you do. You told him, didn't you? If Isobel was gone, then you could have Joe. That was your plan, wasn't it?"

"She wasn't for Joe," my mother sniffed. "I'd met him first. Only then, the SOE sent me over to France. I should never have left him. It all went wrong. She was sent over, too, a couple of months after me. After London lost her radio signal, Joe came over to find her. There was no helping him as long as she was there, don't you see? I could have hidden him indefinitely, kept Braun's people away. But Isobel had to go."

"And so you told Colonel Braun that there were four Jewish children and their teacher at the convent, and he found them and had them sent to Drancy and then to Auschwitz. That's what happened, isn't it, Mother? Only you miscalculated, because Joe ended up getting caught in your net, too."

A low, guttural cry rose in her throat. Her hands gripped the arms of her chair and her face went white.

"Tell me!" I cried. "You betrayed Joe, too, didn't you?"

"He wasn't supposed to be there! It was that old fool's fault."

"What old fool?"

"Viau. He'd grown fond of Joe, as I said. When Joe told him how much he wanted to see Isobel, the old fool convinced the Mother Superior to let Joe inside the convent so the two of them could have some time together. I had no idea he'd be there when Kurt and his men showed up, or I never would have breathed a word. Oh, the fool! The fool!" my mother cried. "Why did he have to do that?"

My heart sank. "Colonel Braun found Joe Meade along with Isobel and the children. And Joe was taken away and shot as a spy, while the women and children ended up in Auschwitz. Oh, Mother...what did you do? What did you go and do? You betrayed women and children and the man you loved, and you slept with their killer and bore his child—me. And yet you still sit there and tell me you were in control of the whole show? Are you mad?"

She sat up straighter in her chair and gave me a defiant look that burned through her tears. "I was in control at the end," she said bitterly. "I had my revenge."

"What revenge? You weren't imprisoned at Drancy when the Allies came into Paris. I already know that."

"No, I was with Kurt. He was one of the last Germans to leave the city. I wanted to get away myself, back to England. But first, I had to make sure he paid for what he'd done to Joe."

"Paid how?"

"With his life," Mother said, her voice icy. "I would have killed him myself as he slept, but there were so many soldiers around him all the time that I knew I'd never make it out of the building alive. If I could get him alone, though, out in the streets, there would be a way to do it."

Suddenly, I remembered what Bernard Cohn-Levy had told me in Paris—that Colonel Braun had been beaten to death by a mob at the Porte de la Villette as he attempted to escape the city. I recounted to my mother what Cohn-Levy had said.

She smiled. "Yes, I know. I was there."

"You were? But how—?"

"I told you, Jillian—Kurt loved me. He'd have done anything to have me. He wanted me to go with him back to Berlin. He was going to go in the staff car along with several other officers, but I convinced him we'd be safer leaving together, just the two of us. I had to get him alone without his bodyguards, you see. In the end, we took a separate car and only the driver, no one else."

"And—?"

"And," she said triumphantly, "when we got to the Porte de la Villette and the car slowed, I threw off my coat, ripped my dress, then jumped out, screaming that I'd been kidnapped by the infamous Colonel Braun, the cousin of Hitler's mistress and the butcher of the lycèe children. You should have seen me, Jillian. It was an Oscar-worthy performance, truly. You can't imagine how quickly the crowd gathered. Some men began rocking the car. Someone else started ripping up the cobblestones and throwing them through the windows. Kurt and his driver were dragged out. He still couldn't believe what was happening. He pleaded with me to help him. Called me his *Liebchen,* if you can believe it. That's when someone put a cobblestone in my hand and I heaved it at the bastard. Hit him square in the head. Then another stone was thrown, and another and another. And someone set the car on fire." She leaned back in her chair, wearing a triumphant expression. "So you see, I really was in control. And I made him pay."

I probably could have killed my mother that night. I was shocked and repulsed and disgusted by every word that came out of her mouth. Even more shocked than I had been before, when I thought the worst she'd done was bear a Gestapo Colonel's baby, then pass me off as the child of American flyer Joe Meade.

But as horrified as I was, I realized, too, that she was morally bankrupt and quite possibly mad. I couldn't spend another minute in her presence, so I ran out into the night and started to walk. I didn't know where. I just had to get away from her. I was wearing only jeans and a sweater, my feet bare inside brown leather loafers, but I didn't notice the cold. Not for quite some time, anyway—long after I had passed the last house on Lakeshore Road. Finally, as the snow began to fall, I turned around and made my way back, determined to gather up my suitcase and get the hell out of there.

But when I reached my mother's house, I found it dark. I kicked off my soaked shoes in the vestibule, and as soon as I entered the kitchen, I smelled smoke and saw a red glow coming from the living room. I called for my mother and started to run to find her, but rounding the kitchen table, my heel hit a wet patch on the floor and my legs went out from under me. I tried to grab a chair for support, but it went over. The last thing I remember is the pain of my head striking the ceramic tile rim of the counter.

Then—I don't know how much later—Nils was at the back door, calling my name, and he got me out of the house and went back in for my mother. And then, I followed him back in and saw her dead blue eyes.

From that moment on, I've wanted to be dead, too. Like my mother. Like my father. And like all the others whose blood was on their hands.

CHAPTER 34

Paris, France
Monday, January 15, 1979

Cruz was off the FBI clock. Just before boarding the plane for Paris, he'd called in and left a message with the Bureau's weekend watch, saying he needed personal time to deal with an urgent family problem—failing to mention that the family in question wasn't his own. It was lame as pretexts went. He knew it wouldn't stand up to even the most superficial scrutiny, and after their conversation Sunday morning, Kessler would be particularly irritated. But with luck he'd be back in D.C. in a day or two, at which time he could see if the job was salvageable or if it was time to start scanning police want ads. In the meantime, he wasn't going to let Berglund's attacker walk, and he wasn't going to lose track of Jillian Meade—not as long as there was a chance of pulling her out of the swamp she was drowning in.

If he was cut off from access to Bureau resources and acting in no official capacity, he still had one old ace up his sleeve. This time, the Mindel card played out even faster than he'd hoped.

Cruz had just deplaned at Roissy-Charles deGaulle around 8:00 a.m. local time when he heard his name being broadcast over the airport's PA system, requesting he report to the El Al counter. From there, a ticket agent—or one of Mindel's people working in guise of a ticket agent—led him to an empty and isolated back room of the Israeli airline's administrative offices, where the man pointed to a telephone with a light flashing on the base.

"Your flight was late arriving, Mr. Cruz," the agent said. He had carrot-red hair and so many freckles that they might have made for a decent Malibu tan if there'd just been one or two more. "Your caller has been most impatient to speak with you."

"Thanks," Cruz said, waiting until he'd left and shut the door before picking up the receiver.

"Alex, finally!" Mindel's voice boomed down the line. "Are you trying to give me another stroke?"

"Sorry about that. The pilot decided to fly around some North Atlantic winter storm system. I was getting ready to jump and swim. What have you found?"

"Plenty. And by the way, this is a scrambled line we're on."

"You never cease to amaze me, Z'ev."

"I try to be helpful. I'm afraid we have a little problem, though. Our Mexico City station just called to say that Edelmann and your Jillian were spotted boarding a charter flight for Paris just before midnight last night. Edelmann's got Jillian traveling on a false Canadian passport. The agent with you there tells me the flight was due to land in fifteen minutes."

"That's not a problem. It's ideal. I can scoop them the minute they arrive."

"Afraid not. Their plane, unlike yours, landed twenty-five minutes early—and at Orly Airport to boot."

"Damn! That's on the other side of Paris, at least thirty miles from here."

"I've got people heading over there now, but I think we've missed them."

"It would've been too much to hope for, anyway." Cruz raked

a hand through his hair. "I'll just have to track them down in the city like I planned. At least we know they're here. So much for our all-points alert system. Obviously they got across the U.S. border."

"Feh! I could have told you they'd make it. Take it from me, my friend, getting into your country undetected requires a little ingenuity, but getting out is a piece of cake."

"Oh, yeah? So how many times have you done it in either direction?" Cruz held up a hand. "No, belay that. I don't want to know."

"Probably better you don't. So, what now? Any idea where they might be headed?"

"I gave it some thought on the way over. If Jillian tripped alarms when she was here last month tracking Grace's past, my best guess is that it was the lawyer, Cohn-Levy, who alerted our boy to the fact that his quarry had finally emerged."

"I don't know the man myself, except by reputation," Mindel said. "It's certainly possible."

"Guy's a dedicated Nazi hunter. Seems like a logical candidate for membership in Ariel's Claw, wouldn't you think?"

"You could do worse than pay him a visit," Mindel agreed. "But Alex, you think Edelmann might have spotted you when you were in Minnesota? Maybe you want to be keeping a low profile when you make your approach, in case Edelmann is there?"

Cruz nodded. "It could be a problem. The town was full of strangers when I was there. Edelmann obviously managed to blend in, but it's pretty safe to say I didn't—not that I was particularly trying to. I had a feeling off and on that I was being watched, but I put it down to a small town and suspicious local cops. Now, I'm wondering. At the very least, if Edelmann was keeping the hospital where Jillian was on lock-down under surveillance while he waited for his chance to get at her, he may have seen me there with the deputy police chief."

"You'll be sorry yet that you didn't take me along to Paris, bubbelah. I could've watched your back."

"You're already helping plenty."

"I'll make sure you get whatever backup you need, my friend. I have to tell you, though, I'm confused. If Edelmann's objective was to take down the collaborator who betrayed his mother and those kids at the convent, once he accomplished that, why go after the daughter?"

"Sheer bloody-mindedness, maybe? He didn't hesitate to take out those two old women in the U.K., did he, when he was trying to locate Jillian, hoping she'd lead him to Grace—which is exactly what happened. Maybe killing her wasn't enough for him. Maybe he wants to wipe all trace of Grace Meade off the face of the earth for what she did during the war—including her offspring." Cruz had another thought. "Unless..."

"Unless what?"

"Did you manage to track down that other information I asked about?"

Mindel grunted. "Oof! I nearly forgot. I did, and you were dead right about Edelmann's mother and her baby."

Cruz felt every hair on the back of his neck stand up. "Son of a... Okay, Z'ev, that's a great help. Might put his actions in an entirely different light."

"I don't get it."

"Long story. I'll explain later. I don't know whether it makes things better or worse, anyway. This Edelmann's a violent guy. Seems to me he could tip either way at this point. Right now, Jillian's promise to lead him to that Nazi gold may be the only thing keeping her alive."

"You know, she's some researcher if she figured that one out. A lot of people have tried and failed."

Cruz frowned. "The problem is, I've read and re-reread that journal of hers a dozen times now and I don't see anything there to suggest she actually *does* know where the gold is."

"You think she was bluffing?"

"Yeah, I do. Not that she wouldn't be capable of solving the puzzle, I suspect, but the gold wasn't her focus when she was over here last month. Grace was. I think it's more likely she made up a fast lie to try to save the deputy's life. The fact that Edelmann still has her in tow must mean he hasn't twigged yet, but if she is bluffing, he's going to find out very soon."

"I'm wondering if he wants that gold for the war chest of Ariel's Claw or to feather his own nest."

"No idea."

"Well, wearing my official cap, I'm hoping it's personal greed. If those fanatics get their hands on that much operational dough, our people are going to have a big headache trying to rein them in."

"Far as Jillian's concerned, it doesn't make much difference. One way or the other, if the gold is what Edelmann's after, it's a pretty safe bet that once he gets his hands on it, she's dead. And if she can't lead him to it, she's equally dead. Sooner or later, Jillian Meade will have outlived her usefulness to him."

Bernard Cohn-Levy behaved like a man who'd either been targeted for assassination in the past or received more than his share of death threats. He'd obviously had some training in personal security measures, Cruz decided.

He'd headed to the man's residential address near the Place des Vosges that Mindel's people in Paris had given him along with the keys to a dusty gray Fiat. Edelmann was a Mossad mess, Mindel had said, and if Cruz was going to help clean it up, the least Mossad could do was provide a few tools. The Fiat's rearview mirror told Cruz those tools included a tail—discreet and at a distance, but noticeable enough to leave him feeling crowded.

He arrived at the lawyer's address just in time to see a big, white-haired man who fit Jillian's description to a T emerge from the entrance of a narrow, elegant apartment block. He was alone. Cruz watched as Cohn-Levy paused at the curb next to a black

Citroën and withdrew a hand-held mirror from his pocket, then bent low to check under the chassis. After satisfying himself that there were no bombs strapped to the undercarriage, he walked around and unlocked the driver's side door, slipped behind the wheel, relocked the door, then ducked down, probably to check the steering column and brake pedals for signs of tampering. When he seemed satisfied that all was in order, he started the engine. Cruz was sitting half a block away, but even from that distance, he could see the old man wince in the nervous split second it took for the engine to kick over. Tense business, the daily life of a crusader.

As the lawyer pulled out into the road, Cruz put the Fiat in gear and followed, keeping a couple of cars back as they headed in the direction of the Seine and, he guessed, Cohn-Levy's office. Sure enough, they crossed the Pont Neuf a few minutes later, and Cohn-Levy headed left toward St-Germain-des-Prés. By the time he'd parked the Citroën and gone through what seemed to be his routine vehicle lock-up routine, Cruz had whipped the tiny Fiat into an open wedge of space on the boulevard and sprinted over. The solicitor was just withdrawing his keys from the door lock when Cruz took him by the elbow.

"Excuse me, M. Cohn-Levy, don't be alarmed." The older man was obviously startled, but to his credit, he didn't back away. Cruz held up his leather ID folder. "I'm a federal agent from the United States, FBI Special Agent Cruz. I wonder if I could have a moment of your time?"

Cohn-Levy studied his identification. "You're in a rather extra-jurisdictional situation here, are you not?"

"Yes, sir. In fact, I'm not here in any official capacity, but since I gather you've had some security problems in the past, I wanted to identify myself and reassure you that I pose no danger to you."

Cohn-Levy waved a dismissive hand. "I spend very little time worrying about that. If my enemies haven't managed to kill me by now, they might as well let God take care of this worn-out old carcass."

"Yet you do take precautions," Cruz noted, nodding at the mirror poking out of his coat pocket.

"Oh, a few, for my wife's sake. She worries. But life is too short to spend it living in constant fear, don't you think?"

"Yes, sir, I do."

"So, what was it you wanted to talk to me about, Agent...Cruz, was it?"

"Is there somewhere private we could go? Your office, maybe?"

"I am in the habit to taking an espresso at that café over on the corner there before I face the madhouse that is my office. We could get a table where we won't be seen or overheard, if that's a concern."

"Fine," Cruz said, ready for some caffeine himself after a turbulent nine-hour flight.

Once they'd settled at a corner table and ordered coffee from the waiter who'd sprinted over at the sight of the solicitor, Cruz got straight to the point. "I'm here about Jillian Meade. Do you remember her?"

"Jillian? Yes, of course, I do," Cohn-Levy said, smiling broadly, leaning forward the small, round zinc table. "A lovely young woman. She was in Paris, oh, a month or so ago, I think it was. I hope she's doing well?"

"I was hoping you could tell me."

"I don't understand."

"Do you know a man by the name of Simon Edelmann?"

"Edelmann? It doesn't sound familiar. Who is he?"

"How about Ariel's Claw?" At the mention of that name, a shadow fell across Cohn-Levy's features and he sat upright in his chair. "I see you've heard of it," Cruz said.

"What is this about, please?"

"What is your connection to that organization?"

"Am I being accused of something?"

"Have they been in contact lately?"

"I ask you again, Agent Cruz—of what am I being accused? What kind of game are you playing here?"

"No game. I'm trying to find Jillian Meade."

"Is she missing?"

"Yes, she is. She arrived in Paris this morning with Simon Edelmann. I want to know where they are now."

The waiter arrived with their espressos, but Cruz's eye never left the lawyer, who waved off the waiter and pushed his cup to the side. "Is she in some sort of legal trouble? Is that why you followed her here? Because if so, I will be the first to volunteer to represent her, and I can assure you, she will receive the fullest protection afforded by French law. She is a fine woman and—"

"I believe she's in serious trouble. She's been effectively kidnapped by this Edelmann and her life may be in immediate, grave danger. So rather than you and I continuing to toss challenges back and forth, if you're as fond of Miss Meade as you claim to be, do you think you could help me out here?"

"You say she's been kidnapped?"

"Yes. I think you know something of Miss Meade's research into her mother's dubious wartime service with the French Resistance?" Cohn-Levy nodded soberly, and Cruz continued. "Not long after she met with you, this Edelmann apparently picked up Jillian's trail and followed her back to her mother. Grace Meade was subsequently murdered in what appears to be a revenge killing for her wartime collaboration, which led to the deaths, among others, of four young Jewish girls."

"Jillian's mother has been murdered? And it had to do with those little girls hidden by the nuns at Gentilly?"

"Exactly. It turns out the teacher arrested with the children was the mother of this Simon Edelmann, so there seems to be a personal angle here. Now, Edelmann has Jillian and he's brought her back here to Paris."

"Why?"

"Because he thinks she'll lead him to a cache of gold stolen from the Nazis in 1944. When he finds out she can't—and I really don't think she can—he's probably going to kill her."

Cohn-Levy crossed his arms over his barrel chest, his white brows knitting together. "This is really beyond the pale, even for those outlaws."

"Ariel's Claw, you mean?"

"Yes, of course."

"You're saying you don't support them?"

"Absolutely not. They're common assassins, nothing more."

"I gather the group is dedicated to hunting down Nazi war criminals. Isn't that your main focus, as well?"

"There is a great difference between their methods and mine," Cohn-Levy said indignantly. "I hunt war criminals, yes, but I use legal weapons to bring them to justice. I follow the laws of humanity, not the law of the jungle. It is slow and tedious business, gathering evidence, building cases. Often our targets disappear or die before we can bring them to trial, but it can't be helped. They destroyed my own family, you know. And I will admit, there was a black time when I wanted to take necks in my bare hands and...."

Cohn-Levy's hands had lifted off the table, and his beefy fingers clenched the air for a moment in a way that left little doubt they still possessed the strength to throttle the life out of his enemies. Then, they dropped back into his lap.

"The Nazis perverted the laws of civilized conduct," he said, "destroying people's lives at will. I came to the realization that if we behave in the same way, we are no better than they were. We would deserve to be dumped on history's garbage heap, just as Hitler and his followers have been." The old man sighed heavily. "So, no, Agent Cruz, to answer your question, I do not support the activities of Ariel's Claw, nor anyone else who thinks they have the God-given right to serve as judge, jury and executioner over another human being, no matter how they justify it."

"Then I apologize for suggesting you did, sir. I take it you are aware of the organization, though. Have they approached you?"

The lawyer took a sip of his coffee, then set the cup down on the round table and nodded. "Once or twice, but not for many years now. I think the word is out that crazy old Cohn-Levy is a bit of a procedural fanatic with little patience for lynch mobs."

Cruz reached into his pocket and pulled out the picture of Edelmann that Mindel had given him. "Have you ever seen this man?"

Cohn-Levy studied the photo, then shook his white mane. "This is the man who has Jillian? So young to be involved in such ugly business."

"He's never come to you?"

The lawyer handed back the photo. "No, never."

Cruz tapped the picture against the rim of his cup. "Well, someone here in Paris had to have been in contact with him. He picked up Jillian's trail not long after she left here. We think he backtracked and killed two of her contacts in the U.K. in an effort to learn where she and her mother lived. Who else would have known about Grace's collaborationist activities and tipped him off?"

"Oh, well—that list could be quite long, actually."

"How so?"

"I made some more inquiries after Jillian left," Cohn-Levy said. "It turns out a number of people in that Gentilly neighborhood had come to the conclusion this 'Sylvie Fournier' was the one who'd betrayed those convent refugees. Apparently someone spotted her with Colonel Braun just a day or two after the Gestapo sweep of the neighborhood in which she and so many others were picked up for questioning. Word soon got around that, while others from the neighborhood were languishing in jail, 'Sylvie' was out shopping for truffles."

"Everyone knew?" Cruz said, sitting up straighter.

"So it seems."

"That's not what Jillian's journal says."

"What journal?"

Cruz drew the nubbled black notebook from his inside pocket. It was getting dog-eared by now from all the times he'd gone through it.

He explained to Cohn-Levy about Jillian's suicide attempts and how she'd wanted to leave a record of what she'd learned about her mother's activities. "In it, she talks about the help you gave her. But after she left you, she went over to Gentilly to try to find someone else—anyone—who could offer an alternative explanation for what had happened back in '44. It seems there weren't too many original residents left, but she did meet a fellow who ran a bar. His name was..." Cruz flipped through the pages until he found the right entry. "...Jacques Aubert. He was apparently a nephew of a Resistance member who was shot after that gold heist. This Aubert was just a kid at the time, but he said he remembered 'Sylvie Fournier' well because she was a real beauty and he had quite a crush on—" Cruz smacked the table. "That's it!"

"What?"

"Aubert! He pumped Jillian for information on her mother's whereabouts. Kept pouring drinks, she said, invited her to dinner. Jillian's journal is a little disjointed in places where she was working off the effects of the meds they'd given her at the hospital, but I think she was trying to say she'd been distraught by the time she ran into Aubert, and she worried how much she might have told him while he kept refilling her glass. Somewhere in the back of her mind, she must have realized there was a chance she'd spilled her guts that night and mentioned she'd been in touch with those two old friends of her mother's. How else would anyone have known to go after them? People here had no idea that 'Sylvie' was actually an English SOE operative. Aubert has to be one of the informants Edelmann had engaged to keep an ear open for any word on her whereabouts."

"I can get you the location of this man's bar, if that would help," Cohn-Levy said.

"It would, thanks," Cruz said, draining his cup in one swallow. Cohn-Levy followed suit and they paid their tab and left the café heading for his office. En route, Cruz shared one other bit of information. "There's something else that's been bothering me about all these accounts of Grace's activities here in France. Aubert may be just the person to clear it up."

"What's that?"

"Between her work with the Resistance and her collaboration—partying at the Moulin Rouge, bedding Colonel Braun at the George V Hotel—when did she have time to be pregnant? Was she drinking champagne and dancing right up to the day she dropped that baby? It's what Jillian wrote in her journal—the numbers aren't adding up, and numbers don't lie."

"Now you've lost me."

"Put it this way—how likely is it that a twelve-year-old boy had the hots for a pregnant woman? Have you ever known a kid that age who wasn't embarrassed by the very idea? I haven't. And think about this, the Drancy files you showed Jillian said just one baby was born there on Bastille Day, which she's always believed was her birthday, and that was to a woman named Isobel."

"Isobel Kempf, the teacher arrested with the children at the convent."

"Exactly. Isobel was the lover of Joe Meade, the American pilot Grace claimed to have married. As I told you, Isobel is also the mother of Simon Edelmann. She emigrated to Jerusalem after the war, remarried after she learned Joe and her baby had both been killed, and had Simon in 1949. There's nothing in Jillian's journal to say whether that Bastille Day baby born at Drancy was male or female, but a friend of mine who works in Mossad was able to find out that Edelmann's lost half sibling was, in fact, a girl."

Cohn-Levy stopped dead in his tracks, prompting curses from pedestrians behind them on the sidewalk, who nearly collided with him. "Jillian was Isobel's baby!"

"I think so."

"Grace Meade stole the baby?"

"It makes sense, if you think about it. Joe Meade was so desperate to find Isobel when her radio signal was lost that he ditched his plane to come looking for her. Why? He loved her, yes, but he also must have known she was carrying their child. When he arrived in Paris, the Resistance put Joe up in the house of Viau, the printer. Even if Grace never laid eyes on Isobel while she was in hiding in the convent, there's a good chance Joe might have told her Isobel was pregnant. Then, after he was killed and Isobel was arrested and sent to Drancy, the Allies landed in Normandy and the tide of the war started to turn. Grace was smart enough to know the days of German Occupation were numbered. It didn't take a genius to figure out how collaborators would be dealt with afterward, so she started to plan her escape. England was too close, but if she could escape to America—"

Cohn-Levy's eyes went wide and his hands cupped his face in horror. "So she pretended to be Joe Meade's widow and the mother of his infant child."

"Right. Had he written to his folks back in the States to tell them he was going to be a father? Who knows? And whether or not he had, Grace knew the baby would be her ticket to freedom. Who could resist a beautiful widow with a tiny, fatherless babe in arms?"

"Isobel and the baby were already in the transit camp by then. How would Grace have gotten her hands on the child?"

"Would Drancy have fallen within Colonel Braun's jurisdiction?"

"Very likely," Cohn-Levy said, nodding. "At the very least, a permit from a Gestapo colonel authorizing the transfer of an inmate, even an infant, would not have been questioned by the commandant at Drancy, who was a much more junior functionary."

"And Grace was a forger, don't forget, in a position to pilfer all kinds of official Gestapo stationery through her relationship with Braun. He wouldn't have had to know a thing about it."

"She had to have taken the baby before Isobel and the others were shipped to Auschwitz—before the infants in the nursery were murdered," Cohn-Levy added quietly. He turned to Cruz. "And therein lies the irony, does it not? If Grace stole the baby to save herself, in doing so, she also saved Jillian's life."

Following Cohn-Levy's directions, Cruz reached Aubert's brasserie in Gentilly just after ten. By then, an advance team of what he was coming to think of a "Mindel's Merry Men" had already arrived and had the place staked out—alerted, no doubt, by the tail who'd been following Cruz since the airport. Cruz, grimly satisfied that his old jungle fighter skills weren't entirely gone, had stolen up from behind and surprised them as they waited for him to emerge from Cohn-Levy's office. One of the men in the tail car turned out to be the redheaded ticket agent from the El Al counter—Solomon, he said his name was. Cruz had brought him up to speed on where the hunt was leading.

As he and his tail pulled into a side street that gave access to the bar's front and back entries, one of the pre-positioned watchers slipped over to meet them.

"The suspects are here," the watcher told Solomon. "They went into the brasserie about thirty minutes ago and sat at a corner table, drinking coffee until the morning patrons cleared out. About ten minutes ago, the owner turned the sign in the window to Fermé, locked the front door and pulled the blinds. There's been no movement since."

"Edelmann will be armed," Cruz noted. "Possibly the owner, as well."

"And the woman?" Solomon asked. He seemed to be the team leader.

"Absolutely not. We need to be clear on this. She's a hostage here. Our first priority is to extricate her safely."

The four Mossad agents exchanged glances. "We're under

orders to separate Edelmann and take him into custody," Solomon told Cruz.

"He's wanted for murder in the U.S. and he's also a suspect for two homicides in the U.K. You people are planning to turn him over, aren't you?"

"I don't know what happens next, Agent Cruz. Our orders are to take him out of commission."

This wasn't right, Cruz thought. Was Mossad planning to spirit Edelmann back to Israel? Deal with him themselves in an effort to try to minimize damage to relations with the U.S. and Britain? Or, it suddenly occurred to him, were these Merry Men actually Ariel's Claw, here to rescue one of their own? Mindel had arranged the backup and Cruz was confident his friend was clean, but Mindel had said himself there was no knowing who belonged to that secret cabal.

"The first order of business is ensuring no innocent bystanders get hurt," Cruz told Solomon. "Otherwise, you're going to have the French strip your hides as well as Washington and London. Are we agreed?"

"Agreed," Solomon said reluctantly.

"So here's how it's going to go down. I'll go in alone, scout things out, see if there's a chance to talk Edelmann out peacefully. You guys give me one of your walkie-talkies and stand by. If he starts firing in there, or you don't get a signal from me in twenty minutes, you come in."

Solomon's red head wobbled dubiously. "I don't know...."

"I'll go to the back door. You keep an eye on the front. If all hell breaks loose, you can go ahead and charge the place—and then be prepared to be thrown out of the country faster than you can say persona non grata. Deal?"

"All right. But I'm giving you ten minutes." Solomon glanced at his watch. "Starting now." He handed over a radio.

Cruz hooked it on his belt and headed for the bar's back entrance. The door there was locked with what looked to be a sturdy dead bolt. Next to it stood a pile of empty Kronenburg beer cases. High on the wall overhead, a narrow window stood propped open an inch or two. Cruz glanced around the empty alley, then arranged the beer cases in a two-step pile and climbed to the top, gripping the windowsill to steady himself on the wobbly crates. He was eye level to the window now. It was about two feet wide, big enough to slip through if he could open it all the way. He unlatched the retaining bar to open it as far as it would go, but he got only a couple of extra inches out of it before the bar, fastened to the sill, stopped it from swinging wider.

Cruz reached into his pocket for the Fiat's keys and glanced at his watch. A minute and a half already gone. Using the cut edge of the key, he worked at the screw holding the locking bar, but it was rusted in place and there was no turning it. He cursed under his breath and was about to climb down off the crates and try his hand at the dead bolt on the back door when he noticed the wooden sill plate under the metal bracket holding the locking bar. The paint was striated and peeling, and when he poked at the wood with the key, he found it water-damaged and half rotted away. He dug around the base of the metal plate until he had worked a hole beneath it and his key struck the threads of the screw holding it down. From there, it was short work to dig the hole a little wider and jimmy the plate loose. When it was free, the window swung wide, and he was hit by the combined pungent odors of chlorine and urine. He found himself down looking into a grimy bathroom.

As a truck lumbered noisily down the cobblestoned street at the end of the alley, Cruz hefted himself up and over the sill, landing lightly on the tile floor on the other side. He paused, listening, but except for the receding rumble of the truck outside, there was only silence. He glanced once more at his watch. Four more minutes lost. Damn. Withdrawing his gun from his waist holster, he moved to the door and pressed an ear against the wood. Nothing. It opened a crack, and he peered out into the bar.

The white shades were drawn against the morning sun and any prying eyes. Light gleamed off the polished steel beer spigots and off the rows of glasses stacked on glass shelves against a mirrored wall behind the bar, but the place seemed empty.

Cautiously, he stuck his head out farther. The back door was to his left, still locked, and there wasn't a soul in the place. How could that be? Solomon's people had had both doors under surveillance ever since Edelmann and Jillian arrived. They'd also seen the owner.

Then, Cruz spotted another door at the far end of the bar. Ducking low to keep the bar between him and it, he threaded his way between tables, plastering himself against the door frame, gun poised and ready. He paused again to listen. Nothing. He reached with his right hand and slowly depressed the handle. The latch gave, but when he pushed against the door, it didn't budge.

Frowning, he turned to face it and only then noticed the bolted latch high on the frame. He slid the bolt off quietly, and this time, when the latch released, the door opened. Inside, he found a small, dark, windowless room, crowded with a steel desk and chair, a file cabinet, and walls lined with crates of whiskey, gin, Pernod and vodka. Hardly enough room to walk in, and no Edelmann, no Jillian, no Jacques Aubert.

Frowning, he closed the door and turned back to the empty bar. Where the hell could they have gotten to? He'd come in through the only rest room, and the back door was sealed. This little office was the only other room in the place. He went to the front window and peered out through the edge of one of the blinds. Across the street, he could see Solomon's red head as he sat behind the wheel of his car, pretending to read the morning edition of *Le Monde*. Cruz nodded, and Solomon dropped the newspaper and looked ready to move out, but Cruz held up a restraining hand. *Wait.* The agent settled back into his seat, frowning.

Cruz dropped the blind and turned back to the empty room.

Moving to the end of the bar, he lifted the latched counter section. As he stepped through, the floor under his foot shifted a fraction of an inch. Cruz's gaze dropped to see that he was standing on a trap door. A rubber mat that must normally cover it was rolled back and tucked under the bar. A wine cellar, he decided. And what else had Jillian written about? Tunnels. There was a rabbit warren of tunnels down there, evidently dug by the Resistance during the war to connect various safe houses in the neighborhood.

Crouching low, he hooked a finger through the iron ring embedded in a recessed hold, lifting the heavy trap door just enough to see below. A damp, musty smell rose to meet his nostrils. Wooden steps led down to a packed earthen floor, and although the cellar seemed dark, when his eyes adjusted from the bright filtered sunlight of the bar, he realized there was a faint light down there. He listened again. Nothing.

Opening the hatch wide now, Cruz dropped his head in to look around. He could see little from his high vantage except the base of what appeared to be row after row of wine racks, dimly lit by a single clear light bulb suspended from the ceiling. Taking a deep breath, he scuttled down the wooden steps. The wine cellar was about twenty feet long and nearly as wide, all of its brick walls lined with dusty wooden bottle racks, except the one on the back, which held three enormous oak brandy barrels laid on their sides, embedded right into the white plaster. The earthen floor was packed hard, muffling his step as Cruz moved forward cautiously, ears pricked.

And then he heard it, and froze. A low murmur of voices, coming from...?

From behind one of the wine racks on the other side of the cave. He crossed over and peered around the end of it. It stood flush against the brick wall, and yet now that he was closer, he heard the distinct murmur of voices. A man, and then, briefly, a woman. Jillian, he was sure of it. But how—?

He pushed against the rack and immediately it gave way. There was an open bolt hole in the floor and, he now saw, a raised, heavy iron bolt cleverly attached to the back of the rack between the bottom row of bottles where it would be all but invisible to anyone who didn't know it was there. As he swung the false door wider, he saw an earthen tunnel beyond, reinforced at intervals by wooden shoring, curving away to the right about fifty feet in. A pale light shone from the bend. Cruz stepped into the tunnel and moved forward, sidestepping an electrical conduit that ran the length of the tunnel, grateful for the earthen floor, less well packed here than in the wine cellar, that softened his footsteps.

When he reached the bend in the tunnel, he paused, listening.

"...says you know." A male voice, speaking English with an accent that reminded Cruz of Mindel's. Edelmann.

"But I do not!" Another male voice, heavy French accent. Aubert, obviously.

Cruz ducked low and peeked around the corner. The passageway continued straight for another thirty feet or so, then seemed to come to an abrupt end, the wall bricked up. There was obviously a chamber of some sort off to one side, however, illuminated by an electric light that seemed brilliant compared to the gloom of the tunnel, although Cruz guessed it was probably the same sort of single bulb that he'd seen in the cellar. He rounded the corner and inched his way along the tunnel, keeping his back to the wall and holding his gun at the ready.

"You might as well tell him, M. Aubert." Jillian. Her voice was clear. She sounded all right. "He'll get it out of you one way or another if you don't. Is it really worth it? You'll lose the gold, but surely that's better than losing your life."

"But I do not know! Simon, I swear, if I had known, would I not have told you?"

"Would you?"

Cruz smiled. Nice job, Jillian. She was trying to turn them against each other.

"Yes, of course!" Aubert protested. "It was our deal, no? I have searched and searched. I have reopened meters and meters of tunnel bricked up after the war. Ten years I have been looking, but if it was hidden down here, I have not found it. I thought you said she would know what happened to it!"

"I said she might."

"And I got in touch with you, did I not, just as soon as she showed up?"

"Not bloody soon enough, Jacques."

"But I called the number you left! Is it my fault you didn't get the message for nearly a week?"

"You put me to a great deal of trouble. All you had to do was find out where Sylvie was. And what do you tell me? 'In Minnesota.' Do you have any idea how big Minnesota is? Why not just say she's somewhere in America?"

"She said Sylvie lived now in a small town!"

"Minnesota is a state, you fool, half the size of France."

"How was I supposed to know that? Anyway, I gave you names of those women who should have known. And you did find Sylvie, I think?"

"Only after going to a great deal of trouble. Fortunately, she did lead me back to 'Sylvie.'"

"There, you see?"

"But Sylvie—or Grace, I suppose we must call her now," Edelmann said, "claimed to have had no part in the Resistance operation to steal the gold. She was bargaining for her life at that point, so I tended to believe her."

"But it was obviously a lie. You must know this, I think. Otherwise, why would you have brought the daughter along?"

There was silence for a moment. Cruz took a chance and peered around the corner. There was a short passage off the main one, maybe six or eight feet, and then a broken brick wall. Beyond, in a small room that might once have been part of the cellar of a neighboring building or just a Resistance hidey hole, he saw the three of them. Jillian was all in black—black dress, open black coat, black boots. Probably the outfit Dr. Kandinsky had brought her to wear to her mother's funeral. She was perched on the edge of a crate off to one side of the room, looking hot and tired, but otherwise alert. Cruz recognized Edelmann from Mindel's photograph—curly hair, mustache, wearing a brown leather jacket and blue jeans, looking for all the world like a musician or a young professor, except for the 9mm Beretta in his right hand. Aubert, bald and bullet-headed, had on a white shirt, black vest and a nervous expression. He was seated on another crate to Jillian's left.

Edelmann stepped in front of Jillian and paused for a moment, reaching to smooth the soft bangs at her forehead. She recoiled and brushed his hand away. "I had my reasons for bringing her," he said. "She's been a naughty girl. She told me at first that she knew where the gold was." He turned to Aubert "But en route, she said it was actually you who'd admitted when you were drunk that you had it."

"I am never drunk," Aubert said indignantly. "And if I had forty million francs worth of gold in my possession, do you imagine I would spend all day on my poor feet tending working-class patrons in a poor little brasserie in Gentilly? This is madness, Simon, surely you see that! Miss Meade, tell him it was you who drank too much that evening. Obviously you have made a mistake."

She shrugged. "I remember what I remember, but if you'd rather go on denying it, M. Aubert, I don't see that I can do anything about it. I'm sorry," she added to Edelmann, "I guess you went to all this trouble for nothing. He doesn't want to tell you where he's put it, so you won't have your blood money, after all."

"But I do not have it!" Aubert cried.

"Shut up, Jacques!" Edelmann snapped. "And you," he added to Jillian, "you're making me very angry, after all the trouble I went through for you. You said you had discovered where the gold was."

"I would never waste a minute of my time hunting for that gold," Jillian said contemptuously. "It's blood money. Those people it was stolen from were murdered. You know that, Simon! Mourn them, not the damn gold. I hope it really was thrown down a well and lost forever. I only said I knew where it was so you'd leave Nils alone—but then you went and shot him, anyway. And for what? For nothing. This has all been for nothing."

Edelmann sighed. "No, not for nothing. After all, I did find her at last, didn't I?"

"My mother."

"Don't call her that!" he said angrily. "She was a demon."

"That makes me the demon child, doesn't it? So why don't you just finish what you started? Go ahead, kill me, too." She waved her hand at Aubert. "Then the two of you can rip each other's hearts out, as far as I'm concerned. Oh, no, sorry, my mistake. You have no hearts, either of you. You couldn't possibly, if you killed those two poor women in England. They were innocent."

"The one in London sent that whore over here!"

"Vivian Atwater was a great woman, brilliant and kind and one of the true heroes of the war. Her work helped save millions and win the war. How dare you presume to sit in judgment of her? And what about poor Nellie Entwistle? What did she ever do?"

"She was a fool. I might have left her alive if she'd told me what I wanted to know. Instead, she blathered on and on and on about dear, sweet, wonderful Grace and what an angel and a heroine she was. Such garbage coming out of that woman's mouth! She wouldn't shut up. And when I told her the woman was a bitch and a murderer, she became hysterical. What was I supposed to do?"

"What you do best, I guess. So, go ahead, Simon. Kill me now, too."

"Shut up!"

"Go on, do it."

"I don't want to kill you!"

"Yes, you do. I'm the bastard child of that whore and her Nazi butcher lover. Go ahead. You'd be doing me a favor."

"Shut up, I said! Don't open your mouth again, or I swear, I'll—"

"What? Shoot me? Do it!"

"No!" Cruz yelled from the tunnel.

Edelmann spun and fired, but the bullet ricocheted off the brick opening. Cruz returned one shot before Edelmann leapt to the side, yanked Jillian to her feet, and wrapped his free hand around her neck. The Beretta was at her head as Cruz stepped around the opening in the cave. Aubert had dropped to the floor and was cowering against the far wall.

"You!" Edelmann cried.

"It's all over," Cruz told him. "The outside of this place will be crawling with French flics any minute, Edelmann. There are Mossad agents out there, too, come to take you down. There's nothing for you here. Give it up."

"Not a chance. You back off or I'll kill her."

Cruz glanced at Jillian, but her face was utterly calm, and the sickening realization dawned on him that she was utterly ready to die. She didn't know. She really didn't know. She was so grief-stricken over what Grace had turned out to be that she hadn't been able to see what was right there all the time—that Grace's legacy of betrayal and death didn't belong to her.

"You won't kill her," Cruz told Edelmann. "Not when it's taken you all these years to find her. How could you kill your own sister?"

There was a moment of silence. Then Jillian whispered, "What are you talking about?"

Cruz turned his gaze on her pale, pale face. "His mother is Isobel Kempf. Edelmann here was born in Israel in 1949, but he was Isobel's second-born child. Her first was a baby girl born in the Drancy transit camp on Bastille Day in 1944. Isobel

Kempf was the woman Joe Meade loved, not Grace. Isobel was the woman he came to France to find. That baby girl born at Drancy was Joe's daughter. That baby girl was you, Jillian."

"Don't call her that!" Edelmann bellowed. Jillian flinched, but he held on to her tightly. "It's not her name! It's just the name that whore gave her."

"Oh, of course. That makes sense. I'm sorry," Cruz said, as calmly as he could. Jillian looked as if she were going to pass out any minute, but he needed to keep Edelmann talking. "What did your mother name her, Simon?"

"'Joelline.' That woman perverted it, changed it to Jillian. My mother called her 'Joelle' for short. Joelle, not Jillian."

"After Joe, I'd imagine. That's a nice name."

"What are you two talking about? How could I..." Jillian's voice faded.

"Edelmann, sit her down, for God's sake," Cruz said. "Can't you see she's in shock? She really doesn't know."

Edelmann backed her toward the crate and lowered her onto it once more, but he kept a close grip on her and the barrel of the gun never left her temple.

"You should let her go," Cruz said.

"I can't do that. Not now. From here on in, we stay together, she and I."

"Simon, explain yourself," Jillian said. She drew a deep breath and her color was a little better as she sat up straighter. There was some fight left in her yet, Cruz thought. Good. She was going to need it. "We only met on that plane from Washington," she said. "I'm not totally stupid. I thought it was odd you were so friendly on that flight. Now, of course I know it's just because you were using me to get to my mother."

"She wasn't your mother, Joelle!" Then, Edelmann shook his head and a bemused look crept over his face. "Although to tell you the truth, I didn't know that, either, until I actually saw you. I had no idea. We'd tried for years to convince Maman that her baby girl had died at Drancy. Everyone had been telling her that since the end of the war, but she refused to believe it. She kept saying that an angel had come to take her baby away and keep her safe. All these years, we thought the poor woman was delusional. She's always been frail, you know, since the concentration camp. But then, I tracked you down at the museum where you work. What a shock, to actually see you."

Edelmann loosened his grip for a moment, and his free hand stroked her head gently. "You look like her—like our mother. It was quite an extraordinary moment. I realized she'd been right all these years when she kept insisting you were still alive. That's why she left me and my father and came back to France, you know. She thought you were still here. She was trying to find you. Poor woman! How could she have known that Sylvie wasn't Sylvie at all—much less an angel—and that she'd stolen you and taken you all the way to America?"

Jillian shook her head. "Oh, no. Simon, I'm sorry for what happened to your mother, but that can't possibly be. You must be mistaken."

"No, I think he's right," Cruz told her. "I read your journal. Most of the pieces were there, only you couldn't see the pattern because you were too close to it all. It never occurred to you that Grace might not be your mother. I did some checking on my own, and through someone I know inside Mossad, the Israeli intelligence service, and it all fits. Joe and Isobel were your parents, not Joe and Grace—and certainly not Colonel Braun. Grace forged a permit on Braun's Gestapo letterhead allowing her to remove you from the Drancy camp. She forged the marriage certificate to convince the U.S. Army to treat her as a war bride and ship the two of you to the States. She was desperate to get out of Europe before the post-war recriminations started. You talked to Tom Newkirk. So did I. He never believed Joe married Grace, but he kept quiet because he wanted to see Grace in Havenwood. He told me he knew Joe had fallen in love with a French girl name Isobel. The only thing he didn't know was that they'd had a child together."

Still, Jillian looked dubious. And little wonder, Cruz thought. But there might be one way to convince her.

"Aubert here knew the woman who called herself Sylvie when she worked with the Resistance. You showed him Grace's picture," Cruz reminded her. "Didn't she, Aubert?"

"Yes," the barkeep said meekly from his perch in the corner.

"And this Sylvie—you said you were infatuated with her as a boy, didn't you?"

"Oh, yes, very much so. She was so beautiful."

"And you saw her frequently around the neighborhood right up to the day she disappeared?"

"Mais, oui."

"And in all that time, did you ever see her pregnant? Expecting a baby?" Cruz added, when Aubert seemed confused.

"Enceinte? Mais, non. Never. Sylvie—you could enclose her tiny waist with your two hands. She was slim and beautiful, always."

Cruz turned back to Jillian. "So, you see—"

Suddenly, an ear-splitting bang shattered the air and the chamber filled with smoke. Cruz hit the ground and rolled toward Edelmann and Jillian, knocking the Israeli's legs out from under him and simultaneously pushing Jillian to the ground. He was deafened, but he could see the muzzle flash as Edelmann opened fire, backing toward the only escape route, the opening in the brick wall leading back to the tunnel. Cruz dragged Jillian behind the crate and threw himself over her as muffled thumps sounded in his ears, over and over. Wood splinters flew off the edges of the crate, and the bricks and mortar kicked up sparks and dust like a meteor storm. They were pinned down under the fire, and all he could do was wait until Edelmann's clip ran out or he had an opening to return fire.

It seemed to go on forever, but then, as suddenly as it had

started, it was over and there was an eerie stillness. Smoke and the smell of cordite hung suspended in the air as Cruz looked over the top of the crate. Aubert was rolled into a fetal ball on the far wall, just to the left of the cave opening, trembling but apparently unhurt, sweat gleaming on his bald head.

Edelmann had not fared as well. He sat slumped against the far wall of the tunnel, eyes open, blood streaming down the wall behind his head from the fatal shot he looked to have taken just above the right ear.

Light filled the tunnel, coming from the direction of Aubert's wine cellar, and Cruz hesitated as a shadow moved across it. Then, Solomon, the redheaded Mossad agent, appeared in the opening to the cave, smoking pistol in hand. Back-lit as he was by the bright lights his comrades had brought down into the tunnel, he looked as if his hair were on fire, and Cruz couldn't help thinking of Grace's father, the way she and Nellie Entwistle had found him in that Dover street that night of the Blitz.

Solomon turned to Cruz and mouthed something, but Cruz pointed to his ears and shook his head. Solomon lifted an inquiring thumb and telegraphed the question. You okay?

Cruz reached back a hand and helped Jillian to her feet, then watched Aubert unroll himself on the floor. "We're okay," he said, nodding, "or we will be in an hour or so, when the hearing comes back."

Jillian looked around, confused, then her gaze settled on Edelmann. Her hands flew to her mouth, and she must have let out a cry, but Cruz couldn't hear it. He steadied her as she stood, rocking slowly, her shocked gaze on Edelmann. Finally, she dropped her hands and took a deep breath. Stepping away from Cruz, she crouched before this half brother she'd known as such for only moments before he was killed—staring into his face as if trying to memorize his features.

Their hearing would return in a couple of hours after the effects of the shock incendiary wore off, Cruz thought, watching her reach out and close Edelmann's eyes, but the losses she had suffered were far greater and more permanent. Her life had been ripped apart at an early age by atrocities of war and acts of incredible, selfish cruelty. How long would it take her to come to terms with all the paradoxes and 'what ifs'? What if Grace's fiancé, or her father, hadn't been killed in the war? She might have lived her life as a vain and doted-upon publisher or a naval officer's wife, scanning the Queen's Honor Roll for titles she thought should be hers.

What if Joe and Isobel had managed to escape from occupied France? Edelmann here would never have been born.

What if Isobel had accepted that her baby girl was gone and been able to be the mother to Simon that she'd wanted to be to her little Joelle? Edelmann might never have turned angry, vengeful and murderous.

And what if Grace Meade had never stolen a baby girl to save her own skin? Jillian might have perished like all the other child victims of the Holocaust, and Helen and Arthur Meade would have been doubly bereaved, losing their only son and never knowing their beloved granddaughter. This exceptional woman before him would never have lived—and that, Cruz thought, would have been the greatest tragedy of all.

POSTSCRIPT

People get lost in time of war. Some lose their lives. Some lose their homes and their families. Some lose their moral compass. Maybe the last is the worst of all.

It's been a month since I returned to Washington, and I'd be lying if I said I'm dealing well with all of it. I don't know if I'll ever fully come to terms with the twists of fate that have brought me to this place.

But at a certain point, I think, we either accept the past or it buries us. We choose whether to be victims or survivors—that's what Bernard Cohn-Levy and Alex's friend, Z'ev Mindel, have both said during the hours I've spent talking with them since the day I learned the truth about who I am. I'm sure they're right.

I can't help wishing I weren't the only survivor of my family, though. First of all, there's the guilt, which both Bernard and Z'ev have talked to me about at length, both of them experts on the subject after all the family they lost in the Holocaust. It's guilt-inducing and it's lonely—but then, I remind myself, many people are left alone every day, one way or another. And as Z'ev also says (he seems to have an appropriate aphorism for every occasion, that old rascal), "When all is said and done, sweetie, we're about as tragically lonely as we make up our minds to be."

I wish my mother—my real mother, Isobel—could have understood that. Her life since the war seems to have been so sad. After Simon was killed, I went to see her in the convalescent home in Tours, south of Paris, where she'd been living for the past year or so. They say her health, both physical and mental, was never very good after Auschwitz. She'd suffered two heart attacks last year, and just a couple of weeks before I saw her, she'd had a massive stroke. When I arrived, she was failing badly, virtually comatose, her eyes open but staring vacantly. She seemed so small, lying in that big, white hospital bed—long-legged, like me, but utterly wasted by the illnesses that were carrying her away before we could ever get to know one another. Even so, I could see what Simon had meant when he'd said I bore a resemblance to her.

They say hearing is the last sense to go, so I tried speaking to her, though my college French seemed wholly inadequate. Still, when I leaned over and kissed her and said, *"Maman? C'est Joelle,"* she seemed to focus on me for a moment, and a hint of a smile appeared briefly on her lips. I think it did, anyway. I'm not really sure.

But I held her hand all that afternoon and into the evening, stroking it and telling her how sorry I was that we'd lost each other all those years ago. Talking to her about anything and everything, switching finally to English when my French vocabulary gave up the gnost. There's magic, they say, in the language of mothers and children. I like to think she understood me. I especially like to think that she knew I was there when she drew her last breath. I hope she knew she wasn't alone.

And then, there's Grace. If I was angry with her before, it was nothing compared to what I felt when I learned the full extent of what she'd done. When I thought about her lying next to my grandparents in the Meade family plot back in Havenwood, there was a moment when I even considered having her body exhumed—preferably to be flung to the wolves. But then, I decided to let the past—and Grace—lie in peace.

Maybe it was talking to Tom Newkirk that did it. I'd actually called him after I got back to find out how Nils was doing but inevitably, the subject of Grace came up and the whole ugly truth came tumbling out of my mouth. Poor Tom. He sounds as if he's aged two decades since she died, and in spite of everything, he's still in love with her. And, as he pointed out, she did save my life, regardless of her motives, and she did bring me and my grandparents together.

I'm not a saint, and there are nights, I admit, when I lie awake thinking about all the times Grace belittled me, and I hate her for her pettiness and jealousy—especially now that I know it was Isobel she was seeing every time she looked at me. But I also know that if I don't let go of that anger, it'll eat at me forever, and in the end, she'll have won.

So I'm not going to let Grace rule me anymore—but I won't dig her up, either.

As for Nils, it seems the bullet that settled in his back missed severing his spine by a hair, although the swelling and bruising still hasn't subsided and he's going to need months of physiotherapy. He's expected to make a full recovery in the long run, though. I called Sharon Berglund, too, to make sure she understood that nothing had happened or was going to happen between Nils and me at her dad's farmhouse. I just panicked the day of the funeral and couldn't go through with the charade of mourning Grace after everything I'd learned about her, and I needed to tell Nils what had happened the night of the fire. Sharon said that's what Nils told her, too, and she saw no reason not to believe him. She's a wonderful person. Their marriage is strong. May it be long and happy.

Sharon and Tom both mentioned that Chief Lunders has had to retire from the police force for health reasons. And since Nils is going to be laid up for a while, he apparently recommended that the town council offer the chief's job to Alex Cruz. I passed the message on, but Alex says that having survived his probationary period, he thinks he'll stick with the FBI for now—despite the Bureau's disapproval of his methods (which did allow him to close three homicide cases single-handed, however). Mostly, he doesn't think he's constitutionally fit to live in a place where people have to drill holes in the lake to catch fish.

I'm glad to hear it, since I've gotten used to having him around, and I certainly don't see myself ever moving back to Havenwood. There would be far too much explaining to do to satisfy the curiosity of the ladies of the St. John's Auxiliary and the Set 'n Style Salon. There's a lot to be said for the anonymity of a big city when your family history is as complicated as mine has suddenly become.

As for Special Agent Alex Cruz, we've gotten close, he and I— surprising as that seems. He's been wonderful these past weeks, coming by every evening after work, just to talk. And, oh, how we've talked, about things that have happened to both of us. He's told me about an incident that happened over in Vietnam—a murder in his unit. How his father still thinks he should have kept his mouth shut and not reported it. And how the worst thing about it was the fact that the men in his unit said they'd murdered the lieutenant for *his* sake. Apparently, when Alex left them to find the sniper who'd been attacking them and didn't come back, they thought the lieutenant's recklessness had gotten him killed. Listening to Alex I thought about how Grace always used to tell me she'd sacrificed her life for me. We both agree there's no worse guilt than being the beneficiary of someone else's needless sacrifice.

And that's about all there is to this little piece of history—except I said I was the last of my family, but that's not entirely true. I have an aunt in Israel, it turns out—Isobel's sister. Z'ev Mindel tracked her down for me, and we've spoken by phone three times in the last month—well, twice, really. The first time, we were both crying so hard that not much conversation took place. I'm planning to go over in April for a visit. Alex says he'll go with me, and Z'ev is planning to take some home leave at the same time.

"Think the Negev Desert in springtime," Z'ev told us. "It's beautiful at that time of year, and you know, a motorcycle is the perfect way to see it. I could give you the grand tour."

We've told him it sounds like a plan.

Jillian (Joelle) Meade
February 17, 1979
Washington, D.C.